A MOMENT OF MADNESS

Also by Hilary Bonner

FICTION

The Cruelty of Morning
A Fancy to Kill For
A Passion So Deadly
For Death Comes Softly
A Deep Deceit
A Kind of Wild Justice
When the Dead Cry Out

NON-FICTION

Heartbeat – The Real Life Story
Benny – A Biography of Benny Hill
René and Me (Gordon Kaye)
Journeyman (with Clive Gunnel)

HILARY BONNER

A MOMENT OF MADNESS

St. Martin's Minotaur
New York

 For information, address St. Martin's Press, 175 Fifth Avenue, New York, N.Y. 10010.

www.minotaurbooks.com

Bonner, Hilary.
A moment of madness / Hilary Bonner.—1st St. Martin's Minotaur ed.
p. cm.
ISBN 0-312-33948-8
EAN 978-0-312-33948-7
1. Police—Great Britain—Fiction. 2. Women detectives—Fiction. 3. Journalists—Fiction. 4. Rock musicians—Crimes against—Fiction. I. Title.

PR6102.O56M66 2005
823'.92—dc22

2006042504

First published in United Kingdom by William Heinemann

First U.S. Edition: May 2006

10 9 8 7 6 5 4 3 2 1

THIS BOOK IS DEDICATED TO FRIENDSHIP

in memory of:

DAVID NATHAN	1926 to April 2001
GINA WEISSAND	1946 to June 2001
DAVID MIDDLEMISS	1921 to September 2001

With thanks to:

David Thomas and Gordon Hines of the Herald Express, Torquay; Detective Sergeant Frank Waghorn and Detective Superintendent Steve Livings of the Avon and Somerset Constabulary; Detective Constable Phil Diss and Detective Sergeant Pat Pitts of the Devon and Cornwall Constabulary.

A MOMENT OF MADNESS

One

A uniformed police officer was at her side as she hurried from the house. She moved with an easy elegance, her head slightly bowed. The policeman opened the door of the waiting squad car for her and she stepped inside, sliding effortlessly across the back seat so her escort could sit beside her.

Kelly raised his binoculars to his eyes and focused them on her.

She was staring straight ahead, not looking at anything or anyone. Her short cropped hair was peroxide white. It changed colour almost from day to day, though, he knew that. Like Madonna, she was into changing her image with the wind. Yet this was no international star, no latter-day icon. She had been married to one, that was all. The only fame she had ever achieved in her own right had been when she was just a kid, and hardly anybody even remembered those early movies any more. John Kelly did, but he wasn't a man who forgot easily. And he reckoned there had always been something about her, an aura almost, that had made her a star too.

Her face was very pale. He was struck at once by her beauty. He thought she looked a bit like a Victorian porcelain doll, fragile, slightly unreal. He had seen countless photographs of her, of course, over the years. And there had been that one meeting, brief and long ago. Even his memory of that, although it would never leave him completely, had faded with the passing of time. Even he had forgotten, he realised, the impact she could have in the flesh. She was breathtaking. It was almost as if shock and grief added somehow to her beauty. Her skin had a translucent quality to it. There were heavy dark shadows beneath the almond-shaped eyes – her only imperfection, but that came as something of a relief, confirmation, almost, that she was real.

The squad car began to move in a kind of circle round the gravel courtyard, kicking up a shower of tiny stones behind its rear wheels, as it headed for the electronically controlled security gates outside which Kelly stood watching. Very slowly, almost as if somebody were operating her too by remote control, just like the big iron-barred gates, she turned her head towards him.

Her eyes were violet. That was the only colour to describe them, like Elizabeth Taylor's, only even more remarkable, Kelly thought. They were very dark, so dark it seemed almost as if there were no definition between pupil and iris, just big violet circles, deep and fathomless. For a few seconds she seemed no longer to be gazing vacantly into space but to be looking straight at him, staring at him. That's how it felt, anyway, although he knew that was probably just an illusion. She wouldn't actually be seeing anything, he supposed, let alone a tired old local newspaper hack, not after what had happened in her house the previous night.

The gates opened and the squad car came slowly through, while several uniformed policemen hovered in the short driveway, intent on preventing any renegade fans from entering the grounds of Maythorpe Manor. Kelly stepped back, as did the fans, although at least a couple seemed intent on committing suicide beneath the wheels of the police car, which continued to move steadily forward. Self-preservation eventually saved the day. Even the most tenacious of the fans moved out of the way just in time to avoid any real chance of injury. The car turned left up the lane, still travelling at an almost leisurely pace, allowing the assembled cameramen and telly crews easily to snatch photographs of the woman in the back seat as it passed them by. Kelly was mildly surprised that the windows had not been blacked out.

Her facial expression did not change as a cacophony of flashbulbs exploded all around the vehicle carrying her. The newly widowed wife of the rock icon was well used to that sort of scene.

It had never been Angel Silver's way to hide.

Two

Kelly watched the squad car disappear up the hill, the tall Devon hedges obscuring it from sight as it rounded the first corner.

Many of the people in the crowd, mostly women, but including a number of men, were weeping uncontrollably. Some had thrown themselves prostrate on to the ground, undeterred by the fact that the uneven surface of Rock Lane was still damp and muddy from an earlier heavy shower.

Several of the photographers took off at a run for their cars, in a hurry either to dispatch their pictures or give chase. Fat chance of that, thought Kelly.

He shivered, and thrust his hands into the pockets of his Barbour jacket. No warmth in it. He'd had one of those fancy linings once, but God knows where it was now. It was a cold damp morning, and before Angel Silver had been brought out he had been standing outside Maythorpe Manor for almost four hours.

Kelly was forty-eight years old and looked it. At least. He had grown a slight paunch, his once nearly black hair was thinning and had turned grey at the temples, his pale blue eyes had been dulled by the passage of time. Kelly had once been a shining light in his chosen profession and had seemed destined to be doing something far different by the time the big five-O approached. As it was, his life had been a roller coaster ride with rather more downs than ups. And there he was, still standing on doorsteps. Waiting. Watching. Freezing half to death.

The lane was particularly narrow by the turning to the grand Georgian house, and Kelly had been forced to leave his old MG in the tourists' car park down in Maidencombe village, so he had been unable even to sit in it and be protected a little from the elements while he watched and waited. A reporter's lot, hanging around for hours, just in case, regardless of the weather, but it didn't get any easier as you got older.

With more than a little reluctance he removed his left hand from his pocket. He wasn't wearing gloves, of course, because gloves were the kind of thing Kelly could never remember. In his fingers he clutched his mobile phone. Once he'd had to know every phone box, pub and public convenience on his patch. Nowadays mobiles had cut out the need to move away from a stakeout at all, except for calls of nature. There was no longer an excuse to spend hours in the nearest boozer. But perhaps that wasn't such a bad thing, he reflected wryly, thinking about the effect too much alcohol had once had on his life.

Kelly leaned against the iron bars of the gate, which had closed again in silent precision, and thought for a moment or two. He was interrupted by the *Evening Argus*' staff photographer at the scene, Trevor Jones, a bright-eyed young man with ginger hair. Trevor was full of the excitement of working on what was already undoubtedly the biggest story of his brief career.

'I got a great one of her, Johnno,' he yelled excitedly. 'She looked straight at me.'

Kelly grinned. Like Princess Diana, Angel had that knack. No doubt every snapper on the case thought the same thing, as indeed he himself had. But he took pleasure in Trevor's reaction. He liked the boy, and invariably felt himself fired by his boundless enthusiasm, even on routine stories. The photographer was a big gangling lad, half a head taller than Kelly, and a bit like a Great Dane puppy, Kelly reckoned, eager to please with soft brown eyes that still smiled easily, and inordinately long legs and arms.

'I'd better get my film back to the factory,' continued Trevor. 'If you get any leads, you'll give me a bell, won't you, Johnno? Leave it to the Picture Desk, and with my luck I'll be doing a golden wedding this afternoon.'

Trevor looked quite downcast at the thought as he shouldered his cameras and turned to leave.

'Will do,' Kelly called after him. He meant it. Given a choice he'd rather work with Trevor Jones than any of the other *Argus* snappers, in spite of the lad's inexperience. He liked working with photographers who didn't clock-watch and would do his bidding without too much argument. At least some of the time.

Trevor glanced back over his shoulder, ginger curls bouncing, flashed a smile of gratitude and gave a thumbs-up sign.

Kelly smiled. As he watched Trevor amble off down the hill he became aware that almost all of the journalists were now starting to leave the scene, believing presumably that there was no more mileage to be got here. A TV news team hurried past him. The cameraman trod heavily on Kelly's right foot.

'Watch yourself,' Kelly yelled. He didn't like the TV boys. Never had, since his very first days as a young reporter. They believed totally not only in their own superiority but also that it gave them the divine right to shove everyone else out of the way. Or just walk on them, Kelly thought wryly, tentatively wriggling his bruised toes inside his shoe.

'Fancy an early pint?' said a voice in his ear. 'Can't see much more happening for an hour or two.'

Kelly turned to face Jerry Morris, the *Mirror*'s veteran area man, a reporter of the old school, who either never remembered or simply didn't care that Kelly had quit drinking alcohol years ago.

'I'll catch up with you,' Kelly said. 'Got a couple of calls I want to make.'

Jerry waved him a careless farewell and set off down the hill in Trevor Jones's footsteps.

Kelly switched his attention to the fans gathered outside the big house, forty or fifty of them already. Soon only they would remain. In spite of a natural cynicism finely honed by long years in newspapers, Kelly was quite impressed by their early presence.

Scott Silver, Angel's rock star husband, had died in the early hours of the morning and the first reports of his death, ambiguous and hedging all bets, had broken on radio and TV breakfast news some time between 7 and 8 a.m., just three or four hours earlier. None the less the first wave of mourning fans had swiftly metamorphosed. Many were clutching photographs and posters of their dead idol, others carried flowers. The weeping and wailing, which had earlier reached a peak when their hero's body had been carried off in the coroner's van, had subsided now into a kind of low moaning. There was already a row of floral tributes on either side of the big gates. The towering manor house provided an imposing backdrop, and through the trees which surrounded it you could just glimpse the sea, iron grey that morning, a shade darker and even more forbidding than the wintry sky.

Kelly studied the scene idly as he punched just one button on his phone.

'Meadows.' Detective Chief Inspector Karen Meadows, already appointed the chief investigating officer on the case, always somehow managed to sound sharp, even if she had been roused from her bed in the middle of the night, as Kelly knew she had been.

'Thanks again for the early tip,' he said.

'Yeah, but you didn't call to thank me. What do you want?'

'A few minutes of your time?'

'You have to be joking. I don't have any time. Not even a few minutes.'

'So it is a murder inquiry, is it?'

'Well, loosely speaking. Two killings. One murder probably, in the strictest sense of the word.'

'Look, Karen, everybody's speculating. All I've picked up since you tipped me off that Scott Silver was dead is what I've heard on the TV and radio news, which was bugger all, and a load of rumours out here at the house. Why don't you put me straight?'

He heard her sigh.

'OK. Then you get off my back, John, all right? We found two bodies at Maythorpe Manor. One is Scott Silver and the other is almost certainly an intruder who broke into the house during the night. It looks fairly certain that he murdered Silver and was killed in self-defence.'

'So you reckon they killed each other in the struggle?'

'I didn't say that.'

'Well, how else do two men kill each other?'

'I didn't say that either.'

'You're talking in riddles, Karen.'

'And you don't listen, Kelly. There was a third person present, wasn't there?'

'Good God. Silver's wife!'

'At last. Your brain's not been completely pickled then. Yup. We believe matey killed Scott Silver and that Angel Silver then killed him.'

Kelly's right hand dropped involuntarily, letting the phone fall away slightly from his ear. He didn't respond any further for a moment or two.

'Kelly? Kelly, are you there? Stop mucking me about.'

He raised the phone again. 'Sorry, Karen. Yes, I'm here. Just thinking, that's all. You told me they'd both been stabbed, though, didn't you?'

'Yes, that's right. The intruder was stabbed over and over again.'

'And she did that? Angel?'

'Yup. Looks like it.'

'What will happen to her?'

Kelly was still adjusting to the idea that the slight, almost frail woman he found so captivating could have killed a man.

'As long as everything adds up she'll be charged with manslaughter. We've got to charge her with something sooner or later, whatever people may feel about justification, particularly in view of the way in which the second man was killed. I reckon she'll plead self-defence, though, and get away with it.'

Manslaughter. So with the right judge she would probably end up with a suspended sentence, or even a conditional discharge, even if she pleaded guilty or was found guilty. But with the wrong judge, she could still end up with a custodial sentence. Angel Silver in jail. Now that would be a story.

Kelly reckoned Karen Meadows would probably prove to be right: that Angel would plead not guilty on grounds of self-defence and that almost any British jury would find in her favour. A woman who had watched her husband brutally killed by the man she had then attacked would be bound to get the sympathy vote, after all. Either way, Kelly's antennae were waggling. Whatever happened it would make a decent change from parish council meetings and magistrates' court. Kelly had been through the mill, God knows, but he'd never lost the nose for a good yarn. Nor the taste for it.

'Where are they taking Angel?' he asked.

'Torquay Police Station. Where d'ya think? Oh, and I shouldn't bother. You'll not get near her. I'll see to that.'

Kelly chuckled. He was starting to enjoy himself. Karen and he went back a long way.

Back to what for him would always be the good old days. They'd been close, very close. Kelly's chuckle stretched into a fond smile at that memory. But it was more than that. Karen Meadows owed him. He'd probably saved her career at what might then have been the expense of his own, and she'd never forgotten it, bless her, unlike most of 'em. Hence the tip-off, hence the instant access to her through her mobile. She also understood him, of course, knew his driving force, knew what made him tick, and knew how to play the game too. Kelly wanted this one, and he suddenly became quite determined to get it. It was nice to feel as if he were back in the big time again. And what he wanted more than anything else was to get to Angel Silver. Karen had twigged that at once. Of course. She'd always been exceptionally bright and an astute judge of character. Except once, and that had nearly brought her down. Nearly, but not quite, thanks to Kelly. They'd been friends ever since, and it was a friendship Kelly valued as much as almost anything in his life – and that included his partner, Moira, his son, Nick, and even the job he still loved in spite of everything.

'I'll just have to wait then, won't I?' he said lightly. 'Don't suppose there's anything else you can tell me?'

There was a pause.

'I need something back.'

'Whatever it is, you've got it,' he replied glibly.

'The intruder was one Terry James, 24 Fore Street, Paignton. Big boy, late twenties, but he still lived with his mum. Funny how often they do, his type, particularly from that sort of family. You may know 'em; we certainly do.'

Kelly thought hard. He was pretty sure he did know the James family. They were in and out of magistrates' court on a regular basis, if he'd got the right bunch. Pub punch-ups and petty theft, that was their mark. And if Kelly had the right man in mind he had indeed been a big boy, well over six feet, and built like a stevedore.

'I think I do, Karen,' he said.

'Got one conviction for GBH and several for minor thieving,' Karen went on, echoing the thoughts running through Kelly's head. 'Be surprised if you hadn't seen him in court.'

'Reckon I may have.'

'Well, anyway, our lads recognised him at once, but he's yet to be formally identified. His brother's on the way to the morgue as we speak, and the SOCOs are at the Jameses' home, doing a search. Been there since the early hours. The place is still sealed, so if by any chance you're planning to bowl over there give it a couple of hours, will you? I can't keep a search team there any longer than that in any case, not with the resources we've got left after that last round of cuts. I need them at Maythorpe.'

'OK,' said Kelly, grinning at the phone. If by any chance, he thought. She knew darned well he'd be off to Paignton like a shot. 'And what is it you want from me then?'

'I want to know exactly what the family say to you. If you know the James lot you'll also know they won't give us houseroom. Look, this case seems clear enough, but I don't want any mistakes. It's too high profile. So just report back, John, every spit and fart, not just from the James family but anything else you come up with, you devious bastard. It might mean more to us than you.'

'For you, Karen, anything.'

Kelly pushed the end button on his phone and punched the air gleefully with his free hand. Not only was he working on a potentially huge story but he already had a big lead. Life was looking up. Suddenly he didn't feel cold any more.

He checked his watch: 11 a.m. on the dot. The only

problem was that he really didn't want to wait a couple of hours before heading off to Paignton. The days when provincial evening papers produced a last edition in the late afternoon were long gone, and, in any case, Kelly never liked holding back on a story. An overdeveloped sense of urgency was programmed into him and all of his kind. But when you had someone like Karen Meadows on your side you didn't mess it up. If you made a deal you kept it. Well, more or less.

He would, he decided, compromise slightly and give it an hour and a half. The *Argus*' final deadline was 2.30 p.m., which was actually a hell of a lot later than many evening papers. If the James family were halfway amenable he should still make it, and he'd certainly have no problem filling in the time. He had already filed an early story to the *Argus*, but there were also several nationals he wanted to send stuff to. He had the edge because some of them had not even managed to get staff men to the scene yet. It was not only the provincials that were run by cost cutters in suits nowadays. In Kelly's day all the nationals had had a network of staff area men all over the country. That was no longer the case. Jerry Morris, a real survivor, was one of the last remaining. So Kelly reckoned it was time he cashed in on the inadequacies of modern newspaper management and started making the kind of money off this story that he had already promised himself he would.

He walked back down the hill, favouring his right foot, which was throbbing unpleasantly thanks to that TV cameraman, and through the pretty little thatched village of Maidencombe to the car park just up from the beach. The old MG gleamed wetly, raindrops from the earlier downfall still visible on its flat surfaces. Kelly kept the twenty-five-year-old car immaculately. It was his pride and joy. He had always loved MGs, and it was nice to have a car that went up in value if you looked after it, rather than down.

He unlocked the driver's door and climbed in. He had learned the art of filing copy off the top of his head over the phone many years previously, and it didn't take him long, sitting there in the car park, to send all that he had so far to the copy-takers of several London newspapers.

'The widow of rock star Scott Silver, killed at his home in the early hours of yesterday morning, was last night at the centre of a bizarre double murder drama . . .' he recited over the airwaves. And he knew it must be gripping stuff by the rapt attention of the copy-takers, who were generally far more cynical than any journalist.

Kelly still remembered during his early days in Fleet Street the copy-taker on his newspaper who invariably interrupted his stories with a muttered 'Much more of this?'

Perhaps he was improving at last, he thought, as he finished filing his final story and then called Trevor Jones, mobile to mobile.

'Twenty-four Fore Street, twelve-thirty,' he told the snapper. 'And if you get there before me, park down the road and don't even move out of that tip of a car of yours until I get there.'

'You got it,' yelled Trevor over the airwaves. Kelly moved his phone a few inches further away from his ear. Trevor continued to bellow at him.

'What've you got, Johnno?' he asked excitedly. 'Who lives there then?'

'I'll share that with you when I see you – and tell your desk you're going off chasing fire engines or something. OK, mate?'

Kelly ended the call before Trevor could question him any more. Kelly had been weaned into Fleet Street by an old-fashioned news editor who had operated under such a strict policy of secrecy that it had driven his staff mad. None the less, Kelly had learned the lesson well enough that if you wanted to keep an exclusive you told nobody, not even your bosses, until the last possible minute. Don't talk about it, write it, was the creed that had been drummed into him.

He started up the MG, enjoying as ever the unique throaty noise that it made, and motored back through Torquay, choosing to take the slower seafront road to Paignton rather than the ring road. He wasn't in a hurry, after all. Along the way he stopped at one of the few seaside caffs that stayed open all year round, bought a cup of tea in a paper cup, and propped himself against the sea wall. A gusty breeze had blown up. Kelly balanced his cup on the wall and clapped his arms against his sides to warm himself up. He really must buy some proper cold weather gear, he told himself for the umpteenth time. But it was worth the chill in his bones just to stand there and watch the ocean that day. It was quite spectacular, an unusually big sea for South Devon. Huge waves roared up the beach, crashing into the wall against which Kelly was leaning. A particularly massive one sent a shower of salty spray on to the pavement, and Kelly beat a hasty retreat, just managing both to rescue his tea and get out of the way without a soaking. He found that he was smiling. There was, he thought, nothing more exhilarating than an English seascape on a day like this. The clouds were moving fast and a sudden break in them revealed a brilliant shaft of pale winter sunshine. Like the beam of a giant cinematic light it illuminated a big circular patch of water, changing the colour momentarily from dark grey to aquamarine, and reflecting off the white tips of the waves so that they turned into gleaming silver. Cecil B. de Mille could not have managed it better, thought Kelly. He felt his heart do a little flip. If there was greater beauty in the world than in this wild and wondrous scene, he really didn't know what it was. There were some compensations to a backwater job on a backwater newspaper in a backwater town, he thought.

He checked his watch once more: 12.21 p.m. Fore Street was just a few minutes' drive away. He reckoned he had given the police and the James family plenty of time, and he could feel his heart thumping in anticipation as he drove into Paignton along Esplanade Road and swung a right towards the railway station. But when he reached Fore Street there was a police squad car parked outside number 24. Kelly battled to keep his natural impatience under control. He'd have to wait again. He could not expect to get any result except a rocket from Karen Meadows if he knocked on the door while there was still a police presence.

Kelly drove slowly past the house. At the far end of the street he spotted Trevor Jones's battered green VW Golf already parked there. The photographer raised a hand to him as he passed. Where Fore Street met the main drag Kelly manoeuvred a swift U-turn and pulled in against the kerb behind Trevor. Trying to look as casual as possible, Kelly clambered out of his own car and made his way to the passenger side of the old Golf. Trevor pushed the door open for him. Between them the two men shifted a pile of old newspapers, chip papers, chocolate wrappers and discarded film packets into the back of the vehicle so that Kelly could clamber in, his feet instantly becoming buried in even more debris.

Kelly passed no comment. He was used to the state of Trevor's car. Instead, he quickly gave the younger man a précised version of what he had learned from Karen Meadows.

'As soon as the bogies have gone I'm in,' he said. 'I don't want 'em frightened by cameras so you wait here until I call you. Got it?'

Trevor Jones nodded, albeit a little reluctantly. Photographers were a nervous breed. They didn't like waiting outside closed doors while reporters had access.

'And you snatch anyone, anyone at all, going in or out,' Kelly continued.

Trevor shot him a slightly reproachful look. The young snapper was already sitting with a camera ready, its 500-mil lens balanced on the dashboard and no doubt already focused on the door to number 24. Kelly smiled.

'OK, OK, I'm sorry,' he said.

Trevor might be relatively new to the game but he had been a quick learner from the start, and already didn't miss too many tricks, even without coaching.

Kelly settled into the passenger seat. The assorted rubble on the floor made crackling noises as he shifted his feet a little. Suddenly there was a bang almost like a pistol going off. Kelly nearly jumped out of his seat, instinctively jerking his legs up so that his knees almost touched his chest, and covering his face with his hands.

'It's OK,' he heard Trevor say. 'I knew I'd lost a flashbulb in here somewhere.'

Kelly removed his hands from his face, shaking his head in mild disbelief.

'You pillock,' he said. 'Apart from putting the fear of God into me, we're supposed to be keeping a low profile here. You really are going to have to get this tip fumigated.'

Trevor mumbled something apologetic. Kelly glanced along the street in all directions. There was nobody about. If anyone, including the police, had heard the bang as the flashbulb had exploded they had apparently not thought it worth investigating. Very tentatively Kelly stretched out his legs again, once more checking his watch. If they were forced to wait for long they'd never make that deadline, he thought. But little more than ten minutes later a young uniformed policeman emerged from the James house accompanied by a man in a suit, who Kelly assumed was CID, and an older woman wearing grey trousers and a cream linen jacket whom he recognised as a detective sergeant he knew vaguely. She seemed to glance in the direction of the Golf. Kelly hunkered down in his seat and gestured to Trevor, who had already knocked off a few frames, to do the same. Kelly didn't want to have to explain himself to Devon and Cornwall's finest, and he had deliberately slotted the distinctive MG in behind Trevor's car where it could not easily be seen from number 24. There were a lot of people around who would recognise Kelly's MG straight away.

Kelly stayed in the half-crouch until he heard the engine of the squad car burst into life. He peeped cautiously through the side window as the police vehicle motored slowly away, fortunately proceeding in the direction it had been facing, which meant that it would not pass the two watching journalists and their cars. He waited another couple of minutes to be sure the coast was clear. Then he was in like Flynn, moving fast in spite of his bruised right foot, which was still causing him to limp slightly, out of the car, along the pavement, up the steps, through the patch of rubble which passed for a garden, and knocking on the door with its peeling blue paint.

A young man, equally as tall as Kelly remembered Terry James, eventually opened the door and looked him up and down with some distaste. From his vague memory of the dead man this could almost have been Terry James, although even more thickset and maybe a few years older.

'If you're looking for your lot they've just gone,' growled the man, aggression oozing from his every pore.

'I'm not police,' said Kelly quickly.

'What the fuck are you then? The Sally Army?'

Kelly smiled. 'No, not exactly –' he began.

'I've got it, you're a fucking vulture.'

'I'm press, if that's what you mean.'

'Well, we've got nothing to say to yer. My brother's just been murdered. Our Terry's dead. Haven't you got no respect?'

'I just thought –'

This time Kelly was interrupted by the arrival at the door of a small dark woman, face tear-stained, hair dishevelled.

'Who is it, Kenny?'

'Some toerag reporter, Mam. Don't worry, I'll get rid of him.'

'Mrs James,' said Kelly quickly, taking an educated guess, 'I'm so sorry about your son. I just want to find out what happened to him, every bit as much as you do, really. Things aren't always what they seem, are they?'

'No, they're not,' said Mrs James.

'Well, I'd like to get the family's side to things now, find out what really happened, put the record straight on your behalf,' Kelly offered, coming out with the oldest line in the business. Nobody had been charged with anything yet; there was even a possibility that nobody would be. Terry James was dead, after all, so he couldn't face trial, and who could tell how Angel Silver would ultimately be dealt with? None the less Kelly wanted a swift result while he still didn't have to worry about *sub judice*.

'Come on, Mam, let's leave it,' said Ken James, moving between the woman and Kelly and at the same time pushing the door with his shoulder in order to shut the reporter outside.

Kelly put his good foot in the door jamb and as he did so wondered if he might be making an extremely dangerous mistake. He wasn't sure if he'd ever actually put his foot in a door before, and he wouldn't have done so then if he hadn't sensed that he could get through to Mrs James, that she wanted to talk. He certainly didn't want to take her son on. But it seemed that he had. Kelly could feel the full weight of Ken James as the big man leaned heavily against the door, pushing it against the reporter's now trapped foot and looking down on him menacingly.

'Do you know what they're saying about Terry, Mrs James?' asked Kelly desperately, pushing his face against the now painfully narrow opening in the doorway.

Even Ken James hesitated. To Kelly's immense relief the pressure on his trapped foot, encased in its flimsy shoe, eased. Kelly had banked on both Ken and his mother wanting to know what was being said. They weren't the sort of people who had much trust in the police, after all. Karen had told him that, as if he had needed telling.

'What are they saying?' asked Mrs James, and Ken opened the door a few inches, freeing Kelly's foot altogether. The reporter removed it swiftly. There was a limit. The way things were going in the foot department that day he was likely to end up unable to walk at all if he didn't watch it.

He could see Mrs James quite clearly beneath her son's arm, which Ken had stretched across the gap in the doorway, just in case Kelly was mad enough to attempt to barge in – which, in spite of a fairly cavalier track record, he most certainly was not. The woman's glance was almost pleading.

'Well, if you let me inside, I'd tell you everything,' Kelly remarked in his 'I'm a really reasonable and helpful bloke' voice.

In response Ken James glowered at him with even more hostility. 'The only reason we've got to talk to you lot is for cash, and lots of it,' he growled.

His mother rounded on her son then. 'You'll not make money out of your brother's death, Ken,' she said, not loudly but with a force and an authority which surprised Kelly. 'Not while I'm alive, at any rate.'

Ken James did not reply but bowed his head slightly as if in acknowledgement.

'You'd better come in,' said Mrs James to Kelly.

Her son stepped back, albeit with apparent reluctance, removing his arm and allowing the door to swing fully open again. Mrs James was little more than half the size of her son but there wasn't much doubt about who was in charge in this household.

She beckoned Kelly into the hall. He was struck at once by the extreme cleanliness and order of the place, which came as something of a surprise after the neglected exterior. The floor of the hall was covered in plush dark red carpet which looked freshly vacuumed, the walls washed plain cream and covered in family photographs. Mrs James led him to an unexpectedly large kitchen at the back of the seemingly small terraced house. The kitchen was smart, modern, well equipped and gleaming. Obliquely Kelly found himself wondering where all those shiny new white goods might have come from. A second, younger woman was sitting at the table. She was sobbing gently into a wodge of tissues and barely looked up as Kelly entered. More than likely a sister to Terry and Ken, Kelly guessed. He knew the James lot were a large family. Two small boys, possibly the younger woman's sons, appeared to be fighting to the death in front of the washing machine. Kelly was aware of the towering figure of Ken James right behind him, literally breathing down his neck. Nobody else in the room seemed to notice the huge commotion the two children were making.

'Hello,' he said to the woman at the table, putting on his 'I'm a nice journalist' face. 'John Kelly, *Evening Argus*. So sorry to intrude at such a sad time.'

'Like fuck,' said Ken James loudly.

Kelly ignored Ken. The woman ignored Kelly.

'May I sit down?' he enquired, doing so without waiting for anyone to reply. He knew how to get himself established inside somebody's home well enough.

'So what are they saying about our Terry?' asked Mrs James for the second time as she lowered herself into a chair opposite Kelly.

'They're saying that Terry broke into Scott Silver's house, that he was disturbed by the rock star, whom he then stabbed to death in a struggle, and that Scott's wife, Angel Silver, then killed Terry in self-defence,' explained Kelly succinctly. He hadn't been a top tabloid hack for nothing.

'We fucking know that,' growled Ken, who appeared to use only one adjective.

'Yes, but do you believe it?'

'No we don't,' said Mrs James. 'Not for one minute. My Terry wouldn't have hurt that Scott Silver. Never.'

'He never hurt anyone, not Terry, except maybe in the pub or summat,' interrupted Ken in what for him was presumably a normal sort of voice. 'Even then the filth never got it right. He only ever fought back when people picked a fight with him, did Terry. There's a sort who like to show how tough they are after they've had a few beers. They like to push big blokes like Terry. I know. I get it too. But Terry never wanted it, never went looking for it. Not like me. I can be an evil bastard, me.' Ken looked quite pleased with himself at the thought and uttered the last words with considerable pride.

'I don't doubt it,' replied Kelly as pleasantly as he could manage. Very casually he slipped a hand into one of the side pockets of his Barbour and withdrew a small tape recorder and a notebook. He put the recorder on the table and switched it on. Nobody objected, which was a result in itself.

'But Terry does have a record both for grievous bodily harm and for theft, doesn't he?' Kelly continued conversationally.

'Yeah, but you can always make things sound worse than they really are,' responded Mrs James. 'You heard what our Kenny said. When he got done on that grievous bodily harm charge it wasn't Terry's fault at all. There was a load of lads down the Pier Arms who decided to take him on and my Terry sorted the lot of 'em out. Then he was the one got done. He wasn't into violence. He didn't like it.'

Kelly sighed. 'So why was he carrying a knife when he broke into Scott Silver's house, Mrs James?'

'I don't believe he was. I've never known him carry any kind of weapon, have you, Ken, honestly now?'

'No,' said the big man. 'Definitely not. It weren't Terry's style. He must have been fitted up.'

Kelly sighed again. He wasn't getting very far. Classic denial. Strange how often it was that the seriously dodgy families were the ones who could kid themselves best.

'Look, your Terry was surprised in the middle of the night while breaking into the Silver home. I understand the police found a suitcase he'd already filled with stuff. I'm not saying he meant to kill Scott Silver, but there doesn't seem to be any doubt that he did.'

'Kill Scott Silver?' Mrs James produced a hollow mirthless laugh. 'He'd never have done that. He wouldn't have stolen from him either.'

Kelly had his notebook on his knee now and a Biro in his right fist, but so far the only mark he had made on the page was an uninspired doodle of something vaguely resembling a cat. Kelly liked cats.

'Well, what do you think your son was doing in the Silver mansion last night then? He wasn't exactly an invited guest, was he?'

'Look, Mr Kelly, Terry was not the brightest of my boys . . .'

Kelly made a huge effort not to look at Ken. The thought of an even less bright version was a disturbing one.

'He was a big softy, though. That was my Terry. He had a heart of gold. He didn't go round hurting people, and that Scott Silver – well, Terry really loved him. Honest he did.'

Terry James loved Scott Silver? What the hell did that mean? Kelly was alert now. He wasn't sure where Mrs James was leading but this was beginning to get interesting at last.

'Look, let me show you something,' the woman continued.

She ushered Kelly out of the kitchen, along the red-carpeted hallway, up the similarly red-carpeted stairs, past more immaculate cream walls dotted with yet more family photographs, and led the way into a small bedroom overlooking the street.

As she opened the door Kelly felt the familiar tingling sensation in his spine that he always got when his journalistic antennae were waggling on overdrive.

The room was a shrine to Scott Silver. Every inch of the walls was covered with posters and photographs of the rock star. If it hadn't been for bare patches indicating that several photographs had been recently removed, almost certainly by the police, Kelly thought, you wouldn't have been able to see the mid-blue-painted walls at all. There were old concert tickets drawing-pinned to the front of the wardrobe, piles of Scott Silver LPs in one corner and a neat stack of his CDs next to the state-of-the-art music centre. Even the rug thrown over the bed bore Silver's picture.

Kelly hadn't expected this. Neither, he thought, would the police have done. Terry James was known as a petty criminal, not the type who would be expected to be an obsessive fan. The tingling in Kelly's spine had extended right the way up his back and he was sure the hairs on his neck were starting to stand on end.

Lost in his own imaginings for a moment he could only just hear Mrs James talking to him. 'You can see what I mean, you can see it, can't you?' she said.

Kelly saw all right. He saw a completely different scenario to the one with which he had expected to be confronted. He saw a potential stalker story. It had to be, surely. He no longer saw a petty thief-turned-killer in a blagging that went wrong, but a young man obsessed with his hero – so obsessed that he could be driven to almost anything. It happened. All the time. It was the curse of the modern celebrity. And it turned an already hot story into something else.

'Did Terry ever try to get close to Scott Silver?' he asked, casually checking that his tape recorder, which he had picked up off the table and was carrying in his left hand, was still running.

'Oh yes, he went all over the country to concerts and stuff. He used to hitchhike, sleep on pavements to get tickets, anything,' Mrs James told him chattily. 'Then he'd wait outside the stage door, that sort of thing. He'd got loads of photographs of himself with Silver. Started being interested in him when he was a teenager, you see, and it just went on and on.'

'Did Terry ever go up to Maythorpe Manor?' Kelly asked.

'Oh yes, he was always going up there, couldn't keep away.' Mrs James chuckled. She was so determined to portray her son as a misrepresented nice guy she didn't seem to realise at all the disturbing interpretation which could be put on her words. 'Sometimes he'd come home and say that Scott had spoken to him, or maybe his wife, that Angel, and he'd be pleased as punch. Then in the last few months he started helping out in the garden a bit, doing odd jobs and that. He was handy like that, was Terry . . .'

Mrs James's voice tailed off and fresh tears started to form in her eyes. Kelly waited in patient silence for her to speak again, trying to look deeply sympathetic while he was actually thinking obscurely that Terry hadn't appeared to be very handy in his own garden. After a minute or so, Mrs James produced a paper tissue from somewhere and blew her nose loudly. Then she continued, albeit a little more shakily.

'H-he didn't talk about it a lot – not a great talker, Terry wasn't. But it was almost like he regarded them as friends. And my Terry was as loyal a man as ever walked this earth. You don't hurt your friends, not our sort. He'd have died for his friends, Terry would . . .' She paused as if at last hearing what she was saying.

Kelly butted in quickly, before she had time to think too much.

'Maybe that's exactly what he did, Mrs James,' he said gravely, realising that the remark made absolutely no sense whatsoever. But Kelly was good at saying what people wanted to hear. And from the look in Mrs James's eye that's exactly what he had done.

'Maybe he did,' she said. 'That would have been just like my Terry.'

'Do you mind if I get a snap taken of this room? I think it says a lot about Terry, don't you?'

'Yes I do,' said Mrs James. 'It shows what he was really like, and what a big fan he was of Scott Silver. It shows that what I said was true, that he'd never have hurt Scott, never, don't you think?'

'Oh yes,' said Kelly ingenuously. 'It really does. So it's OK if I call my photographer in, is it? I made him wait outside. Didn't want to push things.' He smiled reassuringly. Or at least tried to.

Mrs James just nodded. Kelly used his mobile to call Trevor Jones on his. The photographer responded even more swiftly than Kelly would have considered possible, ringing the doorbell within seconds. He must have been standing by his car on starting blocks, Kelly reckoned. Ken James, looking rather less enthusiastic than his mother about it all, showed Trevor up to the bedroom.

The snapper was all smiles and bouncing ginger curls, the kind of young man surely nobody could ever regard as a threat, which was another reason why Kelly liked working with him.

'I'll just rattle off a few frames then,' said Trevor, doing so speedily before the Jameses had a chance to change their minds.

Kelly watched with one eye as Trevor shot the room from all angles, and then charmed Mrs James into posing for close-ups with some of the memorabilia. He really was turning into a smart operator, thought Kelly admiringly. Trevor failed to persuade Ken to be photographed, though. The big man merely responded with a sulky 'Fuck off' and kept himself determinedly out of shot.

'I don't suppose you have any of those pictures of Terry with Scott Silver, have you?' Kelly asked Mrs James.

'The police took most of them, I think,' she replied, gesturing at the bare patches on the wall. 'But there may be one or two in that drawer by the bed . . .'

She started rummaging around and eventually, under a pile of magazines, came up with a photograph which she studied morosely for a second or two before passing it to Kelly.

The reporter couldn't believe his luck. In his hand he held a clear colour snap of the two dead men, both smiling for the camera. Scott Silver, whose ragged good looks had made him such an icon, along with his unusual high-pitched singing voice, even had an arm loosely around the neck of Terry James. Terry had been considerably taller and Scott had had to reach up to do so. His body language suggested that he was making a joke of their height difference. Already wearing cowboy boots with small heels, he was standing exaggeratedly on tiptoe. James was beaming from ear to ear. It was a good picture. And to make it absolutely perfect it had been taken outside Maythorpe Manor. The gates of the waterside mansion could be seen quite clearly in the background.

Gold dust, thought Kelly, wondering why the police had not taken this photo too. Maybe they had found and taken away another just like it, or maybe they'd overlooked it. Kelly knew of more than one occasion in the past when specialist police search teams had missed the obvious. Even experts were susceptible to human error. But Kelly didn't really care what had caused the police to leave this picture behind. He was just so glad to have it.

Mrs James was still talking to him. 'Yes, my Terry always carried his camera with him when he was going after Scott,' she remarked.

Going after Scott. The words hit hard. That was how the world would see it – Kelly had realised that from the moment he had been shown Terry James's bedroom. Now the man's mother had actually said the words.

Kelly couldn't wait to get away now. He had work to do. And he had all he needed to make a huge splash not only in the final edition of the *Argus* today, but also across just about every darned morning newspaper in the country tomorrow.

He extricated himself and Trevor Jones from the James family home as quickly as possible and only just prevented himself from running back to his car.

'Right, first give the *Argus* all you've got, then send your stuff to Scope, including that pick-up pic,' Kelly instructed Trevor. Scope was one of the major picture agencies and Kelly had already been on to its boss, Peter Murphy, that morning, just in case.

'Murphy's expecting you to wire,' Kelly went on. 'And your Desk won't quibble because they'll know what you're doing is down to me. Any flak, send it my way. OK?'

'Right,' yelled Trevor as he flung himself into his car and gunned the engine. 'I'm on it.'

Kelly grinned. Trevor too would earn a few bob out of this, but what the younger man really wanted, more than cash,

Kelly knew, was to see his by-line on a major exclusive in a big daily.

He checked his watch for the umpteenth time as he settled into the driver's seat of his MG: 1.30 p.m. Bags of time. Kelly opened the glove compartment and pulled out the hands-free kit for his phone. He'd start filing on the run. It was second nature to him. First the *Argus*, in plenty of time for its final deadline, and then the nationals. That small-minded prick of a news editor wouldn't like it, but that was tough. Kelly would do his duty, give all he had to the *Argus* first, but he wasn't going to miss the chance of a major crack at the nationals. No way. Hansford would just have to put up with it. Nobody else would object to him making a few bob for a change. It could be quite a few bob too, he reflected cheerily, for him and young Jones. This story was getting better and better.

Kelly headed into Torquay town centre while he talked into his phone and drove around until he found a convenient parking space as close as possible to the police station on the corner of South Street. When he had finished filing he phoned Karen Meadows to give her a full report on his visit to the Jameses' house, as promised.

'And what the fuck do you want now?' Karen yelled into her mobile. It had been a long day already and it was far from over. Karen had been called out at 3 a.m. and had been on the go ever since. Not only that, but she couldn't quite get her head around the double killing. Angel Silver was still being interviewed by two of Karen's team, but the rock star's widow, understandably enough, Karen supposed, seemed unable to tell her story in a lucid way. She remained in shock, of course, and Karen was unsure how much longer she should hold her. Since that darned Human Rights Act had become law the previous year, police officers had to be even more careful than ever how they dealt with suspects – particularly one as high profile as Angel Silver, who also looked so frail you couldn't help thinking she might fall over at any moment.

This was the kind of case which could turn round and bite

you really hard unless you took great care. Scott Silver had been an icon, the circumstances of his death were unusual and highly dramatic to say the least. The eyes of the world were going to be focused on the way the Devon and Cornwall Constabulary handled this one, and Karen knew it.

She was alone in her office at Torquay Police Station, desperately trying to collect all her various thoughts together into a manageable package. At the very least it was vital in a situation like this to stick to correct procedure and ensure that no corners were cut. A senior police officer's career could be all too easily terminated nowadays by an ill-considered move or lack of attention to detail. And Karen knew how high the stakes could be in an investigation as big as this one. She had been going over and over in her mind every course of action she had so far instigated as SIO, and attempting to assimilate everything she should do next.

Karen was an experienced detective with a reputation for being cool under pressure, but the exhilaration at being handed such a hot potato, which had so far carried her through the day, had temporarily evaporated. She was experiencing that energy slump most high fliers are prone to at some stage following an adrenalin rush. She felt tense and on edge, and the last thing she wanted to do was to talk to a journalist. Even to one she genuinely regarded as a friend.

'Uh – I thought it was you who asked me to report back to you,' Kelly replied down the airwaves, his voice calm, even very slightly amused.

Christ, thought Karen, so she had. But Kelly didn't sound too offended. No man with his sort of background would, after all.

'Sorry, I'm up to my ears,' she continued more mildly, but not all that apologetically. 'Just make it snappy, will you?'

'OK. First thing, the family are quite adamant that Terry James never went out tooled up, not with a knife, not with anything,' Kelly remarked.

'They're almost certainly right,' Karen replied. 'We think the knife he used was taken from a set in the kitchen of Maythorpe. Out of character or not, it looks like he picked it up when he broke into the house and when he was challenged by Scott Silver he certainly didn't hesitate to use the thing.'

'A panic attack,' said Kelly.

'Something like that.' Karen chuckled without much humour.

'But you guys obviously know by now what I found out at the house. James had some sort of fixation with Silver. I've gone on the stalker angle.'

'Now there's a surprise. Did you get anything else my lads might have missed?'

'Dunno. Apparently James helped out at Maythorpe doing odd jobs –'

'Yeah, we got that,' Karen interrupted.

'Still, how the hell did he get into the place in the middle of the night, Karen? It's like Fort Knox out there.'

'It should be, but not the way the Silvers have operated their security system. There's a control panel on the wall outside which opens the gates, isn't there? It seems that half the work force of Torquay had the combination. Angel is vague about whether or not she gave the number to Terry James, but I suspect that she did. And in any case, although there's an alarm system both around the perimeter walls and at the house, connected with the security firm HQ in Newton Abbot, when they were indoors the Silvers were apparently lax at even setting it.'

'Yes, but surely . . .'

Karen Meadows never heard what Kelly had to say. The detective she regarded as her right-hand man walked into her office looking worried and at the same moment her landline rang.

'Can't get any sense out of her, boss,' DS Cooper began.

Karen waved him silent, ended her mobile call from Kelly with an abrupt 'Got to go' and picked up her desk phone.

The call lasted only seconds.

'Right,' said Karen finally. 'Seven o'clock it is then.'

DS Cooper didn't speak. He knew better. Instead he just looked at her enquiringly.

'The chief constable wants to see me at HQ in Exeter, Phil. This evening. As if we all didn't have enough to do.'

'Dead right, boss,' responded Cooper. 'Predictable, though. Bet all the brass have got their knickers in a twist over this one.'

'Yes, let's just make sure we guys on the ground don't, shall we? And as for Angel Silver, well, that was never going to be easy, and we'd better keep our carpet slippers on too. I'll be along to have a go at her myself in a few minutes, OK?'

'Very OK, boss.'

Cooper looked relieved, thought Karen, watching him leave the room. Even good officers liked nothing better than to pass the buck upwards, but the higher you got in the pecking order the harder that became. In any case, it wasn't Karen Meadows' style.

She leaned back in her chair and closed her eyes. If she could catnap for just a few minutes it might clear her head. It seemed the day could become even longer than she had thought it would be.

Not for the first time Karen was almost glad that there was no one in her life to whom she was answerable, nobody who might be tricky about the crazy demands put upon her by her job. Sometimes she felt lonely returning at night to a home she shared only with her cat, but at least she didn't have to explain herself.

With a wry shaking of his head Kelly put his mobile phone in his pocket, climbed out of his car and walked thoughtfully along to the big square building which housed Torquay Police Station. As he joined the group of press, onlookers, and distraught fans who were already waiting on the station steps, he had no idea whether or not Karen Meadows was inside. But clearly Angel Silver was still being detained.

Angel Silver. An extraordinary name for an extraordinary woman. Yet Kelly knew that 'Angel' was not some affectation of the music world, but just a shortening of the name her parents had given her. Angelica. Absurdly grand for the daughter of a Billingsgate fishmonger.

A second *Argus* snapper, Ben Wallis, was already on a watching brief and was able to tell Kelly that there had been no developments at the station except the earlier release of a predictable official statement confirming that Angel was helping police with their inquiries.

Kelly shoved his hands deep into the pockets of his inadequate coat and settled into the waiting game again. As time passed the day became even chillier. By late afternoon he felt that his feet were turning into blocks of ice, particularly his sore right one. His back ached too. He was getting too old for this lark, he thought. That cup of tea and the bun from the seaside caff seemed like ancient history. He managed to persuade a girl reporter from the *Western Morning News* to nip to a sandwich shop on condition that he both promised to cover for her and paid. She returned with coffee and half a dozen hot pasties in a bag. Kelly attacked the coffee so eagerly he burned his lips. The pasties contained very little meat and the pastry was distinctly stale but Kelly barely noticed, and neither did Ben Wallis, who gratefully accepted one of them.

As darkness fell and six o'clock came and went, Kelly found himself mildly surprised at how long Angel was being held. He reminded himself that two men had died, and he wondered what the police were asking her and what she was telling them about the high drama that had unfolded in her home during the night.

Disconsolately he stretched his arms and legs, and hopped about a bit from one foot to the other in a bid to get his distinctly sluggish circulation going again. The bruised toes of his right foot continued to throb dully. Kelly was beginning to feel extremely weary. After all, he'd been on the case since his call from Karen just after 6.30 a.m. For a moment or two he considered giving up and going home. He didn't suppose anyone at the *Argus* would notice or even care. They'd merely pick up from the dailies in the morning. But Kelly hated that sort of reporter. He always saw a job through and he'd never liked second-hand information, which he reckoned invariably led to trouble. Kelly liked to make his own mistakes.

At around eight o'clock it started to rain again. That, Kelly thought, was the final straw. There was no shelter worth mentioning. He had neither hat nor umbrella. Naturally. Icy raindrops cut through his thinning hair and ran down his neck beneath his shirt collar. He began to shiver uncontrollably.

Then, quite suddenly, there was a flurry of activity. Angel Silver emerged through the police station's big doors. Several policemen escorted her as she began to walk down the station steps, one of them holding an umbrella over her. The couple of dozen or so assorted press, snappers, reporters, radio journalists, and TV teams pushed forward as one body. The area around the station, lit only by standard streetlamps, was suddenly flooded with film-set-scale illumination as cameras flashed and the lights of the TV teams burst into life.

Angel walked with a straight back, head held high, looking resolutely ahead, face even paler than before, if that were possible. Once more Kelly was struck by her beauty and the way she seemed able to isolate herself from all that was happening to her. He knew that she must be knocking forty now, but, even under such great stress, she looked years younger. There was an ageless quality about her.

Kelly was aware that at the rear of the police station there was a police parking area off public limits, where it would have been possible for her to be discreetly bundled into a vehicle and swept away without anyone having a chance to get near her. He suspected that it would have been Angel's own decision not to sneak out of a back door.

A squad car came roaring around the corner and squealed to a halt as close as it could get to the station steps. One of the policemen escorting Angel stepped ahead to open the near-side rear door. The noise in South Street was every bit as overwhelming as the blazing light. The reporters, TV and written press were all calling out to Angel, desperate to persuade her to tell them what had happened and how she felt. She did not respond and, indeed, gave no indication that she even heard. The snappers and the TV cameramen were hassling each other for the best position for a final shot. Angel bent down to climb into the car and, as she did so, seemed to stumble slightly. A policeman immediately put an arm under her elbow to steady her. She looked round and slightly up at him as if in thanks and then her gaze wandered by him and it seemed almost as if she were taking in the extraordinary scene around her for the first time. It was then, for the second time that day, that Kelly got the impression she was staring straight at him. Certainly their gazes met. Kelly knew all about the Diana factor, but he really felt sure of it. There was something so hypnotic about those violet eyes, their intensity somehow enhanced by the dark shadows beneath them.

'Angel, what happened in the police station?' he called out as loudly as he could, aware of his own voice rising above the commotion. 'Are you being charged with anything?'

Her gaze remained steady. Then she smiled. Well, it was almost a smile. Just an enigmatic lifting of her lips at the corners. A Mona Lisa smile. Slight, yet deep. Unfathomable. But it brightened her whole face.

Then she was gone. Into the car and sandwiched on the rear seat between two extremely large police officers.

Some of the pack ran to their motor cars in order to attempt to give chase. Kelly took his time. Thoughtful. It seemed more than likely that Angel was simply being returned home to Maythorpe, and, in any case, he knew from long hard experience that you could almost never successfully follow a police car.

He started back towards his MG, picking up a bag of chips, which he ate with one hand while he drove out to Maythorpe Manor. No wonder he was growing a paunch, he thought to himself.

Around the gates of the big old mansion probably upwards of a thousand fans of the dead rock star were now gathered in silent vigil, almost every one of them carrying a lit candle. The whole area was bathed in a kind of ethereal light.

Kelly had expected many more fans than had been gathered in the morning. None the less, he was amazed at the sight which confronted him as he approached the house on foot from the car park down in Maidencombe village. Involuntarily he slowed his pace, taking in every detail of the scene. Then suddenly the rather eerie silence was abruptly broken. The gathered fans burst almost as if by prearrangement into a song – probably Scott Silver's most celebrated recording, certainly so well known that even Kelly, not a man with a great knowledge of contemporary music, recognised it at once.

It was a ballad, a hauntingly poignant number made all the more so by the circumstances in which it was being sung.

Gone but not forgotten
Like fallen blossom
In the springtime,
Gone but not forgotten
Safe in my heart
For all time,
Gone but not forgotten . . .

The haunting strains dripped like liquid through the night air. Kelly couldn't make out all the words, but did remember that the song was a typical Silver number that had actually been about lost love rather than death. On this night, sung by this particular choir, it was a moving funeral dirge.

Kelly moved forward into the throng. People of all ages seemed to be gathered now. Scott Silver's appeal spanned the generations. Many of the women and even a few of the men were weeping copiously. Kelly had never quite understood, even as a young man, the adulation many people feel for distant heroes, public figures and celebrities they don't know – film stars, rock icons, royalty. He had never understood it but sometimes he envied its simplicity.

Certainly this was an extraordinary night. Those gathered seemed united in their sorrow. Kelly pressed his way further forward, almost bumping into Trevor Jones who greeted him warmly.

'I knew Ben was at the police station so I thought I'd come straight out here just in case,' the photographer explained. 'Got a great shot of her arriving, Johnno. What a stunner, eh!'

'She's here then,' Kelly murmured, almost to himself.

'Oh yeah,' nodded Trevor. 'Arrived about fifteen minutes ago in a police car, which left almost straight away. We think there's still a police presence in the house, though.'

Kelly nodded. There was sure to be, he thought. They'd

never leave Angel alone there. After all, the whole place was still a crime scene. He reckoned she'd only be allowed to use the rooms they'd already cleared, and neither she nor anyone else except the scene-of-crime boys – the SOCOs – would be allowed near the area where the two men had died.

'Well done, mate,' he remarked absently to Trevor, as he moved on through the crowd. He didn't really want to talk. He preferred to look, to listen, and to drink in the atmosphere. With some difficulty he pushed his way through to the front and found himself once again right up against the iron railings of the gateway where the smattering of floral tributes of the morning had now grown into a mountain of multicoloured blooms.

He crouched down beside them to read some of the messages. The candles and the bright security lights around Maythorpe, although they cast their own deep shadows, meant that he could do so quite easily.

'We always loved you, Scott.' 'We will mourn you for ever.' And some even more melodramatic: 'Life without you will not be worth living.' 'My life is over now, as yours is.'

Quite quickly the muscles in Kelly's calves started to ache and one of his ankles locked. With some difficulty he got to his feet and, forgetting that his right one was bruised and sore, he put rather too much weight on it. The pain caused him to stumble and he reached out desperately with his right arm in the general direction of the iron fencing, seeking support. In doing so he lurched against a figure, dressed in what appeared to be a long dark robe, pressed against the bars.

'Sorry,' he muttered automatically when he regained his footing.

There was no response. Kelly took a closer look. He only had a back view but he somehow guessed from what he could see of the figure's build that this was a young woman. Certainly her nearly black hair, much the same colour that Kelly's had once been, hung long and straight almost to her waist – not that hairstyles always told you anything. Her face must be shoved right into the railings, Kelly thought. She was standing completely still, apart from the rest of the crowd and without what seemed to be the almost obligatory candle. Her black hair and dark robe caused her to half disappear into the quite confusing shadows and rendered her almost invisible from even a short distance away. Kelly had not noticed her until he had bumped into her.

'Sorry,' he said again, a little louder. Still no response.

He shrugged and backed off, turning his attention once more to the rest of the gathered throng. They were singing another Scott Silver number now: 'Why I'll Always Love You'.

Kelly stood amongst them for several more minutes, silently listening. Somewhat to his surprise he found himself quite moved.

He glanced across to the big house safely cocooned behind its security gates and a ten-foot-high wall. Only it hadn't proved to be quite so safe, had it? Terry James had breached the defences of Maythorpe Manor, albeit, it seemed, with the unwitting assistance of its owners, broken into Scott Silver's home and killed him.

Kelly was desperate now to know exactly what had happened during the previous night. He stared steadily at the old grey mansion. Maythorpe, he knew, dated back to Tudor times but, following a fire, had been almost totally rebuilt during the Georgian era, hence its geometric design, which doubtless enclosed big high-ceilinged and well-proportioned rooms. What tragic secrets did the ancient manor hold within its lofty walls, he wondered.

A light behind one of the house's ground-floor windows suddenly snapped out. Somewhere else another flicked on. Seconds later elsewhere on the first floor there was a flash of light and then just a little chink remained.

Kelly concentrated hard on that narrow slice of light. Then, after just a minute or so, that too disappeared. Inside the house someone had pulled back a curtain in order to look outside, he was sure of it. Then, to get a better view and in order to remain unseen, the light inside the room had been switched off.

Was that person still there, looking out, taking in the scene Kelly had just been marvelling at?

Angel Silver was inside there. Was it her at the window? How was she feeling? What was she thinking?

Kelly tried to put himself inside that beautiful porcelain head, convinced she was watching. He shut his eyes to concentrate. He could see her pale face quite clearly. But it told him absolutely nothing at all.

Three

Moira Simmons retreated gratefully into the little office at the rear of Torbay Hospital's children's ward. It had been a busy and distressing night. In the early hours little Timmy Jordan, just seven years old, had finally lost his battle against leukaemia. Timmy had been ill on and off for almost two years and, like so many of the staff at the hospital, Moira had got to know him and his family well. Though the boy's death had been inevitable for weeks, it was a bitter blow.

Moira felt drained. She had spent some time comforting Timmy's devastated parents, whom she had come to regard as friends and whose grief she genuinely shared. They too had known that their son could not survive, but it had not made his eventual loss any easier for them to bear, and neither would Moira have expected it to.

She sank wearily into a chair and closed her eyes. Moira was small and blonde and had never even been threatened by the weight problems which affect most people in middle years. She had retained both a girlish figure and a youthful zest for life, the latter maintained in part at least by an ability to find humour in almost all that life had thrown at her. Which had been quite a bellyful over the years. That morning, though, Moira was leaning far more towards tears than laughter. Only her innate resilience, combined with the professional discipline of her many years in nursing, made it possible for her to stop herself breaking down.

One of the worst aspects of being a night sister was that all too often the sick seemed to die at night when their defences were at their lowest. Moira, perhaps because she knew only too well from personal experience what it was like to deal with despair, had a reputation for being particularly adept at comforting the bereaved. She had the knack of displaying just the right blend of concern, sympathy and professionalism. Only it wasn't a knack, not really, rather something that came quite naturally to her.

After a few seconds she opened her eyes and gave herself a little shake. There were a whole load of tasks in the wards to be completed before she went off duty and the day staff came on at 7.30, and there was also her ritual morning wake-up call to be made.

She checked her watch: 5.55 a.m. That at least was perfect. She always made the call just before six. She reached for the desk phone and dialled a number which rang for well over a minute without reply. Eventually John Kelly, in bed in his three-bedroomed terraced house in St Marychurch, high above Torquay town centre and the seafront, answered with little more than a sleepy grunt.

Moira smiled indulgently. For the last seven years she had shared her life with Kelly, and she reckoned she knew him pretty well. Evening paper journalists have to start work early, but Moira was only too aware that it didn't come naturally to Kelly. He was an old morning paper man more at home working late into the night than rising at dawn.

'And a very good morning to you too,' said Moira, realising that as usual her cheery tone gave little indication of the harrowing night she had endured. That was down to a mixture of training and experience.

'Thank you very much,' muttered the sleepy voice in St Marychurch, and with little more than a few further grunts and a couple of yawns, Kelly hung up.

Moira had not expected him to ask after her welfare at that hour of the morning. She was used to his slow awakenings, although she somehow thought he would bounce into action a little more readily than usual today. She knew that he had been excited to be involved in a big story again the previous day, and that the Scott Silver case was already intriguing him. She was used to his pre-occupation with his work, too.

But that morning she had wished that, just for once, he had enquired about her work.

With a small sigh she rose from her chair and made her way back out to the wards.

Kelly forced himself to get out of bed almost at once. As Moira had guessed, the promise of another day being involved in such a cracking good story made the process less painful than usual. None the less, he was still yawning and rubbing his eyes as he made his way downstairs, picked up the newspapers in the hallway, and dumped them on the living-room floor on his way through to the kitchen to brew a pot of tea.

His first job in the morning was to read the papers. That was what he always did. He had the lot of them delivered and he had a special arrangement with his newsagent, involving prolific bribing of various delivery lads, to ensure that they arrived by 6 a.m. When the tea was ready he carried it back into the living room and sat as he always did in the chair by the fireplace. It was habit for Kelly. But that day the papers were a particularly gratifying read. His bank manger was likely to think so too.

'Stalker kills rock idol Scott Silver', 'The crazy obsession of wild man Terry', 'How my boy stalked Scott Silver, by his killer's mother'. That last one was going a bit far, thought Kelly. Skirting the edge of the law. But then that was what editors did, had always done.

The telephone rang for the second time just after 6.30. He ignored it. Moira, who Kelly knew would be immersed in what was inclined to be the busiest period of her shift, never phoned again after making her wake-up call until she came off duty. There was only one other person it could be at that hour. Kit Hansford, provincial boy wonder, newly appointed news editor of the *Argus*, and the kind of journalist in a suit Kelly simply could not stand.

Kelly glanced again at the front page of his own newspaper, lying crumpled on the floor by his side. He had given the *Argus* all he had yesterday afternoon, but the young news editor would also know that he had filed to the nationals and that Trevor Jones had sent them his pictures. In addition, the approach of the major dailies was so much more sensational, so much more direct, that it left the *Argus* looking lame.

Well, that wasn't his fault, thought Kelly. He was a bit surprised that Joe Robertson, the *Argus*' hard-hitting and imaginative editor, had not given it a bit more top spin. But even Joe had to keep his well-honed journalistic instincts curbed nowadays. The hidden agendas of newspaper proprietors no longer focused merely upon getting great stories and getting them first – which was the only kind of journalism Kelly had ever completely understood. The *Argus* was as much about keeping the advertisers happy as anything else, which meant lots of meaningless advertising features about everything from holiday hotels to shopping malls.

Hansford had no idea of the work that Kelly had already put in on the Silver story. Nor would he care. He didn't know that Kelly had stayed on the case until well after midnight. But Kelly did not clock-watch when he was on a story like this one. That was another habit; the training of long ago. A kind of compulsion.

Kelly spooned sugar into his tea. He liked it so strong and sweet that the dark brown liquid became almost a syrup. He took a deep drink and concentrated on what he was going to do that day. His first thought was to stick to Angel Silver. Wherever she was, whatever was happening to her, she was the key, he was sure of it. And he saw no need to discuss his plans with the *Argus* yet. Or not with Kit Hansford, anyway. Kelly only discussed anything with Hansford when his back was absolutely against the wall.

He hauled himself out of his chair, scattering newspapers across the floor like over-sized confetti. Moira always said that she reckoned one day it would be impossible to get into Kelly's house because of the piles of old papers. Kelly thought that might be one of the reasons she insisted on keeping her own home just a few streets way. Or was it he who had ensured that they had never quite set up a proper home together? Kelly was no longer entirely sure. Certainly he barely noticed the newspapers and magazines, which seemed to scatter themselves, unaided by human hand, he sometimes thought, all over his house. He picked up his car keys off the hall table and reached for his Barbour jacket, which was hanging on the stand behind the door. Then, abruptly, he turned on his heel, walked back across the hall and up the stairs to the spare bedroom where he kept his computer.

'It might not be much of a job, but it's the only one you have and are likely to get, old son,' he muttered to himself.

'Following new lead, mobile phone not working, will be in touch soonest,' was the brief message he e-mailed to his long-suffering boss. The simple duplicity of it, which would not fool Hansford for a second, cheered Kelly.

He drove straight to Maidencombe then, this time turning off the main Torquay road directly into Rock Lane. There were probably even more fans outside Maythorpe Manor than there had been the previous night, despite it being so early in the morning. They parted reluctantly, pressing themselves against the perimeter walls of the big old property on one side of the lane and into the tall Devon hedge on the other, as Kelly motored slowly through them. A lone policeman, a large man close to retirement age, stood by the locked gates. It seemed that the Devon and Cornwall Constabulary recognised the peaceful nature of the crowd and were not expecting trouble. Kelly hopefully attempted to manoeuvre the MG into a corner of the gateway. The policeman, his body language weary, stepped unenthusiastically forward and waved Kelly on with one impatient movement of his right arm. Kelly grimaced wryly and continued slowly down the lane through Maidencombe village to the beach car park. He had no alternative but to trudge up the hill again to Maythorpe and, for the second day running, stand in the lane freezing half to death along with the fans. Although mercifully not raining, it was a cold damp day again, but many of the gathered crowd lay on the ground, huddled in sleeping bags or covered in coats. In spite of the chilly conditions it was clear that some had just stayed there through the night and had been joined by yet more.

Kelly shivered at the thought of such a vigil and hugged his Barbour around him, wondering if there was anyone in the world he would stay out all night to mourn in the middle of a wintry November. He knew the answer. There wasn't and never had been. Not even his only son, Nick, whom he adored. Kelly knew how to keep his feelings buttoned inside him. By and large, that was how he'd coped with the world throughout his life.

As ever he looked carefully around him, taking in the scene, watching out for those little details which can take a story into another dimension. He didn't know if he was being fanciful, but it seemed to him that the crowd was giving off a kind of steamy haze. It was one of those very English wintry days that threatened never to become fully light. Cigarette ends glowed in the gloom. He seemed to be the only journalist there. He wasn't surprised. It was 7.30 in the morning, most of the daily guys would reckon they didn't need to be there until later, even if their News Desks thought differently, and his was the only evening paper in the area. He walked nearer to the railings to have another look at all the flowers. Involuntarily he glanced at the spot by the gates where that rather strange-looking young woman had stood alone last night. She was no longer there, though he did notice that there were two pints of milk in a box by the locked gate.

A minor commotion behind him alerted him to the arrival of the day's first TV news team, probably putting together a piece for breakfast television. Kelly observed with a jaundiced eye. An eagerly bright-eyed young woman reporter puffed up with self-importance was leading a harassed-looking cameraman through the throng towards Kelly, who instinctively shuffled his feet out of imminent danger.

The duo passed by him without incident or damage, and Kelly turned his attention to Maythorpe. Nothing seemed to be moving in the house or its grounds. The big Georgian building had a sleepy locked-up look about it. Kelly always had the feeling that houses could speak to you if you let them, although he was rarely inclined to share that thought with any of his fellow newspapermen or women, who would merely reckon he had completely lost it. Kelly stared hard at Maythorpe. The old house didn't want to wake up that day, he was sure of it, and he was equally sure that the woman inside, the woman who had somehow survived a night of unspeakable horrors only to be forced to spend an entire day detained in a police station, would not want to wake up either.

He took a few steps towards the huge wall which surrounded Maythorpe, interrupted only by the iron-railed gate area, and leaned gratefully against it, as usual hunching his shoulders inside his inadequate coat. When would he ever learn, he wondered, glancing down at his lightweight leather-soled shoes as he settled for a long wait. Half an hour or so later a familiar red van arrived and a slightly bemused-looking postman unloaded two mail sacks and carried them to the gate. The large police officer, who had dealt with Kelly in such a perfunctory way when he had attempted to park outside Maythorpe, punched a code into the control panel by the gates, which swung slowly and silently open, allowing the postman to pass the mail inside. Letters of condolence from fans, Kelly assumed. Two sackloads of them already. His thoughts turned to Angel, yet again. Scott Silver's mesmerising, captivating widow. Would she want to see the letters, let alone read them, he wondered, as the big gates swung closed again with a small but forbidding clunk.

And would she, he wondered, want to see the letter he had written, which was tucked in the inner pocket of his Barbour? Even less, he guessed. He glanced towards the letter box inset in the end of the wall to the left of the gate, only an arm's length away. Well, he had nothing to lose, he supposed. He reached inside his coat, removed the envelope containing his letter, stretched out and posted it into the box. The letter simply asked Angel for an interview, which, in common with all the rest of the press, was what Kelly wanted more than anything else. But Kelly had met Angel before, and it had been an unusual meeting to say the least. They had a brief but maybe exceptional shared history, of which he reminded her in his note. In spite of this he knew how heavily the odds were stacked against him. He also knew what a full talk with Angel Silver would be worth. It would be a seriously hot property. If Angel was charged with manslaughter within the next few days, which he had already been told by Karen

Meadows was the most likely outcome, no newspaper would be able to print such a story until after her trial because it would be *sub judice*. But if Kelly got that lucky he would not find it difficult to be patient.

He realised suddenly that he had been fantasising and forced himself to return his attentions to reality. For a while he concentrated on trying to put another early background story together in his head – something that could be used right away, something that could be published now, before Angel was charged. If indeed she was charged.

Suddenly, at around 8.30 a.m. the monotony was momentarily broken. A police car arrived. All the gathered journalists pushed forward trying to see who was inside. Kelly managed to get quite a good look at the four people the car contained. In the back were two men wearing non-descript grey jackets and ties, almost certainly CID, although Kelly didn't recognise either of them, and in front Karen Meadows, wearing something red to add a flash of colour, sat next to a uniformed driver. The DCI was staring straight ahead, her chiselled features stern beneath her glossy dark hair, which was shaped, as usual, into an almost geometric, rather seventies-style bob. Although she remained an attractive woman, Karen Meadows' appearance invariably gave an impression of severity, which Kelly always assumed was her intention. The policeman by the gate turned his attention to the control panel again as the squad car approached and the electronic gates opened, allowing the vehicle to sweep through.

Two women fans made a half-hearted attempt to run after the car. The big policeman merely put out one arm and stared them down. He had about him an air of slightly bored authority. You knew there was no point in quarrelling with him. The fans retreated meekly, as indeed Kelly had done earlier when confronted by the same approach. A few spots of rain began to fall. Kelly felt them not only on his forehead but also through his thinning hair as usual. He sighed in glum resignation as he looked up at an increasingly threatening sky.

He forced himself to retreat into the half-trance he had developed over the years in order to get him through long, tedious, and often seriously uncomfortable doorstepping sessions. After a bit he virtually ceased to notice the steadily falling rain and nearly an hour passed before he checked his watch again. It was almost 9.30 a.m. His deadline would shortly become pressing, but he decided to give it until eleven before leaving the scene. None the less he suspected that, at the best of times, Angel Silver would be a night bird, unlikely to surface much before the afternoon – and that didn't bode well for an evening paper man.

However, just before 10.30, during a break in the rain, a tall bearded man wearing jeans and a leather jacket emerged from the house and made his way up the drive towards the gates, which opened as if by magic as he approached them, so that his stride did not even have to falter. They must have been operated from inside the house, thought Kelly. The tall man seemed to be framed by the slowly parting gates as he strode through, the massively imposing house looming behind him. Suddenly, as if on cue, the black clouds overhead parted momentarily and a brief shaft of pale autumn sunlight, much the same as Kelly had witnessed lighting up the sea the previous day, illuminated the man, causing his reddish hair and beard to gleam. The wonders of English weather, thought Kelly. Yet again it was almost as if the scene had been stage-managed.

Kelly was amused; Scott Silver had been renowned as a wonderful showman. Kelly felt that he should know who the tall bearded man was. He seemed to have been cast from the same mould as the legendary rock star – there was certainly something theatrical about him. There was, however, also something indefinably camp about him, quite unlike the legendarily heterosexual Scott, and as he stepped out into Rock Lane, his fairly flamboyant body language made it clear that he wanted to speak.

'Any press here?' he yelled. His voice had a mellow quality in spite of its high volume.

Kelly pushed forward. So did the others. There was a second TV crew now, and a smattering of print reporters and cameramen, together with a young woman from Radio Devon.

'I'm Jimmy Rudge, Scott's business manager,' announced the tall man. He was very thin and had a nervous tick in one eye, which somewhat belied his bold stride and loud confident voice. As soon as he introduced himself Kelly remembered him. He had, of course, seen Rudge in countless press photographs with Scott and being interviewed on TV. From what Kelly could recall, Jimmy Rudge had always been rather more than a business manager. He had certainly been a public spokesman for the rock star on many occasions, and it seemed that role was going to continue even after Silver's death.

'Angel has asked me to come out and talk to you,' Rudge began. 'She is devastated, of course, by the tragedy that has happened here and is far too distraught to make any statement herself. In any case, as you know, the police are still investigating the two deaths which occurred here at Maythorpe Manor, and she is unable to comment for legal reasons.'

Rudge paused and continued in an even louder voice as if trying to project himself to the whole crowd of people: 'However, Angel has asked me to thank all Scott's fans who have come here to pay their respects. She watched you last night, saw the candles, listened to the singing, and she was very moved. She feels you paid a fine tribute to Scott.'

There was a kind of murmur of approval. So, thought Kelly, almost certainly he had been right. Angel Silver had been peeping through the curtains last night, watching, listening. He had felt it. He really had.

Rudge started to speak again, this time in a more normal tone of voice.

'Angel would also like to thank the ladies and gentlemen of the press for your interest and for the kind things you have written about Scott . . .'

Half true, thought Kelly. The obituaries of the rock star, already in almost all of the papers that morning, had without exception spoken of his immense talent and charisma, and they could do no other. Scott Silver had been a legend on legs. But Kelly couldn't believe Angel really wanted what Rudge had somewhat euphemistically described as 'the interest' of the press in her present situation. He rightly guessed what was coming next.

'. . . But as for legal reasons she is unable to co-operate with you in any way, and indeed her shock and distress is such that she would in any event not be capable of doing so, she would really appreciate it if you would respect her privacy at this terrible time.' Rudge looked around appealingly. 'So please, guys, go home, go back to your offices,' he pleaded. 'There really is no point in hanging around here, there honestly isn't.'

Kelly had been half looking over Rudge's shoulder as he talked, studying the big house behind the business manager. Suddenly he saw a curtain twitch in the same window from which he believed Angel had been looking out the night before.

She was there again. He could feel those eyes, he really could.

On an impulse he stretched out an arm and shook a rather surprised Jimmy Rudge by the hand.

'Of course, Mr Rudge, I quite understand, as I'm sure do my colleagues,' he said. 'I'm John Kelly of the *Evening Argus* and I will gladly co-operate with you and leave Mrs Silver alone until she wishes to make some kind of public statement.'

'Thank you very much, Mr Kelly,' replied Rudge, but, being a man not unfamiliar with dealing with the press, he did regard Kelly with some astonishment. Not nearly as much, however, as the other newsmen and women gathered outside Maythorpe Manor. Most of them knew Kelly – he'd been around a long time in all sorts of different guises – and were completely bewildered by this display of obedient co-operation that was quite out of character.

Kelly didn't give them time to start questioning him. Leaving them looking uncertain and muttering to each other, he merely turned on his heel and began to stride purposefully back down the hill. With his back safely turned his face broke into a broad grin.

Kelly knew all about giving the right impression. He had planned to leave the house by eleven anyway. It was already twenty minutes to, and it suited his purposes well to be able to create the impression of being one of the good guys.

But while he knew the gates to Maythorpe were still in sight, Kelly turned around for one last look. Rudge had already retreated into the grounds. Swiftly Kelly produced his binoculars and lifted them to his eyes in order to study the grand old manor house for a final time while he still had the chance. He focused on that window. Yes, he could just make out a figure standing there. And he was almost certain that it was Angel Silver. He was also pretty sure that she was studying the scene outside her home through a pair of binoculars.

Did suddenly bereaved women who had been involved in an horrifically violent crime in which they had almost certainly killed a man, albeit in self-defence, usually behave like that? Kelly had no idea. But he had the feeling that Angel Silver was a uniquely cool customer.

Four

Kelly was thoughtful as he drove back towards Torquay and the industrial estate near the hospital which housed the offices of the *Evening Argus*. Coincidentally his first job as a boy reporter thirty-odd years ago, before he graduated to Fleet Street, had been on the *Torquay Times*, a weekly newspaper with offices right in the centre of town. Those had been the days, he reflected a little sorrowfully. Nowadays virtually all newspapers, from most of the nationals down to the few non-freebie weeklies that still existed, had been relegated to bunkers somewhere soulless.

The *Torquay Times* had gloried in the address of Upper Fleet Street, and the town's evening newspaper back then had been right next door. Kelly had no idea whether the term Upper Fleet Street had been an invention, not to mention an affectation, of the two newspapers. Certainly the grandly named piece of road, a suspended terrace just off and above the town's main shopping street of Fleet Street, was really just the bottom bit of Braddons Hill Road. Now the *Times*'s rather splendid old building had become the curiously named Bondi Beach Bar, and the only glory that remained was apparently represented by a load of surfers painted on its once-proud façade. The *Torquay Times* itself was long gone too – as was the glorious career Kelly had once seemed destined for.

He opened his car window and lit a cigarette. He kept trying to give up, and, indeed, had not smoked for several days again, but a man had to have some vices. The idea of a completely viceless John Kelly was rather awful, he considered. He'd given up the drinking – out of necessity, of course, not choice. They'd told him he'd die if he carried on. Not maybe. Or within a few years. But inevitably. And soon.

So he'd knocked it on the head. And he'd quit gambling too. Well, almost. He allowed himself a few quid on the horses on Saturdays only, and limited the stakes to what he could afford to lose. Which was not much, that was for certain, and therefore deeply tedious, because it also meant that what he won was barely worth winning.

He had given up the women too. Apart from Moira. For many years after he and his wife had parted company Kelly had lurched from one short-lived relationship to another, sometimes managing to keep more than one going at a time and fit in the odd one-night stand as well. He had, of course, in those days been drinking for England and gambling constantly. No wonder his career and his marriage had both hit the skids. But now at least he had regular employment again, doing the job he had always wanted to do, albeit at a comparatively low level, but in a lovely part of the world.

And then there was Moira. She was his rock, and Kelly was well aware of the stability she had given him and the state he might still be in, were it not for her. He loved Moira. In a way. In his way. But without that edge of danger which came with high passion, which he had last experienced so long ago he could barely remember it. The trouble was that although Kelly knew well enough that he would still be falling about in a gutter somewhere had he failed to get his life back on an even keel – with not a little help from Moira, whom he had met just a year after joining the staff of the *Argus* thirteen years previously – he was still an adventurer at heart. Still a chancer inside his head. It was what, once a very long time ago, had made him such a good reporter. Good reporters, the really great ones, were not often anything but chancers. They had a boldness about them, a belief in their own immortality, their own omnipotence. But when that belief was shaken it was often hard for them to hold themselves together. Kelly was the sort who had hung on to his own particular brand of greatness by little more than a single thread. When that thread had broken, so had Kelly. And he had long ago accepted that he would never be that man again.

As he swung the MG into the *Argus* car park and pulled to a halt, Kelly struggled to snap out of the morose mood he had slumped into. He was aware that he had acquired a tendency towards self-pity. He'd have to watch that. He disliked it in others and even more in himself. At least he had a really good story to bury himself in. It was a long time since he'd worked on anything as big as this.

Stepping out of the car he took a last couple of puffs from his cigarette and inhaled deeply, before tossing the fag end casually on to the ground. The offices of the *Argus* were, of course, non-smoking. God, how Kelly hated the health-conscious, squeaky-clean, political correctness of modern life. He strode briskly through the big swing doors into the streamlined modern reception area that could have been the entrance to any factory or office block. Nothing indicated press at all. As ever, Kelly allowed himself a brief moment of nostalgia. He was, after all, old school, local-paper-trained, Fleet Street-honed. Hot metal was in his blood and he longed for the noise and the dirt and the sheer exuberance that had once been so much a part of newspaper life.

He made his way unenthusiastically through the ground-floor advertising department and climbed the stairs to the editorial offices above. The journalists produced their newspaper out of one big anonymous grey room. Pale grey walls framed a highly regulated working area in which mid-grey computers sat on lines of dark grey desks. Everything about the *Argus* newsroom was grey – including the atmosphere, Kelly always thought. There was the usual soft mechanical buzz, which was just about the only buzz you ever got from the place, he reckoned. Reporters sat quietly at their terminals with their heads down. The subeditors had tired eyes, too few of them dealing with too much copy, much of it supplied by reporters who weren't really worthy of the job description, in Kelly's opinion.

On his way to his own grey desk Kelly passed the photographers' room. He almost bumped into Trevor Jones, who came hurrying out, camera bag over his shoulder.

'Back to normal for me today,' muttered the younger man glumly. 'I'm off to cover the opening of that new supermarket. I don't think they like it when you get an exclusive on this bloody newspaper.'

Kelly smiled sympathetically. Kit Hansford certainly gave that impression sometimes. And Kelly was under no illusions about the young news editor's opinion of him.

He switched on his computer, logged in, and began to put together a final piece for the midday edition. When he had finished he went on-line to check recent material about Scott and Angel Silver. Having avoided the office the previous day and had no time to use his own computer at home, this was his first chance. On the Net, predictably enough, the principal stuff was fan-based. He plumbed in to the archives of all the national newspapers he could access. The trouble with the Net was that you could only get out what somebody else had put in. Kelly was well aware of the value of the Internet but was wary about the high level of misinformation it contained. He trolled through anything relevant that he could find, and then checked the archives of his own newspaper. The Silvers had lived in Maidencombe for almost ten years, and the *Argus* had given their various exploits considerable coverage.

But Kelly learned little that was new to him. He had a computer for a brain when it came to storing tabloid-style trivia in his head, although he needed sometimes to remind himself of precise details.

There was something in particular he had been looking for, although he wasn't sure what use he would be allowed to make of it. The name jumped off the screen at him. Mrs Rachel Hobbs. A spread in the *News of the World*'s colour supplement featured a half-page picture of a small bejewelled woman with big platinum-blonde hair and an even bigger smile perched on the edge of a large sunken bath, the central feature in the pink satin bedroom of her Essex home. At least most of it seemed to be made of pink satin. Including the wallpaper. No, surely not. Kelly peered more closely at the photograph. Well, it looked like pink satin to him.

Rachel Hobbs. Angel's mother. There was also a mother-and-daughter picture featuring Angel as a truly angelic-looking teenager. It was an old story, dated 12 August 1979.

Kelly remembered vaguely how the Hobbs family, enriched by Angel's earnings as a child star, had moved into that big flash house. Then when Angel's bubble had burst, only two or three years after that article had been printed, they had moved back to the same little terraced house in Clerkenwell where Angel had been born and brought up, which, for whatever reasons, the family had never sold. Angel was thirty-nine now. She would have been sixteen then, her mother forty-eight, according to the *News of the World* report. The various archives were full of material on Angel, including a number of stories concerning her disastrous first marriage to James Carey, a Hollywood actor thirty years her senior. There was even a photograph of her wedding to Carey showing Angel standing alongside her mother, smiling broadly again, and her embarrassed-looking father, Bill, who being a year or so younger than his wife had apparently been exactly the same age as the bridegroom. There were many others tracing Angel's life since her marriage to Scott but no more at all featuring her mother, except a brief item recording the death of Bill Hobbs, which carried only an old picture of him and his wife. Kelly remembered Rachel Hobbs as having been the archetype showbiz mum, but she seemed to have dropped totally out of sight.

He had been to the Clerkenwell house once many years ago. He wondered if Mrs Hobbs would remember. He suspected she would. It had, after all, been a pretty memorable visit. Suddenly Kelly wanted nothing more than to bowl up to London and talk to Rachel Hobbs. About what it was like to be the wife of a Billingsgate fish porter with a daughter like Angel and then a son-in-law like Scott. About the double killing at Maythorpe Manor, which must surely have turned her world upside down almost as much as it had her daughter's. He had a strong feeling that Rachel Hobbs could somehow lead him to her Angel.

He phoned one of the few old mates he had left in The Street, a reporter on the *Sun*, who he was sure would be able to confirm for him whether or not Rachel Hobbs still lived at the Clerkenwell address. He could, and she did. None the less, the odds were against Kelly going anywhere except on his own patch. That was how life was in provincial journalism. To travel outside the *Argus*' meagre circulation area was a rare thing indeed.

Kelly looked across at his news editor. Kit Hansford was twenty-five years old, little more than half Kelly's age. A career provincial man, had it written all over him already. There was a good life to be had in the provinces now if that was the type of journalist you were. The remains of Fleet Street was tougher, more competitive, more cut-throat, more in a hurry than ever before, while in the provinces a man with application and not a lot more could become a big fish in a little pond pretty swiftly.

Hansford was cut out for that. Hand-tailored. Absolutely. Sickening though he found the prospect, Kelly would happily have bet a month's salary that Hansford would be editor-in-chief of the *Argus* group within ten years. And on the board, of course. Then maybe he'd go into politics, local councillor, mayor, even stand for MP. Kelly wasn't sure about the last, though. That might lead to a big pond, which wouldn't suit Hansford at all. Kelly couldn't imagine the mentality of a talented young man who could ever be content with anything except at least attempting to break into the biggest time going. But then, he was still inclined to think about talent, which almost certainly ruled Hansford out. And even if it didn't, Kelly had to admit that he himself was no great advertisement for the so-called big time. He'd been among the best, but look at him now.

The familiar self-pity, which he tried so hard to defy, surged through him in an unwelcome burst.

Hansford looked up from the screen he had been scrutinising. His eyes caught Kelly's. The older man strove to make his face expressionless. Kelly knew better than to make enemies at his time of life, but it was hard to disguise the lack of respect bordering on contempt that he felt for the young news editor.

Hansford wore round metal-rimmed spectacles. Behind their inadequate disguise he blinked a lot. His fairish hair, already thinner than Kelly's, was shorn in a trendy crop, but the rather plump face wasn't strong enough to carry off the look, nor was the head a good enough shape. Hansford's cheeks and jowls were fleshy, but his lips were narrow, a curious mix. He had pale creamy skin and looked as if he barely needed to shave. In some ways he could be even younger than his twenty-five years. But his body was lean and spare as if he spent every spare moment in the gym training hard, which Kelly knew that he did. Hansford was image-conscious and they were living in the age of the body. It wasn't just the gay guys and the sporty types who were intent on the body beautiful nowadays.

Kelly leaned back in his chair and gave his present situation some thought. He was still arrogant enough to believe that he was the only man on the *Argus* who really knew how to handle the Silver story. Did he care enough to push it all the way? He wasn't sure.

While he was thinking, Hansford stood up abruptly and began to walk across the office towards Kelly. Now what? thought Kelly. It wouldn't be anything sensible, that was for sure.

'Are you clear, John?' Hansford asked.

Kelly suspected that he was about to be baited and determined not to rise to it.

'Did you like yesterday's Scott Silver exclusive?' he asked none the less.

'Oh yeah, good stuff,' muttered Hansford, looking vaguely embarrassed. News editors were never inclined to issue many compliments, as Kelly well knew, but with Hansford there always seemed to be this lurking resentment of Kelly, which the older man only half understood. After all, Hansford had it all in front of him. Kelly had left his best days well behind. He had come to terms with that long ago but it still rankled on a bad day.

'I've nothing more to file for tonight, if that's what you mean,' he replied edgily. 'Not yet anyway. But as this is the biggest story there's been on this patch since they found Bruce Reynolds living next to a house full of so-called trainee journalists just above the old offices of this very newspaper, I thought you might like me to carry on working on it. We are having a newspaper tomorrow as well, aren't we?'

Kelly was aware of the note of sarcasm in his voice becoming more and more apparent as he continued talking. He really hadn't meant to rise to Hansford, but he found it so hard not to.

The news editor merely stared at him levelly and handed him a sheaf of papers. Kelly barely glanced at them. He knew what they were and he could hardly believe it. Council minutes.

'There's a meeting of the planning committee at two o'clock. I want you there,' Hansford said. 'We're expecting a crucial decision *re* that proposed new shopping mall there's been so much hullabaloo about. This is a solid provincial evening newspaper which maintains an extremely high circulation through wide and comprehensive coverage of local news. And I'm employed to keep things that way. The Scott Silver murder will be dealt with appropriately and given the right amount of coverage and no more. There are other stories. We're not a red-top Fleet Street tabloid, John.'

Kelly didn't reply.

'Oh, and, John, you didn't waste much time getting that exclusive into the nationals, did you? They had a field day this morning with it. You won't forget who pays your wages every month, will you, old son?'

'No I won't,' replied Kelly evenly, ignoring the 'old son', which he knew had been intended to provoke. 'And you won't forget that I have an agreement with the editor that I retain my own copyright and get to sell on anything I do for this newspaper on the condition that I make sure the *Argus* gets to print it first, will you, Kit?'

This time it was Hansford's turn to make no reply. Kelly waited until the younger man was safely back at the head of the news desk before getting to his feet and setting off across the room for the editor's office. He could feel Hansford's eyes on the back of his neck. The news editor was going to dislike him even more now. Kelly was about to do his best to go over his head, and it wouldn't be the first occasion.

'Fuck it,' Kelly muttered to himself as he passed by the desk. 'No more Mr Nice Guy. There really is no point with that little prick.'

Joe Robertson's office door was ajar as usual. The big man, minus his jacket, was leaning back in his chair with his feet on his desk. His forehead glistened with sweat even though it was not particularly warm in the *Argus* office. Joe was a good six foot five tall and from certain angles appeared to be almost as wide. The jacket of his suit, slung over the back of his chair, was charcoal grey; as usual, his tie, in the colours of the beleaguered Torquay United football team, had been loosened, its knot an inch or two below the opened neck of his immaculate white shirt. He wore red braces and smoked an overly large cigar. The editor's office was the only place in the building where the no-smoking rule was allowed to be broken. The management pretended not to notice. It was probably either that or lose their editor. Joe Robertson was that kind of guy.

Kelly smiled appreciatively as he hovered in the doorway. Joe still looked every inch of the old-fashioned Fleet Street production man he had once been. He and Kelly had worked together in the Street of Shame many years previously when Joe had been the youngest night editor in Fleet Street history and Kelly one of the brightest stars on the road. There had always been tremendous mutual respect between the two men, and it was thanks to Joe Robertson, already editing the *Argus* when Kelly had somewhat spectacularly fallen from grace, that Kelly had been given the job on the Torquay newspaper that he had so far managed to keep. Kelly studied Joe for a moment. The other man had had very different reasons for ending up in a job way below his talent and ability. Robertson's wife, whom he adored, suffered from a rare mental disorder which resulted in severe panic attacks. Only in her home town of Torquay, among friends and family stretching back to her childhood, did she manage to hold herself together sufficiently for the couple to share anything like a normal married life and successfully raise their two children. And that to Joe had been far more important than his high-flying career. He had chucked it up without a backward glance and thrown himself wholeheartedly into a provincial editorship that barely touched the edges of his vast talents. He had stuck at it, though, with impressive success. In an age when local papers were folding all over the place, the *Argus* had gone from strength to strength under Joe's leadership, which had now lasted almost fifteen years. The various awards the newspaper collected almost annually were scattered around the big man's room.

Robertson was watching the lunchtime regional news bulletin on TV. When he became aware of Kelly watching him his face broke into a wide grin. His eyes sparkled with excitement. Joe Robertson had printers' ink running through his veins. Just like Kelly. Or like he had once been, anyway, Kelly thought wryly.

'Great yarn, John,' Joe roared. He had always been incapable of speaking at anything like a normal volume, particularly when his blood was up on a story. Joe's voice, like everything about him including his personality, was big. 'Well done on the stalker angle. Let's keep it up, shall we? It's great to beat the nationals at their own game, isn't it? This is our patch, after all.'

Kelly's heart lifted. Joe was playing right into his hands. He had known the editor would think the same way as he. Just about the only time Kelly and Robertson had not seen things the same way had been when the editor of the *Argus* had appointed Kit Hansford as his news editor just over a year previously. Mind you, Kelly understood well enough. Joe had wanted a solid provincial man to news edit his solid provincial newspaper. The comprehensive coverage Hansford had wittered on about earlier was indeed the backbone of the *Argus* – its structural frame. Robertson had the flair and the originality to make the *Argus* special on a good day; he didn't need his own clone running his news team. Kelly supposed reluctantly that Hansford was perfect for the job, an ideal foil to his boss.

'I have another lead or two, Joe,' Kelly lied. It came naturally to him to lie to editors and news editors about the progress he was making – or lack of it. You never let the backroom boys get in the way of the story. That was another of Kelly's golden rules.

'Yes?' Joe responded eagerly, his eyebrows raised in query. Expectant.

'Well, Angel's the key to it, but we're not going to get to her for some time, I reckon. I'd like to have a go at her mother. I have a feeling she might be the way to Angel, too.'

'And she lives where?'

'London. Clerkenwell. Moved to Essex once when Angel was big as a kid, the obligatory flash showbizzy gaff, but now she's back in the house where she brought up Angel. Quite poetic, really.'

'London?' queried Joe. 'You need a special pass for that.' He was still grinning, though, which Kelly found encouraging. 'What makes you think she'll talk to you anyway, John?' the editor continued. 'The pack will be camped out there, for sure. I don't really have the staff to send a man up to town on a wasted journey.'

'It won't be wasted, I promise you. I've got an in with the old lady.'

Robertson shook his head almost imperceptibly. 'Have you indeed?' he murmured. 'And where've I heard that before?'

'Honestly,' said Kelly.

Robertson was still grinning. He liked chancers. Kelly knew that. Liked the guys with the extra edge. Even though he promoted machines like Hansford to jobs they should never be given a sniff of in Kelly's opinion.

'All right then, off you go. You've got a day and a half. I want you back in here at seven a.m. Thursday morning.'

'Deal,' said Kelly. 'And I'll need a snapper, young Trevor –'

'Forget it,' interrupted Robertson. 'You'll have to do your own pix. Borrow that digital camera for idiots from the picture desk.'

Kelly shrugged resignedly. He'd already got more of his own way than he'd expected. He turned as if to leave, then hesitated. 'Just one more thing . . .'

'Yes?'

Kelly waved the council minutes which were still in his hand at his editor. 'I'm supposed to be at County Hall at two p.m., according to Hansford . . .'

'You really are a crafty bastard, John, but then you know that, don't you?'

Kelly didn't respond.

'All right, tell Kit you're off all other duties until I say so. Oh, and don't score points, John, all right?'

'Now would I?' Kelly asked over his shoulder as he opened the door to his editor's office.

And as he closed it behind him he could still clearly hear Robertson's bellowed response.

'Not much!'

At about the same time Karen Meadows was arriving at the chief constable's office at the Devon and Cornwall Constabulary's Exeter HQ. She was furious, although she knew better than to show it.

Her previous evening's meeting with Harry Tomlinson had been cancelled at the last moment, and she had only received the call on her mobile phone when she was already halfway to Middlemore. Then, while she had been with Angel Silver earlier that morning Karen had once more been summoned to his presence, and had had to leave her colleagues at Maythorpe Manor.

As far as Karen was concerned the whole thing had already become a monumental waste of valuable time. She had a shrewd idea of what she was in for, too, which didn't help her mood at all.

'A very good day to you, Karen.' The chief constable was a rather short plump man who all too frequently had an air of forced cheerfulness about him. He had a slightly military manner and Karen could easily imagine him as the sort of commander who would lead his men to certain death with a merry quip.

'Sorry about yesterday. Got tied up with the Home Office, if you know what I mean.'

Karen knew. She had expected the Home Office to get involved.

'So, right then, you'd better give me a progress report on the Silver case.'

'Yes, sir.' Doing her best not to let her frustration show, Karen gave a full and detailed account.

'It's quite difficult to get an accurate picture from Angel

Silver's version of the tragedy, and that is all we have, sir,' she said in conclusion. 'But she admits that she killed Terry James after he attacked her husband, so it's primarily a matter of deciding what steps to take next.'

'Have you talked to the CPS?'

'Briefly, sir. I plan to give them a more detailed report later today and talk it through with them fully then.'

'Well, I've had the Crown Bench Prosecutor on to me already, and he's adamant that we have to charge the woman with manslaughter at least. As you well know, everybody's a victim nowadays, including thugs who attack innocent householders. We have to play this one strictly by the book. He gave me the public interest line, of course. Is that the word you've got?'

'Yes. I don't think there is any choice. Unless we charge her with murder, of course.'

Karen was being mischievous with her last remark, and she found the chief constable's reaction highly gratifying.

'Good Lord no,' he countered quickly, his earlier avuncular approach no longer evident. 'There can be absolutely no question of that. There was enough hullabaloo over the Tony Martin case, and he was an unknown farmer who killed an intruder. God knows how the press and the public would react to Angel Silver being convicted of murder when all she was doing was trying to defend herself and her husband. We're walking a tightrope here, Karen.'

'Yes, sir, and don't I know it. If only detectives could just concentrate on detecting the job would be a whole lot easier, wouldn't it, sir?'

Karen hadn't meant to say that. She was aware of the chief constable shooting her a rather sharp look, but he made no direct response.

'So have you talked to her solicitor?' he asked instead. 'What will she plead?'

'Not guilty on the grounds of self-defence, almost certainly.'

Tomlinson sighed. 'Well, let's hope we manage to get a jury with some brains for a change. We really can't afford to send that bloody woman to jail.'

'No, sir,' said Karen as expressionlessly as she could manage.

The case was developing in the way she had feared. It was no longer particularly important, it seemed, to try to find out exactly what had happened at Maythorpe Manor that night and to prosecute accordingly. Instead, the emphasis was on ensuring that the due process of law was seen to operate in a way that gave the least possible cause for public outrage in either direction. And neither justice nor truth seemed to have much relevance.

Karen gritted her teeth. Politics all too often seemed to dominate policing nowadays. She was used to it but she'd never get to like it.

Five

Kelly had parked the MG at the far end of the *Argus* car park where he always did. There was a tall wall there which protected the little motor somewhat both from sunshine and the worst excesses of weather.

He paused to light a cigarette as he approached it, and was vaguely aware of a figure taking off at a run and vaulting over the fence into the main road.

Instinctively Kelly sensed trouble. He quickened his pace slightly. His fears proved justified. Both the tyres on the driver's side wheels of the MG had been slashed. They were completely destroyed.

Kelly kicked one of them in frustration, unlocked the driver's door, flung in his lap-top computer and the digital camera duly acquired from the picture desk, both of which he had been carrying over one shoulder, then used his mobile to phone the MG specialist who looked after the car for him. The good news was that Wayne from Torbay Classic Motors had two of the right tyres in stock and would bring them straight over. The bad news was the price: £200. Ouch, thought Kelly. He supposed that he could claim for them on his insurance, but he had a £100 excess. It could have been worse, of course, and Kelly had little doubt that it would have been had he not interrupted whoever had vandalised his car. The MG could have been totally wrecked. Kelly supposed he should report the incident to the police. But for reasons he couldn't entirely explain he didn't want to. He had no real idea who might want to vandalise his car but he somehow felt sure it was connected with the Silver story. It occurred to him at once that it could be members of the James family. They wouldn't be too pleased with him after his stalker story. The interpretation that he had put on what he had learned from his visit to their Fore Street home would not have pleased the family at all. And they were the sort who liked to take the law into their own hands.

On the other hand, of course, the tyre slashing could be just indiscriminate vandalism, but Kelly didn't think so.

Kelly climbed thoughtfully into the driver's seat. He preferred to wait there for his new tyres to arrive rather than going back into the *Argus* office. Hansford would only gloat and Kelly could not really blame him. As Robertson had predicted, Kelly had not been able to resist doing a bit of gloating himself when only a few minutes earlier he had returned those council minutes to Hansford and given him the editor's message.

Wayne from Classic Motors was as good as his word and arrived less than half an hour later with two replacement wheels.

Within just a few minutes they were fitted and Wayne, a tall angular young man who was one of the best mechanics Kelly had ever encountered, loaded the original pair with their damaged tyres into the back of his van.

When he had finished Kelly asked him if he would just take a look underneath the car and check that nothing else was damaged. Wayne stroked a chin that had never quite recovered from a bad attack of teenage acne and regarded Kelly thoughtfully. But he made no comment, until, after spending several minutes both lying on the ground underneath the little motor and prodding around inside the bonnet he eventually spoke.

'Looks OK to me, John,' he said in his squeaky high-pitched voice. 'Don't forget you're overdue for a service, though.'

Kelly nodded. 'I'll drop her in as soon as I get back from London.'

He drove back to St Marychurch then to pick up an overnight bag and leave a message for Moira. In the beginning, when they had first met it had been Moira who wouldn't quite make the commitment of moving in with Kelly. She had, after all, only one major relationship behind her, a marriage to a man who had turned out to be a violent bully, and she told

Kelly that after that she had vowed never to make herself vulnerable to any one man ever again. Then later Kelly suspected it had been him who wouldn't quite make the commitment. They had settled eventually for a slightly disjointed way of life which seemed none the less to suit them well enough. Moira was one of the good ones, and not for the first time Kelly resolved to let her know more how much he valued her. When he got back from London, that was.

The first thing he noticed when he opened his front door was the smell of fresh paint.

As he closed the door behind him a blue-spotted blonde head appeared over the banisters.

'I thought I'd start on the spare room,' Moira called, then added with just a small note of anxiety, 'You did say blue would be OK, didn't you?'

She didn't look surprised to see him turn up in the middle of the day. But then, she wouldn't be. Kelly invariably seemed to manage to come and go from everywhere, including his place of work, on his own terms.

'Sure,' Kelly replied, peering at her up the stairs. 'You know I reckon you always get it right. Shouldn't you be home in bed, though?'

'I just want to finish the first coat,' she replied. 'I've still got time for my seven hours.'

Kelly knew that all too often, particularly if she'd had a tough night, Moira felt unable to go straight to bed to sleep after coming off duty. Virtually the whole of Kelly's house had been revamped that way. Moira enjoyed decorating and rejuvenating a home. And there had certainly been plenty of scope in Kelly's house which he'd rented when he first came to Torquay and then managed to buy on a mortgage a few years later. She had eagerly taken on the task of giving his home a face-lift, and continued to regard periodic redecoration as a running task. It was a pleasure for her, she told him. It was how she unwound.

Kelly smiled up at her paint-spattered face. Moira was more or less free to come and go as she pleased, but she never took too much for granted. He liked that. And he liked Moira. A lot.

'The blue suits you, by the way,' he said.

Grinning, she held up her hands for him to see. They were both blue too. Moira was very good at painting and decorating, but she always seemed to give herself a coat of paint as well.

'I've got to go to London,' he said. 'I've just popped back for a bag, and I was going to phone your machine and leave a message.'

When Moira was sleeping during the day she set her telephone answering machine to take calls with the ringing tone switched off.

'Well, you can tell me to my face,' she told Kelly, trotting down the stairs. She moved very quickly, almost jerkily. Perhaps that was why she got so much paint over herself, Kelly thought obliquely. She had a small pretty face, which matched her build, a fresh complexion, a ready smile and kind eyes, but there was something in them that made you instantly aware that she had suffered pain in her life.

Kelly had always vowed never to cause her any more.

When she reached the hall he leaned down to kiss her – she was a good six inches shorter than he was – taking care to find a patch of face which was not blue.

'You're supposed to paint the walls, not yourself, you know,' he told her affectionately, stroking her blue-spotted hair.

'I know, but all of us need brightening up,' she responded.

Kelly shook his head in resignation. Then he studied her more closely. The shadows beneath her eyes were very dark that morning, and although she was smiling at him there was a strained tightness about her mouth. He knew that Moira's cheery manner and apparently light approach to life frequently belied the weariness and stress of her job. He was also aware, particularly when he was working on something which excited him, that he was inclined to forget to give her the kind of support she undoubtedly needed.

'Are you all right?' he asked.

'Of course.'

He touched a patch of blue-painted face with his fingertips.

'Hard night?'

'Yup.'

'Anything you want to tell me about?'

Moira was silent for a moment, then she reached out and pulled him close to her.

'Little Timmy Jordan died,' she said eventually.

She didn't tell Kelly much about her work, although he wasn't quite sure whether that was his fault or hers, and he was in any case just as bad about his own job, but she had told him about Timmy. He knew that the boy's death, although expected, would have hit her hard.

'I'm sorry,' he said, and kissed her again.

After a few seconds she drew away from him and held him at arm's length. He could almost see the conscious effort she was making to shrug off the events of her night on duty. Not for the first time he marvelled at her. The NHS just wasn't good enough for Moira and all the others like her, he thought.

'So why London so suddenly, John?' she asked.

'It's the Scott Silver murder,' he told her. 'One or two leads to follow up in town.'

Instinctively he did not elaborate. Old habits died hard. It really was ingrained in Kelly that you gave away as little as possible about a story. Not to anyone. Not even the woman you shared your life with.

'I didn't think you local paper guys were allowed off your patch. You've grumbled about it often enough.'

'I've got a special pass,' he grinned. 'I've been given my freedom – but for less than a couple of days, though, so I'd better get a move on.'

'You're back when? Tomorrow night then?'

'Gotta be. Back to jail the following morning.'

Moira chuckled. 'I'll be off duty. Would you like me to come round and cook you a meal to come home to?'

'You bet,' he said, and he meant it. In spite of his terrible track record, and his apparent reluctance to bring about any permanent changes in his more or less independent lifestyle, he always preferred not to come back to an empty house.

He eased his way past her then and loped up the stairs to

the main bedroom where he slung a couple of spare shirts, a sweater, his toilet bag, and a few other bits and pieces into an overnight bag. Moira followed him.

'Will you have some coffee before you go?'

'I think I just want to get on,' he said.

'Aren't you going to admire my handiwork first?'

'Of course.'

When you paint walls which had previously been murky cream a kind of mid blue, it's hard to tell what the finished results will be after just one coat. All you can see are cream and blue streaks. But Kelly dutifully expressed his admiration.

Back in the car Kelly found himself relishing the long drive, and put aside his lurking anxiety about who had damaged the MG. At least, thanks to Wayne, he could be fairly confident that there was no further unseen damage which could jeopardise him and his car. In fact, safely cocooned in the little motor, and heading away from Torquay towards the motorway, he almost convinced himself that it probably had been just a random act of vandalism. Only almost, though. He didn't really believe that, but sometimes all you could do to keep paranoia at bay was to kid yourself a little. Meanwhile he had four hours plus all to himself to think, to work on his game plan.

He had come to love the West of England, and Torquay, the English Riviera, the splendid old seaside town with its faded grandeur, as much as anywhere he had ever lived. But to Kelly neither Torquay nor any other provincial metropolis could ever really compete with London, the city he had always somehow regarded as the centre of the universe. He still remembered his first job there, twenty-five years ago, a local-paper-trained grammar schoolboy with very little knowledge of life but a bellyful of ambition.

He'd been just twenty-three years old and full of hope and enthusiasm. He'd already got himself a young wife, Liz, his childhood sweetheart, who was drop-dead gorgeous, turning heads wherever she went, and a thoroughly nice human being as well. Too nice for him, probably. He never valued Liz as much as he should have done, of course. Never really valued her at all. And in some ways he had never really valued the job either. It had all come too easily to Kelly back then. Liz remained probably the best-looking woman he had ever been involved with. Their only son, Nick, was born almost precisely nine months after the marriage, and he had been the perfect baby, beautiful and bouncing with health, although Kelly had never appreciated him. He had been too busy doing other things. His natural ability as a journalist quickly won him star status on the *Daily Despatch*. It was Kelly who jetted off all over the world at the drop of a piece of copy caper. Kelly who dashed off to all the hottest trouble spots. There had been Cyprus, Israel, Northern Ireland, of course, revolutions, riots, famine, plague, and other national disasters world-wide, and finally the Falklands. That had been one of his last big ones before the rot set in.

Kelly could no longer quite remember how or why it had all gone wrong. There had been no specific incident. Burn-out, people called it nowadays. But Kelly wasn't even sure if it was as simple as that.

Kelly had been rocketed into the very highest level of journalism at a very young age. He had always been extra-ordinarily able in his chosen trade. He had never countenanced failure. On the big foreign stories he always had to be the one who got closest to the ousted president, interviewed the tortured dissidents in their Argentinian police cells, stood by as they cut a woman's hand off for adultery in Saudi Arabia, and gained access to the cell of execution when they sent an American serial killer to the electric chair.

Huge stories, huge tasks, taking a mammoth toll on all around them. But Kelly hadn't even realised he was under pressure. He had been plunged into an extraordinary working life, and not until years later did he realise just how extraordinary it had been.

For almost ten years Kelly did not stop. The awards came flooding in. He won reporter of the year, foreign correspondent of the year and feature writer of the year. But he could barely even remember the various awards ceremonies. They went by in a flood of alcohol accompanied by endless banter. Once, weary, unshaven, and just a little drunk, he had fallen off a plane returning from some now forgotten war, and an office car had picked him up from Heathrow to rush him straight to the Grosvenor House Hotel in Park Lane to accept a major award from his peers. Kelly had attacked his stubbled face with his electric razor as he was driven through the streets of London, and the long-suffering Liz had met him at the Grosvenor with his dress suit into which he had changed in the gents, at the same time managing fortuitously to acquire a hit of cocaine from a kindred spirit which enabled him to get through the evening and even, miraculously, make a halfway lucid speech.

The excitement was such and the demands on his time and his energy levels so overwhelming that those early years of his marriage were all a bit of a blur. To his eternal shame, he later believed, he had regarded the birth of his only son more as an encumbrance than anything else. Nick's arrival had been an accident. Kelly had not wanted children then – his life had seemed already to be too full and too busy – and maybe he also realised that his lifestyle did not lend itself well to fatherhood. When little Nick had come along, Kelly had barely paused to take notice.

Kelly had survived everything on a heady cocktail of large gin and tonics, adrenalin, and as the years passed, cocaine. There were women too, of course. Kelly had an apparently glamorous job, plenty of opportunity to play away from home, and plenty of money in his pocket.

At first it was the drinking and the drugs which got him through the long hours, the overnight flights followed by mad races to catch a deadline before you could even allow yourself to grab a few hours' sleep, and then gradually, the drinking and the drugs began to make it more difficult for him to do his job, rather than easier.

Once in a central African state torn apart by revolution he had lain comatose in his hotel room after a particularly heavy binge just at the moment when the president and his entire cabinet were summarily executed. Kelly had been blissfully unaware of his colleagues filing copy down below. But those had been the days of teleprinter machines, and everything that all the other reporters had written lay in long curled strips on the floor of the office which housed the hotel's machine. The hotel's night porter, a legendary character who had gained such experience of the way the press worked during his country's troubled history that he had ended up knowing almost as much about newspapers as many of the correspondents he encountered, had gathered up those remnants of everybody else's copy, lumped them together, and sent them over to the *Despatch*.

The man had had a big soft spot for Kelly. People were drawn to him in those days. He had always had the ability to be both warm and charismatic if he chose. It was just his family and those close to him back then who were beginning to suffer the downside of his crazy lifestyle. The night porter did a good job. Kelly had received a hero-gram by return. Only he didn't know it straight away. He had still been flat out.

Inevitably, perhaps, Kelly became overwhelmed by his excesses. Whatever he did in life he seemed to do to excess. Looking back he sometimes thought that because the thrill of his job had been so amazingly extreme, he had wanted that in every area of his life too.

The miracle was that he had not permanently destroyed himself during those heady days. But by God, he thought to himself as he approached the Chiswick flyover, a stone's throw from his old London home, that hadn't been his fault. He'd tried hard enough to kill himself in every way. And he'd had to sink right to the bottom of the pile before he could even begin to climb up it again. But Kelly still hated even to think about that.

He took his old route into town. Along the Cromwell Road, straight through Knightsbridge, down Constitution Hill past Buckingham Palace.

Then he decided to indulge in the sweet torture of driving along Fleet Street to Ludgate Circus. The wave of nostalgia he usually felt in this part of London was not as great as it would once have been, however. So many years had passed that the pull had lessened, and most of the buildings that had once meant so much to him were either long gone or had taken on an identity so different that he barely recognised them. The bulk of the pubs were still there, though, the King and Keys, the Old Bell, the famous Cheshire Cheese up that little alleyway on the left.

He swung a left, north up Farringdon Street and then right past Clerkenwell Green where he pulled in to check the route to Chain Street in his *A to Z*; his one visit to the Hobbs family home had been so long ago. His memory refreshed, the destination proved easy enough to find and just a few minutes later Kelly turned slowly into the street where Angel Silver's mother lived.

A small group of men and women, some with cameras, were standing around outside what was sure to be her house. Robertson had been right, of course: the pack would have been doorstepping Mrs Hobbs from the moment the story broke. But their continued presence indicated that they hadn't got what they wanted yet, and that at least was good news for Kelly. He pulled to a halt in a conveniently empty slot in residents' parking and sat thinking for a moment or two. He'd get one crack at it, he reckoned, and he certainly didn't want to get involved with the pack. The nationals would already have offered a bundle of dosh, for sure, and he had no money at all. In fact, he'd be lucky to get the expenses to pay for this trip.

He reached behind his seat for his overnight bag and removed a sheaf of notepaper. Swiftly he wrote a brief note. Then he got lucky. His first news editor had told him he only employed lucky reporters. Perhaps that had been at the root of Kelly's demise, he thought to himself wryly. His luck had certainly changed, that was for certain. A bored-looking lad of twelve or thirteen, carrying a large canvas sack over his shoulder, turned into the road and pushed a circular of some kind through the letter box of the first rather twee front door that he came to. Then the second.

Kelly was out of the car quick as a flash.

'Hi,' he said. 'Delivering something, are you?'

The boy, who had cropped brown hair and eyes which somehow indicated that they had already seen too much, studied him suspiciously.

'Wot's it look like?' he enquired sullenly, his thin face setting into a deep frown.

Kelly glanced down at the bag. The words *Clerkenwell Chronicle* were printed in big blue letters on the grubby grey canvas. The local giveaway newspaper, Kelly guessed. At least he was working for a regional newspaper which still made an effort to be the real thing. At least people still paid for it and its staff still got a proper wage. Well, very nearly. But it could be worse.

'Delivering to number forty-four?' he asked.

'I might be.'

He was the sort of kid Kelly would like to shake. That wouldn't help, though. Instead Kelly put his hand in his pocket and produced a five-pound note.

'If I give you this,' he said, waving the fiver enticingly in one hand and the sheet of folded notepaper in the other, 'would you put this through number forty-four's letter box for me?'

The boy looked unimpressed.

'Make it a tenner,' he said.

Shaking was too good for the brat, thought Kelly. A good kicking would be better. He paid up.

The boy grunted and carried on down the street, Kelly's note stowed in his bag along with the giveaways.

There was nothing to do now but wait. Kelly climbed back into the MG, reclined the seat as far as it would go and almost immediately fell asleep. He was tired from the long drive and he had not spent very much of the previous night in his bed. It was long ago on the road that he had learned the knack of catnapping, grabbing your rest where and when you can.

He was woken by the strident ring of his mobile. Instantly awake, he picked it up and looked at the display panel. It was Hansford. Well, he certainly didn't want to speak to him. Kelly settled back into his seat and let the phone ring until it diverted to his message service.

He peered down the road. The scene outside number forty-four had not changed. He wondered if he was wasting his and his newspaper's time, just as Joe Robertson had feared. More than likely his ploy would have no success at all. It was almost six o'clock. The last of the wintry sun had dropped behind the tall buildings of Clerkenwell and the City to the east more than an hour ago. Kelly shivered and wrapped his arms around himself. He realised suddenly that he felt quite cold. It was November, after all. His excitement at being involved in a major story after so long had faded as well. Waiting did that to you.

When the phone rang again it woke him up. He reached out with a stiff arm. The movement sent a shooting pain down his back. He realised that he was now seriously cold. He was also cramped into an extremely awkward position and his whole body was aching. He had no idea how he had ever managed to fall asleep like that. Trying not to think about his discomfort he once more glanced at the phone's display screen. It was Moira. He didn't bother to answer her either. He wasn't in the mood. He would call her later when he could choose the moment.

He really didn't want to stay on this doorstep any longer. There was a limit, even for Kelly. Rachel Hobbs had his mobile number, and whether she called him or not Kelly would return to Chain Street in the morning. He rubbed his chilled fingers together, wondering why on earth he should ever have realistically thought that one encounter all those years ago would make any difference to either Angel or her mother. Suddenly, he no longer felt optimistic at all.

Six

Kelly checked into the Grand Hotel in Southampton Row for the night. Cheap and cheerful. If you could call £70 for a small single room for the night cheap. But it was by London standards.

As soon as he had dumped his bag in his room he walked along to Soho, ordered a pint of Diet Coke in the French House, and wished as ever that it was a pint of Guinness. Kelly always seemed to be meeting reformed alcoholics who said that not only would they never touch a drop again, they didn't even miss it. Kelly missed it terribly. He missed what he considered to be the unique refreshment of a pint of cool bitter, he missed the clink and the fizz of a well-made gin and tonic, long and icy in a decent glass, he missed the warmth on the tongue of a fine claret and the taste it leaves behind, and most of all, of course, he missed the burn and the buzz of a shot of whisky as it hits the back of the throat.

There was nobody in the bar that he knew, except Gavin, the manager, who had once run Scribes Club just off Fleet Street. Kelly allowed himself a brief moment of nostalgia before he swallowed the last of his Coke and left. This was not a drink to linger with, and neither was a bar empty of familiar company. Then he wandered up Greek Street to an Indian restaurant of which he had fond memories. The lack of first-class ethnic restaurants was one of the things Kelly missed terribly about life in the sticks and he reckoned a good Indian meal would cheer him up.

Indeed, the food he ordered looked and tasted excellent but he had only just started eating when his mobile phone rang.

A central London phone number which he did not recognise appeared on the display. Rachel Hobbs?

Kelly's mood changed at once. He felt the adrenalin course through his body as he pressed the speak button.

'John Kelly,' he said.

'You'd better come and see me,' said a woman's voice.

Jesus Christ, he thought. It's her.

'I'd love to,' he said as levelly as he could manage.

'How soon can you be here?' she asked.

Automatically Kelly checked his watch. It was just gone 9.30. 'Half an hour, maximum,' he said.

'Thought you wouldn't be far away,' said Rachel Hobbs, as she hung up.

Kelly didn't wait for her to change her mind. He threw a handful of cash at a surprised-looking waiter, soaked his nan bread in his barely touched chicken Madras, the rest of which he sorrowfully abandoned, and, munching his improvised sandwich, hurriedly left the restaurant. He didn't even consider bothering to retrieve the MG from the multistorey car park in which he had earlier installed it at considerable expense. Instead he grabbed a black cab.

At Chain Street there was still a small group of reporters and photographers outside number 44, and they gathered around as Kelly's taxi pulled to a halt. The house was neat and well decorated, but without the twee front door and window boxes of most of the others in the road. Chain Street, built in the late Victorian era as a row of down-market workmen's cottages, was now at the heart of London's inner city rich-pickings real estate market. Indeed Mrs Hobbs' tiny terraced house was probably worth almost as much as a big house in Essex nowadays, thought Kelly, shaking his head at the irony.

When he rang the doorbell a couple of reporters stepped forward to ask him who he was. As he had expected, there was nobody outside the house who knew him. Kelly was history in national newspaper terms.

'I'm just a friend,' he said.

Seconds later the voice he recognised from the brief telephone conversation called from the other side of the door, asking the same question.

'It's John,' he replied, thinking how convenient it was

sometimes to have such an anonymous Christian name. Not that the other guys were likely to know his name.

He heard a key turn in the lock, then a bolt shoot back. The door opened an inch.

'C'mon in – and hurry up,' said the voice.

Kelly pushed the door a little more and slid through the gap, shutting it swiftly behind him. Then he saw Mrs Rachel Hobbs for the second time in his life, standing at the foot of the stairs looking steadily at him. He knew she was now seventy years old, and had naturally expected her to have changed with the years. He knew that during much of her early life she had worked extremely hard, as a seamstress in a nearby factory. And he also knew, as well as any outsider probably, just some of the turmoil she had already faced concerning her extraordinary daughter. He supposed he had expected a little old lady, somebody overwhelmed by being at the centre of media attention again. Nothing could have been further from the truth.

Rachel Hobbs was dressed in a crimson shirt which looked as if it was made of silk, and a short black skirt. The two were divided by a broad gold belt. Big jewellery dripped from her neck and wrists. Her hair was also big, just as it had been twenty years earlier, still platinum blonde and sporting two jewelled combs. She wore very high-heeled shoes and sheer stockings. Her legs remained good. Her figure could have been that of a woman little more than half her years. Only her face gave her age away at all. It was a face that had been lived in, but a good strong one. High cheekbones. Deeply etched laughter lines around almond-shaped eyes, similar to her daughter's but more blue than violet and not nearly so remarkable, which were fringed by thick lashes heavy with mascara. False lashes? Kelly couldn't be sure. Full lips painted ruby red. It was all a bit overwhelming for a terraced house in Clerkenwell.

'Hi,' he said. 'Nice to meet you again.'

Something in his voice or the way he looked at her must have given his surprise away.

She smiled quizzically. 'What did you expect, a Zimmer frame?'

He smiled back. 'I didn't know what to expect,' he said evenly. 'You've kept a low profile for a long time. The only pictures I could dig up were over twenty years old and it must be getting on for that when we last met.'

She nodded. 'I made a deal with Angel when she married Scott. The deal was simple. I had to keep out of her public life or she'd cut me out of her private one. I couldn't argue about that really. Angel saw me as a threat, her brassy mum from East London.' She paused. 'She's a good kid at heart, though, always was. She'd have given me and her dad anything . . .' She paused again and the mask slipped. For a moment she looked almost vulnerable.

Kelly was fascinated. It was suddenly quite hard to grasp the reality of why he was visiting Rachel Hobbs again. The woman's son-in-law had just been killed and her daughter was likely to stand trial for the manslaughter, at the very least, of the man believed to be his killer.

As if reading his mind Rachel Hobbs pulled herself together. 'Right, we'll talk in the kitchen. And this had better be good,' she said. 'Not that I don't know you're conning me.'

'I don't reckon I'd dare.'

'Oh, you'd dare,' she said. Then she smiled again.

'It's been a very long time,' he ventured.

'For both of us,' she said. Then, as if considering: 'I thought you'd be an editor by now.'

'So did I,' he said.

'You were destined for the top,' she said. 'That was the impression you gave, anyway. I followed your career for a bit. Then you just seemed to disappear.'

'I certainly did.' He didn't want to go into that. Not even with her. Perhaps particularly not with her.

Rachel Hobbs' accent was definitely London but not quite as strong as Kelly had remembered. Maybe even his memory had become governed by clichés.

'Right,' she said again when they were seated on either side of the kitchen table, 'I've decided to trust you, so let's get on with it. What do you want to know?'

'I want you to tell me about Angel,' he said. 'Everything

about her. What makes her tick, what she was like as a child – everything you can.'

'Well, you know some of that, don't you?' she replied. 'An awful lot more than most.'

She glanced down at the kitchen table. Kelly saw that his note was lying on top of a small pile of papers.

'"I helped Angel once, please let me do so again",' Rachel Hobbs read out loud. She looked up again at Kelly quizzically.

'Moral blackmail, I think,' she said.

Kelly shook his head. 'No, I don't intend to reveal any secrets, whatever you do or don't tell me today,' he replied, knowing he was only telling half the truth. It was true that he had never intended to reveal the little sequence of events he and Angel and her mother had become embroiled in all those years ago. It was also true that he knew how to call in favours. That had always been the name of the game for Kelly.

'I just want to write about Angel how she really is, the Angel probably only you know. Not her image. But the person. I want you to start at the beginning for me, to pretend that I know nothing at all.'

Rachel Hobbs studied him in silence for several seconds. 'OK,' she said eventually, leaning back in her chair and averting her eyes so that she seemed now to be staring into the middle distance without really saying anything. 'Everybody knows Angel's beginning as a child star, and what a star she was, John. God, she was a gorgeous kid. I'd always wanted to do it myself, you know, go on the stage. I was the classic stage mum. I realise that. And I didn't blame Angel when she made her stand. Did you know about that?'

Kelly shook his head. If he'd ever known he'd forgotten. It hadn't shown up in the cuttings he'd managed to get hold of. And it certainly wasn't one of the secrets he'd referred to.

'The diaries picked up on it. One of Angel's so-called friends must have blown the gaff, I reckon, but not Angel, and not me either, so nobody could ever make a lot of it. I'd wanted too much for her, I suppose. She showed talent, real talent, but then everyone knows that. You remember the way she was, I expect. Cute, they call it now, don't they? We did it all, Angel and me: theatre, TV, that Hollywood movie. Then suddenly she was sixteen and nobody wanted her any more. I think it was me who was more upset, but Angel almost didn't seem to realise that it was all ending. She went wild really. Wouldn't stop spending. The money soon ran out. I suppose we should have had more control, but she was a determined kid. We had to sell the big house, and come back here along with my old dad, which was quite a squash in this little place, on top of everything else. It didn't suit Angel, that was for certain. She was never going to stay.

'Her name was still big enough to give her entry to the in-crowd and that was how she met Jimmy Carey, her own Hollywood superstar. Only he was a bit more faded than Angel realised. He was forty-seven and she was seventeen. I should have stopped it, or at least tried to. Me and her dad, we both should have done. But Angel had made up her own mind, as usual. She was just determined that she wasn't going to stay in a little house in Clerkenwell with a fishmonger for a father.

'We barely saw her for the next four years or so you know. Then she came back one day looking like death and with a black eye to boot. Just twenty-one and a battered wife with a drug problem. I could see it all at once, but Bill, her father, couldn't. She was always his little girl to him. I wasn't as shocked as I should have been. Well, I'd got her back, hadn't I? I took her to our doctor – they're used to drug problems round here – and with his help we weaned her off. She said she was going to divorce Carey and take him for every penny he had. She always had a practical streak, did our Angel. Then Carey died, didn't he? He died of an overdose and there was that big scandal. Angel went back to the States for the funeral and to see to his affairs, as she put it. That was the biggest shock of all, I suppose. Carey had been a big star. He lived in a Hollywood mansion. He lived the high life. I guess we'd all assumed he was filthy rich but he'd gambled it all away. There'd been horses and casinos and, on top of it, bad business deals. It seemed he'd been on the brink of going under when he'd died. There was even talk that the overdose wasn't an accident, of course, that he'd done himself in.

'Anyway, Angel ended up with much, much less than she'd expected. Enough to buy a nice flat in the Barbican and put a tidy sum in the bank, but not nearly enough for the kind of lifestyle she wanted. She'd never had an agent or anything, just me managing her, but I didn't know how to begin to reinvent her, and that's what was needed, more or less. So I went back to the contacts I'd had in the business and fixed her up with Jack O'Sullivan. You've heard of him?'

Kelly nodded.

'Straight as a dye, Jack, and one of the best, but he just couldn't get her off the ground either. She struggled around the fringes for a while, putting on a brave face, but that wasn't Angel. She wasn't born to struggle, to graft hard. Not our girl. There were a succession of men, of course, who were no damned good to her, and I knew she was dabbling in drugs again. But somehow she kept up the lifestyle, kept it all going. It wasn't till you came along that I knew what was really going on.' Rachel Hobbs looked at Kelly anxiously.

'That's not what I've come for, you should know that,' he said.

'I suppose I do or I wouldn't have invited you in.'

'Go on.'

'Well, she hit rock bottom you could say, couldn't you? But then she got lucky, no doubt about it. Amazingly lucky. She could always attract men, of course, always looked so great. Still does, doesn't she?'

Kelly nodded again.

'She met Scott Silver at a party and that was that. They were soul mates, she said. I'm sure he was hers. He was rich, attractive, and a famous rock star. Angel's dream man. Just a week after they'd met she told me she was going to marry him. And she did. I wasn't invited, of course. Nobody was. Ran off to Vegas, didn't they? I never even met him till after the wedding. They'd managed to keep it a secret too. They came here late one night. They'd just flown back, they said. I'll always remember it. They couldn't keep their hands off each other.

'Scott was not at all what I'd expected, you know. Surprisingly shy away from the spotlight, I thought. He was polite and friendly but you could tell he wasn't a bit interested in me or Bill. Just wanted to get our Angel home to bed. She was ecstatic. He went upstairs to the lavatory and that was when she said it.

'"I've got it all, Mum, now," she said. "You won't spoil it, will you?" I told her I didn't know what she meant, but I did, of course. "I'm going to put that child star bit behind me. I just want to be Scott Silver's wife. I'll never cut you out of my life, but I don't want you involved in the public side of it at all. If you carry on living off me I'll never see you again."

'She was right, of course, I had lived off her. And not just financially, either. That wasn't what she was getting at. She was always generous by nature, was Angel. It was more that I liked the glitzy side of things so much, all I ever wanted was to be involved in the showbusiness world. I'm honest enough now to admit that I revelled in her stardom. We've always been two of a kind, me and Angel. I knew she meant it, though. I have never since spoken about her publicly until now. Never. And this may be a mistake.'

'It won't be, Rachel. I won't let Angel down. I didn't before, did I?' Kelly admitted to himself as he spoke that there was indeed an element of moral blackmail there. But they did owe him, Angel and her mum. And in any case, the curious thing was that he meant it. He was as captivated as he had been the very first time he saw Angel.

'So let's get some facts straight,' he went on, giving Rachel Hobbs as little time as possible to dwell on her doubts. 'Has she been in touch with you?'

'Right after she called the police. Phoned to prepare me for the news to break, to tell me she was all right, and what had happened.'

Rachel Hobbs ran the fingers of one hand nervously through her hair. 'I couldn't believe it,' she said. 'It's almost as if there's some kind of curse on Angel, you know. Just when things seem almost perfect the bottom falls out of her world. But this, this . . . it's just so dreadful. I was horrified as much by what Angel told me she'd done as by Scott being murdered.'

Kelly felt all his antennae waggling. 'Can you remember exactly what she said?'

'What do you think? Not that she said very much actually. She wasn't hysterical or anything. Her voice was quite calm. But it was as if she just wasn't functioning properly. Well, she wouldn't have been, would she? It was all quite mechanical, I think.

'She said that she and Scott had woken to find an intruder in their bedroom. A burglar, she assumed. He had a knife and he attacked Scott. Stabbed him. When Scott collapsed the bastard turned on her. She'd been terrified. There was another struggle and somehow she managed to get hold of the knife. She has no idea how really. She said, she said . . .' Rachel Hobbs' control wavered a little. There was a quaver in her voice. 'She said she supposed that she must have stabbed him. The next thing she knew he was lying on the floor and she was covered in blood. But she didn't know what happened. She couldn't remember it clearly. She said she supposed she must have stuck the knife in him, that was how she put it . . .'

'What did you think, Rachel?'

'What do you think I thought, you daft bugger?' There was fire in her voice again. She had never been short on pluck, Kelly reminded himself.

'I thought it was all some awful nightmare,' Rachel continued. 'Can you imagine being phoned up in the middle of the night by your daughter and told something like that? It still hasn't sunk in, to tell the truth.'

'But were you surprised that she was capable of such a thing, even in self-defence?'

Rachel Hobbs studied him with something verging on amusement.

'No, I wasn't surprised about that,' she said. 'And I don't know about self-defence. She didn't know that Scott was dead, did she? She was defending him, that's what she told me. Angel would have done anything to defend Scott Silver, anything at all. She didn't just love him. She worshipped him.'

*

Back in his Southampton Row hotel room Kelly was on such a high that he had completely forgotten his abandoned Indian meal and certainly felt no hunger. What he felt was elation. He always did when he knew he had a lead on the pack. He lay on his bed and contemplated what he had now on the Scott Silver case, and what he was going to do with it. He had been right, after all. He had had an edge. He had had a special way in to Rachel Hobbs. For once he had not been lying to his editor. He couldn't have known whether she still cared about what he had done all those years earlier, but he would have bet six months' wages – if he'd still betted like that, of course – that she would remember. And she had.

It had actually been almost exactly seventeen years ago. Kelly had still been the number one fireman on the *Despatch* then, but he was already drinking more than anybody knew. He was also on the coke by then whenever he could get hold of it, anything to keep the energy levels up, to keep him motoring. The cracks were beginning to form, of course, only he had yet to become aware of them. He'd thought, if indeed he'd thought at all, that he could go on for ever on his crazy tightrope of thrills, chasing fire engines throughout the world on a diet of booze, girls and coke.

The job that had led to his one previous meeting with Angel Silver's mother had seemed routine enough when the news editor had asked him to go undercover on a hot tip. A former child star, famous for playing cute little kids, was allegedly working as a prostitute, pulling punters at a bar in a big London hotel. It was Angel Silver – only then her name was Angelica Hobbs.

The paper's aim was to check out the tip and, if it was true, to expose Angelica in a big way. Kelly's task was to find her, get close to her, and get pulled. It was not the kind of assignment he liked but it went with the tabloid territory. And he had appreciated it for the seriously great yarn that it was.

Angel hadn't been hard to find. On only his second night hanging around in the bar the paper had been told was her regular haunt, he had spotted her. He did not immediately recognise her. Angelica Hobbs' hair had been raven black rather than its familiar blonde. Indeed, it was during that period of life that her chameleon tendencies had evolved. She had been wearing tinted glasses and heavy makeup, something for which she had not previously been known. After all, Angelica had actually once been described by a major film critic as 'the fragile English rosebud of our cinema'.

She had walked straight to the bar, mincing slightly as she did so, and a glass of pink champagne had been provided by an unsmiling barman as soon as she sat down on one of the tall stools. If this young woman was indeed a prostitute – and there was something indefinable about her that suggested that – then her visit was probably business for the barman too, Kelly had thought wryly. He watched her take a packet of cigarettes from her handbag and light one up. Perhaps she had felt Kelly's eyes on her. Abruptly she took off her glasses and looked right at him. Christ, it really was her, he thought. Angelica Hobbs. You could never mistake those eyes: almond-shaped and brilliant violet. Like Elizabeth Taylor's, he had thought then as he had again when he had encountered her all these years later. And she was so beautiful. Most women wore heavy makeup in an attempt to enhance their looks. It was almost as if Angelica Hobbs had plastered the stuff on her face to tone hers down. Instead of the flawless porcelain complexion Kelly remembered from her films, Angelica's skin had the matt look which usually indicated bad skin coated with thick layers of slap.

She remained stunning, though. Although too thin. Far too thin.

For several seconds the two of them stared at each other. Eventually Angel's eyebrows rose in some silent query. Was that the come-on? Kelly had felt awkward, embarrassed, unusually unsure. He looked away. He needed to watch her for a bit. And, to be honest, he needed a few more drinks before he felt he could take this one any further.

He glanced over his shoulder. The photographer he was working with was sitting in a corner of the bar with a virtually untouched beer on the table in front of him. Kelly jerked his head slightly in the direction of Angelica Hobbs and gave a small nod. Michael Phildon, one of the *Despatch*'s hot shots, nodded back even more discreetly.

Phildon's job now would be to snatch what pictures he could of the young woman, preferably with a punter or two on her arm.

Kelly remembered that Phildon hadn't had long to wait. A man appeared as if by magic at Angelica's side. Kelly guessed that he was an Arab and he had that air of confidence about him of the seriously rich who have never had cause to lose their certainty that money can buy anything.

Kelly saw Mike Phildon slip out of the far door of the bar. Phildon had been a good twenty years older than Kelly, but he was the kind who never went off the boil, an expert in his trade. A photographer with years of experience behind him of working on investigations and exposés, including more than his share of sex exposés like this one.

A few minutes later Angel and her Arab punter also left the bar. Kelly had known that Phildon would be lurking somewhere unseen in the foyer. He'd have the pair of them on celluloid in a flash without either of them knowing they'd been had. They didn't call Mike Phildon Super Snatcher for nothing.

Kelly stayed at the bar patiently waiting. Less than an hour later Angelica returned alone. Ready to pull another trick, no doubt. Kelly watched again as she settled on to the same bar stool and the still unsmiling barman provided her with another glass of pink champagne. She had passed him a wad of notes, a considerably greater amount of money than the price of a couple of glasses of pink champers, even in that rip-off joint, Kelly had reckoned.

He had stared hard. Again she took off her glasses and gave him the come-on. This time he pulled his stool closer to hers and offered her another drink.

It was not very long before they were leaving the bar together. She had been quite direct, businesslike almost.

'Do you have a room here?' she asked.

'Yes,' he said. It was a two-bedroomed suite, in fact, equipped in anticipation of a result with another photographer and state-of-the-art recording equipment in the locked second bedroom.

They walked to the lift together. He realised that she was

swaying slightly. She stumbled and he grasped her by the elbow to prevent her falling. Her bones were so thinly covered by flesh that they felt sharp to his touch. He had already noticed how thin she was, but it was more than that. Angel was quite emaciated.

She leaned against him. The dark glasses slipped down her nose and he could see her violet eyes close up for the first time. There was a blankness in them, and her pupils were dilated. He wondered what on earth she had been taking. Her black silk dress had slipped off one shoulder. He could see an ugly black bruise over her collar bone. Out of the corner of an eye he glimpsed Mike Phildon stepping softly forward from a shadowy corner beneath the staircase, camera at the ready. On an impulse Kelly pulled Angel closer to him so that Mike Phildon would be unable to snap her without the protection of her tinted specs.

Then, even more impulsively, he heard himself speak. There was something about her, the way she looked at him, her fragility, which made it impossible for him to throw her to the wolves.

'C'mon,' he said. 'I'm taking you for something to eat. You look starving.'

Kelly had surprised himself. He was, after all, a dedicated tabloid hack, top man, and his behaviour had been completely out of character.

Angel made no protest. She had probably been unable to. In the taxi it became apparent that she was beyond eating. She just slumped in the seat beside him, passing no comment when he redirected the taxi driver from the restaurant he had planned to take her to, giving him instead the address of a hotel he had used before. Somewhere where the staff were used to couples with no luggage turning up unannounced.

In the room he swiftly acquired he had poured himself a Scotch from the hip flask he invariably carried and only gave her one when she insisted.

'I know who you are,' he told her.

She did not argue. 'Add to the thrill, does it? Would you like me to put on a gym slip?'

He'd shaken his head, wondering why she made him feel

so sad. At one point she began to undress. He'd stopped her, thought about telling her who he was and then thought better of it in case he frightened her.

'Why are you doing this?' he asked.

'Girl's got to make a living,' she told him, and shortly afterwards said that she needed to use the bathroom.

She seemed a long time. He tapped on the door. No response. Eventually he tried the handle. The door opened, she had not even bothered to lock it. Inside she was slumped on the lavatory seat, a syringe on the tiled floor beside her. He picked it up and smelled it. Smack. He had thought as much.

Angel looked at him with unfocused eyes, a silly smile on her lips. 'I feel better now,' she said.

He helped her to the bed and she lay back against the pillows. 'I think you should go home,' he told her. 'Have you got anyone to look after you?'

She had shaken her head and fallen deeper into her drugged stupor.

Kelly was quite full of sorrow for her by then. He remained unable to explain to himself why this waif of a girl moved him so, but she had done from the very beginning. From the first moment he had looked into her eyes she had had this effect on him.

He went through her handbag then. There was a diary with some phone numbers and addresses at the back. Rachel Hobbs had been listed there – Angelica's mother. Kelly had known all about her. Everyone did in those days – the archetypal pushy stage mum, generally regarded as being of the opinion that she was as much a star as her daughter had once been.

Kelly called Rachel Hobbs' number. It was 2 a.m. An irritable voice, heavy with sleep, answered. But the irritation turned to what seemed like genuine concern when Kelly told her who he was and what had happened, exactly what her daughter was doing and the state she was in. However, being media wise, Mrs Hobbs was not just concerned about her daughter's welfare.

'You're going to make a meal of this, I suppose, in that rag of yours. Well, I have no comment to make to add to whatever rubbish you're going to write. Just tell me where my daughter is and I'll come and get her.'

'That won't be necessary, Mrs Hobbs,' said Kelly. 'I'm bringing your daughter home. Oh, and I didn't ring you for a quote, by the way. I don't intend to run with this story. I rang you because you're not only Angelica's mother, you made her what she is. So now you're the one who has to get her sorted. If you don't, there will be other reporters, I promise you. If she goes back on the game to fund this habit of hers it will only be a matter of time before she gets found out big time. Mind you, she mightn't even live that long.'

Kelly had not waited for Rachel Hobbs to reply. Instead he called a cab, wrapped his jacket round Angel, helped her out of bed, and bundled her down the stairs and out of the hotel. She was still only semiconscious when they arrived back at that same terraced house in Clerkenwell, the house the family had moved back to when Angel's child star bubble had burst, the house Kelly had revisited earlier that night, seventeen years later.

Kelly had helped Angel into the house, half carrying her. Mrs Hobbs had put her to bed and made him a cup of tea.

'I had no idea she'd gone on the game. I had no idea it had got that bad,' Rachel Hobbs told him, and she had looked at him quizzically. 'Are you really not going to write this?'

'No,' he said.

'Why not?'

'To tell you the truth, Mrs Hobbs, I'm not sure I can answer that,' he had responded honestly. And he had never been able to answer it, really. It had always been inexplicable. Kelly hadn't been a soft touch for a sob story, that was for certain – not in those days, anyway.

'I'm grateful,' she'd told him. And he'd known that she had been.

The next day Kelly informed his bosses at the *Despatch* that there'd been a mistake. The girl looked like Angelica Hobbs, but it wasn't her, he was sure of it.

The news editor had not been best pleased. He'd wanted to know why Kelly hadn't taken the girl up to the suite they'd hired at great expense. Kelly had said she'd refused to go with him there. He didn't know why. She'd insisted they go back to her flat. The news editor was suspicious, Kelly knew that, but his reputation had yet to be completely destroyed. He was still the *Despatch*'s leading fireman, after all, and his version of events had been reluctantly accepted. More or less. They'd pored over Mike Phildon's photographs, but they were snatches, albeit good ones, and none had caught Angel without the dark glasses. Kelly had made sure of that.

He knew that they'd sent another team round to the same hotel bar for a few nights, but he'd hoped that Angel would never be found there again. And she wasn't.

He'd often thought of her, even then, and wondered how she was getting on. One of the other dailies picked up the story that she'd been booked into the famous Priory rehabilitation clinic. He'd supposed that had been inevitable. At least she and her mother were trying to do something. Three months later he'd received a phone call.

He'd recognised her accent at once, Hollywood Cockney meets stage school English.

'My mother tells me I owe you a thank you,' she said.

'Think nothing of it,' he replied.

'I can barely remember that night.'

'I'm not surprised.'

'In any case I just want to blank the whole thing out. You really did me a big favour, you know. When I realised how close I'd come to be splashed all over the *Despatch* even I knew something had to be done.'

'Didn't you want to do it just for yourself? You were on a free fall to destruction. That stood out a mile.'

There had been a brief pause, then she'd said something which had sent a little shooting pain right through his heart.

'I guess I never liked myself that much, Mr Kelly.'

He struggled to find the right reply. 'And now?'

There had been another pause, and when she eventually spoke again she carefully avoided answering him properly.

'I promise you one thing, Mr Kelly, I'll never get in that state again.'

Then she'd thanked him again and hung up. He'd sat at his desk thinking about her even more, trying to work out why she captivated him so much, and wondering why he hadn't invited her out to dinner or something. Perhaps it was because he recognised that she was just a fantasy for him. Perhaps because one side of him was disgusted by her behaviour and yet he recognised a lot of himself in her. Maybe he'd realised even then that he was sliding down a similar slippery slope.

But less than a year later Angel met and married Scott Silver after a whirlwind romance, and their marriage had always been represented as one of the great love affairs of the showbusiness world. Kelly had never met or spoken to Angel since, nor seen her except on TV and in newspaper photographs, until the killings at Maythorpe Manor.

The next morning Kelly e-mailed his story back to Torquay, along with the up-to-date snaps Rachel Hobbs had allowed him to take of her with the digital camera which he was able to connect directly to his lap-top, in time to catch the first editions of the *Argus*. He'd written his piece the previous night before going to bed, but it didn't do to give 'em copy too early. They thought you hadn't worked hard enough for it. Kelly'd learned that long ago as well as so many other tricks.

He had nothing more to do in London, but when he spoke to Hansford he invented a story about meeting contacts. He had no intention of reappearing at the *Argus* office until the following morning, as agreed with the editor. After a quick breakfast he rescued his car from its extortionately expensive car park and set off through the heavy London traffic, heading west across the city towards Chiswick and the start of the M4.

On the way he called Karen Meadows on his mobile. If they were about to charge Angel Silver all his hard work could be wasted – for the time being, at any rate.

'She's going to be charged, almost certainly, but I can't tell you when or even exactly with what, John,' said Karen. 'You'll be all right for tonight's edition, though, if that's what's worrying you.'

'And tomorrow morning?'

'What've you got, John? Something you've flogged to the nationals, I presume.'

'Not yet,' said Kelly lightly. And that much was true. He would file just as the lunchtime edition of the *Argus* hit the streets. The paper did pay him a regular monthly wage, after all, even if it was a pittance compared with what he had once earned.

'I'll tell you what I want –'

The DCI interrupted him. 'You don't have to, I know. But even Angel Silver isn't mad enough to give you or anyone else an interview right now. Anyway, I've got someone with her. For her own protection, you understand.'

Kelly understood. 'And the post mortem – did that tell you anything you didn't know already?'

There was a pause. Then she went formal on him. 'You'll have to wait for that, John. Our inquiries have only just begun.'

'Forensic?' he queried. 'DNA?'

'Already?' she responded. 'You've got to be joking. Only in the movies do you get forensic results this quick. And DNA, as you well know, takes three weeks or more. Look, John, we've got a double killing here. I'm really not going to be able to help you any more until we're damned sure we know exactly what happened.'

'But you do know, don't you?' Kelly was always persistent. 'That's what you told me, anyway.'

'Well, yes. It seems straightforward enough. But two men have been stabbed to death on my patch and one of them was one of the biggest rock stars in the world. This is not a good case to make mistakes on. I've already got the chief constable on my back, and he's got the Home Office on his.'

'Now why doesn't that surprise me?' said Kelly as he ended the call.

He knew that any major crime was always surrounded by people working to their own agenda. The police were no exception. In this case there really seemed to be very little detection to be done, but Karen Meadows would be only too well aware of how high profile the case was, and she was obviously determined that nothing was going to go wrong. That would be disastrous PR.

Kelly drove to Torbay without a break and headed for Classic Motors. It might have been his imagination, but he'd reckoned the MG had sounded a little rough on the way home, so he decided to heed Wayne's warning about the overdue service and drop the car off straight away.

Wayne lent him his courtesy car as usual, which was rather a posh term for the overly large elderly Volvo, which felt to Kelly rather like a tank after the MG. None the less he decided to continue on out to Maidencombe, to the Silver home. The Volvo seemed particularly huge and clumsy as Kelly manoeuvred it through the village and down the slope to the beach car park. He had deliberately avoided attempting to negotiate Rock Lane, where, as he had expected, a number of fans and a smattering of press were still gathered outside Maythorpe Manor. Kelly mingled with them for a bit, soaking up the atmosphere, picking up a few quotes, gathering what information he could.

Nobody had caught sight of the rock star's widow since the police had escorted her back to the old manor house after she had been questioned at Torquay Police Station.

Trevor Jones was there again. In fact, looking at him, Kelly wondered if he had been home at all. The young photographer was unshaven and slightly dishevelled-looking, his bright eyes hooded with tiredness. Even his normally unquenchable enthusiasm seemed to have waned slightly. Doorstepping did that to you, thought Kelly wryly.

'Has Jimmy Rudge been out again?' he asked.

'Nope,' replied the the youngster flatly. 'The police come and go. The SOCOs have only just left. God knows what they were doing in there. The postman's been already with another two big sacks of mail. And that was today's big thrill.'

There was still a lone policeman on duty by the gate, and Karen Meadows had indicated a further presence inside. The mound of floral tributes to the murdered rock star had grown into a small mountain.

Kelly wandered over for a closer look. It was then that he noticed the same young woman he had accidentally collided with on the night after the murder, the one who had stood apart from the rest. She was standing apart now, but this time leaning against the railings looking unseeingly towards the crowd rather than into the grounds of Maythorpe Manor.

Kelly had not seen her face before but he was sure it was the same young woman. She had the same long robes and the same long lank hair. Several strands of beads hung round her neck and she carried a further strand in her left hand, like a rosary. She looked like a kind of sixties throwback.

He took a couple of paces nearer to her. She was prettier than he had at first thought, but she wore no makeup and everything about the way she dressed and the way her hair hung untended, almost straggly, indicated someone who took little interest in their appearance, and certainly someone who made no attempt to look attractive.

She was very dark, her hair almost black, her skin olive brown. The shape of her eyes suggested that she might have some oriental blood. They were red-rimmed and her cheeks were tear-stained.

Kelly was standing right in front of her now, but she gave no sign that she was even aware of him being there.

'You look very upset,' he said.

There was absolutely no response.

He tried again. 'Scott must have meant a great deal to you.'

She glanced at him then, as if suddenly surprised by his presence. 'Yes,' she said in a quiet, distant sort of voice. 'He did. A great deal . . .' Her voice tailed off and she turned and walked away from Kelly.

'Miss, miss,' he called after her, 'I'm from the *Argus*. Would you talk to me? Will you tell me who you are?'

Her shoulders stiffened and her pace quickened. Kelly did not attempt to follow her.

When Kelly eventually returned home he walked, as was his habit, straight through the hall, and up the stairs to his spare-room office in order to check his telephone answering machine. A disconcerting message awaited him.

'I may owe you a favour from half a lifetime ago but don't you ever go near my mother again.'

That was all. Nothing else. A woman's voice, but the caller did not leave her name.

She did not have to. The accent, still Hollywood Cockney mixed with stage school English. The slight lisp. Such a distinctive unusual voice. Such an unusual woman.

Seven

Kelly played the tape over and over again. There was anger in Angel's voice, but also the familiar vulnerability.

He wondered if she had got his note, or if it had merely become buried in fan mail as he had suspected. If not, it seemed likely that she had spoken to her mother and Rachel Hobbs had given her his number. Old hack that he was, he found himself oddly disturbed that she was angry with him. Also, although it was unlike him to give a damn, he hoped that he had not caused her to be angry with her mother, whom for some reason he quite genuinely liked.

Kelly frowned in concentration as he attempted to sort out his thoughts. He was so engrossed he did not even notice Moira, standing quietly in his office doorway.

For two or three minutes Moira watched in silence as Kelly kept pushing the play button on his digital answering machine. She had been in the kitchen when he had arrived home, but she heard him open the front door and run up the stairs, and had followed him, intending only to greet him in a normal fashion. But there had been something in the intensity of his manner as he kept playing his message which had stopped her.

Suddenly he seemed to become aware of her presence and swung round to face her. He looked mildly surprised.

'I – I didn't hear you,' he stumbled.

She smiled uncertainly. 'Hello,' she said.

'Yes, hi.'

'Good trip?'

'What? Oh yes.' He was distracted, and it showed.

'I saw the paper. It looked great. Got what you wanted, I assume?'

'Yes,' he said again, still looking as if his mind were somewhere else.

She walked across the room to him then, and, standing on tiptoe, stretched up to kiss his cheek.

'Welcome back,' she said.

'Thanks,' he replied, abstractedly stroking her hair, almost the way he always did but not quite.

She pulled away again and studied him carefully. 'You'd forgotten I was coming round, hadn't you?' she enquired.

'Course not,' he replied swiftly.

But she knew it was a lie. She knew him too well, well enough certainly to know how selfish he was when he got stuck into a story. He'd told her many tales about his time on the *Despatch* and although most of them were great entertainment she was well aware that he must have been a real monster to live with back then. Even without the booze and the drugs, and even though he was no longer a big-time operator, Kelly still had a selfishness about him when he was working. He hadn't called her at all while he had been away, even though she had left two messages on his mobile voice mail.

'Sorry I didn't phone,' he said then, almost as if he had been reading her mind. 'I meant to last night, then Rachel Hobbs called, late . . .'

His voice tailed off. He was still preoccupied. Well, thought Moira, she was never going to change that in him so she might just as well make the best of it and take an interest.

'So who was that on the machine?' she asked.

He told her.

'And why do you keep playing the message?'

'I, um, don't know.'

Kelly sounded as if he didn't want to talk about it. Taking an interest was obviously not going to win her many bonus points on this occasion, thought Moira, just as Kelly abruptly changed the subject.

'You cooking?'

'Of course. That's what we agreed, and I remembered, even if you didn't.'

If he was aware of the acerbic note in her voice he certainly did not show it.

'Tell me what's for dinner then, beautiful?' he asked her. 'I'm absolutely ravenous. I haven't eaten since breakfast.'

Moira couldn't help smiling at that. It could be infuriating, but there was something appealing in the boyish enthusiasm Kelly still displayed about his work, an enthusiasm which had remained undampened against the odds.

'And I bet you didn't remember that until now, either,' she countered.

He grinned at her. 'You're not wrong,' he said.

Then the phone rang. Kelly pounced on it, not bothering to look at the display panel, instead grabbing the receiver as if afraid the caller might not give him time to pick it up.

'Hello, hello. Oh, it's you.'

Moira detected a definite note of disappointment in his voice. She looked at him enquiringly.

'It's Nick,' he mouthed to her.

Moira was surprised. She didn't think she had ever seen Kelly anything but overjoyed to hear from the son he had only in recent years been reunited with. So who had he been expecting or hoping the caller would be? Angel Silver was the only person Moira could think of, although judging from the message she had heard Kelly play, that seemed pretty unlikely.

After only a minute or two more Moira headed back to the kitchen to tend the leg of lamb she was roasting, leaving Kelly to talk to his son in private. She was aware of him making a conscious effort to sound interested. That really was unlike him.

He must be seriously caught up in the Scott Silver case, she thought to herself as she removed the lamb from the oven, threw on more rosemary and garlic, and piled some potatoes and parsnips around it to roast alongside.

Well, she thought indulgently, it must be a good feeling for him to be involved with something other than council meetings and magistrates' courts again.

Nick, alone for once in his dockland apartment, had also been surprised at the way his father had greeted him. He had grown accustomed to warm enthusiasm from Kelly.

'Everything all right, Dad?' he asked.

'Of course, Nick. Couldn't be better.'

'Right. Good.'

'And you?'

'Yeah. Fine. Really fine. Got another big bonus this week. I'm thinking of trading the Porsche in for that new model I told you about that they've just brought out.'

'Oh great, yeah.'

It wasn't the words, but the lack of expression in them which puzzled Nick. Kelly shared his son's love of sports cars. In his father's case it was classic British racing cars, particularly MGs, of course. But Nick knew that he had also developed an interest in the Porsches his son so adored. Kelly was highly unlikely ever to be able to afford such a vehicle himself now, and Nick thoroughly enjoyed chucking his father his car keys and watching Kelly turn into a boy racer. On this occasion, however, there was barely a note of enthusiasm or any interest at all in Kelly's voice.

Nick ran the fingers of one hand through his thick sandy hair, an inheritance from his blonde mother, and tried again. 'You know we talked about you coming up to town for a weekend, well, if you could manage it within the next two or three weeks I'll try to arrange a test drive.'

There was a pause. 'I don't think I'll be able to, Nick,' Kelly replied eventually. 'Not that quickly, anyway. There's this big story, you see . . .'

Nick felt his shoulders tense. During the relatively small amount of time that he had spent with his father as a boy this was all he remembered hearing. Kelly was invariably away on some big story. Only as he'd grown older Nick had learned that that was not always the truth. All too often his father had been drunk or stoned, or with a woman other than Nick's mother. Frequently all three, Nick reflected.

Nick had been ten when his mother and Kelly had finally split for good, but even before the final breakdown of his parents' marriage he had seen very little of his father. When Kelly had not been away allegedly working, he would still, more often than not, arrive home only in the middle of the night and sometimes not at all. After the divorce Nick had seen virtually nothing at all of him until, a grown man of twenty-one and a young army officer, he had sought his father out of his own volition.

He still didn't know quite why it had been so important to him to build a relationship with Kelly. Neither did he know why he had still cared. After all, looking back he didn't even know whether his father had loved him at all during those early years. But it had been important. Possibly the most important thing in Nick's life. And he had cared, desperately.

Kelly had tried to explain how the whole fatherhood thing just passed him by. He had pronounced himself overjoyed to be reunited with his only son and had told him: 'It was only guilt and shame that kept me away from you. I honestly thought you and your mother would be better off if I didn't go near either of you.'

Nick, all too aware of the depths his father had sunk to, had been moved by that. And he certainly had no doubt that his father loved him now. He could see it in his eyes, hear it in his voice, every time they met or even talked on the phone.

Which was why this conversation was so peculiar. Kelly was so distracted. Ever since their reunion Nick had been aware of being at the centre of his father's universe. Not today, though. And that disturbed Nick. He had grown to love Kelly every bit as much as he believed his father now loved him. It was more than love, really. It was an acute need for a part of his life he had previously felt to be missing.

Nick was twenty-seven, tall, fit, and well aware of his own attractiveness as well as his abilities. He had both charm and looks, and he knew it. He also had money. He had left the army two years previously and had since pursued a much more lucrative career. Nick liked the good things in life. During his time in the army he had been trained as a computer expert. The modern army, he had learned, no longer marches so much on its stomach as on its software, and Nick learned skills which he found to be much valued in civilian life. His official title now was 'business consultant', which covered all manner of territory. The reality was that he moved with rare ease among people he regarded to be the real movers and shakers of the world, and that he provided specialist services with a rare aplomb. Nick was the kind of young man who seemed to have been born with an old head on his shoulders, which, combined with the energy and daring of youth, had led to him already being very successful. His spacious and luxuriously appointed penthouse apartment, with its views down the river to Greenwich, was just one of the many trapping of that success. His Porsche was another.

Nick was the guy who had everything. And neither his business associates nor the succession of glamorous young women he dated would have believed just how much his relationship with his father meant to him.

Nick tried to ease the tension in his shoulders, moving them in a kind of circular movement to loosen the muscles.

Kelly was still talking. '. . . It's this Scott Silver case. I don't know if you've seen any of my stuff in the nationals. It's the best yarn that's come my way since God knows when . . .'

Nick listened absently. He just hoped that was all it was. He knew his father was proud of him, but wondered if Kelly realised that Nick too was proud of him for the way in which he had rebuilt his life. Nick didn't just love his father, he liked and respected the man he had only been able to get to know just a few years previously. And Nick was pretty sure his father wouldn't have any idea how frightened Nick got at the remotest prospect of Kelly turning back into the distant, thoughtless, shadowy creature of his boyhood memory. Nick was always afraid that his father would start drinking, fall back into his old ways. And Nick didn't know if he could handle that. Not again.

'Sure, Dad,' he said. 'I understand. No problem. Maybe I can get down to you guys soon.'

He made his voice bright and brisk, determined that his disappointment and fear wouldn't show. Nick was good at hiding how he felt. That was another of the reasons for his success.

When Kelly walked into the *Argus* office early the next morning as promised, he received an excellent reception. Even Hansford congratulated him on his coup, albeit in his usual grudging way, and Robertson was ecstatic.

'Great stuff, John,' enthused the editor. 'Seems like you haven't lost your touch after all.'

Kelly liked compliments as much as the next man, albeit barbed ones. And he didn't mind banter a bit. After all, he'd been weaned on it. But the most important thing that came along with his latest exclusive was that nobody, not even Hansford, was likely to suggest that he worked on anything other than the Silver story for a bit.

He had already had his usual quick run through the national dailies at home, but sitting at his desk he had another more thorough look, particularly at the *Sun* to which on this occasion he had filed exclusively. The *Sun* News Desk had asked him to give them the chance of an exclusive on any fresh material he came up with and he had done so. They paid well, from experience he found them less likely to mess freelances about than most of the rest, and he still had a couple of good old mates there, in senior positions now, whom he dealt with directly. Only the early issues reached Torquay, but Kelly felt sure that all the papers would have followed up his *Sun* stuff in their later editions. He had been more interested to see if any of the other nationals had anything that was new to him.

The *Mail* had an interview with one Mrs Sheila Nott, Angel and Scott Silver's daily who had waxed lyrical about what wonderful people they both were and how, when she had said goodbye to Scott on the morning preceding his murder, she had had a premonition that it would be the last time she would ever see him. Nonsensical crap, thought Kelly.

Much more intriguingly the *Mirror* had a fairly detailed account of what they claimed to be the post-mortem reports on both Scott Silver and Terry James. Somebody must have had a good contact at the hospital, Kelly thought, turning the pages. Of course, there was no guarantee of the accuracy of the *Mirror* story, but Kelly doubted very much that any paper would go big on a flier with a tale that could have as many repercussions as this one.

It seemed that both Scott Silver and the man believed to have broken into his home had been the victims of frenzied attacks. Both of them had been stabbed several times. Scott Silver had suffered a total of eight stab wounds all over his body, primarily around the area of his heart and in his belly, but also in his upper arms, suggesting he had been trying to defend himself. Terry James had suffered even more wounds, possibly as many as ten.

Kelly thought about it for a moment or two. Karen Meadows had refused to tip him off about the results of the post mortem before the official report that would be given at the inquests into the two deaths, but he was fairly sure she'd be prepared to tell him if the *Mirror* story was fundamentally correct. He decided to phone her at once. She was her usual self, brisk, in a hurry, and gratifyingly straightforward.

'As near as damned,' she said in reply to his question.

'So both of them were stabbed repeatedly? It must have been a blood bath out there.'

'Yup. God knows how those bastards at the *Mirror* got hold of so much detail at this stage but that's journalists for you.'

'Good at their jobs, you mean,' Kelly countered mischievously.

'Good at being devious,' she responded.

'Any chance of a meet?' he went on, not bothering to react to that one.

'Now? In the middle of a murder investigation? You have to be joking.'

'Nope. Thought you might like to talk to somebody you could trust.'

'Is that another joke?'

He smiled and remained silent. He knew that she did trust him, and liked him. They wouldn't have been having this conversation otherwise.

After a few seconds she seemed to relent.

'I don't even have any time to spend with myself right now, Kelly,' she said. 'But maybe soon, OK?'

'OK.'

Kelly was thoughtful as he replaced the receiver. He was also slightly taken aback. From everything he had gathered about Terry James, he quite believed, in spite of the family's protestations, that the man would not only strike out in self-defence, but also use a knife with no compunction at all in order to avoid being caught. Kelly had not swallowed the gentle giant stuff for one second. But he was surprised that the man would have stabbed Scott quite so many times. He had somehow imagined that when Scott had awoken and surprised the intruder, Terry James had hit out instinctively, once, maybe twice, and then stepped back, perhaps frozen by the horror of what he had done, and somehow given Angel a chance to grab the knife from him. It had also not occurred to Kelly, even though Karen Meadows had told him that James had been stabbed several times, that Angel could have launched a frenzied attack on the scale that the *Mirror* indicated. Rather he had imagined her too lashing out, probably striking James glancing blows with the knife, causing only shallow flesh wounds, before hitting a major artery.

Kelly concentrated, trying to imagine what had happened next. Angel always looked so fragile. But there was a toughness in her. She was a survivor, no doubt about that. And her mother had indicated to him that she would do anything to defend Scott. But Kelly had actually witnessed a frenzied knife attack once – well, a bayonet attack, to tell the truth – and remembered it all too clearly. It had been in the Falklands. Kelly had been yomping across the island with a British battalion. They had come over a rise straight into a group of Argentinian soldiers. Surprise and fear were a heady mix. The first man to be confronted face to face with an Argentinian had been a very young squaddie. He'd got the first blow in, bayoneting the Argentinian in the throat. Blood gushed out like oil from a geyser, drenching the squaddie and spattering everyone near him, including Kelly, who had shaken for days after the experience. Kelly suspected that the other man had died at once, but the British squaddie didn't stop, perhaps couldn't stop. He repeatedly stabbed the Argentinian soldier with his bayonet. It was hard to believe one man could have so much blood in his body. It spurted from every puncture point. Blood pressure. You had to see a human being stabbed, see the sheer power behind the blood which then bursts from the body, before you ever fully appreciated what the phrase meant. Kelly was all too well aware of just how much blood pressure there was within the human frame. The other soldiers had to pull the lad off. And when they did his appearance was ghoulish. He had looked as if he had been bathing in blood.

Kelly shuddered at the memory. He tried to imagine what it must have been like for Angel. How could she have done anything like that? He wondered if she'd been on coke at the time. Or did she still do smack? She certainly didn't look like a druggie. She looked wonderful, in spite of her ordeal. But then, apart from that one time when he had done his best to rescue her from herself, she always had looked wonderful.

Karen Meadows hadn't mentioned drugs. Neither had anyone else. Kelly knew that during the last year or two of his life Scott Silver had become a born-again Christian of some kind. Maybe that had meant he no longer did drugs, although there had been no doubting his involvement in the drug scene as a younger man. But Angel? Was she clean? Kelly had no idea. If drugs were involved that would affect any prosecution against her. He'd got the impression from Karen Meadows that the police were pretty sympathetic towards her. Drug involvement would change all that.

Whatever the truth, Kelly wondered what kind of effect having killed someone in such a way would have on Angel. He knew about how sometimes it was the apparently weakest amongst us who became the strongest when under attack, and were capable of acting with a viciousness that would normally be completely out of character. He would always remember seeing for the first time the picture in a newspaper of the man who had broken into former Beatle George Harrison's home and attacked him. George's wife, not a big woman, had leaped to her husband's defence, and given his attacker a real hammering. The picture had shocked Kelly. He'd imagined, as was so easy for him to do, how the man must have spurted blood all over her, and yet she had just gone on hitting him. Some woman, he'd thought at the time.

What Angel had done was even more extreme. And it had led to a death.

He would see her face for a long time, pale, beautiful,

almost translucent, surprisingly calm, as she'd been loaded into the police car that morning. He could hear her words on the answering machine. Angry. Afraid maybe, too. All of that.

He switched on his computer terminal and started to type. He wanted to send Angel another letter, to explain, to apologise. He'd done nothing to apologise for. He was a working journalist, after all. But it was important to him that she would realise that he was a friend as well as a hack – at heart always had been a friend to her – that he was on her side, and that she could depend on that.

It took him several attempts to get the words right, to explain how he felt, and find the right way of convincing her that he honestly believed her mother's story would win sympathy and support for her. To try to make her believe that he really wanted to help her.

Finally he again asked for an interview. Well, he couldn't help himself, could he?

'You'll have to talk to somebody sooner or later, Angel,' he'd written. 'Make it me. Make it somebody you already know is a friend, somebody who won't let you down. I didn't before. And I won't this time.'

There was an element of moral blackmail there again, of course. Angel was well aware now of exactly who Kelly was and the secret he knew about her. This was the second time he had reminded her, and her mother had almost certainly done so too. Angel must realise that, if he chose, Kelly could write about her days as a prostitute at any time. He had first-hand knowledge. The photographs of her would still be on file at the *Despatch*. She probably did not know they had ever existed, and he didn't intend to use them against her, never had. But they were there, none the less, and Kelly could confirm exactly who had been behind those dark glasses. He had a few trump cards in his hand. And he was rather hoping that all he had to do was drop a hint or two. Well, he was still a hack, after all. He knew how to walk that tightrope, how to please editors and those on the other side of the fence. He'd always been good, too, at making people like him if he put his mind to it.

He printed out the letter, folded it in his pocket, and set off for Maythorpe to play the waiting game. He didn't intend to risk this latest note getting mixed up with all that fan mail and more than likely opened by somebody other than Angel, like Jimmy Rudge, Scott's business manager, or even, heaven forbid, the police.

He would bide his time, wait till he had the opportunity to pass the letter to Angel personally. Then at least he would know that she'd got it.

He'd been standing outside Maythorpe Manor for almost two hours when Joe Robertson called.

'Fancy a quick one or sixteen?' he asked.

Kelly did. He didn't much enjoy going into pubs any more, now that he no longer drank alcohol, but for Joe he would always make an exception. Kelly liked his editor's company. Joe was one of the few people with whom he could reminisce about the good old days. Both men were inclined to remember the good moments rather than the bad, yet Joe knew all about the lowest points in Kelly's past, and that made Kelly feel at ease with him. Even in a bar.

For just a second or two Kelly wondered about the wisdom of abandoning his stakeout. But he had a gut feeling that there were going to be no developments today. His only real purpose was to await an opportunity to pass Angel his letter, and, realistically, the chances of her walking out through the gates of Maythorpe that night amidst a group of waiting press were about nil.

It took Kelly less than twenty minutes to drive to the office pub. Joe was already standing by the bar, a slightly flushed Trevor Jones in attendance. Kit Hansford was sitting at a table with the picture editor. Kelly felt the news editor's eyes boring into him as he walked in. He rather liked that. Hansford resented the closeness Kelly had with his editor, and Kelly had to admit to himself that he quite enjoyed the occasional opportunity to rub it in.

Joe was full of bonhomie. He also had a large glass of whisky in front of him and Kelly was pretty sure it wasn't his first.

'Well-timed, dear boy,' Joe greeted him effusively. 'Thought I'd better buy you two heroes a few. Pity I couldn't send Trevor here to London with you, John, but there's still plenty of mileage for you on this one, young man, I promise you that.'

Joe clapped Trevor on the back as he bought Kelly his usual Diet Coke. Trevor beamed. Basking in the glow of his editor's approval he had obviously forgotten his earlier dissatisfaction with the *Argus* bosses.

'Now, John,' Joe continued. 'I was trying to remember your story about the cockroach race. C'mon. You take over. I can't even remember where it happened.'

Kelly grinned indulgently. He owed Joe a few good pub yarns. In fact he owed him a hell of a lot more than that.

'Neither can I, not exactly,' he said. 'A run-down bar in a run-down town somewhere in Colombian drug-baron land. There were these cockroaches cowering in a corner and I had this bet on which one would dare to be first to scurry across the room to feast on a bit of old sandwich. I had a hundred quid on it and my little bugger won, no doubt about it. Only problem is I'd chosen to bet with two extremely large mercenaries. One of the bastards plonked his bloody great boot on my cockroach and that was the end of it and my winnings.

'"Your 'orse ees dead," he told me. Well, I know when I'm beaten. I paid up and did a runner. I wasn't entirely suicidal. Not even then.'

'Oh, I don't know about that,' roared Joe.

Kelly smiled easily enough. The stories sounded good. He knew that. They were of the rollicking hell-raising sort. The reality, of course, became very grim indeed. Kelly had indulged in all the vices. And he had gambled for England. It started with casinos in foreign towns, then he became hooked on horse racing – or rather on betting on horses. He had no interest whatsoever in the finer points of the races themselves or the horses which ran them. Eventually he would bet on anything. Hence the cockroach race. Kelly's whole life became a kind of vicious circle. He would get drunk, often in some obscure part of the world, pick up a woman, usually in a bar, sometimes more than one, wake up the next morning next to somebody whose name he could probably not even remember, be overcome with remorse and go home to his wife, probably via a betting shop or two, and have a row. Liz half knew about the women, suspecting more than she would admit even to herself, Kelly had reckoned, and she certainly knew about the gambling. Kelly had been earning big money but he was spending even more. Cocaine, horses, women and whisky are an expensive combination. The debts mounted. The fights between Kelly and his wife became more frequent and more vicious. Kelly had vague memories of Nick in the background at these times, usually yelling his head off. As soon as possible after the fighting Kelly would invariably go off to some bar again and drink himself silly. Then he'd pick up a woman. Then he'd do some coke. Then the cycle would begin again.

Kelly remained mildly surprised by how quickly his downfall came once he started to slide. People think that the reporters of days gone by all spent their time getting drunk. In fact to be incapable of doing your job because of alcohol was a cardinal sin, and drugs were pretty much a no-go area in the Street of Shame, which kept rigidly to its own totally inexplicable code of conduct. After you'd brought in the story of the day, yes, you could get blind drunk if you wished. But not when you were in the middle of one. And if you were unofficial chief fireman like Kelly you always had to be able to pull yourself together because you never knew when the big one was going to break.

The first time Kelly was actually blind drunk in the office and incapable of putting his story together, a couple of fellow hacks ushered him out of the building, and covered for him. They even wrote his story, filing it under Kelly's name.

Kelly doubted he ever thanked them. In fact he wasn't sure if he even knew it had happened until he was told about it years later.

Kelly didn't know how any of it happened really. These were the good old days when Fleet Street employers were about as tolerant and as benevolent as you could get. They checked him into a rehab centre. Not once, but three times. They warned him. Not once but several times. Then suddenly, it was all over.

One day he was the king, largely regarded as the best on-the-road operator in Fleet Street. He had a house in fashionable Chiswick, a beautiful wife, a baby son, and a flash car. He expected to get and was given the best stories. He ate in the best restaurants. On the rare occasions when he took a holiday it was to top hotels in the Caribbean or the South of France. He assumed now that he had thought that he was unassailable and that his glory days would last for ever, regardless of his increasingly erratic behaviour.

The next moment he had been sacked. The job that meant everything to him disappeared as quickly as one snort of the white powder he was so fond of. And his wife disappeared too. Not that he blamed her, after all she had put up with, although classically she went home to her mother leaving him to sort out the mortgage problems with the house and all his other debts. He didn't do any such thing, of course. He failed to deal with any of it. He lost the house and although he had been given a generous pay-off from the *Despatch*, most of it went towards settling as many as possible of his debts, while at the same time keeping his various habits going until it too disappeared.

Within less than a year he ended up with no home as well as no income. He stayed with various friends until they wouldn't put up with him any more. As soon as he got hold of any money he spent it on booze. He could no longer afford cocaine, but in any case coke was an achiever's drug, designed to kill the need for sleep and keep the brain buzzing long after it would otherwise have slumped into oblivion. Kelly didn't even want to achieve. It was only oblivion that he sought, and alcohol did that for him well enough. Women didn't come into it any more. None would come near him. In the end he exhausted all his resources. There were no more friends prepared to pick up the pieces.

His fall from grace was every bit as spectacular as his rise to it had been. He actually did end up on the street. For several weeks he spent his nights in a cardboard box in the

Waterloo underpass and his days begging. He would hang around Fleet Street pubs and offices, waiting for old mates to emerge and begging them for cash. Actually he used to pretend he was only asking for loans – that was the last vestige of his pride. But both sides knew the truth.

The guys he had worked with, once been at the forefront of, were deeply embarrassed, unwilling always to meet his eye. Which suited him. Kelly had not wanted contact, just their money, which they invariably handed over in order to get him to go away.

Looking back it remained a mystery to Kelly how he had got himself in that state. It was also a bit of a mystery how he had pulled himself out of it. He remembered that the first step had been to allow himself to be helped by one of the organisations which ministered to the winos of London. He had moved to a hostel which had been a vast improvement on a cardboard box, he had been persuaded to attend Alcoholics Anonymous meetings, and one day he had just stopped drinking. Simultaneously he had been able to start rebuilding, first finding himself any casual work going, more often than not in hotel kitchens, and ultimately getting back in touch with the few old friends he had not totally antagonised, in the hope of finding more gainful employment. It was then that Joe Robertson had come up trumps with his offer of a job in Torquay. And once Kelly got his foot back on the bottom rung of the ladder he began to climb it again, albeit just a little way, with less difficulty than he might have anticipated. It seemed he had been one of those people who had to sink to the very bottom of the pile before he could even start to recover.

The memory of it still shamed Kelly. And it still frightened him. He was aware more than most of the fragility of his own existence. He would never again have anything like the life he had enjoyed in those early Fleet Street days, he knew that. But although he was revelling in this rare treat of a really big story, he wasn't sure that he would want that back, even if it were possible. The other side of the coin had been just too awful. Kelly had lived on the edge and he hadn't been able to handle it.

Now he had a decent home in a gorgeous part of the world, a decent job, a good woman, and a fairly recently honed new relationship with his only son. He was possibly as near to content as he had ever been in his life.

If ever Kelly was tempted to drink again – and sometimes, watching friends down a gin and tonic at the end of the day or enjoy a bottle of fine claret, he did envy them – he just remembered how close he had come to total destruction. And he knew that he couldn't take the risk.

He took a sip of his Diet Coke and heard Trevor Jones's voice in the background jerking him out of his not-altogether-welcome reverie into the past.

'Tell us about that hotel porter in Africa, Johnno . . .'

Kelly interrupted. 'Not tonight, Trev,' he said mildly. 'I promised Moira I'd be home for supper.'

It was a lie. Moira was on duty. But Kelly was not in the mood for relating any more drunken stories of the good old days. They might make young photographers laugh, and even envy the swashbuckling lifestyle, but all too often they just left John Kelly feeling sad and empty.

Kelly spent most of the next three days, and half the night, doorstepping Maythorpe Manor. Not just professionally, but also personally, he found Angel Silver's involvement in the double killing absolutely intriguing. Her account of what actually happened, whenever it could be obtained and printed, would, of course, make compulsive reading. But Kelly was beginning to accept that his fascination for the woman and for what had happened that night went far beyond his instinctive desire to be first with a great story.

For two days he did not even catch a glimpse of Angel, not even the twitch of a curtain indicating that she might be looking out, and certainly no shadowy view of a figure watching from a window.

Then at about 11 a.m. on the fourth day after Kelly's trip to London, Angel appeared suddenly on the steps to Maythorpe and was hustled into a squad car by two policemen and a policewoman. This time there was not even the merest illusion of eye contact. Not for him, nor for anybody else, he suspected. Angel kept her head bowed. She was wearing a big black hat with a wide brim. He could not even see her face.

The gates to Maythorpe opened and the squad car sped through. Angel was sitting in the middle of the back seat flanked by the two policemen. Kelly caught another glimpse of the hat, and that was about all he could see of her.

One of the local agency snappers had managed to park his motorbike virtually in the hedge just opposite Maythorpe. He ran to it and took off with a squeal of wheels after the police vehicle. Kelly watched with amusement. He was in any case too old for car chases. And he would hazard an educated guess that Angel was being taken to Torquay Police Station again. He tried to call Karen Meadows to confirm but her mobile was switched to voice mail and Kelly didn't think there was much chance of her having either the time or the inclination to call him back. None the less, he decided to follow his hunch, like he always did. The *Argus* Picture Desk had decided they could no longer keep a snapper outside Maythorpe, so, as he made his way down the hill towards the Volvo, Kelly called them and told them to get Trevor Jones to the police station smartish. His success gave him a little bit of authority for a change, he thought, as he drove as fast as he dared into central Torquay.

When he got to the station he found that there was quite a buzz among the small group of journalists already gathered outside. Kelly's hunch had been right: Angel was already inside, and the word that something was happening at last had got around fast. Within an hour of Kelly arriving at South Street, several more reporters and photographers turned up, including Trevor Jones and two TV crews. The group waited for a further two hours before Karen Meadows, as senior investigating officer, accompanied by the Devon and Cornwall Constabulary's chief press officer, came out on to the station steps to give a statement.

'I can tell you that Mrs Angel Silver has been charged with the manslaughter of Terry James,' she announced. 'She will appear at Torquay Magistrates' Court tomorrow morning to be formally charged before the Bench. She has been released on police bail and for your information, ladies and gentlemen, I understand that she has already left the station so there is no point in hanging around.'

Kelly tried to edge forward in an attempt to get a private word with the tall detective inspector, who politely refused to answer any of the questions which were thrown at her. But she was having none of that either, and merely turned smartly on her heel and retreated back through the police station's big double doors.

The news came as no surprise. Karen had looked cool and in control as she spoke, but then she invariably did, thought Kelly. He knew that she must be into her early forties now, just a couple of years or so older than Angel, and he reckoned that as well as being a highly impressive woman, she had also become a first-rate copper. None the less, he didn't believe for one minute that Angel had departed without being spotted. Kelly knew that the snappers had done a deal with each other. There were at least a couple of guys watching the only other entrance. It was just conceivable that Angel could have been hidden in one of several cars which had left through the gates to the yard round the back earlier that afternoon, but Kelly didn't think so, not unless she had been lying on a car floor or something, and that wasn't Angel Silver's style. Not even when charged with manslaughter.

The TV crews were children nowadays. They filmed Karen, then immediately started moving away, as did several of the other journalists. Kelly and one or two of the old hands exchanged glances. Kelly walked up the street a short distance and quickly filed the latest development to the *Argus* on his mobile, giving Karen Meadows' statement very nearly verbatim. He had retained his excellent short-term memory even if his long-term recollection, which had once been brilliant, was not quite what it was. On the way back he stopped at an *Argus* news-stand on the corner and bought a copy of his own paper. Then he walked casually back, half reading the paper as he did so, half looking over it, watching the doors to the station. He was sure she was still in there. And he had his own personal reasons for wanting to get close to her. If they bundled her into a vehicle round the back he might still see her but he had no chance of getting close. He remained convinced that Angel Silver wasn't a back-door girl. The police might be trying to protect her, but he didn't think she'd let them make her look as if she were hiding away.

He positioned himself so that he hoped he was close enough to get to her should he be given the opportunity, but in such a way that he didn't look too conspicuous. And certainly not threatening. He saw that the others were trying to do much the same and that Trevor Jones had set himself up with a 1000-mil long tom in a shop doorway opposite. Smart lad that, he thought approvingly. Grafter too.

Over an hour later, just as Kelly was beginning to think maybe he and the few other know-alls who had stayed at the station stakeout had got it wrong after all and that Angel had been smuggled away, she came out.

Two policemen were alongside her plus two other men. Kelly recognised one of them easily enough. It was Jimmy Rudge again, Scott's business manager. He guessed that the other was probably Angel's lawyer. He looked the type, Kelly thought, but he wasn't really interested in Angel's escorts. Just in her.

Her head was no longer bowed. She held the wide-brimmed black hat in her hand and was staring straight ahead, looking neither to the left nor right. The violet eyes shone. Her face was paler than ever. That translucent skin looked paper-thin, almost as if at any moment it might split over those sharp cheekbones. As usual she wore very little makeup, just the familiar slash of vermilion lipstick.

She was dressed in tailored black trousers with turn-ups, very high-heeled shoes, and an expensive-looking black coat open at the front to reveal a simple white cotton shirt with the collar turned up. The effect was stunning. And even at this surely quite devastating time in her life, Kelly felt quietly certain that she knew it.

The motor-drives of the cameras belonging to the handful of snappers who had remained whirred busily. Kelly lurched forward, much faster than any of the others, even though he was probably the oldest. He was also probably the only one who knew exactly what he was going to do. After all, it was highly unlikely that Angel Silver would talk – and even if she did, nobody could print anything much, not now that she had been charged.

Before the police or the other two men accompanying her could stop him, Kelly was by Angel's side thrusting his letter into her hand.

'This time, please read this and get back to me,' he commanded. 'We need each other.'

He backed off at once, before he was manhandled out of the way, surprised partly by his own vehemence and also by realising that he meant the line he had spun her.

She turned and looked at him. That same look he had first experienced all those years ago when she had been half out of her head in that awful hotel bar, pulling anybody who'd have her to fund her drug habit. It was a look that had haunted him for seventeen years, he realised.

A look that said, 'Can this really be happening to me?'

A look that said, 'I'm not what I seem, really I'm not.'

A look full of vulnerability and contradiction, part hard and streetwise, part cool and controlled, part little girl lost.

It did for him. Just like before.

Eight

Early next morning Kelly was awakened by the sound of smashing glass.

'Stay where you are,' he ordered Moira tersely as he jumped out of bed. He opened the bedroom door and stood for a few seconds listening. Nothing more. He made his way swiftly downstairs. The noise had come from the front of the house. But there didn't seem to be anything amiss in the hallway. Cautiously Kelly opened the living-room door.

There was shattered glass all over the carpet along with a couple of broken china ornaments which had previously stood on the windowsill. Kelly glanced towards the bay window which looked out over Crown Avenue. All that remained of the central panel was a few jagged edges. And in the middle of the debris on the floor was a rather large brick loosely wrapped in a sheet of paper held in place by strips of Sellotape.

Kelly had no shoes on. He stepped gingerly forward, leaned over and stretched out an arm to pick up the brick. He removed the sheet of paper which carried a message stuck to it from letters and words cut out of newspapers. There was, of course, no signature.

Kelly smiled grimly. He hadn't thought anybody used newsprint to form anonymous threatening messages any more. The sentiment expressed was clear enough, though, if a little simplistic: 'Lying bastard. We're going to get you.'

It had to be the James clan, surely, thought Kelly. Then he heard Moira, who naturally hadn't stayed in the bedroom as he had told her to, call out to him from the stairs.

'John, John, are you all right? What's happened?'

Kelly let the brick drop to the floor again and hastily stuffed the note into his dressing-gown pocket as he made his way gingerly out of the room and into the hallway.

'Don't go in there,' he told Moira. 'Not with bare feet anyway. There's broken glass everywhere.'

He opened the front door and peered out. It was only 6 a.m. and there was no sign of anyone at all in the street outside. He glanced towards the Volvo, still parked by the kerbside where he had left it. The car did not seem to have been damaged. Well, it wouldn't have been, would it, he thought. Whoever threw the brick through the window would almost certainly have had no idea that the vehicle was anything to do with him. The MG was still at Classic Motors. Kelly thanked his lucky stars for that. He dreaded to think what damage might have been caused to his beloved old car had it been parked outside.

He was vaguely aware of Moira standing in the hall now peering into the living room.

'Oh my God, John!' she cried. 'Someone's chucked a brick through the window. Who on earth would do such a thing?'

'Just mindless vandals, I expect,' said Kelly, who had no intention of letting Moira anywhere near the note he had secreted in his pocket.

'Aren't you going to call the police?' asked Moira.

'I don't see the point,' replied Kelly.

'For goodness' sake,' said Moira irritably. 'Of course there's a point. It might happen again. And in any case, if you don't call the police you'll have insurance problems.'

Kelly sighed. 'OK,' he said. 'Will you do it, though? You're off again today, aren't you? I really have to get in to work early.'

'Oh John, I told you Paula's coming down from London for the day. I really don't want to be hanging around here.'

Paula was Moira's married eldest daughter. Kelly had completely forgotten about her planned visit, but he did know how close Moira was to all her girls. Yet she hadn't seen Paula, who had a demanding toddler, for months. And her second daughter, Lynne, was off back-packing somewhere exotic, much to her mother's constant concern.

None the less Kelly had no intention of being diverted from his day's work.

'Please yourself,' he said casually. 'But I really would appreciate it if you could get hold of a glazier.'

Moira studied him without enthusiasm.

'Oh, all right,' she said eventually.

Kelly dressed quickly and left the house, doing his best to avoid any further conversation with Moira. He had been threatened before, of course. That was inevitable during a lifetime of the kind of journalism Kelly had been involved in. But he still felt shocked. There was a hollowness in his belly and the palms of his hands were clammy.

He had transferred the threatening note to the pocket of his trousers. He supposed he had concealed it from Moira because he didn't want to frighten her. Not that she frightened very easily, he had to admit. She was a nursing sister, after all.

Also he didn't intend to hand the letter over to the police. He didn't quite know why. He just knew he wasn't going to, that was all.

Later that morning Kelly sat at the press bench in Torquay Magistrates' Court doodling in his notebook while he waited for Angel Silver to be brought in and formally charged.

Her arrival brought a low murmur from the packed public benches. She looked as pale and as beautiful as ever. Her hair was slicked back off her face. She wore a neat grey suit, classic in design, old-fashioned even. Only on her it looked sensational.

She spoke just once during the brief hearing, when the chairman of the magistrates asked her how she pleaded to the charge of manslaughter.

'Not guilty,' she replied simply. Her voice was loud and clear. Surprisingly so. She stared straight ahead and her expression gave nothing away as she was told that she would be sent for trial at Exeter Crown Court and remanded on bail until then.

No surprises there, thought Kelly. He knew that Angel had already given statements to the police admitting that she had killed James in self-defence, but nobody in their right mind could imagine that she would be a danger to anyone else, which was supposed to be the main criterion for remand in custody.

At one point during the proceedings Angel looked across at the press bench and Kelly experienced what he was now beginning to accept as an inevitable reaction. He was sure she was looking at him. Directly and particularly him. But the big violet eyes were blank.

Afterwards they took her out of the court's back door where a car waited for her in the private parking area where neither Kelly nor anyone else could get close to her. She had arrived at the court in the same manner. Maybe even Angel had been unable to face any more press attention. Or maybe the police had insisted. The court had been full to bursting point, of course, and at least a couple of hundred fans were outside along with twenty or thirty photographers, several TV crews and a handful of reporters who had been unable to gain access. In spite of police efforts to control them the assorted crowd spread untidily across Union Street, and the flow of traffic, never very fluent at the best of times in Torquay, was seriously disrupted.

Kelly assumed, as did most of the others, that Angel would be taken home again and he drove out to Maythorpe Manor. A few fans still remained, although it seemed that most of them had either gone home now or decamped to the court. Nobody had removed the flowers around the gate, which were now wilted and decayed. A handful of other reporters and photographers were already there, standing around looking slightly lost. The house had a closed, forbidding look about it. There were no police on duty.

And that, of course, was the giveaway.

Kelly was unsurprised when one of the other hacks told him that nobody had spotted Angel since she'd left the court. The word was that she had gone away and would not be returning to Maythorpe for some time. Judging from the lack of police presence she was not expected.

Kelly found that he didn't like not knowing where Angel was.

Eventually Kelly made his way back to the *Argus* office and started putting together his background, the material that could not be used until Angel was tried but which would be printed as soon as her trial was over.

In spite of Kelly's triumph with Angel's mother in London, Hansford had been prickly with him ever since he had gone over his head to the editor. Kelly couldn't have cared less. If you weren't in a position by the time you got to his age to go over the head of a pipsqueak like Hansford then you really were a seriously sad case, he thought.

The news editor kept trying to read over his shoulder, which Kelly found very irritating. Each time Hansford approached Kelly exited the Silver file on his screen.

'You'll copy me in when you've finished, won't you?' instructed Hansford in that irritatingly authoritarian way of his.

'Naturally, boss,' said Kelly.

Hansford gave him a hard look. Kelly kept his face expressionless. Like Angel Silver. Only he wasn't going to think about her any more. Writing the copy was one thing. Getting obsessed with some silly cow who was famous for being famous and nothing much else any more was quite another, he told himself sternly.

It was mid-afternoon before he had put together just about all the material he had amassed so far in one consummate piece. Unknown to Hansford, of course, he had been working on disk and when he had finished he removed the disk and slipped it in his pocket. And, naturally, he didn't copy Hansford in. After all, that kind of secrecy was second nature to Kelly.

Just before leaving the office he called Moira. He knew that he'd been preoccupied and neglectful ever since the Silver story had begun, and that she was probably still shaken from the events of the morning.

'Everything all right?' he asked.

'I've had the window replaced and the police have been round, if that's what you mean,' she replied, in a not particularly friendly manner, he thought.

'Great. What did the police say?'

'Much the same as you did.'

'Told you so. Just mindless thugs at play.'

'John, are you sure there isn't something you're not telling me?'

'Course not.'

'It isn't to do with the Silver case, is it?'

Kelly hesitated. Moira had always been perceptive.

'Shouldn't think so for one minute,' he replied as lightly as he could and decided to change the subject. He wanted to take her mind off things, and make up a bit for what had happened.

'Do you fancy dinner at the Grand?' he asked abruptly.

'Paula's here, I keep telling you.'

Damn, he'd managed to forget again.

'But she'll be going back on the last train, won't she?' he replied, making a pretty good recovery. 'I thought you might like to go out after she's gone.'

There followed just a few seconds' silence. Moira's voice was still a little flat when she replied but he was fairly sure, none the less, that she was genuinely pleased.

'OK, I'd like that,' she said quietly.

'Good. I'll drive, then you can have a drink. I'll come round to yours around eight,' he replied. 'Oh, and give my love to Paula.'

The MG was ready at Classic Motors and Kelly was able to pick it up on his way, which was a relief, although he cursed himself silently for not having bothered to find a new garage for it after the lease had run out on the one he had rented until mid-summer.

The Grand, as ever, did not disappoint, it was a lovely old hotel in a fine seaside location and boasted an excellent restaurant, and Kelly made a real effort for Moira.

Everything went well until the coffee stage, which he'd ordered along with a cognac for Moira, who had already had a couple of gin and tonics followed by a half-bottle of Chablis with her Dover sole. She seemed relaxed and mellow, and had only mentioned the brick incident fairly briefly in the car on the way to the Grand.

But, somewhat out of the blue, as she sipped her cognac she started asking Kelly about Angel.

'Why are you so fascinated by that woman?'

'I'm not,' he replied shortly.

'Oh, don't be ridiculous.'

'I am not being ridiculous. I am not fascinated by Angel Silver. I am fascinated by the story. It's just such a great yarn.'

'The story?' Moira's voice rose to a considerably higher pitch than usual. Perhaps it was the alcohol that had done that, he thought uncharitably, aware enough of himself to realise that there was nothing in this world more unbearably pious than the converted.

'Shush,' he said.

'No I won't shush. You're getting to be obsessed by that woman, and you won't admit it. Playing her message again and again on your answering machine. It wasn't even a nice message.'

Kelly felt his irritation rise. This really was not the way he had planned things. He was determined not to let the evening be spoiled.

'Even when some bastard throws a brick through your window all you want to do is to carry on working on her story, get yourself to court so that you can watch her –'

Kelly interrupted sharply. He didn't want the evening ruined, and that was the way things were going.

'Look, shall we talk about something else?' he said.

'No, I want to know why you're obsessed with Angel Silver.'

'I've told you I'm not.'

'Humph.' Moira gave a rather silly sort of snort. Her cheeks were flushed. She just wouldn't let go. She'd never behaved like this before, not with him, anyway. 'I know you, John Kelly. You just don't realise how well I know you.'

That was just the sort of comment guaranteed to make Kelly really mad. Moira sounded smug and self-satisfied. After all, he told himself, he had only been doing his job. The anger began to rise in him dangerously.

'If you really know me that well you'd know what I was thinking now, wouldn't you?' His voice was quiet and very controlled. He didn't know whether she realised or not that he was at his most dangerous when he was like that. But for the first time during the evening she looked uncertain.

'All right then, what are you thinking?'

'You don't want to know.'

'Really? Well, I bet I could guess. I bet it's about that Angel –'

He interrupted her then. 'I was thinking that right now I really do understand why that old man of yours knocked you about,' he said coldly.

Her eyes opened wide in disbelief. For just a fleeting second she looked as if he had hit her too. Moira was a strong woman, but Kelly had homed in on her big weakness. Her lower lip trembled.

'Oh for God's sake,' he said. 'Let's get the bill and I'll take you home.'

The next day Kelly woke alone feeling terrible. Why on earth had he reacted so strongly? Moira had indeed been deeply irritating but nothing justified the remark he had made. Absolutely nothing.

Kelly did not have a good track record with women. He had made more than his fair share, particularly his first wife, deeply unhappy. But his problem was that he liked women too much. It was almost beyond his comprehension that any man would hurt a woman physically, and Kelly abhorred those who did.

He'd met Moira at a dinner party organised by Joe Robertson, about a year after he had started working for the *Argus*. Without the prop of alcohol Kelly had found it impossible to build himself much of a social life in the seaside town. Also, when he'd stopped drinking he'd realised that he no longer knew how to pick up women, something he had always rather excelled at. But in any case, no longer fuelled by drink and coke and with damned near unlimited expenses in his pocket, he'd pretty much lost the urge. He'd become a loner. In every way.

Kelly had recognised at once the placing next to each other of an unattached man and an apparently unattached woman of a certain age amid a small group of solid couples for the piece of blatant matchmaking that it had been. But, far from taking offence, he had accepted it as the warm gesture which he was sure his old friend intended and had been touched by it.

Also, he had liked Moira from the start. She was attractive, bright and practical. There was also a sparkle in her eye that suggested that she could be darned sexy too, and without too much encouragement.

'She's just what you need, John,' Joe Robertson's wife had told him in a slightly too loud aside. Even that had not put him off. Moira had flushed slightly. Kelly had winked his commiseration.

He'd taken her home, and they'd travelled in giggling companionship in the little MG, wondering at other people's good intentions – which in fact turned out to be almost totally successful.

Moira had invited him into her home, which had proved to be so conveniently close to his own. Somewhat to Kelly's surprise they'd slept together that same night and he had reflected that Sandra Robertson had actually been quite right. He and Moira were indeed two lonely like-minded souls who needed each other.

Their relationship flourished. It was never a great torrid romance – Kelly had reckoned that they had probably both been through too much ever to experience that again – but rather something warm and comfortable. They gave each other companionship and a level of affection which he felt was as great as anything he could have hoped for. The sex was good too. Surprisingly so. Better than he had thought it would ever be again.

In the beginning he had been almost eager for them to move in together, had wanted totally to share the remains of his life with her. But it was harder for him to win Moira's trust than her affection. She had little reason to trust men, and it was some time before she told him about her monster of a husband who had used her for target practice with his fists whenever the mood took him.

'Why did you stay with him?' he had asked her.

It was the old story. One he had never fully understood because perhaps no man ever could.

'He was a good father to our three girls. Strange, perhaps, but he never laid a finger on them, and I knew he never would. It was just me he'd vent his anger on. And, you know, every time when it was over, he couldn't even tell me why . . .'

Moira was a highly qualified nursing sister, clever and capable, able to make her own way in the world, earn her own living. But she had stayed with the bastard because her girls needed their father. Because he was her husband. Because of all manner of reasons which were quite beyond Kelly.

'He was always so sorry afterwards, John,' Moira told him. 'And then for weeks, maybe months, he wouldn't touch me, and we'd be quite a happy family. Honestly.'

It was more than not being able to understand. John couldn't quite believe people could live like that.

'The girls must have known, surely?'

'I became good at suffering in silence,' Moira explained. 'However hard Pete hit me I never cried out. Never. And he was very organised in his attacks, you know.'

Kelly had thought what an odd turn of phrase that was.

'He only every hit me in our bedroom. He would tell me to go there and I always did so at once because if I didn't it would be even worse. He would lock the door, then he would explain to me exactly what I had done to deserve a punishment, then he would go for me. But only on my body, upper arms, upper legs, the parts of me that would normally be concealed by clothes. He never touched my face. A couple of times I had to go to hospital. He broke two ribs once, and my wrist, but we'd just make up some story about a fall.'

'But you have three intelligent daughters, Moira. They must have known what was going on. Kids do . . .'

'No, John, they didn't.' She had been quite insistent. 'And you must never tell them. Never.'

It was then that he had learned that Moira's daughters, one of whom, the youngest, Jennifer, still lived at home, had not only not known at the time of their father's violent behaviour but neither had they ever been told. Peter

Simmons had died suddenly and unexpectedly of a heart attack three years before Kelly and Moira had met, mercifully releasing his wife from a life of domestic torment, and had been mourned by his family like any other loved father and husband.

To Kelly it was farcical, and he had remained unconvinced that the girls could really have been so unaware. The most he could accept was that Moira's daughters had just blanked their father's outrages out, come to believe only what they wanted to believe. Kelly had got to know Jennifer quite well, of course, and she seemed like any other normal well-adjusted teenager to him – at least as normal and well-adjusted as teenagers ever are – but he had always felt uneasy about those four women, mother and daughters, living out their lie together.

After Moira had first told him about her troubled past, he'd thought to himself that sooner or later the whole family would erupt in some kind of awful delayed reaction. It hadn't happened yet, though. Whatever defence mechanisms they had built up around themselves seemed remarkably effective. Kelly had learned to accept Moira's way of dealing with what had happened to her and not to criticise. In any case, how could he possibly criticise someone who had been through what she had been through?

Now he had quite crassly and unforgivably thrown the whole dreadful thing in her face. He'd actually told her he could understand why Peter Simmons had beaten her. Nothing justified that. How could he have done it?

He reached for a cigarette for courage, and only when it was lit and he had taken the first few essential drags of the day, did he feel able to call Moira. It was just after 6.30 a.m. But he knew she'd be awake too. Her crazy working hours meant that she was more able to sleep during the day than at night, even when she was off duty. In any case, Jennifer had to leave for college before eight. Kelly imagined Moira pottering around her tidy little kitchen making coffee, waiting for Jennifer to come downstairs at the last possible moment as usual.

She answered the phone quite quickly and in a way that indicated that she had guessed it would be him. Well, who else would call at that hour?

'Hi, I just wanted to say sorry,' he said.

'It's OK,' she said, her tone of voice making it clear that it wasn't. He knew he certainly didn't need to explain what he was apologising for.

'You know how I feel about all that, I really am sorry for what I said,' he repeated.

'It's OK,' she said again. 'I think I was a bit drunk –'

'No you weren't.'

'Well, I kept on at you, didn't I? Maybe I wanted to make you mad.'

Was that how she had excused her husband for all those years, he wondered.

'I shouldn't have said what I did,' he went on. 'It was unforgivable. But if you can forgive me, what about trying again tonight?'

'I'm back on duty tonight, John.'

Of course. He should have known that. He'd forgotten.

'Lunch then. I'll meet you in town at twelve thirty. How about that new fish place on the front?'

She had agreed readily enough. But he knew he'd have some bridge-building to do. He lit a second cigarette from the stub of the first. The extraordinary thing was that he and Moira had never really quarrelled at all during their years together. He had always thought that part of the reason for that was probably that they did not actually live together. But there was more, of course. Both of them had had enough disruption and drama in their lives of one kind and another. Neither was probably able to deal with an emotionally volatile relationship. He had always thought that they were more like friends who had sex together than real lovers, but it wasn't until now that he had perhaps realised how important their slightly unusual relationship was to him. It had always worked brilliantly. That was the truth of it.

The incident of the previous night had somehow shaken its foundation. They had both broken the unwritten rule really – that there should be no stress, no intrusive probing, and above all no conflict. Just an easy unformulated sharing of their lives.

And now, for the first time in his relationship with Moira, Kelly felt unsure and uneasy.

He set off rather glumly for work and was horrified to find that the MG seemed to be missing from its usual parking space outside his house. Then he remembered. He was so preoccupied that he'd actually managed to forget that he'd parked the car three streets away as a precaution.

Soon after he'd eventually found it and was on his way to the *Argus* office Karen Meadows called.

'What's all this I hear about a brick being thrown through your front-room window?' she asked.

Kelly sighed. Trust Karen to know already.

'Vandals, what else?' he remarked as casually as he could. He still didn't want to involve the police. Something told him that would stir things up even more.

'In St Marychurch? At five a.m. on a weekday morning?'

'Why not?'

'Yes, well, we checked the brick for fingerprints and surprisingly enough there weren't any. So uniformed are going to send a couple of lads over to have a word with Ken James and any of the rest of his family.'

'I'd rather they didn't.'

'Tough.'

Karen hung up before he could protest any more. She was sitting, in the kitchen of her seafront flat just up the road from the Grand Hotel, with her cat on her lap and a mug of tea on the table before her. Kelly had always been a sharp operator as a journalist but she hoped he wasn't getting in too deep with the Silver case. Reporters all too often thought only about the story and gave little or no consideration to any other consequences.

It was strange that Karen still cared about Kelly after all these years, but she did. She knew that many of her colleagues had picked up on what she had once overheard rather sarcastically described as her 'special relationship' with the reporter.

The truth was that Karen and Kelly had first met when she

had been an eager young detective constable based at the Devon and Cornwall Constabulary HQ in Exeter, and Kelly had been sent back to his old West Country local paper patch by the *Despatch* to investigate organised crime on the English Riviera.

He had discovered that one of the prime suspects, an Irishman called David Flanigan, was indulging in a passionate affair with DC Karen Meadows. Flanigan, it seemed, was heavily into the international trade of both drugs and arms. And it was a little-known fact that the West of England was a world-wide centre for the arms trade, boasting far more than its fair share of weapons factories, often discreetly hidden away in leafy rural lanes. Flanigan had also had a strong IRA connection, Kelly had been able to reveal.

Looking back, Karen couldn't believe that she could have been so naïve, not even then. She also hadn't believed that a newspaper reporter had come up with so much information which the police force apparently did not have, or at least not at her then lowly level. She had been swept off her feet by a sophisticated and handsome charmer. It had been a whirlwind romance – she had known Flanigan for less than three months before the bubble burst – but Karen had been truly in love. She had been aware that there was gossip about him and that his activities had attracted police attention on more than one occasion, but her feelings for him were such that when Flanigan insisted that he was just an honest businessman whose success led to jealous rumour-mongering she had believed him without question. Probably because she had wanted to so much. She still had no idea whether or not David Flanigan had been using her merely for information, but she remained afraid that she had probably, albeit unwittingly, done him several favours.

Kelly had up-fronted Karen first. She had been both astonished and devastated. She had also been surprised by Kelly's reaction. He left her in little doubt that he had been expecting to confront a bent cop. Instead he had encountered a duped young woman who had fallen head over heels in love and behaved like an idiot. Karen had tried immediately to call Flanigan. She couldn't reach him. Had, in fact, never heard from him since. Word was he was doing the same kind of business somewhere in South America. It seemed that he had got wind of Kelly's investigation and done a fast runner.

Karen had expected to be decimated. She waited almost listlessly for Kelly's story to be printed in the *Despatch*. When it was, over several days, to her utter astonishment she was not mentioned at all. There were whispers within the force, of course several of her colleagues were aware at least that she knew Flanigan and had been seen with him, although, mercifully, she had never discussed the true nature of their relationship with anyone. A bit of flak flew, but nobody could prove anything, and Karen's fledgling but promising career was, by and large, unaffected by her indiscretion.

She could still remember calling Kelly in his London office to thank him.

'Don't mention it,' he'd replied. 'It's villains and bent bastards I'm after, not bloody fools.'

And that had been the start of a friendship which had lasted getting on for twenty years. Contrary to general opinion, there had never been an affair at all, although sometimes Karen almost wished there had been. But, then, when a woman cop and an old hack were as close as she was with Kelly, rumours were inevitable.

Karen hugged her cat close. Sophie purred her appreciation. The plump tortoiseshell was the only creature Karen had shared her life with for some time. It was her own fatal flaw that since Flanigan she had probably never really trusted any man again. Except John Kelly.

Angel Silver disappeared off the face of the earth. Or that was the way it seemed to Kelly and the rest of the press pack on the case. Half the journalistic world was trying to find Angel, and nobody seemed to have got close, as far as Kelly could work out. He realised that the police must know, unless Angel had jumped bail, and mad as she was he didn't think she was quite that crazy.

He asked Karen Meadows, who told him he had to be kidding.

'There are limits,' she informed him.

'Even for me?'

'Particularly for you, you old scallywag.'

He smiled at that. Lovely old-fashioned word, scallywag, and not one you could ever take offence at really. Kelly liked words a lot. That came with the territory, a bit, but in his case was another obsession. He hated it when words were wrongly used. Even apostrophes in the wrong place could set him ranting and raving about dropping standards. He had read in the *Telegraph* once about a society for the protection of the apostrophe, which he didn't regard as eccentric or outlandish at all. He even thought about joining it, but Kelly wasn't a great joiner of things. Alcoholics Anonymous had not had the effect on him he'd been told that it had on most alcoholics, many of whom attended meetings for the rest of their lives. Kelly had never been able to get beyond the embarrassment of it. In the end, and only after he'd sunk to the bottom of the pile and realised that the only alternative was death, Kelly had dealt with the drink the way he dealt with most things in his life. Alone.

Kelly waited for Angel Silver's trial with a kind of numb anticipation. Following the Narey Report, which had come into force earlier in the year, major criminal cases were already being fast-tracked into crown courts without the old bureaucratic procedures of magistrates' court committal proceedings. The purpose was to prevent the Human Rights Act violation of keeping suspects on remand in jail for months on end, but it also applied to Angel, even though she had been bailed. Her trial was therefore scheduled to begin at Exeter Crown Court during the second week in January, just eight weeks after the double killing at Maythorpe. And she was expected, as Karen Meadows had predicted from the start of it all, to continue to plead not guilty on grounds of self-defence.

Kelly carried on working intermittently on the Silver case, even though there was actually very little to do until the trial began. He checked all his police contacts regularly and occasionally phoned Mrs Hobbs who was friendly but guarded.

'Madam wasn't best pleased with me even though I thought your piece could only have helped her. At first she told me she thought I'd promised never to interfere again. But I told her this was different. It wasn't some daft show-business story. It was my daughter facing a manslaughter charge, and I'd help her as much as I could, in any way that I could, whether she liked it or not.'

'What did she say?' Kelly had asked.

'Do you know, I think I heard her laugh. She's a rum one, that girl of mine. I'll never fathom her. She calmed down. She said: "Right, I'll let you off then. But if you shoot that mouth of yours off again I'll be round with that carving knife." '

Kelly had been amazed. How could she make a crack like that when she was on a manslaughter charge for stabbing a man to death – and with a carving knife too? Kelly certainly couldn't understand Angel Silver and he wasn't at all surprised that her mother couldn't either. Angel was extraordinary, she really was.

'Don't you even think of printing that, John,' said Rachel Hobbs quickly. 'It's off the record, all right.'

'I wouldn't dream of it,' said Kelly. And he meant it, although he wasn't entirely sure why.

He asked Mrs Hobbs several times where Angel was and each time she replied patiently that she didn't know and she wouldn't tell him if she did. Kelly was inclined to believe her on both counts.

The weeks passed more or less uneventfully. Once Kelly returned home to find the words 'lying bastard' painted in white on his black front door, which he managed to swiftly repaint before it was seen by Moira. There were no other attacks of vandalism against him, but Kelly was wary of letting his guard down. Perhaps the police warning to the James family, if indeed they had been the perpetrators, had done the trick after all. Perhaps they'd just got bored. Perhaps not.

Christmas approached, Angel remained hidden away somewhere, and her name remained unspoken between Kelly and Moira. True to the way in which their relationship was conducted the Grand Hotel incident was never mentioned again. Not by either of them.

At first there was just an edge of tension between Kelly and Moira. But after a bit things returned pretty much to normal. The easy familiarity, lack of stress, lack of demands, which seemed to suit them both so well within their relationship, returned. Although Kelly always felt that the incident in the restaurant of the Grand continued to hang between them.

Nick was expected for Christmas, much to Kelly's delight. It even took his mind off the Silver case for a bit.

The rekindled relationship with his son was indeed one of the best things in Kelly's life. He had thought often enough about his only son but had not dared to approach him as a boy. He hadn't even troubled, or perhaps again dared, to get to know him when he had grown into a man. But when Nick had contacted him Kelly had been overjoyed. He had jumped at the opportunity, well aware that he would never have had the nerve himself to make an approach. In any case, rejection was one of Kelly's great fears. It hadn't been when he had been young and bold and full of belief in his own immortality. But after the cracks had formed and his world fell apart he had never quite been able to believe again that anyone would ever want him for himself.

His professional confidence, on the rare occasions he was ever given an opportunity nowadays to test himself beyond the mundane, remained fairly strong. But his personal confidence was non-existent. Moira, with her steadfast friendship and obvious deep fondness for him, had raised that confidence a little, but he was aware that the very fact of her loving him, and he had no doubt that she did, devalued her slightly in his eyes. He knew that was wrong. It made no difference. He didn't love himself. That was the problem.

Kelly's son shared many of his father's dreams, and Kelly just hoped that unlike him, Nick, who certainly seemed to have already made a big success of his life even though Kelly didn't really understand what his work entailed, would live out more of them than he'd ever managed to do.

Father and son had discovered so much in common. The love of words, for one thing. Nick didn't write, but was an avid reader. Then there was that shared love of fast cars and of fast horses too – although Nick, to Kelly's relief, did not seem to have inherited his father's near compulsion for gambling. And they seemed to share the same sense of humour too, the same appreciation of the absurd in life.

Kelly was greatly looking forward to Christmas with Nick, and Moira, who had managed to get leave for the festive period, had agreed to cook a traditional Christmas dinner at Kelly's house. Moira and Nick got on well. But then Moira got on well with almost everyone, thought Kelly with some satisfaction.

In preparation Moira insisted on giving the kitchen a fresh coat of paint and helped him clean the house, erect a Christmas tree in the living room, fill the fridge with food and the cupboard in the dining room with booze.

'Just because I can't touch the stuff doesn't mean you and Nick can't,' Kelly had announced magnanimously.

He was extremely glad that Moira was doing the cooking. In his younger days Kelly had never cooked at all. He'd either eaten meals cooked for him by his wife or dined in smart restaurants with a variety of guests he more often than not shouldn't have been with at all. Necessity had turned him into a reasonable cook since he'd rebuilt his life in Torquay, but he was not quite confident enough to prepare the kind of Christmas feast he had in mind for his son. There was to be quite a gathering too. Jennifer would be there, of course, and Moira's eldest daughter, Paula, was coming home from London with her husband, Ben, and their toddler son. It would be like a proper family gathering and it gave Kelly a nice warm feeling to think that he did have a family of sorts nowadays. Against all the odds.

Nick arrived on Christmas Eve at more or less exactly the time he had said he would. And Kelly, although he would have denied it if challenged, had been watching through the living room window for his son's Porsche. He was impressed by Nick's lifestyle. Kelly had visited the Thames-side apartment. He knew that Nick holidayed in the Caribbean in the winter and the smarter parts of Europe in the summer, and although he did not seem to have a regular girlfriend his father had got the impression that Nick did not suffer from shortage of women.

John Kelly was truly proud of his only son, whom he greeted with a handshake as usual, and a cautious smile which completely belied the strength of his feelings.

'And how's my favourite nurse,' said Nick, flashing the endearing little-boy smile which he had inherited from his father, and which Kelly, well aware of its effect, had used mercilessly as a younger man both professionally and personally on the various women in his life. Moira stepped forward at once and gave Nick a big hug, to which he responded warmly. They looked so natural together and laughed together easily. Kelly envied Moira. For all that had happened in her life she still had that open quality and seemed always able to give affection without a problem in the world. He wished he could be as comfortable with his only son as she seemed to be.

He hoped that time would help, and that very soon he too would feel able to greet Nick with a big hug instead of a handshake. How he wished that he could. It was mainly guilt, of course, a feeling that you could not rewrite the sins of your own past just like that, which stopped him.

Lunch, however, was a great success. Moira had a calmness about her. Perhaps that came with her job. Certainly cooking a turkey, with all the trimmings, for six plus a noisy toddler determined to get under your feet at all times, did not faze her at all.

The meal was perfect. Nick was as nice and funny as ever. He wanted to help wash up but Moira protested that he should talk to his father, that they didn't see each other often enough. Then the girls said Moira wasn't to do any more either, they'd clear up and make coffee.

So, with Nick unconvincingly protesting that he felt like an Eastern potentate being waited on by his handmaidens, the three of them did as they were told. Kelly produced a box of Cuban cigars and passed one to Nick, who then had to quell Moira's loudly expressed fears that Kelly would give his son a habit as bad as his own.

'I like the occasional cigar, but I don't seem to get hooked,' he said. 'I guess I'm just lucky. Non-addictive.'

Then, realising what he had said, Nick shot an anxious glance at his father.

'Don't look at me,' said Kelly. 'Apart from smoking I'm so darned vice free nowadays if I got too clean there'd be nothing left to hold me up.'

The afternoon stretched easily into evening. Paula and Ben took their young son back to Moira's house to put him to bed. Jennifer was watching TV with the sound low. Moira had dozed off. Her irregular sleeping pattern meant that she would occasionally be overwhelmed by drowsiness, and that combined with the good lunch and quite a lot of wine was proving to be a fatal combination.

Kelly and Nick chatted easily and unchallengingly, enjoying each other's company.

Then, some time around 10.30 the phone rang.

'I'll get it,' said Kelly automatically. He was never able to leave a phone unanswered. No journalist could.

'House of Kelly,' he announced cheerily.

'My mother seems to think you're a good ally,' said a voice. He knew who it was at once.

'Hello, Angel,' he half whispered. In the background he was vaguely aware of Moira stirring in her armchair.

'W-what, who is it?' she enquired of nobody in particular, just a reflex action upon being suddenly woken by the phone, while probably not even fully aware of what had awoken her.

But Nick had heard what Kelly had said. 'Somebody called Angel,' he responded with apparent innocence.

Kelly winced. Moira would not be pleased. The truth, however, was that he didn't care much. This call, even though it was Christmas, was suddenly the most overwhelmingly important thing in his life.

'How are you?' he enquired into the phone.

'I've been better. I just have this awful feeling, in spite of what everyone says, that things may go pear-shaped.'

'Even the police are on your side, Angel,' he said.

'Yes, and why doesn't that fill me with endless confidence?'

He laughed.

'Look, John, I've got to talk to someone sooner or later. And I need someone to be able to put my case, to know what really happened, to tell it like it is if anything . . .' she paused, '". . . goes wrong in court". I read your note. I know you've fed me all the old lines. None the less, you're the lesser of most evils, I reckon.'

'Thank you,' he said. 'Do I take that as a compliment?'

'You do,' she responded. 'So how about it? How'd you like it to be you I talk to?'

'I'd love it,' he replied truthfully. 'When do you want to meet?'

'What's wrong with now?'

'Angel, it's Christmas night –'

'So?' she interrupted. 'I might change my mind tomorrow . . .'

Everything he had ever read about her, everything her mother had told him, suggested that Angel had developed into a manipulative bitch since his brief liaison with her all those years previously. This exchange backed that up.

'Why would you do that?' he asked, not giving up entirely without a fight.

'Because that's what I do,' she responded without further explanation.

It was then that he caught something, just a slight inflection, in her voice, which suggested to him that she might be high. And it really was quite likely that when she came down she would change her mind, he thought, already justifying to himself what he knew he was going to do.

'All right,' he said. 'Where are you?'

'Where do you think I am?' Her voice was taunting, slightly mocking.

'I've been trying to find that out for weeks,' he said.

She laughed. 'Jimmy Rudge hid me away. A cottage in Norfolk miles from anywhere and a whole gay network to look after me. The gay community still knows a lot about hiding things, you know.'

'Sounds interesting.'

'Boring as hell actually. But I had plenty of outings. Amazing how a wig and makeup can change your appearance.'

He said nothing, but he knew about her chameleon qualities.

'And they found me company when I needed it,' she went on.

There was something provocative in her voice which made Kelly unsure of what she meant by that and even more unsure if he actually wanted to know.

'OK, so where are you now?' he asked again. 'At Maythorpe?'

'Oh, clever boy!'

He ignored the sarcasm. 'How long have you been back?'

'About ten days,' she said. 'And nobody's even noticed. I'm not an old story already, am I?'

More mockery. Was it really that long since he'd checked out the old manor house? He supposed it must have been. He had been preoccupied with Christmas and his son's visit. So Angel was half right. Even he had lost interest a bit after so long with nothing happening.

None the less he told her, 'You'll never be an old story, Angel.'

'So I'll expect you then?'

'I'll be with you in half an hour.'

'Make sure you hurry.'

She hung up without giving him time to say goodbye. Typical, he somehow suspected. She'd sounded almost flirtatious. She'd also sounded annoyingly sure of herself, sure that he would drop everything and run to her. Which, of course, was exactly what he was going to do.

He replaced the receiver with exaggerated care and turned round very slowly to face Nick and Moira. Jennifer had slipped into the kitchen to put the kettle on and he could hear her arranging mugs.

'I'm sorry, guys, I've got to go out for a bit,' he said, spreading his arms in apology. 'Work, you know.'

'Yes, of course,' Nick replied quickly.

Moira looked at him steadily. 'She's back then,' she said flatly.

Kelly nodded, trying to keep his face expressionless. When he spoke again he addressed Nick, barely looking at Moira.

'It's this Scott Silver story, biggest thing in these parts for years. I'm on a major exclusive here, Nick.'

'Sure, Dad,' said Nick in a tone of voice which gave his father no indication at all of what he might be thinking.

'Yeah, I should be no more than a couple of hours maximum. Sorry, Moira, I'll be as quick as I can.'

'Whatever you say, John,' she replied stiffly.

'I'll be back for that cup of tea later,' he said over his shoulder as he headed for the front door.

Moira followed him out into the hallway, but his thoughts were already racing away from him when he heard her say quietly, to herself really, 'Only it's not Scott Silver, is it, John? It's Angel. She's snapped her fingers and you're going running. On Christmas Day, for God's sake.'

Kelly didn't reply, pretended he hadn't heard. He told himself Moira didn't deserve a reply. He was chasing a big story, the biggest he had encountered in years, that was all, though he was just about honest enough to admit to himself that there might be some truth in what Moira had said.

Angel Silver had summoned him and it was as if he had no choice.

Nick went to the sideboard in the dining room and poured himself a whisky, which he drank in one swallow. He usually drank very little, knowing only too well the damage the stuff could do.

With his head swimming slightly he sought out Moira, who had retreated to the kitchen, where Jennifer was pulling on her coat.

'Don't think I'll wait up for the old bugger,' he told her casually. 'I feel like an early night. It's been a great day. Thanks for everything you've done.'

Nick was invariably courteous and thoughtful with people. He worked at it. He liked to get people on his side, and even as anxious as he was becoming about his father, it was automatic for him not to forget to thank Moira.

But all she said in response was: 'OK, Nick. Good night then.'

She sounded preoccupied and Nick didn't blame her. Neither did he want to talk to her, however. He just wanted to be alone with his thoughts.

There was something about the way his father had reacted to that phone call. It reminded Nick of the old obsessive behaviour patterns which he still recalled so clearly from his childhood.

Nick felt anxious as he climbed into his pyjamas, which he had that morning folded neatly on the pillow. Nick was very tidy and liked order. That partly came from his army days. It was also, he suspected, a legacy of his childhood when, thanks to his errant father, he had known very little order at all.

He lay down on the bed, still thinking the evening through. Probably he was worrying over nothing, he told himself. Kelly was certainly still dry, Nick was sure that he would know if he'd been drinking at all. And naturally a man with his background would be delighted to be involved in such a big story again.

Nick just hoped that was all it was. Moira already seemed to regard Angel Silver as some sort of threat. Nick didn't know whether she was or not. Not yet, anyway.

Nine

It was very dark outside Maythorpe Manor. The security lights were off, and if there were any lights on inside the house the curtains must have been tightly drawn because Kelly could not see even a chink at the windows. The place was deserted. No police. No fans. No press.

Well, it had been empty for weeks and people get fed up with standing outside an empty house. Even journalists.

Kelly slowed almost to a halt outside the towering electronic gates and was about to stop the car to get out and speak into the intercom when the gates opened before him as if by magic. At the same moment the lights blazed on.

Had Angel been watching from inside, seen his headlights approaching, Kelly wondered. Or maybe she had heard the engine. No motor in the world had a more distinctive sound than an MG.

He drove into the grounds of the imposing old house. It felt strange to be an invited guest after having stood on the doorstep for so long. He motored slowly across the gravelled forecourt and pulled to a halt outside the pillared front door.

Thanks to the neon glare of the security lamps it was almost like daylight as he stepped out of the car. From what he could see of the garden it already did not look as well cared for as when he had last studied it. The white paint of the front door was peeling slightly. Only the daily help, Mrs Sheila Nott, had been retained, Kelly understood. It seemed that everything had started to fall apart.

He fastened the zip of his battered old leather jacket as he stepped out of the car. A bright and sunny Christmas Day had turned into a cold damp night.

The front door opened just as he reached for the bell pull on the wall alongside it. Suddenly she was standing right in front of him. He withdrew his hand and stood looking at her.

Her hair was wispy blonde again, close to its natural colour perhaps. He wondered if even she knew what her natural colour was any more. The violet eyes studied him in that slightly mocking way which seemed to come naturally, even when she would appear to have absolutely nothing to be mocking about. Her mouth was, as usual, a vermilion slash in that translucent porcelain skin. It parted in a slight smile of greeting, the lips curling almost imperceptibly in the corners.

'Don't just stand there, come on in,' she said.

He took a step forward. His legs felt weak, slightly shaky. There was something about getting close to someone you had trailed from a distance. He had spent so much time thinking about Angel Silver and what had happened to her, trying to get inside her head.

'Close the door behind you,' she commanded, stepping backwards, still looking at him. She was a woman fully aware of the effect she could have on men.

Kelly did as he was told, and a little voice inside his head sent him a message that this was how it would always be with Angel Silver. Trouble was, he didn't even care.

She led him into a big high-ceilinged sitting room which looked as if it could do with a good clean. Its décor was the first surprise. Absolutely traditional English furniture. One or two rather good antiques, Kelly thought. Two chintzy sofas, a rocking chair, a beautiful mahogany desk in the corner, heavy velvet drapes at the windows, richly coloured Indian rugs scattered over a dark wood-block floor, cream brocade wallpaper.

Kelly was not sure what he had expected to find in the home of a rock icon and his beautiful if slightly weird wife, but this was not it at all. It was so conventional. He had just assumed that he would be confronted by something outlandish, he supposed.

Music played softly in the background. Another surprise.

'Mozart,' he said.

She nodded, the eyes even more mocking.

'Didn't you think Angel Silver could appreciate classical music?'

He noted the use of the word 'could' instead of the 'would' that might have fitted rather more naturally.

'I hadn't thought about it,' he said, trying to sound casual. He looked around again. There was no sign at all in the house that it was Christmas Day. Indeed, when they had spoken on the phone earlier it had been almost as if she were unaware of that until he had pointed it out.

'Have you been alone today?' he asked.

'Yes?' she replied questioningly, sounding surprised that he should bother to make such an enquiry.

'Well, nothing, but it is Christmas . . .' he stumbled uncertainly.

'Just another day to me,' she replied quickly. 'Particularly this year.'

Of course, he thought, wondering if he had been insensitive.

'I suppose so. I'm sorry,' he said.

'Don't be. Can I get you a drink?'

'Coffee maybe?'

Her eyebrows had lifted. 'Coffee? Is this the wild man of Fleet Street that I remember?'

Everything she said to him seemed to be mocking, or teasing at the very least. She was wearing what he could only describe to himself as a sort of little-girl frock in an almost fluorescent pink silky material. On any other woman of her age it would have looked ridiculous. Angel got away with it. She looked gorgeous. The dress was low and displayed an enticing glimpse of small pert breasts. Kelly tried not to look. They were very white. A vivid image of what they would be like fully exposed – small but perfect, with dark hard nipples – suddenly flashed in front of his eyes.

As if on cue her hand went to the front of her dress. She tugged at it slightly, revealing just a little more pale flesh.

He flinched, and made a real effort to pull himself together. Could she read his mind?

'I'm surprised you remember me at all.'

'Why? Because I was out of my head?'

'No, I didn't mean that –'

'Yes you did, but it's all right.'

She invited him to sit down, and disappeared somewhere to make coffee, leaving him alone with thoughts which were already confused. She had been flirting with him, there was no doubt about that, and he wasn't sure whether he hoped she would stop or not. He had no illusions. He suspected flirting was just a reflex action for her. None the less he found it terribly disturbing. He fiddled with his tape recorder, making sure it was working properly, and checked unnecessarily that his notebook and pen were in his jacket pocket.

Angel seemed to be away a very long time. Kelly wondered how used she was to making coffee for herself. It was somehow difficult to imagine Angel Silver undertaking any mundane household task. Eventually she returned with two large porcelain mugs on a plastic tray.

'Instant OK?' she enquired in a voice which suggested that it didn't much matter whether it was OK or not, because it was all he was getting.

'Sure,' he said.

She tripped slightly over the rug by the sofa. Kelly leaned forward and grabbed the tray, steadying it, then taking it from her. The two mugs each sat in a brown puddle now. She reached for a box of paper handkerchiefs on the little table next to him and mopped up the tray, very carefully. As she leaned over him the flimsy pink dress gaped even more and he could see her breasts even more clearly. The nipples disproportionately large, very dark brown, and standing out. Hard. Inviting. Much as he had imagined them earlier. He made himself look away.

'There,' she said, behaving as if she'd accomplished a momentous task as she finished cleaning the tray, screwed up the paper handkerchief and tossed it into the already littered grate of the unlit fireplace. Then she sat down on the sofa next to him, closer to him than most people would sit, he thought. Her eyes were unnaturally bright. She was breathing quickly. She gave a little sniff and lifted one of the mugs to her lips. He studied her. He had a pretty fair idea of what she had been doing which had kept her so long while she'd been allegedly making the coffee. He'd done enough coke himself to know the signs. He made no comment, of course. What could he possibly say? That he'd always had her down as one who'd never really be able to kick all her bad habits, somebody who would never even want to face every day of the rest of her life without that something extra, without something to bend her mind, without that buzz, that lift, that you can get from a little packet of white powder? Yet Angel seemed to survive, and to continue to function, whatever she was doing, whatever she was on, whatever got her through the days. If she still had a habit she must at least have retained some control over it, he reckoned. She looked so good, for a start. Perhaps she was one of the ones who could handle it after all, at least well enough to kid themselves that they could. And maybe she'd had to sink to rock bottom first to get even that far, just like he had done not so long afterwards. She still looked so absurdly young although it was almost seventeen years since he'd plucked her from the gutter. And since then he'd been there himself.

He picked up the other coffee mug and took a sip, moving the tray from his lap on to the floor at their feet.

'So, are you going to switch that thing on or what?' Angel asked, gesturing at the tape recorder, taking charge again.

You'd think she was the one conducting the interview, Kelly thought. He gave himself a mental talking-to. If this was going to work he had to take control.

'If you're sure you're ready,' he said. 'I'd like to start with you taking me through the night when it all happened. When Scott and Terry James died. Your own version of events –'

'What do you mean, "version"?' she interrupted sharply, snapping at him, no mockery now in her eyes, just a fast-blazing anger.

'Whoa. That's just a turn of phrase, that's all.'

'Well, you watch your turn of phrase then. I thought you were supposed to be an expert with words.'

'Shall we try again? Would you just tell me what happened from the beginning?'

'Where do you want me to start?'

He had a feeling Angel was deliberately testing his patience. He didn't rise.

'Wherever you think you should.'

She nodded, leaning back on the sofa, and seemed to go off into a kind of dream.

'Scott and I had spent the evening here alone, listening to music. We weren't mad ravers any more, you know. We liked our home, just being together. A nice meal, a decent bottle of wine. Maybe a video. We were just like any ordinary married couple.'

She glanced at him appealingly. Anybody less like half of 'any ordinary married couple' than Angel Silver was difficult to imagine. Kelly did not speak. He just gestured her to continue.

'We went to bed about midnight, I suppose. I'm not sure. We both fell asleep quite quickly, I think. The next thing I knew was I felt Scott stir, I think he sat upright, and he must have flicked the bedside light on. It was probably the light which woke me, or it may have been when he cried out, "What the fuck?" That's what he said. "What the fuck?"

'I suppose neither of us was quite awake. It was like a bad dream. There was Terry James standing in the middle of our bedroom just looking at us. He was carrying a bag in one hand – the police said later it was full of our things – and he had this knife in the other. I recognised it. Can you believe that? At that moment I recognised it as one of our kitchen knives, he'd just picked it up, apparently. I was kind of mesmerised by him just standing there, couldn't take it in as real, but Scott leaped out of bed and threw himself at him. He was always like that, Scott, fancied himself as a bit of an action man. He was the first person I knew to try bungee jumping, before most people had even heard of it. Scott liked danger. He was never afraid. It was just like him to act first, then think later . . .'

Angel's voice tailed off. Her eyes still had that faraway look. Kelly didn't want to break the spell. He kept silent, waiting for her to speak again.

'There was a struggle. Scott was very strong, you know, tough, wiry. He had hold of Terry James's knife arm, and with his other arm he was going for him, clawing at him, punching, going for his eyes, it looked like. James was shouting, "Get off me." I just watched. I can't believe now that I didn't manage to do anything else. I could have helped. There was a panic button by the bed. I might even have had time to phone the police. But I didn't do anything. I just watched.

'Anyway, although Scott was strong he was half Terry James's size. James got his knife hand free and started lashing at Scott. He cut him on the cheek, I think, just a glancing blow, but Scott cried out in pain and he sounded scared then. I think he finally felt afraid, realised what he was taking on. He just turned away, cowering. James brought the knife up from under, and stabbed him in the side of his back, low down, right in the kidneys, the police said. That first blow, that . . .'

She broke down then. Tears started to pour down her face. Kelly stared at her, fascinated. She wasn't sobbing, not weeping at all in the conventional fashion, but these huge tears were just pouring down her face. He passed her one of the paper hankies. She took it but did not attempt to use it. It was almost as if she did not fully realise that she was crying.

'That first blow, they told me, that alone, may have been fatal. B-but, he didn't stop. It was like he went mad. Scott started to fall, James was half holding him up, and he just kept sticking that knife into him, over and over again.

'Then suddenly he let go. Scott fell in a crumpled heap, and it was as if James suddenly realised what he had done. He seemed rooted to the spot, just staring at Scott, the knife dangling from his hand. For a moment it was like he had forgotten that I was there.

'Sc-Scott was making this funny gurgling noise. He was covered in blood. It was spurting out from all over his body, out of his mouth too, sort of bubbling out. But I didn't think that he might be dying, might be more or less already dead. I just wanted it all to stop. I had to protect him, I thought. It was down to me to make it stop.

'I half fell out of bed and I grabbed James by the arm and took the knife from him. I think I took him completely by surprise. I got the knife from him quite easily. Suddenly I had it in my hand. It was covered in blood, of course, thick gooey blood, but I don't remember caring about that at all.

'James made this sort of grunting noise, as if suddenly becoming aware of what I had done, or even that I was there at all. Then he said, "C'mon, give it me back," and he said it quite gently, which made it all the more frightening, somehow. I kept walking away from him, backwards, watching him all the time. I don't know quite what I intended to do – maybe throw that dreadful knife out of the window, anything to get rid of it. Maybe I was too shocked to have any intentions. I didn't take my eyes off him. He was like a wild animal. I kind of thought as long as I had eye contact it would be all right, that he wouldn't charge. But he did, you see. That's exactly what he did. Suddenly he came at me . . .'

The tears were flowing more freely than ever; liquid was flowing from her mouth and nostrils as well. She was not crying prettily. At last she started to sob properly and her shoulders began to heave. Her eyes were red and swollen. This was a bitter heartfelt outpouring of grief. It could, Kelly felt, be nothing else. But still he did not intervene. He didn't know what to say, for a start.

The paper hankie he had passed her was screwed into a ball in her right fist. He passed her another one, silently. She took it, dropping the first one on the floor, and this time blew her nose loudly. Then she mopped the worst of the tears from her face. He watched as she struggled to regain control. It was two or three minutes before she started to speak again.

'He came at me,' Angel repeated, her voice low and distant. 'He just charged at me. This huge powerful man. I don't think it occurred to him that I would use the knife on him. I don't think it occurred to me either. I was just trying to protect myself, to protect poor Scott, to make sure he didn't hurt us any more. He charged and I just thrust out the knife. He more or less threw himself on it. He took almost the full blade in his stomach. It just went in so easily . . .'

Her voice became even more faraway. She started to sob again. Kelly waited but she made no attempt to speak again.

After a while he took her hand lightly in his. 'But Angel,'

he said very gently, 'it's been reported that Terry James was stabbed at least ten times. How did that happen, Angel?'

She stopped crying at once, turned to look at him full face, and quite deliberately removed her hand from his. The vermilion slash of her mouth was smudged now, lipstick smeared across her face. Like blood, he thought. Only nothing was like blood, except blood. And Kelly knew that better than most.

Her voice surprised him when she finally spoke again. But then, Angel Silver was full of surprises. Always had been. Suddenly she sounded quite hard.

'I pulled the knife out of him. It came out as easily as it had gone in. He started to fall to the ground. He was clutching his belly. Scott kept making this dreadful gurgling sound. Suddenly I wanted to hurt the bastard, just like he'd hurt Scott. I lost it. I know I lost it. I can't believe what I did. I stabbed him again. And again and again. I just couldn't stop. I couldn't, couldn't stop.' She paused. He waited.

'So, does that make me a monster too, John?'

'No,' he said, and he meant it. He knew what fear could do to people, decent people, he knew how shock and blind terror could make them behave in ways they would not think themselves capable of. But he also thought she was probably lucky to have got away with a manslaughter charge. Like the chief constable and Karen Meadows, although for different reasons, he thought about the farmer Tony Martin, who, a couple of years earlier, had shot a young tearaway in the back when his home had been broken into. He'd been charged with murder, found guilty and been locked up. Obliquely Kelly wondered if that farmer would have faced the same charges had he been the beautiful wife of a rock icon instead of an unknown middle-aged man who presented a none-too-attractive image.

He took Angel's hand again. This time she didn't remove it. He must concentrate, make sure that he did not antagonise her. He needed more detail.

'There must have been an awful lot of blood, Angel,' he remarked, leading her forward as much as he dared.

She nodded and started to cry again. 'I'd never seen so

much blood. I didn't know there was so much blood in a man's body. There was Scott's blood, and Terry James's blood. It was just everywhere.'

'You were lucky not to be injured yourself,' Kelly continued, gently pushing and probing.

'Lucky was one word for it. After what that bastard did to Scott, and when I realised fully what I'd done to him, when it all started to sink in, well, I wished that I was dead, John. I really did.'

'So then what did you do, after you'd stabbed Terry James, what did you do next?'

'I went to Scott. I tried to stop him bleeding. I pulled one of the sheets off the bed and I sort of wrapped it round him, as tight as I could, like a big bandage. Stupid, I suppose. I didn't know what I was doing. Then I phoned for the police and for an ambulance, and I just sat with Scott until they came. It was terrible, John. I watched the blood gush out of him, watched his life just drain away. There was this dreadful gurgling sound and his eyes were wide open all the time, staring at me. That's how it felt anyway, as if he were staring and staring at me. Yet I knew he couldn't see anything. I just knew that. And then, and then, eventually the gurgling stopped. I felt his body go cold, I felt him go cold, John. I don't remember much else. I know that the police came and the paramedics. I don't remember what they did. What I did. I know they took my clothes away, but I don't remember undressing. I know I was examined by a doctor but I don't remember it happening. They told me later they'd taken a DNA sample from me, but I don't remember that at all. I know somebody put me in a bath, washed me. But it's all just a vague impression. At some stage I fell asleep. Can you believe that. I fell asleep. The body's great defence mechanism. I fell asleep.

'The next thing I remember clearly is the following morning – well, later that day really – being taken to the police station, being questioned. I felt like I was the villain. Like I was the murderer. And I had killed a man. But I'm not a murderer, I'm not, am I, John?'

There she was again, that poignantly charismatic mix of the vulnerable and the manipulative.

'No you're not, Angel, of course you're not,' he said. And again he meant it. Kelly believed that all too often victims were turned into villains. He had seen it happen. The law did that, and all its well-meaning hangers-on, the sort who get IRA murderers thousands of pounds in damages because their human rights have allegedly been violated.

He wanted so much to reassure Angel. He only narrowly resisted an absurd urge to take her in his arms and cuddle her. Instead he made himself concentrate on the matter in hand. He was an old-hand hack, for God's sake, an accomplished interviewer, and this was one hell of a story.

'Will you tell me about you and Scott, Angel?' he asked. 'I want to know about your time together, about your marriage.'

She nodded. Her face lightened slightly and her eyes brightened as she began to speak. 'Scott was everything to me,' she said. 'You know what I was like before, don't you? You know as well as anyone. Better than most. I don't know what would have happened to me if it hadn't been for Scott. Shall I tell you about how I met him?'

Kelly nodded. He'd heard versions of this story, including her mother's, but never directly from her, of course.

'I'd cleaned up my act, after . . . you know.' She looked at him anxiously. 'You won't write about that, will you, not ever, John? I just couldn't bear it. Promise me?'

There she was, vulnerable again. Pleading. Irresistible. Little girl lost in a big bad world.

'Don't you think I would have done so by now if I'd ever intended to?'

'I've never been up on a manslaughter charge before.'

She was sharp. Even at a time like this, even after having just disintegrated into near-hysterical tears. And she was right, of course. Everything in her past was suddenly of much more interest than it had ever been before.

She sighed, and started to smile.

'I'd cleaned up my act,' she said. 'I'd moved back in with Mum in Clerkenwell. We'd sold the flat and invested what was left after I'd cleared my debts. I didn't have much, but I was free again in every way. Mum found me this agent and I was even starting to work again. They got me this pantomime in Croydon. I was the puss in *Puss-in-Boots*.

'Scott had this sister he was mad about who was also in the show. The word went round one night that he was in the audience. I couldn't believe it. I'd always been crazy for him, you see, since I'd been a little kid. Me and half the rest of the world. He came back stage afterwards and his sister introduced us. The first words he said to me were, "Angelica Hobbs, I've been in love with you ever since I saw your first movie."

'And I said, "I've been in love with you since I heard your first record." It was incredible really, looking back. I don't suppose either of us was entirely serious, but he just looked at me with those come-to-bed eyes of his and I melted. I went with him that night, of course. There didn't seem to be any choice, not for either of us, I don't think. In the morning I woke up with him and I thought, You bloody fool, Angel, you've done it again. Easy lay, as ever. You're just another groupie to him, you fool. If you weren't before you will be now.

'Then he woke up and we made love again. Well, there wasn't much point in resisting then, was there? In any case, it was so good with Scott. Always was. I could never say no to him.

'Then afterwards he said, "How do you feel like waking up to me every morning for the rest of your life?" I thought it was a really sweet thing to say. But it didn't occur to me that he meant it.'

She picked up her mug and took a long drink from it. The coffee must be cold by now, Kelly thought. Her eyes were brighter than ever. Sparkling. The tears just a memory. She was transformed, smiling as she talked.

'He did mean it, though. Three months later we were married in Vegas. It was all my dreams come true. He was the man of my dreams, he really was.'

She sighed deeply. Kelly studied her more closely than ever. From almost anyone else the words would be at best trite at worst a cliché and Kelly's natural cynicism would have kicked in. But she got away with it in his book; the words were all right, somehow, coming from her. And he did not doubt her sincerity. Not for a moment.

'Can you imagine losing that, John?' she asked. 'And in such a way?'

Kelly couldn't. He didn't think he had ever had anything remotely like the way she had described her relationship with Scott to lose.

'Was it really that perfect?' he asked, the cynic shining through just a little.

She looked at him directly. 'Yes, I suppose it was,' she said. 'Hard to believe, really. Somebody like me, somebody like Scott. We were soul mates.'

'Didn't you ever quarrel?'

She looked puzzled. 'We didn't have anything to quarrel about. We had a wonderful life. All this . . .' she gestured at the opulent home, 'a house in LA as well. We travelled when we wanted, did what we liked when we liked. Scott never needed to work again to keep it all going either. Anything he did was because he wanted to, no other reason. No pressure at all. And we had each other.'

From anyone but Angel it would have sounded sickeningly smug. She seemed quite ingenuous. Then her face clouded over.

'There was only one thing that wasn't perfect,' she continued. 'We wanted children. But you'd know about that. The whole world knows about that.'

She was right too. Angel Silver had suffered a series of much publicised miscarriages in the first few years of her marriage to Scott. The best fertility brains in the country were not able to sort the problem out. The final miscarriage almost killed her. Both Angel and Scott had talked publicly about their anguish. There had been one high-profile interview in which Scott said he had made the agonising decision that they would stop trying for a child.

'I cannot risk Angel any more,' he had announced memorably. 'I can live without a child but I cannot live without my wife.'

Kelly stayed for another hour or so, going over with Angel

half-forgotten details of her past, and going through again the night of the killings.

A couple of times Angel made an excuse and left the room for several minutes, reinforcing Kelly's suspicion that she was taking cocaine. He decided to confront her, to let her know that he was not a fool, and that he remained as streetwise as ever.

'I didn't know you were still doing that stuff,' he remarked mildly.

She looked startled.

'C'mon, Angel,' he went on, keeping his voice very gentle. 'It takes one to know one.'

'It's only coke,' she said sulkily. 'I'd never get back on the smack. Never. This stuff I can handle. And it's helping me get through all this. God knows I need something . . .'

She shot him that vulnerable, appealing look. He tried not to fall for it totally.

'But you weren't on it the night it all happened?'

He knew she'd been tested clean when she was charged with manslaughter four days after the killings. The police were well aware of Angel's track record and if there'd been any kind of drug angle she'd never have got off with a manslaughter charge.

Angel shrugged. 'I can take it or leave it.'

Kelly doubted that somehow. But maybe she believed it. Who knew?

'The police searched your house. That's routine. They didn't find anything, though, did they?'

He knew that to be the case, and it was beginning to puzzle him more and more.

Angel scowled. 'Even druggies run out of stuff sometimes.'

Her voice was hard-edged, heavy with sarcasm. He supposed she had a point. He changed the subject. He didn't want to antagonise her. He had a great interview. And he had a feeling there would be more to come. He needed to keep her sweet. Oh, and to hell with it, he had to admit it, he didn't want to upset her unnecessarily, to give her more grief. He wanted everything to be all right for her.

Ten

Kelly was on a high when he left Maythorpe Manor, and he didn't know how much of that was due to having landed an interview with a woman half the world's press were chasing, and how much of it was caused simply by having spent almost three hours in her company. He found Angel Silver mesmerising.

He was undoubtedly preoccupied, his excitement making him drive a little faster than usual, when it happened.

As he sped through the gates and swung a right, passing out of the illuminated area around Maythorpe and into the shadowy darkness of Rock Lane, a figure loomed suddenly in his headlights. Kelly was taken totally by surprise. A woman, long hair, long clothes, was standing quite still in the middle of the road directly in front of him. She seemed frozen, like a startled rabbit, her face lit up starkly. Kelly slammed on the brakes. There had been a heavy shower while he had been in the house with Angel and the road surface was still wet. The back wheels of the MG locked solid. The car went into a skid. Kelly gripped the steering wheel so hard his knuckles turned white as he struggled to regain control. It was hopeless. The little car started to spin.

'Jesus Christ Almighty!' Kelly cried out involuntarily.

He was quite sure he was going to hit the woman. But at the last possible moment he was aware that she seemed to come to her senses and throw herself out of the way. It still seemed an age before he gained control of the MG again. And when he did he was facing the wrong way, albeit miraculously still on the tarmac and not smashed into one of the banked hedges on either side. Kelly and his car had turned a complete 180 degrees in the narrow road outside Maythorpe. Obliquely he thought that if he was offered a million pounds to complete a turn like that deliberately in the limited space available he would be unable to do it.

He stopped the car and jumped quickly out. There was no sign of anybody else around.

'Are you all right?' he called into the black nothingness. The darkness away from the bright security lights of Maythorpe was dauntingly total. He reached back in the car for the torch he always kept in the glove compartment and shone it around the now apparently deserted stretch of road.

Perhaps he had hit her after all. He didn't think so, but he couldn't be sure. Perhaps she was lying there injured, or worse. Perhaps the force of the impact had thrown her into the hedge.

But there had been no impact. He knew that really. He was just in shock. She must be around somewhere though, mustn't she?

Maythorpe Manor was quite isolated. Rock Lane was the sort of opulent semi-rural road the residents of which rarely left their dwellings by any means other than a motor car. Except when all the fans and press had been gathered outside the Silver home you were unlikely to meet any pedestrians, and certainly not at that time on Christmas night. Fleetingly, Kelly wondered if his imagination had been playing tricks on him. But he knew better.

There had been someone there, all right – a young woman whom he had very nearly killed. And he was pretty sure he recognised her as the one he had tried to talk to outside Maythorpe Manor in the days right after Scott Silver's death, the woman who had always stood out as different to the rest of the fans, strangely apart and alone. What on earth was she doing there on Christmas night, he asked himself.

'Hello, are you there?' he called again.

No response. Was she hiding? Had she run off? If so, she must have moved faster than he had been able to after that near miss.

He turned and looked back towards Maythorpe. The gate had closed behind him. But he could see through the railings that Angel was still standing by the big front door. A frail-looking figure, white and pink, not moving.

He walked back to the gate, already closed behind him, and shouted to her through it.

'Hey, did you see that?'

Even as he spoke she turned round and disappeared into the house, the big door closing behind her with a slam.

It was almost two in the morning when he got home. Boxing Day had started, and he expected he was not going to have a good one. The house was in darkness. He was relieved. Moira might, of course, have retreated to his bed but he thought that was unlikely. As he was out, she would almost certainly have gone back to her own home, particularly in view of her feelings about his visit to Angel Silver at such a time on such a day. Rather disloyally, he hoped that she was no longer in his house. He was not in the mood for explanations, he was still in shock from his near collision with that young woman outside Maythorpe, and he much preferred to face Moira in the morning when he would have had time to collect his thoughts. He was also glad that Nick seemed to have gone to bed.

One way and another Kelly's adrenalin was racing, and he didn't feel tired even though it was so late, so he thought he would make a pot of tea and maybe read for a bit, try to settle down. The kitchen was beyond the living room, and as soon as Kelly switched on the light there he saw her. Moira had not gone home. She had fallen asleep in the big winged armchair by the window. And as the light snapped on she woke with a little jump.

Kelly tried for normality, tried to behave as if nothing out of the ordinary had happened.

'Sorry, I didn't know you were there,' he said.

She nodded, rubbing her eyes sleepily.

'Nick gone on up?' he enquired.

'Yes.'

'Jennifer gone home?' He was aware that he was slumping into banality but it was the best he could do at that hour of the morning. He was just desperate to avoid confrontation.

'Yes.'

Oh dear, he thought. This was hard work, and the

temptation just to walk away was almost overwhelming, but he reckoned Moira deserved better than that.

'Sorry I was so long, I just couldn't stop her talking,' he said lightly.

Moira glanced at her watch. 'Did you want to?' she asked edgily.

'Not really. It's a great story.'

'John, you're supposed to be building bridges with your son. He comes to be with you for Christmas, to spend time with you, and then you just disappear. For hours. And you return in the middle of the night.'

'It was work, Moira.'

'That's one word for it.'

Kelly felt his patience begin to run out. 'Look, I just don't understand why you're being so bloody difficult about this. It's the best bloody story I've got near for years. What do you expect me to do, give up on it?'

'No.'

'What then?'

He could see her relenting a little. Nobody understood the importance of work more than Moira, although he supposed his paled into insignificance alongside hers.

'I don't know. I just didn't like the way you dropped everything and went running when that woman called you. And Nick was completely bewildered –'

'It wasn't like that, Moira, and you know it,' Kelly interrupted.

'Do I?'

'Oh, come to bed for Christ's sake,' he said, making one last attempt to restore the situation.

Somewhat to his surprise she agreed to do so, and without passing any further comment. But he suspected that it might be only because she was too sleepy to be bothered with getting herself back to her own home.

Kelly didn't get to see Angel Silver again until her trial three weeks later. It wasn't for want of trying, but when he phoned all he got was her answering machine. Her mobile seemed never to be switched on. He wrote again but received no reply.

It became an almost daily routine for him to drive out to Maythorpe and just look. He never even got a glimpse of Angel. Several times he stopped his car and tried to use the intercom system on the gates. There was never any response. After a bit he didn't bother any more, and instead merely drove slowly by.

Once, that now familiar young woman, whom he was so sure he had nearly hit on Christmas night, was again standing in silent vigil by the gate, staring towards the house. He pulled up alongside.

She turned to look at him but gave no sign of recognition.

'Hi,' he said. 'I think we had a near miss, you and I.'

She just stared at him blankly.

'Christmas night?' he tried again.

Her eyes remained blank.

'Why did you run off?' he asked her.

He thought just a flicker of some indefinable reaction crossed her pale face, but he wasn't even sure of that. Then abruptly she turned her back on him, pressing her face against the railings as he had seen her do before.

He switched off the engine of his car and climbed out.

'Look, will you please talk to me? You nearly got yourself killed, you know. Frightened me half to death. You must have been frightened too, surely?'

Still no reply.

He took a couple of steps forward, reached out a hand and placed it on her shoulder. It was supposed to be a gesture of reassurance. But it didn't quite work out. She jumped away from him and turned to face him again, her face full of alarm.

'Don't touch me,' she cried. It was the first time he had heard her speak. She had a strong northcountry accent at odds, somehow, with her slightly oriental features.

'I'm sorry,' he told her, removing his hand at once. Her eyes blazed at him for a few seconds, then she dropped her gaze to the ground, and once more turned away and pressed her face to the railings, almost as if he wasn't there.

'Who are you?' he asked gently. He expected no further response and got none. He was beginning to get very curious about her, that was all.

'Why do you keep coming here?' he persisted.

She didn't turn, she didn't move, and he only just caught her words, she spoke so softly.

'To pay my respects, of course,' she said.

Only minutes later Nick called his father on his mobile. At once Kelly started to talk about the Silver case.

'There's this young woman, I'm sure she's involved, sure she's more than a fan, but I just can't get her to talk to me.'

'Not everybody in the world wants to talk to journalists, you know, not even such a celebrated one as you.' Nick knew that he was being heavy with the sarcasm but his father hadn't even bothered to ask how he was, and he was already used to being the centre of attention as far as Kelly was concerned. His father's obvious lack of interest in him both offended and irritated Nick.

'If only I could get to Angel. I have this feeling there's so much more to all of this. I don't even know where the bloody woman is . . .'

Nick was only half listening. He couldn't believe it. His father hadn't appeared to take in Nick's deliberately cutting remark. And he seemed to have only one topic of conversation.

After four or five minutes of much the same Nick ended the call abruptly. His father did not even seem to notice.

He really is obsessed, thought Nick glumly. He just hoped that Kelly had the strength not to fall into any other old traps.

Exeter Crown Court was packed for the trial. And there were hundreds more onlookers crowding the streets around the ancient walls of Exeter Castle within which the modern courtrooms had been constructed. Kelly had a coveted press pass and a seat inside the court. Part of the public gallery as well as the normal press bench had been allocated to press because of the exceptional interest in the case.

From the moment Angel was led into the court Kelly was riveted. As ever, everything about her mesmerised him. She was impassive. Her face gave nothing away. The violet eyes were bright but expressionless. On the first day of the trial she wore a simple pale beige shift dress. Her hair was still peroxide blonde, much the same as it had been when he had visited her at home three weeks earlier, although perhaps a little longer already, parted at one side and combed straight and flat to her head. The effect was as stunning as ever. Yet her arms were so painfully thin, accentuating somehow that air of fragile vulnerability which was so much a part of her.

Angel pleaded not guilty to manslaughter on the grounds of self-defence, as had been expected. She had a leading London barrister, Christopher Forbes, representing her. And from the way the red-robed judge, Lord Justice Cunningham, looked at Angel from the start Kelly felt little doubt that Forbes' task would not be too difficult. The judge seemed quite captivated by Angel. Another one, thought Kelly, who knew the feeling.

When Angel was put on the stand she gave her evidence clearly but quietly, faltering only twice – first when she described seeing the initial knife blow struck against her husband, and secondly when she told how she had grabbed the knife from Terry James and plunged it into him.

'It wasn't just that I was trying to protect Scott. I was terrified. I – I thought I was going to be next.'

It was dramatic stuff, made all the more dramatic by an outburst at that point from the public gallery. Ken James, his mother, and other members of the clan were up there, and they weren't best pleased with what they were hearing.

'My brother never hurt anyone,' shouted Ken James.

There were other cries of 'Shame' and 'Lies' and even 'You lying bitch'. At least it looked as if the angry attentions of the James family were being diverted from him, thought Kelly disloyally.

Lord Justice Cunningham, a distinguished-looking man used only to obedience, acted swiftly.

'Anyone perpetrating any further outbursts from the public gallery will be removed from the court,' he thundered. 'I will not tolerate this kind of behaviour.'

The gallery subsided into a reluctant silence. At least for the time being.

Angel looked up at the James family as if mildly interested

in something which had nothing really to do with her. Kelly wished she would look at him. He wanted to see directly into those eyes again, to try to fathom the unfathomable.

But by and large Angel's attention was firmly focused on the judge and the two counsels. Kelly thought the prosecuting counsel was amazingly gentle. It was almost as if even the prosecution already regarded the result of the trial to be a foregone conclusion – a conclusion which would cause the police, the legal system, and the government, he thought, the least trouble. It occurred to Kelly that there was an element of show trial about the proceedings, or as near as you were ever likely to get to that in the UK, anyway. Kelly always looked for hidden agendas, and he was bloody sure there was one here. Up to a point he understood it, and probably agreed with it, though even Kelly himself had given Angel a slightly harder time when he had interviewed her, he reckoned. There was, of course, no mention of drugs. How could there be? None had been found and Angel had been clean when tested on her arrest.

Prosecuting counsel did ask, as indeed Kelly had asked Karen Meadows, how Terry James had been able to gain entry to such an apparently well-protected property undetected.

'Scott and I were probably always too trusting of people, particularly people who work for us,' Angel had replied winningly, and she had gone on to explain how she and her husband had somehow lost the habit of setting the zoned house burglar alarm, with its window-and-door-alert system, when they were indoors.

'Maythorpe was our home, and we always felt safe there,' she said. 'And we didn't know how wrong we were to feel that until it was too late.'

The judge seemed completely satisfied by Angel's answer. As indeed he did with all her answers.

About the only moment when Kelly thought the jury might even consider an unexpected guilty verdict came when the weapon was passed among them. Several of the jurors looked uncomfortable and one woman visibly blanched. The carving knife which had been used to kill the two men at Maythorpe Manor on that terrible November night really was a lethal-looking weapon. And when prosecuting counsel asked Angel why she had used it to stab Terry James so many times, Kelly was aware of the jurors studying her intently, doubtless wondering, as he had done from the beginning, how she could have been so brutal. But yet again Angel's reply struck exactly the right note.

'I had no idea how many times I stabbed him,' she said, her voice very quiet and just a little shaky. 'I was fighting for my life, trying to save my husband. I know I kept striking out at him, but I can't even remember exactly how it all happened. I was terrified, I was out of my mind.'

Lord Justice Cunningham actually nodded his bewigged head sympathetically. Kelly was not surprised. He had had previous experience of Cunningham, who was probably the oldest judge on the circuit now and who many involved in both the legal profession and the police force thought should be pensioned off. He could have been hand-picked to handle this case, and indeed most probably had been, Kelly thought wryly. Some judges were seriously into human rights, even the human rights of known villains. Others paid only lip service. Cunningham was one of the others. Only more so. Kelly reckoned that if he could get away with it, Lord Justice Cunningham would like to provide all law-abiding householders with loaded revolvers and sit back while they summarily dispatched anybody at all who dared to violate their homes. Without any interference from the law whatsoever.

The trial lasted only three days. The judge's summing up was so sympathetic that the jury seemed left with little choice but to find Angel not guilty, and a verdict of justifiable homicide was recorded.

Angel reacted hardly at all. Kelly thought there might have been just a hint of her Mona Lisa smile. He made his way quickly outside in order to watch her leave the court. She posed for photographs on the steps, wearing a cream and blue dress with a hemline several inches above the knee that was slightly more flamboyant than the beige number of the previous day. He suspected she might have been fairly confident of the outcome by day two. Angel was always well aware of the effect she had on men. Red judges were not likely to be an exception.

Her solicitor, a local man called Rupert Grant, whom Kelly knew vaguely, gave a brief statement. 'Mrs Silver is, of course, relieved by the decision of the court. There could, however, be only one outcome. Mrs Silver acted entirely in self-defence, and in defence of her dying husband, against an intruder in her home. Justice has been done and Mrs Silver asks now only to be allowed to get on with her life. Thank you very much, ladies and gentleman.'

Grant put a protective hand under Angel's elbow and made to guide her into the waiting car. But she stopped him, making a kind of halt motion with her free hand, leaned towards him, and whispered something in his ear.

Grant nodded.

'Just one more thing, ladies and gentlemen,' he said, raising his voice to be heard above the clamour. 'Mrs Silver wants me to say that she remains quite distraught at having been responsible for the death of another human being, regardless of the circumstances. And she says that she feels for the James family at this dreadful time.'

Kelly looked on admiringly. She was some woman, that Angel. For all her fragility and apparent vulnerability she never seemed to stop thinking. Once again she had been ahead of the game. She had killed a man and she wanted to make it quite clear how she felt about it. Her solicitor hadn't done that, so she had quickly put him right. She knew a thing or two about PR, Kelly thought.

She was probably fortunate, though, that none of the James clan seemed to be in the vicinity. He doubted they would have been much impressed.

Angel stood very still with her head slightly bowed, a sad half-smile flitting around her lips. Grant turned to her questioningly when he had finished speaking. She gave a little nod. He put his hand on her arm again and this time was allowed to guide her down the steps and into a waiting black limo, which departed at once, belting through the portalled entrance of the old castle and down the narrow road leading into Exeter town centre, scattering the crowd before it.

Kelly had no idea whether Angel was being taken back to Torbay and her Maidencombe home or away somewhere again to hide from the fuss.

He really had to speak to her now. He had already written his story, of course, based around her interview, and he was quite gratified to realise that he had obtained considerably more detail than had come out in court. He wouldn't want to run the piece today, in any case, because it would just get caught up with the court material. But he would certainly like to turn it round soon. Public interest was a highly disposable commodity. The attention span of your average Fleet Street News Desk was quite astoundingly short. Kelly was hoping to make some real money with his exclusive, as long as it remained an exclusive, he thought wryly.

He had promised Moira a lavish holiday when the case was finished, and he really did intend to keep that promise. He valued his relationship with her, and he knew it was time he demonstrated that.

But neither could he break his promise to Angel. It wasn't just that it would go against the grain to let her down in any way, it was also that, strangely enough, much of his success as a journalist had been based on keeping promises, not breaking them. In fact, it was when his alcohol- and drug-fuelled state of mind had deteriorated to the point where he could barely remember the deals he had made, let alone ensure that he stuck to them, that his professional life had started to collapse around him and he'd lost the plot.

But that was years ago. He was on the up again now. Occasionally the thought had occurred to him, as he had nursed his cherished exclusive through the weeks of waiting for Angel to stand trial, that maybe he would get a recall to the big time when his story dropped. Maybe some young pip-squeak Fleet Street editor would see that tired old hacks like him did have their uses, that he could still pull in the big one. He didn't really believe it, though. And in any case he remained unsure that he even wanted it any more. He suspected he wouldn't last long, for reasons entirely different from before, in the national press of today. Kelly was old school. He believed in checking and double-checking and not printing until you were absolutely sure. He'd cracked the old joke many times about never spoiling a good story with facts. But it was a joke. In Kelly's book you never risked spoiling one with half-truths either.

He watched the rear of the limo disappear round the corner at the bottom of the hill. First things first, he told himself. He found himself a quiet spot in the castle yard and filed his version of the morning's events. It would be the splash in the *Argus* that evening, of course. No doubt about it.

When he had finished he walked back to the front of the courthouse. Almost everybody had disappeared. There was no sign any more of any lawyers, court officers, or police, and the gathered crowds outside the walls had dwindled away. The photographers had gone to wire their pictures. Only a couple of other reporters, who had also no doubt been using their mobiles to file copy, remained chatting by the gates. So, that was it, Kelly thought. It was all over, apart from getting his exclusive sorted out and making a few bob. That was all that was left now.

He returned to his car, parked in a nearby car park, and began the drive back to Torbay. On the way he decided that he might as well take a run out to Maidencombe. He didn't know where else to look for Angel, after all. He thought that if he were her he would have been tempted to hide away somewhere again until the dust had settled. But he knew better than to try to second-guess her.

The fans had returned to Maythorpe with a vengeance. Hundreds of them were gathered outside the gates, again singing Scott Silver songs. There were flowers once more piled alongside the railings. Many of the fans carried banners. The messages were predictable: 'We will always love you, Scott', 'Gone but not forgotten'. There was also an outpouring of support for Angel: 'Thank you for trying to save him', 'Live your life for Scott'.

Kelly walked amongst the crowd for a while. It was a lovely sunny afternoon, almost like a spring day, even though it was only mid-January, and very different to the bleak wintry weather around the time of Scott's death. There were several journalists there and the usual TV crews. Kelly quickly learned that Angel had returned to her home, but the limo carrying her had raced through the gates, and neither she nor anybody else had made a further press statement. Neither had she posed for photographs this time. Angel knew when to milk it and when not, thought Kelly cynically. She knew how to keep the pack panting.

He pushed his way through the crowd to the gate and stood looking at the intercom for a moment or two, considering if it was even worth trying it.

'Don't bother, it's been switched off,' Jerry Morris, the *Mirror*'s area man told him.

Kelly nodded, unsurprised, and turned to chat to Morris.

It was then that he noticed the young woman he had nearly run over on Christmas night, the one who intrigued him so much. She was standing right alongside, and it was probably only because she was so still and silent, and dressed in her usual dull dark clothes, that he had not been aware of her presence before. As he would already have expected somehow, almost as if he knew her, she carried no banner, and neither was she joining in the singing. She had her back to him and her face was pressed against the railings as usual.

'Hello again,' he said to her.

She did not reply, nor even turn to look at him.

'Well, at least Angel is free,' he went on, trying desperately to coax her into conversation.

There was no response. Nothing at all discernible. Although he thought her shoulders tensed slightly.

'It would have been terrible if they'd locked her up, wouldn't it?' he continued conversationally. 'After all, she was only trying to protect Scott . . .'

The young woman swung round then to face him. Her features were screwed into an expression of pure fury, her arms hung loose by her sides but her fists were tightly clenched. She uttered a strange sound, which Kelly couldn't quite make out. It was a kind of moan. Derisory? Scornful? He wasn't sure.

She was about to talk to him, surely. To tell him what had made her so angry. But she didn't speak. Instead she suddenly raised her right fist and shook it at him. Kelly was quite taken aback. He didn't think anybody had ever actually shaken their fist at him before. For a brief moment he thought she was going to strike out at him. But she didn't do that either. Instead she lowered her arm, pushed past him and half ran up the hill in the direction of the main Torquay road. He watched her reach the first corner and disappear behind the big Devon hedges. Did she have a car, somewhere? Was she on foot? If so, perhaps he could persuade her to let him give her a lift wherever she was going.

He hot-footed it back to the MG, which was parked down the hill in the Maidencombe beach car park again, quickly started the little motor and took off after her, taking the most direct route through the village to the main road. At the top he turned left. He thought that if she had no transport he should be able to see her then. But he couldn't. He motored slowly for about a mile or so in the direction of Torquay. There was no sign of the girl. She could not possibly have got further on foot, and if she was in a vehicle she would be long gone. He turned in a side road, returned to Maidencombe and this time swung off the main drag directly into Rock Lane. Maybe she was still lurking there somewhere, he thought, or maybe she had even returned to stand outside Maythorpe again.

But Rock Lane was deserted, except outside the old manor house, of course, where the waiting crowd parted reluctantly for him. Kelly slowed almost to a halt, looking for her. Still no sign.

Yet again she had disappeared, it seemed. But then, she was good at that.

Eleven

Kelly slammed down the phone. He had spent just about every waking moment for two weeks either trying to get to see Angel or thinking about her.

Now both Angel's mobile, to which he had in any case never got a reply, and the telephone number for Maythorpe, where he had only ever spoken to the answering machine anyway, had been summarily changed.

Kelly really had no idea how he was going to get in touch with her directly ever again. And, mindful of Angel's threat, he couldn't really approach Rachel Hobbs again. His only solace was that presumably all the other journalists he knew who would be chasing the rock star's widow were facing the same problems. The previous evening, on his daily trip out to the big old manor house, he had once again put a note in the big letter box by the gate: 'We must talk. I made a deal with you that I am trying to keep. We really need to talk.'

He didn't just want Angel's permission to print, he wanted her reaction now to all that had happened to her. He was after an up-date. He wanted to know how the trial, relatively brief though it had been, had affected her in addition to everything else she had gone through. How was she getting through her days? Was she completely traumatised? He wondered about that. Maybe that was why she was shutting herself off this way. Maybe her quite horrific experience had unhinged her. Maybe she was suicidal. His interest wasn't just professional, he knew himself well enough to admit that. He found that he was seriously worried for her safety, and deeply frustrated that he could not get near her to find out how she was coping.

The number of fans outside Maythorpe had diminished daily. There was, after all, little there to encourage pilgrims.

He had seen the strange young woman only once more, early one evening just a few days after the trial, and as soon as she caught sight of Kelly she did her now familiar disappearing trick. He hadn't even been given a chance to get near her, not, based on past experience, that he thought it would do him much good if he had.

Contact with the outside world seemed to be limited during that time to a visit from a Sainsbury's delivery van every couple of days, and the ubiquitous Mrs Nott who was frequently in and out. Kelly had approached her a couple of times for the hell of it, but the woman was largely uncommunicative and, when pressed, merely remained fulsome in her praise of her employer. Kelly had been told that she was probably the best-paid daily help in the West of England and that her wages had continued to be delivered in full even when Angel had shut the house up after Scott's death. Angel knew how to buy loyalty, he thought, and was then a bit ashamed of himself because he really had no idea what kind of person Mrs Nott was. It was just that there was something about the small plump woman with her tight little mouth which made him think that money rather than friendship would be her driving force.

He leaned back in his chair and racked his brain to no avail. He did what he so often did when he was stuck. He called Karen Meadows. This time it turned out not to be such a good idea.

Karen was on her way home. She felt lousy. She had a rotten cold and she'd left the station early, intending to take to her bed and fight it off.

'What do you want?' she asked Kelly nasally.

'And hello to you too,' said Kelly.

'Look, I'm not in the mood.'

'I can hear that. Have you got a cold?'

'My God, the man's a genius,' she muttered.

'Sorry. I just wondered if you had any word at all on Angel Silver.'

'Now there's a surprise.'

Kelly ignored the sarcasm.

'Well, have you?'

'Angel Silver was tried and acquitted, in case it escaped your notice, John. She is no longer any of my business.'

'I suppose not. It all went pretty smoothly for her really, didn't it? Nobody gave her much of a hard time, did they?'

Karen made no response to that. She knew what Kelly was getting at and privately she agreed with him. The word from above had been pretty strong. The chief constable had made it quite clear to Karen that there must be no repetition of the Tony Martin case, when public opinion had been so strongly behind the farmer who was at first jailed for life for murder after killing an intruder at his home. Harry Tomlinson had put pressure on Karen, and she knew well enough the pressure he had been under from higher authorities like the Home Office. The processes of law had had to be seen to be executed, but everyone involved had probably known the result that they wanted and, more than likely, everything possible had been done at the highest level to ensure that. Angel had stabbed a man to death and had to be charged with something. Yet, as Tomlinson had said, if Angel Silver had been jailed for killing the man who had killed her husband there would almost certainly have been a public outcry. The jury had fortuitously cleared Angel, and Karen had absolutely no idea just how much the prosecution services had been acting under any particular instructions, but she did know that somehow the right judge had been picked for the job.

There was little doubt that had the jury found Angel guilty of manslaughter, Lord Justice Cunningham would have pronounced the most lenient sentence possible.

'Are you there, Karen?'

'Yes. I'm here.'

'It's just that I made a deal not to print my interview until I'd talked to Angel again. I wondered if maybe you still had some way of contacting her.'

'No,' said Karen abruptly. 'Neither am I interested in your pathetic bloody problems. I've got enough of my own, thank you very much. Now bugger off.'

She pushed the end button on her phone. Her nose was

running. She sniffed miserably and rummaged around in her handbag, open on the passenger seat, for a paper tissue.

She knew she was inclined to blow hot and cold with Kelly, but sometimes she just couldn't help it. Apart from anything else the old bugger always seemed to find her Achilles heel.

It wasn't that she had any real doubt about what had happened at Maythorpe House the night Scott Silver and Terry James had died. And, while believing absolutely that Angel had to stand trial, she also approved absolutely the verdict. Karen stood somewhere in between the wet liberals of the force and the aggressive right. She hoped she stood for common sense. Also she could not help but be aware that her adroit handling of the Silver case had not gone unnoticed.

It was just that whenever politics came into policing, which it so often did nowadays, Karen was left with that uneasy feeling.

By the end of January Kelly was just about ready to break his agreement with Angel. He felt he had kept his end of the deal by waiting that long, and there was no doubt that Angel was giving him the run-around. Then he arrived at Maythorpe one afternoon just as Jimmy Rudge, Scott's business manager, was driving through the gates on his way out. Immediately Kelly swung the MG in front of Rudge's black Range Rover, blocking his way. He quickly jumped out of the little car and made his way to the driver's door of Rudge's much bigger vehicle. Acting on impulse he tried to open the door, which seemed to be locked.

Jimmy Rudge wound down his window a scant couple of inches.

'What on earth do you think you're doing?' he enquired sharply. His voice was calm but his eyes looked a bit panicky.

However, Kelly withdrew at once, stepping smartly backwards, and feeling vaguely ridiculous.

'John Kelly, *Evening Argus* –' he began.

'I know who you are, you bloody fool, you've been around every bloody corner since this thing began,' Jimmy Rudge shouted through the window, his voice no longer calm at all.

It gave Kelly a fleeting sense of satisfaction to see the smooth bastard lose his cool.

But all he said was a quiet: 'I'm sorry.' However, he made no attempt to return to his car, which continued to block Rudge's path.

'Yes, well.' Jimmy Rudge switched his gaze hopefully from Kelly to the MG and back again. Kelly made no move.

'So OK, what do you want?' asked Rudge huffily.

'I just wanted to know how Angel is,' Kelly replied quietly.

'She's fine.'

'Really?'

'Yes really.'

Kelly still didn't budge.

'For God's sake, man, how would you expect her to be?' asked Rudge then. 'Her husband's been murdered and she's just stood trial for the manslaughter of the man who killed him. She's been through hell. But she's coping and she's coping by keeping away from people like you.'

Kelly felt wounded by that remark. Of course he was after a story. But he actually had the story already, or the bulk of it, anyway. He wanted to explain that he was trying to do the decent thing; that he really did consider himself to be Angel's friend; that maybe he had proved that in the past. Perhaps some of that showed in his face. At least Jimmy Rudge sounded marginally less hostile when he spoke again.

'Look, Angel's a survivor – if you know anything about her you'll know that.'

He was right, of course, and the thought cheered Kelly.

He nodded. 'She's given me an interview already, but we made a deal that I wouldn't use it until she gave me the go-ahead. I've tried to keep that deal, but now she won't even talk to me.'

Rudge looked mildly surprised. That gratified Kelly too.

'Any chance of you asking her to call me?'

Rudge chuckled without much humour. 'This is the first time I've managed to get to see her in weeks,' he said. 'And we've got so much stuff to sort out, you wouldn't believe it.'

'Would you try?' Kelly persisted.

Rudge sighed. 'I'll try,' he said flatly.

Kelly was far from convinced but reckoned that was the best he was going to get. He returned to the MG, reversing it out of the way to allow Rudge to pass.

'Thanks,' he called, more in encouragement than anything else, as the two vehicles' paths crossed.

He watched the black Range Rover disappear up Rock Lane. There was nobody else around at all. The fans seemed finally to have deserted Maythorpe altogether. It was the worst sort of January day, cold and dull. The sky grey and low with the imminence of rain. That grim sort of winter weather which made even Kelly, who was totally disinterested in sun-seeking, wonder idly whether life wouldn't be rather more pleasant in a Mediterranean climate. Kelly's head felt as heavy as the atmosphere. There was a tickle in his nose. Suddenly he sneezed, several times. He wondered if, like Karen Meadows, he too was getting a cold. He sniffed and wiped his nose on his coat sleeve. Why did he never have a handkerchief? The weather and his physical discomfort pretty much matched his mood.

It happened just after 11 p.m. on one of Moira's nights off. Kelly had cooked dinner for her. She was a far better cook than him, but she seemed to like it when he cooked and he enjoyed doing something for her which gave her pleasure. He did little enough, after all, and although he and Moira seemed to be muddling along well enough he was aware of a certain strain lurking just below the surface. And he knew how distant and preoccupied he had been for so much of the time ever since he had become involved in the Silver case.

The meal went surprisingly well, one of his better efforts. He had managed to cook the sirloin steaks just how they both liked them, thanks to the iron griddle pan that was his favourite kitchen utensil. They were nearly black on the outside and nicely pink inside, all the juices satisfactorily sealed within the almost charred crust.

He and Moira were sitting together in contented companionship on the big sofa, half watching an old movie, Moira stretched out and leaning against him. He undid her bra and was lazily playing with one of her breasts while she occasionally made appreciative noises. He was about to suggest that they go to bed when they were interrupted by the ringing of the phone in the hall.

Kelly jumped to his feet at once, pushing Moira away. He hurried out into the hall. 'No ID Received', read the message on the display panel of his digital phone. Somehow he just knew who was calling. There was a tingling sensation running up and down his spine. The adrenalin was racing. He was quite sure that it was Angel calling before he even picked up the phone. Certainly it was true that he didn't get too many phone calls at that time of night, but it was more than that. He had a sixth sense about the bloody woman, he really believed that he did.

He pressed the receiver to his ear.

'Hello,' he said quietly, and he could hear the expectancy in his own voice.

Again, she didn't introduce herself. 'You'd better come round,' she said.

'What, now?'

'Whyever not?'

'It's nearly midnight,' he protested mildly, taking care not to say her name, although he might as well not have bothered. As usual Moira was ahead of the game.

'I don't bloody believe it,' he heard her call irritably from the living room. 'Tell her you'll go round tomorrow, for Christ's sake, John.'

Angel was speaking again. Her voice bantering to the point of mockery, yet she somehow managed to sound flirtatious at the same time. 'Ten minutes past eleven. I see you're showing your usual strict attention to the facts.'

'Well, it is late . . .'

If he took off for Maythorpe now he knew what Moira would say to him – that he had gone running again, jumped to Angel's whim. Moira would be right too. He had spent weeks trying to get Angel even to speak to him and now, yet again, she just expected him to drop everything and go to her.

'About to turn into a pumpkin, are you?'

'Well, no, but –'

She interrupted him. 'I don't like buts,' she said. 'Do you want to come and see me or not? It's quite simple.'

An entire choir of voices in his head warned him not to let her have her own way like this, not to let her run rings round him. He reminded himself then that he did have a major story to sort out. Funny how that could be so easily overshadowed in his dealings with Angel. He did have a good professional reason for seeing her, although suddenly it almost seemed like just an excuse to go running, which he was, of course, about to do. So there was little point, really, in continuing to protest.

'OK. I'll be as quick as I can,' he said.

He put the phone down and turned to face the music – in the shape of Moira, who came out into the hall from the living room, buttoning her blouse with one hand, and reaching for her coat from the hat-stand behind the front door with the other.

'Right, I'll be off then,' she said.

'No, don't,' he said automatically. 'I won't be long this time, I promise. Go to bed. I'll be back before you know it.'

'Spare me, John. You'll stay with that woman for as long as you can, and don't think I don't know it.'

'Look, Moira, you know I've got this interview burning a hole in my notebook. It really is work, you know. You don't want me to lose the story, do you?'

'Quite frankly, John, I don't care about your damned story, and I sometimes doubt you do that much, either.'

'Why on earth else would I turn out in the middle of the night?' he asked, realising at once that he had made a mistake.

'John, will you please stop kidding yourself?' Moira replied wearily.

'I'm a reporter and I'm chasing the best story I've worked on in years,' he insisted.

She let him drop her off at her house.

It was fifteen days since the end of the trial and two days since his confrontation with Jimmy Rudge. Kelly had no idea whether Rudge had precipitated the call from Angel or not, and neither did he care very much. Neither did he care as much as he would have expected about the front pages he was, he hoped, about to capture.

Instead, as he pulled away from outside Moira's house and headed out to Maidencombe, the thoughts that filled his head were of seeing Angel Silver again, of getting close to that fragile, so beautiful woman who he knew could wind him round her little finger. Something about which he already seemed to have little control.

This time the gates of Maythorpe Manor didn't open for him immediately on his arrival. He stepped out of his car and tried the intercom. It remained switched off. Angel was still not encouraging visitors.

He waited for a moment, standing there by the gates bathed in the illumination of the security lights. He couldn't see any lights on in the house, but he knew that the drapes were heavy. After a couple of minutes he automatically reached for the mobile phone in his pocket. Then he remembered that the phone number at Maythorpe had been changed and the only mobile number he had for Angel no longer worked either. He cursed himself for not having had the presence of mind to ask for her new phone numbers when she had called. She might or might not have given them to him, but he had been so excited by her call he hadn't even thought to ask. A very elementary mistake for an old hack. Damn and blast, he thought.

In frustration he went back to his car and gave several blasts on the hooter. Nothing happened. He was starting to feel quite angry. He leaned on the hooter. A continuous wail filled the night air. He resolved not to stop until either she opened the gates for him or he was arrested. And at that moment he wasn't entirely sure which was more likely.

After a good minute or so of unremitting noise the front door of Maythorpe opened, revealing the silhouette of a figure. Simultaneously the big iron gates swung apart in their usual magical way.

Kelly roared through them much faster than he would normally.

He came to a halt with a screech of tyre rubber and was quickly out of the car.

'What the bloody hell do you think you're playing at?' he enquired with a forcefulness that quite took him by surprise. 'You command me out here in the middle of the bloody night and then you keep me locked out –'

Her very silence stopped him in his tracks. She was standing quite still, smiling that small smile. It might have been either apologetic or mocking. He wasn't quite sure which. Perhaps a bit of both. She looked pale. No makeup. Hair straggly with dark roots that had not been apparent at the trial now emerging. There were black rings beneath her eyes which had that familiar faraway hazy look to them. She was wearing a flimsy silk dressing gown, almost exactly the same pale flesh colour as her face. Strange how it seemed perfectly normal for Angel Silver to greet a guest to her house in such a garment. She swayed slightly, reaching out a hand for support. Kelly stepped forward, taking it at once. He was pretty sure she was high again. Could she only bring herself to see him when she was half out of it, he wondered. Or maybe she was high most of the time. He really had no idea. He had no idea either how she managed to look so beautiful in spite of the roots and the black rings round her eyes and the very fact that she was plainly continuing to abuse her body.

'I thought it was you who wanted to see me,' she said eventually.

Infuriating bloody woman, he thought.

'You gave me an interview. We made a deal. I've stuck to my part of it. I said I wouldn't print till I'd cleared it with you. I haven't even been able to get near you since the trial.'

Kelly was trying very hard to be professional. She swung away from him without speaking, and walked off towards the living room. He closed the front door behind him and followed her. She was standing with her back to the fireplace, eyes blazing.

'Have you any bloody idea what it's like to go through what I've been through?' she asked.

He shrugged a kind of apology and was about to speak, but she didn't give him time.

'No of course you haven't,' she continued. 'Not you, not anyone. So don't you dare criticise me. Don't you dare. I haven't been able to talk to anyone, you bloody fool. Since the trial it's been even worse. The relief was just so overwhelming. But I think it was only after that I really thought about what happened, what I'd done.'

Kelly nodded, understanding. 'It's just that you always seem to summon me in the middle of the night, that's all,' he said lamely.

'Always? Summon? Middle of the night?'

She had that mocking look about her again. 'It's still not even midnight. You've only ever been here once before, and I don't recall that you needed much persuasion. In any case . . .' she was looking at the floor, lower lip trembling, vulnerable now, '. . . maybe it takes me all day to pluck up the courage to talk to someone like you.'

All day and a load of coke, he thought. He reckoned she was still playing games with him. Quite deliberately he hardened his approach to her, determined to stick to being strictly professional about this and not to let her get to him in any other way.

'Are we on the record?' he enquired, producing his tape recorder from his jacket pocket.

She pouted. 'I suppose so. You're only interested in me for what you get from me, aren't you? You're just using me, you beast.'

She pulled an exaggeratedly hurt face, then half smiled at him again, flashing those violet eyes. She was being very slightly flirtatious, making a little-girl appeal to his better nature. But Kelly was not a complete pushover. Not yet, anyway.

'And you? You're not using me?'

Her brow darkened.

'All right, you miserable bastard, let's get this over with, shall we?'

She sat on the same sofa they had shared for the previous interview. He joined her and switched on his recorder.

'First of all – and there's really no point in continuing if we can't sort this out – do I take it that I have your agreement to run the interview we've already done when I see fit, plus anything you tell me today?'

'Oh, all right,' she said sulkily, taking a cigarette from a packet by her side and offering him one.

He accepted and lit hers. 'Anything else I can get for you?' she enquired coquettishly.

She really was a chameleon. One minute she was one woman, the next another. The way she had spoken clearly implied that she was offering something like coke. He watched her as she leaned back in the sofa, the flimsy dressing gown slipping up her body so that one thigh was exposed almost to her crotch. On the other hand, he thought she could have been offering herself. She had, after all, done that before, freely enough and often enough.

He dismissed the thought. Either way she was a cheeky bitch, he thought. And dangerous. Always dangerous. No doubt about that. He made himself concentrate on the job in hand, ignoring her suggestive query.

'So tell me exactly how you've been feeling since the trial?' he asked. 'You're right: I cannot know. Who could? Tell me how you've been coping.'

'I feel absolutely devastated,' she replied, suddenly disarmingly straightforward, no longer appearing to be playing any kind of role. 'Not only have I lost the love of my life and had to watch him die in such a terrible way, but I killed a man trying to defend Scott and myself and I have had to stand up in a court of law and explain what I did. I have been given a conditional discharge and I walked free and everybody seems to think that should please me. That I should just be able to put it behind me, build a new life. But I can't. I shall never get over it. It will haunt me always.

'In some ways . . .' She hesitated, and those unnaturally bright violet eyes were full of pain. 'In some ways it would have been better if they'd sent me to jail. I don't even have anything to fight against, do I? I have been treated with . . .' she hesitated again, as if searching for the word, '. . . compassion, I suppose. Maybe I would have preferred some sort of punishment, I feel so guilty, you see . . .'

The words tailed off.

'What do you feel guilty about?' Kelly prompted gently. He could guess the answer, of course, but he needed her words.

'I feel guilty because I didn't save Scott, and I feel guilty because I killed a man.'

'In self-defence, Angel.'

'Yes, in self-defence,' she repeated tonelessly.

'And now, how do you get through your days? I wondered that before. I'm surprised that you stay here, rattling around in this big house. Aren't you lonely?'

She turned to face him directly.

'I am more lonely than I ever thought or believed would be possible,' she said, and he just knew that she meant every word. 'I don't know why I stay here. Maybe I won't for much longer. I think I stay because I don't have the energy to leave. And maybe because I always felt closest to Scott here. This house was his dream, and mine, you know, not the place in Hollywood. I'm thinking of getting rid of that. We hardly ever went there and I certainly don't want to go there now. This was our dream, this was our home, this big old English country house by the sea.'

She sighed. 'How do I get through my days?' She sounded almost whimsical. 'I sleep late, I watch videos, I listen to music, sometimes Scott's music, sometimes other stuff. The hours pass. I don't really know how exactly.'

She flashed him a challenging look. 'And I do a little coke occasionally, but you know that, don't you?'

He nodded. Rather more than a little, he suspected.

She was suddenly anxious. Yet another mood change. 'You won't print that, will you?'

'No,' he said.

He asked her some more questions about her feelings, about that terrible night, about the trial, squeezing all the information he could from her, searching for the most emotive quotes, going over and over the old ground in the hope of touching on something new, something more special than the stuff he already had.

He had a kind of checklist in his head of points he wanted to raise.

'Have the fans bothered you at all?' That was just his way in. He had something specific on that subject that he wanted to ask her.

'Not really. They were bound to turn up. Millions of people loved Scott . . .'

Angel had that faraway look again. 'They've been a kind of support, really, a reminder of how special Scott was. They were the only thing that got through to me in the beginning. Were you there, on that first night, when they all had candles and were singing his songs?'

He nodded.

'Yes, I was sure you would have been.'

'There was one fan who was nearly always there,' Kelly said, getting to the point he had been wanting to raise. 'She stood out from the rest, she looked like a kind of hippy throwback – long hair, long robes. I wanted to ask you if you knew who she was.'

Another mood change. A flash of irritation. 'I don't know who any of them are,' Angel snapped. 'They're fans. Scott had millions of them.'

'But this one was different. She was often here when nobody else was, too. She was even outside on Christmas night when I came here. I nearly killed her when I left. She just loomed in front of the car. You were watching, I saw you.'

'For God's sake, I may have been watching but I couldn't see anything. Just shadows. Certainly not enough to recognise anyone. You screeched to a halt, then you drove off. That was all I saw.'

'But for days on end she stood by the railings by the gate, in the same spot, with her face pressed to the fence. You must have seen her then. You couldn't have missed her. She seemed so strange I even wondered if I should tell the police. I was afraid she might be some sort of a threat to you.'

Angel looked bored. 'For God's sake . . .' she said. And then, referring much less warmly to her dead husband's adoring public than she had earlier, she went on, 'OK, maybe I do know the one you mean. She's just some stupid fan, only even worse than most of them. She's in some idiot religious sect. She was always hanging around here trying to get Scott involved. She drove the poor bastard mad, but she's harmless.'

Kelly nodded. He supposed he would have to be satisfied with that. It was plausible enough. Anyway, all the loose ends were more or less tied up now. He really had a cracking piece, and that, he knew, was what he should concentrate on. He could see the headlines as clearly in his mind as if they were already printed: 'How I held my dying love in my arms', 'Scott and Angel, our great passion', 'How I killed for my darling'.

It was gripping stuff and he was going to clean up on this one. He had so much more than had ever come out in court. That good turn of seventeen years ago really had paid off, he thought cynically.

'Right, I'd better get to work,' he said.

He couldn't wait to get home to his computer and feed all the extra material he had gathered into his original copy.

Angel was quiet as she showed him to the door. Yet again he was struck by the paradoxes in her. He was aware that she treated him by and large with a mixture of flirtatiousness and contempt, but as ever it was her vulnerability which melted him. He studied her closely as she stood there in the big doorway, holding the silky gown close to her thin body, white hair lank and wispy, eyes bright from the coke. He thought she looked at her most fragile. And at her most beautiful. Although God knew how.

On an impulse he bent down and kissed her cheek. She did not pull away.

'Be gentle with me, Johnny,' she said.

Nobody, but nobody, had ever called him Johnny before. If anyone but her had made a remark like that to him he would probably have laughed in their face. It was different with her. Everything was different with her.

'Angel, sweetheart, I promise you, when my stuff hits the streets public opinion will be on your side like never before,' he said, genuinely hoping that would prove to be so. 'The whole world is going to love you and feel for you. And the knocks on the door from press and TV will stop, they really will, because there won't be any point, not after I've finished.'

She smiled wanly.

'OK,' she said.

Suddenly he wanted just to take her in his arms and comfort her. But he resisted the urge. In any case, she'd probably slap his face. Waiflike and vulnerable one moment, sarcastic and provocative the next, you never knew how she was going to react, how she was going to be, you really didn't.

He settled for touching her left hand lightly. 'Goodbye then, and don't worry,' he told her.

Somewhat to his surprise she reached up with her other hand and stroked his cheek.

'You're not a bad man, John Kelly. Do you know that? You can come and see me again if you like.'

His heart sang. As he drove away through the big gates he felt so elated that he punched the air. He was glad the hood of the car was up. He wouldn't have wanted her to see that gesture. He just hadn't been able to help himself.

Not only had he pulled off one of the greatest journalistic coups of his career, but Angel Silver wanted to see him again. OK, she was lonely. Kelly was around. She probably saw him merely as someone who was always available for her. And Kelly was a good listener. Kelly was also somebody she could use for her own ends.

To hell with it, he thought. He didn't really care what her reasons were.

Twelve

Kelly's story was huge. He sold the full interview to the *Sun* who paid him handsomely, but not as much as they would have done had he been able to guarantee them total exclusivity. He couldn't do that because he was bound to let the *Argus* publish first, if he wanted to keep his job, that is, and he knew the other nationals would lift what they felt they could get away with from it. But the impact of his coup was enormous. Local and national radio and TV all invited Kelly to go on air to talk about Angel. He was the only person in the media to have got near to her.

It felt as if he were back in the big time. It felt good. Really good.

Even Nick called specially to say well done.

'That Christmas night visit paid off after all, then, Dad,' he remarked without making any further comment.

Kelly was on cloud nine. He felt seriously good towards everyone who was important in his life – Nick and Moira, of course, but perhaps particularly Karen Meadows who had given him more help from the beginning than she had either needed to or even perhaps should have done.

The evening that his story broke, Moira was on duty and Kelly was alone at home in St Marychurch when he suddenly decided on impulse to pay Karen a thank you visit. Deliberately he did not call her first. At best she would be slightly embarrassed, and at worst she would try to put him off. Kelly reckoned the best thing to do was to just pop round to her place. If she wasn't there then he would lose nothing, and if she was he somehow didn't think she would shut the door in his face.

On the way to her seafront apartment he stopped at a late-night supermarket, which he knew had a special pet shop section, where he bought a bottle of champagne and another, more unlikely, present.

Karen's apartment block had an intercom system. Kelly was pleased when she answered swiftly after he rang the appropriate bell, but then not so pleased when she took almost half a minute or so to speak again after he announced himself.

'Come on up,' she said eventually, albeit a little grudgingly, at the same time pushing the buzzer which allowed him to enter.

She was waiting at her front door when he stepped out of the lift on the fourth floor. Her expression didn't give a lot away.

He grinned at her in what he hoped was a disarming fashion, handed her the champagne with one hand and his second offering, in a supermarket plastic carrier, with the other.

'Late Chrissie pressies,' he said. 'The bubbly's for you, and there's something in the bag for the lovely Sophie.'

Karen raised her eyebrows enquiringly, took both gifts from him, and ushered him into the flat. Once inside she led him into the living room overlooking the bay and peered into the carrier bag. When she saw the contents she immediately started to laugh.

Kelly had bought the detective chief inspector's cat a rather sophisticated battery-operated toy mouse.

Karen dangled the creature by its plastic tail and giggled.

'C'mon, Sophe,' she called. 'Your Uncle John has bought you a present.'

There was no immediate response. Kelly glanced around him. Sophie, with her paws in the air, was flat out on her back by the radiator beneath the window. She appeared to be sound asleep and showed no signs whatsoever of intending to arouse herself.

Karen shrugged apologetically.

'It's all right,' said Kelly. 'She's a proper cat, that Sophie.'

'She's certainly that,' replied Karen. She walked over to the window, leaned down and scratched Sophie's head. The cat did not stir.

Karen returned her attention to Kelly.

'I'd offer to share the bottle you've brought if I didn't know it would kill you, you old bugger,' she said.

'I know,' said Kelly.

'So how does coffee sound?'

'Great.'

He gazed idly out of the window as Karen busied herself in the kitchen. Lights flickered all around the bay. It was, appropriately, he thought, a beautiful night. Stars and a half-moon reflected on what seemed to be an unseasonably still sea. Kelly's senses were on full alert, he realised. His nostrils began to twitch appreciatively. There was nothing quite like the smell of real coffee brewing, and, unlike Angel, he thought aimlessly, Karen Meadows would not consider serving anything other.

Minutes later, when they were sitting companionably sipping coffee which was every bit as good as his sense of smell had led him to expect, Kelly apologised for arriving unexpectedly.

'It was just that I thought you might find an excuse if I phoned. I do know how much pressure you've been under, too,' he said. He paused. Then added, rather awkwardly, 'Also, I wanted to say thank you.'

Karen regarded him equivocally. 'For what?'

'You know what. And I do appreciate it, that's all.'

'Bollocks,' said Karen.

Kelly didn't mind. One thing he'd remembered from his AA meetings of years ago was the counsellor who'd told him not to listen to what people said, but instead to observe what they did.

'Bollocks yourself,' he countered easily.

Karen smiled.

'I saw all your stuff in the *Sun* this morning,' she said. 'No wonder you're in such a good mood.'

'Sort of. How about you? At least it's over, after all.'

'Is it?'

'Presumably so.' He returned her steady gaze. 'And you guys got the result you wanted, after all, didn't you?'

'Don't push it, Kelly.'

There was steel in her voice. Karen Meadows was an extremely capable senior police detective equipped with all the grit that her job required. Kelly knew that side of her well enough, but it always took him by surprise when she levelled it at him.

'I wasn't,' he said at once. 'I'm just glad when things work out for people I care for.'

Karen smiled very slightly. 'You know, you really are a tricky bastard, Kelly.'

'I have no idea what you mean.'

'Oh yes you do, you bugger. You come here, an old friend bearing gifts, and the next minute you're starting to pump me like crazy.'

'No I'm not.'

'Yes you are.'

It was Kelly's turn to smile. 'I didn't mean to.'

'Yes you did. And it's getting you nowhere.'

Kelly was still smiling. 'Which is only what I would expect from you, Karen,' he said. 'I give in.'

They were sitting in armchairs on opposite sides of the living-room window. Torbay was a panorama in front of them. Sophie still lay by the radiator on the floor beneath them. Quite suddenly she stirred herself and jumped on to Kelly's lap, her claws digging into his thighs as she attempted to paw a bed for herself.

'There, Karen, see, your cat loves me,' said Kelly.

Karen sank deeper into her chair. 'No taste, that creature,' she said.

'I have to disagree.'

'Naturally.' Karen narrowed her eyes and focused them on him. 'What the hell are you doing here, anyway, Kelly?'

'God only knows,' he said.

'Are you sure?' she countered.

'No.' Kelly didn't think then, just blurted his feelings out. 'There aren't too many of us around who remember good turns, Karen,' he said suddenly. 'You always have done, and I can't get over it sometimes.'

Karen leaned towards Kelly, who did not move, and tweaked one of Sophie's ears.

'You've always been a soft sod for a tabloid hack, Kelly,' she said.

It was only later, at home in St Marychurch, that Kelly wondered if Karen could possibly have been getting at anything else when she'd asked why he'd turned up unexpectedly at her flat.

She probably hadn't. It made no difference anyway. It was far too late now for their relationship to become anything more than it was.

Five days later the bombshell dropped. A new sensation broke in the *News of the World.*

'I WAS SCOTT SILVER'S LOVER.'

It was a major interview with a young woman who claimed to have been Scott Silver's secret lover, and it threw doubt on almost everything that Angel had told Kelly about her relationship with her husband. In fact, it turned the whole public and police conception of what Angel had been through upside down. If you believed even a half of it then it made Kelly's stuff suddenly seem like a carefully orchestrated piece of PR. Kelly found himself wondering suddenly if he had been used in a big way by Angel Silver.

From her picture Kelly immediately recognised the young woman as the silently lurking hippylike creature he had seen so many times hanging around the Silver mansion, and whom he had very nearly run over in his car.

Damn, thought Kelly. His instincts about her had been absolutely right. She had been far more than just another fan. He really should have tried harder to pin the woman down. He was furious with himself.

Her name, it seemed, was Bridget Summers, and she was, as Angel had told him, a member of an outlandish religious sect, One God, One People. There all resemblance between the stories of the two women ended.

Summers claimed that she and Silver were deeply in love and that the rock idol had been about to leave Angel for her. And she had letters, allegedly from Silver, which appeared to prove her case. The *Screws* printed long extracts from the letters, including some, presumably as an indication of authenticity, photographed in their original spidery handwriting.

'My darling Bridget, I cannot wait to be with you all the time,' read one. 'I really am going to free myself from the Crazy One. I have devoted enough of my life to her. I want to move on, I want to be with you, and work with you for all the wonderful things we both believe in.'

Summers claimed that far from being driven mad by her attentions and those of the One God, One People sect, Scott Silver had actually become a devoted disciple. There was indeed a photograph of the two of them together, both wearing the long dark grey cotton robes which was all Kelly had even seen the girl wear, and which were presumably the sect's required wardrobe. One God, One People was an American order, but its British HQ was in Exeter, which, conveniently for Scott Silver, was just half an hour or so's drive from Torquay.

Summers also claimed that she was only speaking out at last because of the lies Angel had told in the interview she had given to Kelly. Knowing how shy she seemed to be, Kelly was quite surprised that she had decided to talk to the press at all. His interview must just have been too provocative, he supposed. He also thought about the damage Bridget Summers could have done had she gone to the police with this information before Angel's trial. And he wondered why on earth she hadn't.

Then he read on. 'I tried to tell the police but they wouldn't listen,' said Summers. 'They treated me as if I was the Crazy One.'

Well, Kelly could half understand that. The woman came across as being thoroughly crazy, whereas Angel Silver could be extraordinarily plausible if she put her mind to it. But if Bridget Summers were telling the truth about that, then someone somewhere in the Devon and Cornwall Constabulary had made one hell of a balls-up.

He hoped that Karen Meadows wouldn't be left carrying the can. Impulsively he picked up the phone and called her.

'I don't want anything, honestly,' he told her hastily. 'I just wondered if you were all right.'

'Oh yeah, great. I've been summoned to see the chief constable again.' Karen managed just a hint of the sarcastic bantering tone she so frequently employed with Kelly, but it wasn't convincing.

'Ah.'

'Ah, indeed.'

'Is it true that Bridget Summers tried to talk to you guys?' he asked.

He could almost feel Karen tense up.

'Off the record, yes,' she said. 'But we were being inundated with fans full of nonsensical fantasies about Scott. I don't know yet who took her statement. I do know that whoever the poor fucker was, he or she will probably have taken at least another dozen statements like it. There will, of course, be an inquiry, but these things are always so damned fucking obvious with hindsight, aren't they?'

'Yeah, I know.'

'Do you? I doubt that, frankly. We'll get Bridget Summers in for serious questioning now. But God knows where we go from there, except deeper into the shit.'

'Me too.'

'Oh, come on, Kelly, you'll come up smelling of roses, you always do.'

He knew the bother she was in and understood her bitterness. None the less he was a bit hurt. Ultimately all he said was: 'I just hope you do, too.'

'Fuck knows,' replied Karen.

Kelly forced himself to return his attention to the *News of the World* and his unease grew as he read on further.

' "That woman Scott married knew he was going to chuck her out. She knew he couldn't stand her wicked ways any more. If you ask me, she'd have done anything, anything at all to keep him. And once she knew that she couldn't keep him, she was prepared to go to any lengths at all to prevent someone else having him." '

The article then made the claim that Angel and Scott had had a pre-nuptial agreement which severely limited his financial obligation to her should they ever part, in fact slashed it to the bare minimum unless there were ever children involved. There were not, of course. And Angel had always presented that as the tragedy which Kelly was sure it must have been. In more ways than one, he now thought cynically.

It was damning stuff. Kelly was shocked rigid. Not only was his story starting to look suspect, but his almost blind faith in Angel had been totally rocked. When he had first heard about the double killing he had considered all the options in a cool professional sort of way and had even voiced them to Karen Meadows. But once he had got close to Angel all such careful reasoning went out the window. Had she just made a complete fool of him? Could the double killing at Maythorpe have been part of some bigger, wider plot than a burglary by a chancer who had worshipped the rock idol and developed a dangerously lethal obsession? Perhaps those vague suspicions Kelly had only ever been able to half form did have some truth in them after all.

Kelly put the paper down and tried to clear his head for a moment. He was still in bed. His Sunday morning treat was to get up when he woke up naturally, without setting the alarm clock, which roused him at six every weekday now Moira was no longer making his alarm call, toddle downstairs and pick up the Sunday papers from the doormat, make himself a pot of tea and retire to bed with the lot. It was both slothful and blissful to Kelly.

Moira usually shared the ritual with him, but she had recently been noticeable by her absence more than anything else. Kelly did not even know whether she had been on duty the previous night or not. He hadn't seen her since he had abandoned her so summarily to interview Angel. Or 'gone running to that woman', as Moira had preferred to describe it.

Kelly sighed and contemplated the mess his life seemed to be disintegrating into again after so many years of calm and order – or as near to calm and order as he would ever get, he thought wryly.

There was nothing slothful or blissful about this Sunday morning. Kelly hoisted himself out of bed, sending a tangle of newsprint to join the piles already on the floor around the bed.

He had to see Angel, and find out what was going on. There must be an explanation. There really must be.

Perhaps Moira was right, perhaps he was obsessed. Certainly he was quite disturbed by the prospect of Angel Silver having deceived him. He knew well enough that there were many sides to her. He just hoped that there was no side to her as dreadful as some of the ideas which were forming in his head.

On the way to Maythorpe Manor Kelly tried to call Angel on the numbers he had finally remembered to get from her at the end of his interview with her. Predictably there was no reply from her mobile and, as usual, all he got from the house landline was the answering machine – no more or less than he had expected. He might just as well not have bothered to acquire her new numbers, he thought.

The pack were already gathered. All the daily paper district boys would have got the call from their Saturday night watchman desks as soon as the *Screws* had dropped, and been told to get on the case straight away. There was a TV crew there already.

Kelly walked through them to try the intercom. It seemed to be connected again, unlike a while ago, but nobody responded when he spoke into it.

Disconsolate, he wandered away, kicking at the ground with one foot.

'Wassamatter, John? Shut you out now she's made use of you, has she?' sneered the man from the *Daily Mail* nastily. The fact that Kelly reckoned the jibe was probably pretty damned near the truth made it all the more unpleasant.

'Up yours,' he remarked in a pleasant tone of voice. He certainly wasn't going to show his feelings to that mob.

Suddenly down the hill roared an ancient battered Jaguar, mostly black with one door panel white and half the bonnet in the orangy-red of anti-oxide, which normally indicates a state of running repair. It was travelling far too fast for safety and scattered several reporters before drawing to a screeching halt in the middle of the road right in front of the gates.

Out jumped an angry Ken James. Kelly was not surprised to see him. He already had reason to believe in the man's penchant for direct action against those he felt had wronged him or one of his. The James family had already been infuriated by Angel's lenient treatment in court; they would presumably have been sent apoplectic by the Bridget Summers revelations. Tactfully, Kelly retreated to the back of the pack. He certainly had no wish to clash with James. Not when the big man was in this mood. Not ever, come to that.

James shouted a command into the intercom. 'Open up, you fucking slag.'

Unsurprisingly, perhaps, this solicited no response. He then started to smash it with his fist. Hard. A knuckle split open. Blood splashed around, spattering on to James's face and his already grubby shirt front. The man gave no sign of feeling any pain.

When he presumably felt he had inflicted enough damage on the intercom he stepped back and began to scream abuse at the house itself.

'I know you're in there, you rotten slag, I know you set our Ter up. I'm going to get you for it, I promise you, you twisted bitch . . .'

There was no police presence that morning, even though Kelly felt it likely the *News of the World* story would at least be sure to lead to Angel being re-interviewed by the police. And watching Ken James's near-hysterical antics Kelly began to wish that the police would turn up a bit sharpish. So, he gathered, from his colleagues' nervous shuffling, did most of them.

Suddenly James turned his unwelcome attentions on them.

'As for you lot, you bunch of vultures, who the fuck do you think you're staring at, eh?'

The big man took a menacing step towards them. He really was huge. Then the worst happened. The reporter Kelly had been hiding behind shuffled smartly to the left, leaving him clearly exposed in James's sightline.

'You, you fucking bastard,' James bellowed. 'You're her fucking lapdog, you are, and you turned my family over, you piece of shit. I've been wanting to get my hands on you.'

He lunged forward. The assembled press parted readily to let him through. Spineless buggers, thought Kelly. Then he took off. At a sprint. Right up the road and into his car, which, without any police to prevent him doing so, he had parked almost in the hedge just around the corner up Rock Lane. Fortunately the hood was down and the car was facing in the right direction away from Maythorpe Manor, allowing Kelly to jump over the door into the driver's seat, gun the engine and be gone seconds before Ken James, who looked as if he would like to dismember him with his bare hands, could reach him.

Kelly watched thankfully as the fuming figure in his wing mirror, standing stranded in the middle of the road and waving both fists at him, disappeared into the distance. He managed a small smile. Kelly had always been surprisingly quick on his feet for a man who was invariably totally out of condition. A very good thing in his line of work, he thought wryly.

That evening she phoned. He had hardly dared to hope that she would. He really needed her to explain, and not just for his professional peace of mind.

'Why don't you come round? I want to put the record straight about that evil cow's rantings,' she said.

Kelly didn't intend to give Angel an easy ride. He didn't like being taken for a fool, and he feared she might have done just that. But he wasn't going to argue with her on the phone. He wanted to confront her face to face. Only that would do. He wanted those big gates to open again and let him into the hallowed inner sanctum of Maythorpe Manor.

It was just after 8 p.m. by the time he got back to Maidencombe. A group of journalists were still hanging around, and so, to Kelly's horror was Ken James. He was just wondering how he was going to get past the man alive when he noticed that there was a police presence at last: two uniformed constables were standing by the gate. Somebody had probably called the police after the disturbance earlier in the day, Kelly thought – Angel herself, one of his colleagues, or perhaps a neighbour. Kelly was relieved, anyway. Even Ken James was unlikely either to attack him or try to force his way into the house in front of a couple of coppers, he thought.

And so, with a show of confidence he did not entirely feel, Kelly drove straight to the gates, stopped the car, stepped out and announced himself into the battered but still apparently operational intercom. James made no move. He just glowered at Kelly, who was considerably gratified that his confidence in the authority of a pair of British policemen seemed not to have been misplaced – although a little voice in his head warned him that he would be more firmly established than ever now on the Ken James hit list.

The intercom speaker uttered no response, and for a fleeting moment he hoped Angel wasn't playing games with him again. Then, in that magical way that they had, the gates opened, and the two policemen stood back, allowing him to drive through.

In spite of everything, Kelly experienced a rush of adrenalin. He couldn't help getting a big buzz from leaving the pack on a doorstep while he was ushered in. Nothing that he might be about to learn could quite take that away.

Thirteen

She was wearing the same silky dressing gown, gaping open. A cigarette hung from her mouth. For once there was no vermilion lipstick; no fresh makeup at all, in fact. Just panda eyes. Black smudges of yesterday's mascara mingling with the dark shadows that almost always seemed to be there.

She led Kelly into the living room and began to pace up and down in front of him. Her hair was all over the place, the black roots all the more evident, and not even combed that morning, Kelly suspected. In one hand she held a packet of cigarettes, in the other a lighter.

'I'm seriously fucked off, John,' she yelled, throwing both arms in the air in a furious gesture. The dressing gown opened even more. Kelly tried not to stare at her breasts. Why did she always do this to him, he thought. It must be deliberate, it really must. Although if Angel noticed his interest in her body she gave no sign of it. Kelly actually thought it possible that, just for once, she was actually unaware of the effect she was having on him. She was steaming angry.

He made himself concentrate, determined not to let her take charge.

'So am I,' he said flatly.

That seemed to stop her in her tracks. Abruptly she sat down on a chair by the window. He suspected that might be a deliberate gesture. On his previous visits she had chosen the sofa where he had been able to sit next to her. She took a final drag on the cigarette in her mouth, took another from the packet she still clutched, lit it from the glowing end of the first, ignoring the lighter in her other hand, and then tossed the butt end at the fireplace. It missed by just an inch or two, hitting the fender and falling back on to the thick cream hearth-rug where it smouldered gently. Angel made no attempt to pick it up. In fact, she leaned back in her chair looking at him steadily, whether genuinely unaware of what had happened or challenging him to let the house burn down he wasn't sure. Probably a challenge. It didn't matter. Kelly wasn't in the mood for playing games. He walked briskly across the room towards the fireplace and stood on the butt, grinding it into the rug. When he removed his foot, iron-grey ash had spread around a dark brown scorch mark.

Then, uninvited, he made his way across to the window end of the room and sat on a chair facing Angel's but several feet away. Both chairs were ornately Victorian and upright. Their seating arrangement was therefore quite formal. That suited him. He put his tape recorder on his knee and, without asking her, he switched it on. Then he just waited. After all, she knew her only hope of repudiating the *News of the World* stuff was to talk to him, or at least to somebody like him. And it seemed she had chosen him again.

Angel shifted uncomfortably in her chair. Kelly already knew how much she liked to be in control.

'It's all a load of crap, you know,' she told him eventually.

'Is it?' he enquired, raising a quizzical eyebrow.

'Yes, it bloody is. I'm not saying Scott didn't shag the silly cow. He'd screw anything that moved, male or female, and it didn't need to move much either. Did you know that?' She glowered at him. Provocative as ever. Always keen to shock. Kelly didn't react. Again he just waited.

It was several seconds before she continued, 'I always knew that about him. I didn't have any illusions. But he sure as hell wasn't planning to leave me. He needed me. Always did. As for those bloody letters, well, Scott would tell you whatever you wanted to hear to get his own way. He was always like that. It never meant anything . . .'

'Didn't it?' It was Kelly's turn to be provocative, and he succeeded.

Angel jumped to her feet. 'For God's sake, Kelly,' she yelled, 'stop being so infuriating. I'm telling you the fucking truth.'

'Well, that will make a change. I'm beginning to think all

I've had from you so far is a pack of lies. What about the dream marriage, then? The great fairy-tale romance? The fucking knight in fucking shining armour?' Kelly could no longer even act cool.

Angel winced. 'I never told you anything like that.'

'As near as damn it,' Kelly stormed. He became aware that he was trembling with rage, and he was surprised at the strength of his anger. Kelly was no stranger to making a fool of himself. Other people had done the job more rarely, and, professionally, hardly ever. Kelly had always been able to do it all by himself. But this one was the tote double. Angel might well have made a fool of him both personally and professionally, he reckoned.

'Look, it was a good marriage,' she insisted. 'All right, it may not have been everybody's idea of a good marriage. I knew Scott played away from home occasionally. And I knew I'd never stop that. I'm not the first woman to put up with the three-card trick because she loves her man to distraction, am I?'

'No. But was that all, Angel? What about you? Did you play away from home too? Did you have a lover waiting somewhere in the wings for you to run to once you'd made sure of collecting Scott's loot?'

The violet eyes blazed. She looked as if she might attack him. Then her demeanour changed. Dramatically. Instantly. In that astonishingly total way he already knew that it could.

She lowered her eyelashes, went all coquettish on him.

'That would be telling,' she half whispered.

'Don't mess me about, Angel,' he commanded. 'Answer the question.'

She stepped away from him, sat down again, and when she looked up at him once more all the teasing coquettishness had left her as quickly as it had arrived.

'Never,' she said. 'Not once in all the years we were together. You can mock if you wish, and I know it sounds like a cliché, but he really was the man of my dreams in every way. I never strayed and I never would have done for as long as Scott had lived. Can you believe that?'

Kelly didn't know what to believe. Even if it were true, he

wondered how far Angel would have gone, what she would have done, in order not to lose a man she had cared for so deeply to another woman. And an erstwhile hippy religious nut at that. His doubt obviously showed in his face.

'I don't give a fuck what you believe, actually,' she told him sulkily.

'I believe you're still holding back on me, Angel,' he said. 'You've made me look a fool in print once, I'm not letting it happen again.'

'But I want to set the record straight, that's why I wanted to see you. I didn't tell you anything that was wrong or untrue. I just left some bits out, that's all.'

She pouted at him, a little girl suddenly. Were there tears in her eyes, too? Kelly wasn't sure, and, in any case, remained unimpressed. For once her wiles seemed to be having no effect on him at all.

'Oh, c'mon, Angel. You left out the minor point that this husband you adored and who allegedly adored you, who you claim you'd killed a man for in an attempt to save his life, was having a rampant love affair. Even more than that, he'd told the new woman in his life that he was going to leave you for her. And whether he meant it or not, the fact that he told her so appears to be a matter of record. There really is little doubt. Don't you realise that changes totally how most people would regard you? Anyone reading Bridget Summers' story is bound to find themselves wondering what really happened here the night Scott and Terry James died.'

'I don't see why. I don't see that it changes anything,' Angel insisted stubbornly. She was still pouting.

'You wouldn't, would you?' Kelly remarked wearily.

'He wouldn't have left me. Not ever. Really he wouldn't. I want you to make that clear.'

'Yes, well, I need more than that if we're going to come up with any decent reply to the *Screws*' allegations. For a start, tell me where you reckon Scott stood with One God, One People.'

'Oh, he was completely under the spell of that lot,' she responded at once. 'You'd have thought he'd have had more sense, wouldn't you? I don't know how he first got involved, but suddenly it was as if they'd taken him over. They have this leader in America somewhere, and that Summers woman is one of the leading lights over here. I have no idea why or how. She's hardly Miss Fucking Charisma, is she? Anyway, Scott even invited her into the house here once, the bastard. I'd already guessed that something was going on. But to bring her here? That was seriously out of order and I told him never ever to do it again. He didn't either. He'd broken our rule, you see. The rule was that he never brought his . . .' she hesitated, something Kelly had noticed her do quite often, as if she were searching for absolutely the right word, and nothing less would do, '. . . he never brought his peccadilloes home with him,' she went on, eventually choosing a word that made Kelly smile in spite of himself. 'That was the rule. But although he never brought her here again, there was always this presence. Her presence, in a way, and also this religious presence, I suppose. It did change him. He considered himself a born-again Christian. They had these weird chants, One God, One People, and I'd find Scott in odd corners sitting on the floor cross-legged chanting at the ceiling. It was pretty disconcerting. It really was as if he was under a spell.'

Now this was better. 'That's good, Angel,' Kelly encouraged. 'Just something with a bit of bite, that's what we need. So you believe Scott was under a kind of spell from the sect? Now what effect do you reckon that had on his relationship with Summers?'

'I think it had a very great effect,' she replied quickly. 'I mean, you've seen her. All you have to do is look at her. Scott always went for the same type – dolly birds, they used to call them once upon a time. Very pretty and very young. The younger, the better. And preferably none too bright. There was more than a touch of the Bill Wymans about Scott. I always pretended, even to myself, not to notice. It was the only way I could cope with it. But I noticed this one because she just wasn't right. She didn't look right. Didn't dress right. Didn't act right. Made no attempt to make the best of herself. Scott would never have touched her if he'd been in his right mind.'

Kelly came back at her fast. 'What do you mean by that? Do you think he wasn't in his right mind?'

'I suppose that I think he was so much under the control of that sect that he may have gone slightly off his head. Yes, there was a kind of madness about him.'

'If you really thought that, didn't you try to do something about it? Get some help? Psychiatric help, maybe?'

She shook her head. 'No, I wasn't worried about Scott, you see. Not really. Annoyed, frustrated, but not worried. I'd seen it all before, remember, or bloody near. I thought it was just a phase. I still think that. If Scott hadn't died he'd have moved on to something else by now, forgotten all about One God, One People, and forgotten all about Bridget Summers. I'd bet anything on it. Scott was always going through phases, getting mad enthusiasms for things. Women, of course. I was the only one he stuck to; we were different, Scott and me. But the others came and went at the speed of light. It was more than that, though. Ideals. Beliefs. He'd get these crazes. Scott just kept on looking for something to believe in. He had this need. I remember when he went through the Indian guru thing, just like the Beatles did. That didn't last either. And nothing changed our relationship. Everything stayed the same between us really. Even though he knew how much I disliked the One God, One People lot, we were still close. It changed his attitude to life in many ways, but it never came between us. Not really. Nothing ever did.'

'OK,' said Kelly, who was beginning to feel slightly better about things. Angel could be very persuasive, very convincing. He just hoped he could put that across. 'There's a couple more things we have to address, though. Particularly this pre-nuptial agreement thing. Now that could be a really damning allegation. I need to know, is it true?'

'No,' she replied emphatically. 'That's a load of bollocks. We never had any such agreement. Scott did love me, you know – every bit as much as I loved him, in his way. I will always believe that, and he trusted me. Absolutely.'

Kelly studied her carefully. 'You wouldn't lie to me about that, would you, Angel? Because if you did, well, it will come out in the end. It'll have to. There must have been solicitors involved, clerks, all manner of people. You'd never get away with a lie about something like that.'

'I am not lying,' said Angel, pouting at him again.

'OK,' he repeated, rising from his chair, switching off his tape and putting his notebook in his pocket. For once he didn't want to stay with her any longer. She'd given him a surprisingly reasonable account of her side of the story, he thought. He just wanted to go home and write it – for his paper tomorrow. It was already too late to catch the last editions of today's *Argus*, and the nationals the day after, in what seemed to be becoming his usual routine.

He walked out into the hall and she followed him in silence. At the door a final thought occurred to him. 'I saw the two Noddy hats at the gate, of course, but have the police talked to you again yet?'

'This morning. DCI Meadows and a detective sergeant. I told them much the same as I've told you. They seemed satisfied. Anyway, there's nothing they can do, is there?'

'Isn't there?'

She looked mildly startled. 'Of course not. I've stood trial and I was found not guilty. It's over.'

'Right, that's OK then,' he responded, mildly sarcastic.

'Yes it is,' she said quietly. 'It doesn't change anything anyway. It can't change anything. I've told the truth from the beginning about what happened that night. I had no reason to lie.'

'All right, Angel,' Kelly responded, relenting a little. 'I'm sure you did. It's just that Bridget Summers has opened a real can of worms here. But you know that, don't you?'

She nodded, then surprised him again by reaching up and kissing him on the cheek.

'Thanks for coming, Johnny,' she said quietly.

Angel's response to the Bridget Summers allegations ran big in the *Argus* and on the following day in all the nationals, as Kelly had known that it would. Kelly tried to get to Bridget Summers, or at least somebody from the sect, and failed miserably. It seemed that the *Screws* still had Bridget locked away.

The copy looked good. It was as strong a reply to Summers' allegations as could possibly have been expected. Kelly felt that at the very least much of his own journalistic credibility had been restored. He had managed also to restore much of Angel's credibility, he thought. He reckoned he might actually have succeeded in making her appear as convincing in the copy as she had been in the flesh when he had talked to her. A woman who allowed her husband to make a fool of her because she loved him so much was not exactly unique, after all. It was a fair bet that Angel would retain her sympathy vote among the public. But Kelly was still not happy.

There were doubts now, holes in Angel's original story, that he had never even suspected, let alone known about. And they were niggling away at him.

He had a strong feeling that the best thing he could do would be to leave well alone now, let Angel sort herself out, let the story and the law, should it decide to step in, run their course. Get out while the going was good. Kelly had done extremely well out of the Scott and Angel Silver saga professionally and had so far avoided getting in too deep personally. What he should do now was to back off. He had no doubt about that, but he also knew, for reasons he perhaps did not want to recognise, how hard that would be for him. Inside his head, and perhaps in his heart, he was already in deep.

He did succeed in holding back for almost a week. Then he called her. He told himself that all he really wanted from her was further reassurance. He wanted to fire questions at her, give her a hard time, and at the end of it he wanted her to come up with the kind of answers which would put all his fears at rest. He also wanted to hear her voice again, of course, but he tried not to think about that.

But, to his surprise and delight, halfway through his message Angel interrupted and picked up the phone.

'I wondered if I could come round?' he asked at once.

'Why?' she enquired. She sounded languid, slightly distant. Stoned again? Kelly was no longer sure when she was and when she wasn't under the influence of some drug or other, or perhaps alcohol. He suspected that she was just a little bit stoned most of the time. It didn't seem to affect the way she functioned very much.

'I want to see you,' he said. 'I have a few more questions.'

'Is that all?'

The flirtatious teasing approach again. Kelly deliberately didn't respond.

'I can be round in half an hour, if that's OK,' he said.

'If you like,' she said, sounding as if she really didn't care either way.

'See you then,' he replied, ending the conversation as abruptly as he had begun it.

He went straight for her as soon as she opened the door to him. He hadn't meant to. But it was becoming increasingly important to him to be sure of her, to know. And he thought the way to do it might be to shock her into some kind of submission.

'Look, you could still be done for murder, you know,' he told her bluntly.

They were standing facing each other in the imposing hallway of Maythorpe Manor. He hadn't even waited to be taken into the now familiar living room before beginning his assault.

'What the hell are you talking about?' she asked, slurring her words slightly.

She was definitely at least a bit stoned. Her eyes had that unnatural brightness about them. She ran the fingers of one hand through her white-blonde hair. He noticed that they were trembling slightly. She was wearing what he thought was a man's shirt, with just one or two buttons done up. The shirt was so long on her that it hung almost to the hem of her short skirt. Kelly made himself not even look at her body.

'Murder, I'm talking about. OK, almost certainly you couldn't be done for the murder of Terry James, because you've been cleared of his manslaughter, but there's always the murder of Scott.'

She looked genuinely astonished.

'The murder of Scott? Me?'

It all came out then, the half-voiced suspicions he had never quite confronted before.

'You have to see how it could look. I'm just playing devil's advocate, honestly,' he told her. 'Your husband is cheating on you and maybe you just can't live with it any more, in spite of what you say. You can't stand even the thought of losing him to another woman. Then you have this intruder. He comes into your bedroom, wakes you both up. Everyone is startled. You think fastest. You grasp the opportunity. You grab the knife. You kill Scott and then you kill Terry James. It's easy.'

She was studying him quizzically, her jaw slack.

'It is? Oh yes. I get it. I understand. I leap out of bed, and tackle this six-and-and-a-half-foot-tall giant, grabbing his knife, which I then use on the husband I love while the giant stands meekly by and then allows me to stab him too. Several times. Easy. Yes.'

'Something like that.' Actually, Kelly had to admit, it did sound pretty silly when put that way. Maybe he just had too highly developed an imagination. He'd often been accused of that. But he didn't mind that it sounded silly. He was, of course, only calling her bluff, seeing how she would react. There was no evidence at all, just the rantings of Bridget Summers, and Kelly doubted she would ever prove to be a very convincing witness. He just wanted Angel to vindicate herself. He wanted that more than anything, and that's what he was trying to shock her into doing. But by voicing his half-formed suspicions he'd probably pissed her off to such an extent that she would never want anything to do with him again. And he supposed he couldn't really blame her.

Her reaction was a complete surprise to him. Suddenly his reverie was interrupted by a great roar of laughter. Angel, head thrown back, was rocking with laughter. Eyes filled with tears, she was laughing so much she was shaking.

He stared at her in astonishment. Had his remarks been that funny?

Then as abruptly as she had started laughing she stopped.

'Why are all the men I get involved with slightly mad?' she enquired lightly.

'I'm not mad and we're not involved,' he said.

'No. Of course not.'

She stepped back, swaying slightly the way she did. Was it coke, or dope, or booze, or just the way she was? It really was true that he didn't even know for sure when the woman was under the influence of some substance or just being herself.

She had another surprise for him. With one hand she started to undo her shirt. While he was still wondering what exactly she was up to, what trick she was playing this time, she removed the shirt and let it drop to the floor. He already knew that she was not wearing a bra. Then, before Kelly could even begin to gather his thoughts, she swiftly removed her short skirt too. She was not wearing any underwear at all. In the blink of an eye she was standing before him stark naked.

He took a sharp intake of breath. Those small pert breasts. The tiny waist. Legs longer than they should be. The small almost imperceptible round of her tummy. Smoothly translucent skin. She was stunning. Quite sensational.

He didn't move. She had been staring at him while she undressed and continued to do so.

'This is what you want,' she said. 'This is what you have always wanted. Why don't you admit it? Why don't you take it?'

'Oh, Angel . . .' He spoke softly, almost sorrowfully. In his head he didn't want her to behave like that. But his body's reaction was somewhat different. He could feel himself becoming aroused.

'What's the matter? Are you afraid to take what you want? Or maybe you aren't capable any more . . .'

There was something unpleasant in her tone of voice – sarcasm and mockery, definitely, and an inflection of something else he couldn't quite make out. But it wasn't nice, he was sure of that.

Not that it stopped him. Not that anything could. She had pushed him too far, which he had little doubt had been her intention. Almost involuntarily he lurched forward and was on her before she could change her mind, indeed before she could move, his hands and mouth all over her. He must have had an erection all the time he had been talking to her, he suddenly realised. Not for the first time probably. He had not felt so urgently virile in years. He had known he was still capable of performing, all right, but not of anything as extreme as this.

He half carried her backwards, pushing her against the wall by the stairs, undoing his flies with one hand. She was so small, so light, so compliant. He manoeuvred her into position with far greater ease than he would have considered possible and entered her straight away, thrusting into her with all his might. Kelly had no time for foreplay. No time for any niceties at all.

She flinched slightly but did not utter a sound. It didn't take very long for him to finish. He pulled out of her and stepped back, using one arm to lower her to the ground. She slumped straight to a sitting position on the polished wooden floor, as if she were exhausted. Her eyes were fixed on his, largely unfathomable, but triumphant somehow.

Kelly was astonished at himself, and a little ashamed too. She had issued the invitation. She had taken the lead. She had undressed before him and clearly waited for him to make the next move. She had even mocked him when he had not done so at once. But when he had eventually responded to her it had been in such a way he could hardly believe it. He had been like an animal, and he had never behaved like that before. But then no woman in his life had ever had that kind of effect on him before.

None the less Kelly felt very uneasy. Invitation or not, it had been almost like rape.

Fourteen

Kelly didn't stay with her. He couldn't. He had watched for a moment as she had sat on the floor, panting slightly. Her expression remained mocking. Then, without speaking, she had pulled herself upright and walked off, still naked, in the direction of the downstairs bathroom. He could only see her back view, but he was sure that her shoulders began to shake as she walked away from him. Then he heard her laugh out loud just before she closed the bathroom door behind her.

He didn't like it. Not any of it. Suddenly he didn't like her, or himself, or what had happened. Not one little bit.

He zipped up his flies, struggling to regain self-control, and swiftly left the house, making no effort to say anything to Angel. It gave him some satisfaction that as he retreated through the big front door he thought he heard her call after him.

It was only when he was in the MG that he remembered the electronic gates. God, he thought, he couldn't even get out of the damned place without her help.

He drove slowly towards the closed gates and pulled to a halt in front of them, leaving the engine running while he contemplated what to do next. Ultimately he had no decision to make. The gates suddenly started to part in that magical way he was becoming used to.

Angel had obviously decided not to attempt to keep him there. Well, that wouldn't have been her style, would it?

There were no longer any police on duty, nor was there any sign of Ken James. Just one lone photographer waited outside. There was, after all, by now, not a deal of point in an across-the-board press presence. Angel had talked. She'd given the interview they'd all been after, and she'd given it to Kelly.

He drove thankfully through the gates, trying to ignore the tingling sensation in his crotch. In one way that brief, almost violent sexual act had been horrible. It had also been extraordinarily thrilling. He had to remind himself that the way it had happened was quite repugnant to him. Or it least it was to the man he had always been, he thought, as little waves of lingering excitement coursed through his body.

He made a vow to himself, a pledge. It was over. Whatever Angel Silver was up to, whatever she had or hadn't done, whatever her future held, he would have no part of it. He would never see her again.

Pledges, however, like rules, are made to be broken. Kelly's good intentions lasted precisely three days, thirteen hours and five minutes.

He had the usual problems getting through to her, ultimately leaving messages on her mobile and her home number and even sending a fax. There wasn't much point in trying not to look too eager. She already seemed to know him too well.

She kept him waiting another day and a half before she returned his call. And during that wait every time his phone rang, at home, in the office, or the mobile he kept in his jacket pocket, he answered swiftly, hoping and praying that the caller would be her. He was sitting at his desk in the *Argus* newsroom when she finally phoned.

'So what on earth might you want?' she asked him, her voice mocking him in the way which already seemed to have become par for the course.

'I want to see you,' he replied throatily.

'Do you indeed, Johnny boy? After the way you left the last time?'

'It was wrong. What happened was wrong.'

'Oh, don't you want to fuck me after all then?' More mockery.

He sighed.

'Not like that, I don't. No. I care about you.'

'Really? Spare me, John. You should have seen the expression on your face. You looked as if you'd wanted to have sex like that all your life.'

He felt empty. She was half right, that was the worst of it. He looked anxiously around him. Even though he knew it was impossible, it seemed to him that everybody in the newsroom could hear her voice as clearly as he could.

'Look, I can't talk about it now,' he said. 'Can I come round tonight?'

'Why not?'

A disinterested approach now, then just a slight change of tone. 'Only don't pretend to be some fucking born-again Christian, will you, Johnny? I've had enough of that crap.'

He arrived at Maythorpe just after eight, and was relieved that there were no longer any journalists at all waiting outside. He didn't want too many questions asked about his visits. The gates were shut so he merely drove the MG up to them and sat waiting for them to open. He was beginning to get the hang of it now – well, the mechanics of getting into the house, if nothing else. The gates duly parted. He drove through, and after just a second or two's thought, parked the car around the side of the house where it could not easily be seen from the road. Now that he and Angel had had sex, of a sort, all the goal posts in their relationship had changed. That was the way it always was. Kelly no longer wanted to advertise his business with her, whatever that might turn out to be in the future.

He walked to the front door, hunching his shoulders against the rain which had just started to fall, and again waited for a moment or two for her to open it in the way that she had done previously when he had visited Maythorpe. When she failed to appear he tugged at the big bell pull to one side. Still no response. Then he realised that the door was not even properly closed. Gingerly, he pushed it open. There was still no sign of her. He walked in, shutting the front door behind him. First he checked the big living room where he had so far spent most of his time in the house. Then he checked the kitchen, the formal dining room alongside it with its gleaming mahogany furniture, and the low-beamed book-lined library, the one room in the house, he understood, to have retained any of Maythorpe's original Tudor structure.

Back in the hall he glanced towards the section of wall against which he had pushed Angel the last time. Against which he had had her in the most direct animal fashion he had ever known.

Almost in defiance of his wishes, because he didn't really want to remember it, the thought of that short sharp fuck caused the desire to rise in him again.

He walked over to the bottom of the stairs.

'Where are you, Angel?' he called.

For a few seconds there was no reply. Then her voice wafted down the stairs, husky, perhaps slightly slurred.

'Why don't you come on up.'

Like Mae West, he thought obscurely, or more likely a spider inciting a fly into her web. It made no difference. He had stopped even kidding himself that anything much could. He mounted the stairs with alacrity. All but one of several doors leading directly off the landing were closed. He walked to the one which stood ajar and peered inside.

She was lying naked on the bed, leaning against the pillows, eyes half closed. In her hand she held an overly plump cigarette. He recognised the pungent, heavy odour of dope at once, even though it had been a very long time since he had smelled it, let alone smoked it. The curtains were drawn and the room was lit only by candles. Mozart played gently in the background.

As ever she looked breathtakingly, wonderfully beautiful. Or he thought so, anyway. The pink glow of the candles flickered enticing over her pale body.

'Do you want a drag?' she asked languidly, holding up the joint.

He remembered how well he had always found dope went with sex. None the less he shook his head.

'For God's sake,' she snapped, her mood changing in a second in that way he was becoming so familiar with. 'I told you not to come here if you were going to be fucking sanctimonious.'

'I can't smoke, Angel,' he said. 'I really can't. I can't handle it.'

'Fuck it, Kelly, I'm offering you a pull on a fucking joint.

It's not a syringe full of smack. I'm not trying to get you mainlining, am I?'

She glowered at him, those eyes blazing again.

He decided just to ignore the offer and get on with what he really wanted to do. He walked over to the bed and sat down on it next to her and began to stroke her. Very soon she started to move under his hands, sensuous as a cat. He couldn't believe how much pleasure it gave him to feel her body like that, just to touch that translucent white flesh. She looked as if she had never exposed herself to the sun in her life, he thought, as he let his fingers trail the downy hair which ran in a thin line along the centre of her belly. Then he started to explore between her legs.

She began to move quite frenziedly. On an impulse he swung himself round, buried his head there and began to use his tongue on her. Almost at once she started to buck violently and to cry out. He was pretty sure she reached an orgasm, but, just as she appeared to do so, she pulled herself away from him.

Then it began. Really began. First she lay face down on the bed and asked him to enter her from behind. Then she made him lie down on the bed and sat across him. From somewhere she produced a silk scarf and wrapped it round his head, covering his eyes.

She continued to ride him while she took first his left arm and then his right and tied them to the bed-head. He didn't even know what she used to tie him up. He couldn't see, after all. He found it disconcerting but also strangely exciting. Certainly he didn't protest. Not until he felt something wound round his neck and be tightened. He started to struggle then. But it was too late.

Whatever his now buried suspicions about what might have happened at Maythorpe house the night Scott Silver and Terry James died, Kelly didn't think for one moment that Angel was trying to kill him. He realised immediately what she was trying to do. He had no doubts whatsoever by now that her tastes in sex leaned strongly towards both the bizarre and the extreme.

He knew all about what he had always regarded as the

quite mad practice of limiting the air supply to the brain in order to increase the sensation of climax. It had killed that gay Labour MP a few years back and had quite possibly killed rock star Michael Hutchence. Kelly had no doubt at all that was what Angel was trying to do to him, and he was terrified.

But by the time he started to protest, with his arms already tied, his struggles proved merely fitful. His vision was fading, and his brain felt fuzzy; however, his other senses did seem to heighten. After a bit he couldn't see at all. There was only blackness in front of him and a grey mist inside his head. But he was sure his erection had grown six inches. He arched his back against her, pushing himself into her moist softness with as much strength as he could muster. The climax came swiftly then and it was truly amazing. The most extreme he had ever experienced he was sure of it. So good it was worth even risking his life for. In that moment of madness he was sure of that too.

Then he blacked out completely.

When he recovered consciousness, he had no idea how much later, but he somehow thought only probably a few seconds, she was still sitting astride him with that familiar triumphant look in her eyes. He felt wonderfully sated, wonderfully relaxed. Of course, he realised suddenly, some of that might be due to the joint she was holding between his lips.

He struggled against the restraints which still tied him to the bed, wanting to sit up, wanting to free himself, wanting to get rid of the joint which was making his head feel even more woozy. Then, equally suddenly, he didn't want to get rid of any of it at all.

'It's just dope, for Gods sake,' she had said.

He felt himself drifting off again. He didn't know exactly what was causing it then, the dope or the effects still of the lack of oxygen to his brain. Neither did he care much. He just allowed himself to float away.

When he next came to, the restraints had gone and he was propped up comfortably against the pillows. He didn't think he would have been able, in his condition, to move into that position unaided. Maybe Angel was stronger than she looked. She lay naked beside him. In her left hand she held another freshly made joint which she offered to him at once. He rejected it, really wanting to clear his head.

This time she did not try to persuade him. Instead she took a deep pull herself and said, 'Time for the film show, then.'

'What?' he enquired, looking at her.

Her eyes were deeply mocking. But there was nothing new about that.

Casually she reached out with one hand for the video and TV control which lay on the bedside table next to her. A picture appeared on the wide-screen TV set into the wardrobe system along the far wall. At first Kelly couldn't quite make out the first image to appear, then he saw that it was Angel, lying spread-eagled on the bed they were now sharing. After a moment he appeared alongside her and started to stroke her pale body. He watched her almost instantly responding to his touch.

'How the fuck –' he began.

'The best of modern technology,' Angel drawled. 'There's also a video camera concealed in that unit. You can probably see its lens if you look closely, in the corner of the big mirror.'

He looked, but still couldn't see it. In any case his eyes were drawn back compulsively to the screen. His head was between Angel's legs now, she was bucking and the sound of her cries of pleasure filled the room. He knew he was becoming aroused again, in spite of himself.

'Scott used to like to watch himself fuck,' Angel whispered. 'I thought you might like it too. I wasn't wrong either, was I?'

She reached out and touched him. He made an unusually fast recovery. For him. He thought he might never have been so hard. He pulled her on to him. He loved her compliance. It was as if he just melted into her. It was just sensational.

The next night, and the night after, and the night after that, he went back for more. He couldn't keep away. Each time the sexual demands she made of him were more and more extreme. Almost always there was bondage involved. Angel liked anal sex. She liked him to hit her at the moment of climax. Whatever they did together she often wanted him to hurt her, it seemed to him. Once she asked him to use a needle on her, piercing her nipples while he slowly fucked her. He nearly did it too. But there was still a limit, it seemed. In the end he just couldn't pierce her perfect white skin, couldn't bear the thought of seeing blood run over her breasts.

Everything else that she asked, he did. And, crazily, he frequently let her use the scarf round his neck, becoming almost hooked, just like she was, perhaps, on seeking more and more sensational orgasms.

He gave up even pretending not to want to smoke dope with her. Not only did it increase his physical senses, it also numbed his mental senses. And he didn't want to think when he was with Angel.

Always, whatever they did in bed, always there was the film show afterwards. He anticipated it too, began to play to the camera. She had been right. He loved to watch himself fuck her, loved to watch her use her mouth on him, loved to watch himself ejaculate over her breasts, into her mouth. Nothing, absolutely nothing, was taboo.

And, by God, afterwards he hated so much of what they did together. Loathed it. Abhorred it. Hated what his relationship with Angel, if it could be called that, was doing to him. But that was only when he was away from her.

When he was with her the sex between them was everything. He existed on a kind of sensual roller coaster.

In spite of everything, Kelly felt an overwhelming tenderness for Angel which did not square with the kind of sex they indulged in, and which certainly did not seem to be returned. Angel shied away from any show of affection, any gentleness at all. When he tried to talk to her about her feelings, she hid behind that façade of distant mocking indifference which he began to feel increasingly irritated by.

Angel had experienced far more than her share of the dark side of life. She was rich, famous, albeit primarily for being famous, and existed now in the lap of luxury. But she also knew what it was like to be in the gutter. She had known emotional turmoil too, and sadness. She'd suffered a series of miscarriages and failed to produce the child she claimed she and Scott had longed for, although Kelly was beginning to wonder about everything now, even that – to wonder how much of all that she had told him was fantasy, or just plain lies. Most of all he continued to wonder about the night of the double killing. He couldn't help it. So much didn't add up.

It was strange, but the greater their sexual involvement became, the greater became Kelly's concerns about what had happened. He also worried for Angel's future.

Angel seemed to believe there was little that the police could do to her, but Kelly feared that he knew better. When it came to unearthing the truth about murder the forces of the law were not inclined to give up so easily.

He called Karen Meadows to ask whether or not the case was being reopened. She was rather abrupt with him.

'I don't know why you're asking me that, John,' she told him curtly. 'You're the one with all the inside information, aren't you?'

And that had been more or less the end of the call. Karen had rung off, saying that she had to go to an urgent meeting.

'Just be very careful, John, OK?' were her last words.

Kelly had somehow been left in little doubt that the detective inspector now knew about him and Angel. He had no idea how, but he supposed he shouldn't be surprised.

Karen had had no urgent meeting to go to. She just hadn't known what to say to her old friend. Kelly had been right, she was well aware that he and Angel were almost certainly having an affair. Even if Kelly didn't realise it, his liaison with the rock star's widow was the talk of the *Argus*. Newspaper offices leaked like sieves, and Kelly wasn't the only journalist around with special police contacts.

Karen stretched out her long legs beneath her desk. She was still reeling from the Bridget Summers revelations in the *News of the World*. The chief constable had already come down on her like a ton of bricks, and she had only with difficulty been able to gloss over Summers' initial approach to the police which, however understandable in the circumstances, did seemed to have been rather pathetically overlooked.

The interviews her team had since conducted with the young woman had also been sorrowfully inconclusive. Bridget Summers stuck rigidly to her story but had been able to tell them little more, and neither had there been any further proof to substantiate her allegations.

The recent new interview that Karen had conducted herself with Angel Silver had not taken investigations any further either, although the picture Angel painted the second time round of her relationship with her husband differed substantially from her original version. None of it was enough, however, for Karen to make any kind of move on Angel in spite of the suspicions which were now beginning to form in her mind concerning the night when Scott and Terry James had died. There was, in reality, no new evidence to justify formally reopening inquiries.

In any case, even if there were, there was probably little that could be done. Angel had already been cleared of the manslaughter of Terry James. There was no way she could be charged with murder under the same set of circumstances.

None the less, Karen continued to have that nasty feeling that the Scott Silver case was far from over. And she didn't like the sound of Kelly's involvement with Angel one little bit. She knew all too well how vulnerable Kelly could be, in spite of his apparently streetwise approach to life and his journalistic cunning. Angel's reputation as a party girl who drank a lot and almost certainly still took drugs, even though Maythorpe Manor had proved to be clean when they'd searched it after the killings, also disturbed Karen. She feared Kelly might prove unable to resist temptation, and that if he were tempted he would not be able to cope.

She also reckoned Kelly's innate decency, good-heartedness and sense of fair play – unexpected always in a tabloid hack but which she had experienced first-hand all those years ago and never forgotten – might well, in the case of Angel

Silver, cause him only trouble. She suspected that Angel was the sort who knew all too well how to cash in on the good nature of others, particularly if she had managed to get them under her spell in the way it was rumoured that she already had Kelly.

'Underneath it all, John Kelly, you're as soft as shit,' the DCI muttered to herself under her breath. 'And I just hope you don't land yourself in it again . . .'

Kelly too had just enough sense left to realise he could indeed be heading for big trouble. The problem was that he was mesmerised by Angel Silver, even though he didn't trust her an inch. He was totally under her spell, as Karen Meadows suspected, and yet he was still honest enough with himself to be aware of it, just about. And occasionally he became overwhelmed by doubt and suspicion. Was Angel just using him? What had really happened that dreadful night? Then he felt disloyal. He adored her, after all. He adored making love to her. Only she never allowed it to be that. It was always that ultimate thrill-seeking fuck, which sometimes he didn't like at all. Not afterwards, anyway.

Kelly was totally confused. He knew what he really wanted to do – the only thing that made any sense. He wanted to clarify events in his mind in such a way that he could exonerate Angel from any blame. He wanted to prove her innocence to himself. That's what he wanted to do. And as long as he failed to do so he was always going to be uneasy in their relationship.

But Kelly was getting nowhere fast with Angel in that regard. He could never get a straight answer from her about anything. He would occasionally drop loaded queries into their conversation, on the rare occasions they had any conversation. He'd wondered whether the police had found the video camera in the bedroom. It had never been mentioned publicly. Kelly supposed it was irrelevant really, but it was just the sort of thing smart-arse lawyers liked to make mileage out of.

One night he asked her about it. 'What would you do if you knew a load of plods were going to come trampling over your life?' she replied. 'I packed it away in its box, of course. There was nothing in the bedroom for them to find.'

He'd thought about that carefully. How could Angel have had the presence of mind to hide away a video camera after what she had seen and done that night? After she'd allegedly watched her husband murdered and then killed his murderer? But Angel Silver was not like other women; she was not like any other human being he had ever known.

On another occasion he asked her again why the police hadn't found drugs.

'You never fucking give up, do you, John?' she stormed at him. 'Why should they have found anything? We weren't fucking dealers.'

No, thought Kelly. And he had no idea where she got her stuff from, although he suspected she did her buying in London, where she was inclined to disappear every so often for a couple of days or so, he had discovered.

'I've never been here when you haven't had plenty.'

'Oh, fuck off, John,' she said.

And he'd backed off at once. He couldn't bear to have her mad at him. He lived for those long wonderful hazy nights when she lay compliant by his side, her pale translucent body so inviting, and begged him to do things to her. Absolutely anything to her.

The mornings were invariably an embarrassment. Sometimes Kelly couldn't quite look Angel in the eye, not after the things they had been doing during the night. They didn't bother her, though. Then there was Mrs Nott, the cleaning lady, who worked at Maythorpe three mornings a week. Kelly's early evening paper hours meant that he normally avoided her, but a couple of times on days off and on one occasion when he overslept he'd had to pass the time of day with her on the way out. Mrs Nott had looked complacently superior. Angel didn't seem to care what the cleaning lady saw, it seemed, but Kelly had a sneaking feeling the woman could be dangerous.

Nothing put the breaks on his lust for Angel, though. Nothing could. One night she persuaded him to let her put cocaine on the end of his penis. He knew the old trick. It would numb the nerve ends slightly, make his erection last longer, maybe even make him harder and bigger.

He let her do it, remembering more vividly than ever all the other effects of the enticing white powder which he had once so enjoyed. He allowed himself to forget the part it had played in destroying his life.

And it was only a matter of time before he joined her in a line. The familiar buzz went straight to his brain. He thought he was the best stud ever. He thought he could conquer the world. He couldn't imagine how he had lived without this wonderful drug for so long.

The need returned at once. But then he had always known that it would. Kelly had never been able to dabble, not in drink, not in coke. Not in sex, it seemed now. Maybe not in anything. He always had to go all the way.

Kelly quickly lost interest in everything in his life except Angel. His relationship with his news editor hit a record low. When he was out of the office, which was most of the time, Kelly had stopped returning Hansford's calls at all, even though he knew he was close to committing professional suicide for the second time in his life. He even started avoiding Nick's telephone calls, in spite of the increasingly anxious tone he detected in his son's messages, particularly when Nick called Kelly at home at times when he would definitely be expected to be there.

His relationship with Moira went from bad to worse. Indeed, since he had begun to have sex with Angel he'd barely seen the woman with whom he had previously shared his life.

He felt sure she knew what was going on but he still went through the pretence of deception. She phoned his home on more than one occasion, and a couple of times called round, when she would have expected him to be there. And twice, although he couldn't believe he'd done it, he made definite arrangement to see her and then just disappeared. To Maythorpe Manor, of course.

He began to invent stories which seemed unlikely even to

him. An unexpected summons to the death bed of an aged aunt who had never before even been mentioned. A meeting with a nameless Fleet Street editor so impressed with his work on the Silver case that he was on the cusp of offering Kelly a truly amazing job.

'Work?' repeated Moira caustically. 'So that's what they call it nowadays.'

But she hadn't pushed the point.

Then one morning he returned to his house after a night with Angel to find Moira sitting at his dining-room table. He was taken by surprise in more ways than one. Moira still had a key to his front door, but it wasn't like her to use it without a prior arrangement. He stood in the doorway just looking at her, unable to think of anything to say.

'I – I just thought it was time we talked,' she stumbled. 'I never seem to be able to catch you now. I've just come off duty, so I thought I'd come round. I just assumed you'd be here . . .'

Her voice tailed off. She looked shattered. Empty. Kelly had little doubt that she knew darned well where he'd spent the night.

But, on autopilot, he continued with the pretence of deception. Desperately he sought for inspiration.

'I just popped out to get some papers,' he managed.

She looked pointedly past him towards the hall. He followed her gaze. The usual pile of newspapers lay against the wall where they would have been pushed when she had opened the door earlier.

'Er, they'd missed one or two out . . . distribution problems . . .' he continued lamely.

Moira looked very weary. She just nodded.

He took a step towards her, tripped over the edge of the carpet, and very nearly went flying. He was aware then of her studying him closely. He was, of course, still stoned, which was getting to become the norm again, and without doubt he shouldn't have driven home. He ran a hand over his stubbled chin, and with difficulty manoeuvred his tongue around the inside of his mouth, which suddenly felt unbearably dry. He had come home to shave, change his clothes, and try to get himself together in order to go to work. It was getting to be more and more difficult to extricate himself from Angel and to come even close to keeping evening paper hours. But so far he had managed it, just about. If only in order, he reflected with a rare flash of honesty, to convince himself that he had everything under control.

His head ached. He was having some difficulty focusing on Moira. Abruptly he made a lunge for a dining-room chair and, with a feeling of great relief, sat down on it.

'Have you been drinking, John?' asked Moira. Her tone of voice suggested concern more than interrogation. She knew all about Kelly's past; she knew how low he had once sunk.

'No,' he answered truthfully.

She peered at him closely. He lowered his eyes. It was always the eyes that were the giveaway.

'What have you been doing then, John? What on earth have you been taking?'

It was guilt and maybe fear that made him fly off the handle.

'Nothing, you stupid woman, and in any case it's none of your fucking business,' he growled at her. And he regretted it as soon as he'd said it.

She recoiled from him. He moaned to himself softly, unable in his befuddled state even to begin to retrieve the situation.

Then, in that plucky way that she had, the way he assumed she had managed to survive with that brute of a husband for all those years, she gathered herself together, stood up and walked to the door, where she paused and turned to face him again.

'You're absolutely right, John, aren't you?' she remarked quietly. 'It isn't any of my fucking business. So I'll just leave you to it, shall I?'

He didn't reply. There was no reply to make that he could think of. In any case his head was swimming. He lowered it into his hands. His brain felt as if it belonged to somebody else, and somebody else he didn't know. After a moment he heard an almost inaudible click followed by a gentle thud –

the noise of the front door being opened and shut quite carefully.

Kelly raised his throbbing head and leaned back in the chair. The ceiling was going round and round.

'Oh shit,' he said rather more loudly than he intended.

Fifteen

Kelly was well aware of the damage that his relationship with Angel was causing to people he cared about. He strongly disliked so much of the effect it was having on him, his life, and those around him. He didn't want to hurt anyone, least of all Moira. And, although he kidded himself it was different now, he knew, as Karen Meadows did, that, for him with his track record, dabbling with drugs was like playing with fire. Yet none of that made any difference. He couldn't keep away from Angel, couldn't stop himself from being with her at every opportunity and doing anything and everything that she asked.

Most nights that they were together they videod themselves having sex and afterwards watched the tape. Kelly continued to be aroused by this, which actually disturbed him considerably. He also had other anxieties.

'I hope you're careful with those tapes, Angel,' he remarked one day, as casually as he could.

'I sell them to this porn shop behind King's Cross station,' she replied, smiling at him mockingly. And just for a fleeting moment he half believed her. Well, she was crazy enough to do almost anything, was Angel. Then her smile widened, she threw back her head and laughed at him, something she did quite frequently. He wished she wouldn't. It wasn't laughing with him at all, but at him. He found that humiliating and on occasions even wondered if it was her intention to humiliate him.

'I don't even keep them, you idiot. I just tape over the same one.'

He was reassured, at least momentarily. But, as ever, he didn't know whether to believe her or not. Certainly he decided to do a little checking. Surreptitiously he searched the bedroom, the big wardrobe which housed the video camera and the widescreen TV, the other built-in furniture in the room, the bedside cabinets, even under the bed. He didn't find any tapes at all in the bedroom, except one unused one still wrapped in its original cellophane, which was encouraging. Maybe she was telling the truth. That was all he wanted to prove really, in every way.

He also checked the living room. One cabinet was filled with video tapes, all meticulously labelled. Some were movies, but most seemed to be of Scott and his band in concert through the years. Once, when Angel was having a bath, Kelly picked a tape at random and played it. It was Scott at Wembley Stadium in 1984. Just as it said on the label. Kelly cursed himself for being so suspicious.

Then one night he arrived unexpectedly. He had done it before and Angel hadn't seemed to mind. He had the code now to open the electronic gates, and was unsurprised to find the front door to the house unlocked. One thing about which Angel was undoubtedly telling the truth was her cavalier attitude to security, which, extraordinarily, had remained much the same even after the shocking events of the previous year, even though her husband might well still be alive had Terry James not been able to enter both the grounds and the house so easily.

Kelly could hear an at first unidentifiable noise coming from Angel's bedroom. Then the sounds became clearer. He feared he knew exactly what he was listening to. It was the sound that Angel made when she cried out during sex, and he could also pick out a low male grunting.

He ran up the stairs, two at a time, not giving himself any opportunity to think through what he was doing, nor even considering how scathing she was likely to be of him, whatever was going on in her bedroom. He was out of breath by the time he thrust open the bedroom door, and stood there panting, looking anxiously in.

Angel was lying naked on the bed. But she was alone. One hand lay languidly between her legs. There was, as usual, a packet of the familiar white powder on the bedside table. Next to it was a rolled-up ten-pound note. She was staring at the TV set as Kelly burst in, her lower body moving in its own rhythm of arousal. Her gaze switched instantly to him. At first her eyes were full of alarm, but as soon as she saw who it was the alarm disappeared to be replaced with what could only be described as cold anger.

The noises were coming from the TV. Kelly swung round to look at it and just caught a glimpse of writhing limbs and a close-up of Angel's own face, screwed into that intense expression, which could be either ecstasy or pain, that he had become so familiar with. Then the screen went blank.

He looked back at Angel. She had the remote control in one hand. She must have switched the set off.

'Who the hell invited you?' she snapped at him, her violet eyes flashing with fury.

'I – I'm sorry,' he said, confused for a moment. At first he had merely been relieved that she was not with anybody else. Then he thought about what he had seen on the TV screen. It had just been a glimpse, but there had been more writhing limbs on that screen than could belong to any two people, he thought. Not that he was either surprised or shocked by that. He had little doubt that Angel's taste in sex would run to orgies, if she thought she could get away with it – in fact no doubt at all.

One thing he had never really believed was her protestation of fidelity to Scott. Maybe he had half kidded himself, but Kelly supposed he had always known better really. He suspected that monogamy just didn't go with the territory as far as Angel Silver was concerned.

He became vaguely aware of her scrabbling at the bedclothes. She was pushing a load of black video tapes under the sheets, he realised. He pretended not to notice.

'Are you spying on me or something?' she enquired, still furious.

'No,' he answered truthfully, still taking in the possible significance of what he had seen. Not yet, he thought to himself. Did she have a secret library of home-made blue videos, featuring herself, her husband, him, and God knows who else? And if so, where on earth did she keep them? He had seen no sign of them. And neither, he wouldn't mind betting, had the police. They hadn't found any drugs either, when they'd searched the place, and Kelly couldn't believe there wasn't always at least a little coke and a few grams of dope somewhere in Maythorpe.

'I just came to see you.' He grinned, which was the last thing he felt like doing, took a step or two forward and touched the hand lying loosely in her crotch. 'Thought you might like some of the real thing,' he continued huskily.

Her arousal was obvious and seemed to take her over then, as it so often did. Her hunger for sex was extraordinary. She was insatiable. Sometimes he wondered how much real satisfaction she ever got, certainly with him. She never seemed to get enough, that was for certain.

Predictably she didn't bother to speak, but just took his hand and guided his fingers into her.

'Whoa,' he said. 'I need to go to the bathroom first.'

He retreated into the en-suite, leaving the door very slightly ajar. Almost at once he was aware of her moving around. The bed squeaked. A floorboard creaked. Very carefully Kelly opened the bathroom door and followed her out through the bedroom on to the landing. As he passed the bed he noticed that the duvet had been flung back and there was no sign of the video tapes he had noticed earlier. He waited until she reached the hallway down below and disappeared into the library, with its rows of designer books which had always looked to him as if they'd never been read, before he ventured on to the stairs, treading with immense caution, and wincing each time there was a creak from the ancient wood.

When he got to the hallway he saw that she had left the library door just ajar. Very gingerly he peered round it. There was no sign of her. Puzzled, he took a cautious step into the room. Then he realised that part of the book-lined wall opposite him was closer to him than it should be. He peered at it closely. It had moved out of the way, revealing some kind of opening behind him.

'Jesus,' he muttered to himself, remembering both his schoolboy history and similar sights he had been shown in old houses. 'It's a priest's hole.'

He could hear sounds from within. What was she doing, he wondered. Stowing those tapes back where they belonged, more than likely. He wondered how the priest's hole opened. He would really like to know what the mechanism was.

Suddenly she appeared from behind the books. Kelly was standing fully exposed in the doorway, but thankfully managed to step back behind the door's protection before she noticed him. He paused, breathing heavily for a moment or two, then decided to take a risk. He'd got this far, but there would probably be little point unless he could see how she closed the bookcase wall. He put his head round the door, moving very slowly and carefully. She had her back to him. With her left hand she was pushing the bookcase, with her right she was fiddling in a gap in the books at the edge of the third shelf from the top. He could see the missing books on the floor, but was unable quite to decipher which ones they were.

The movable wall began to slide back into place. Angel bent down and started to replace the books which had been removed. She wouldn't be long now. Kelly took off up the stairs as fast as he could. He had no time to waste and could not take the care he would have liked to be quiet. The creaking of the stairs sounded loud as gunshots to him. He even feared that Angel might be able to hear the jangling of his nerves, which were rattling for England. Inside her bedroom he removed his shirt and lay down on the bed in one disjointed movement, trying to control his heavy breathing. He really was out of condition.

But if Angel noticed anything amiss when she came in she gave no sign. Instead she came straight to him and put one hand on his chest.

'You took me by surprise,' she said. And that was about as near as you would ever get to an apology for anything from Angel Silver, he thought.

'Where've you been, anyway?' he asked as casually as he could, quite certain that she would have a glib answer. She did.

'I got the munchies,' she said. He noticed then that she

was holding a packet of chocolate biscuits in her free hand. She didn't miss a trick, he thought admiringly.

Angel put the biscuits down and began to attack his flies with both hands.

'God, I feel randy,' she said.

He responded as lightly as he could. 'I'm not surprised, what *were* you watching?'

'None of your fucking business,' she replied.

And then, quite quickly, they both became too busy to talk any more.

Only when it was over, and he was lying sated and sore, with that vague feeling of unease which for him so often seemed to be part of sex with Angel, did he wonder at his own behaviour as well as hers. Without a moment's compunction he had deliberately spied on Angel. This was the woman he could not leave alone, the woman he was obsessed with, and yet it had come so easily to him to sneak after her and watch her.

What did it all mean and where was it all leading? If he distrusted Angel so much, then what was he doing with her? And what exactly did it say about him?

There was one idea in particular that Kelly could not get out of his head. He was almost certain now that Angel kept a library of her own personal porn movies. He knew he would not be able to rest until he confirmed that he was right, and found out just what kind of stuff they featured.

The problem was that Kelly had not been able to stop his imagination taking an unwelcome quantum leap, almost from the moment he had discovered the existence of the priest's hole and what it might contain.

Angel liked to video sex. So, it seemed, had her husband. Born-again Christian or not, Kelly thought wryly, everything that Angel indicated to him about Scott Silver suggested a liking for sex every bit as bizarre as her own.

Kelly's train of thought progressed swiftly. What if Angel and Scott Silver had not been asleep when Terry James had entered their bedroom. What if they had been making love? Scott had at that time apparently been professing undying love to Bridget Summers and even promising to leave Angel, but Angel consistently maintained that their sexual relationship had remained unchanged. And Kelly somehow thought that in that regard at least she was probably telling the truth. Both Angel and Scott Silver would have been well able to dissociate their sexual urges from their emotions, he suspected.

It was, he felt, quite possible that Angel and Scott had been having sex when they had found themselves confronted by Terry James. If that was the case then it was also a possibility that their video camera had been running. And the million-dollar question, a question fuelled by his suspicions of what might be hidden in the priest's hole, a question which Kelly could not get out of his head, was whether or not that tape still existed. Angel was seriously into sexual excess. There were many aspects of that side of her which disturbed Kelly greatly, and he was inclined to be even more disturbed by the alacrity with which he himself joined in. But would even Angel Silver keep a video which possibly showed two men being killed, one of them the husband she had allegedly loved so much, the other his assailant whom she had killed herself? Would she really keep a real-life snuff movie featuring that?

Kelly just didn't know.

Angel kept a spare set of keys to Maythorpe Manor in a drawer in the kitchen. Kelly had seen them there once when he'd been looking for matches.

At the first opportunity Kelly removed the keys and stowed them carefully in a zip pocket of his leather jacket. Angel was not an orderly methodical person, except possibly when it came to labelling and filing her smutty video tapes, he thought wryly. He was fairly confident that even if she looked for the spare keys in the drawer she would just think that she'd mislaid them somehow.

The next time she told him she was going to London for a couple of days, something she did at frequent intervals, he was ready. Previously he had always wished she might ask him to accompany her. He had no idea what she got up to when she went away, or even where she stayed, and she never discussed it with him. He didn't like to think about it too much and in the past had resented her brief trips away from him. But this time he was glad when she told him she was off to London the following day.

He had watched her set the burglar alarm often enough. Since his plan had come into his head he had watched carefully, making a note afterwards of the code she punched in. It hadn't been difficult. Angel made no attempt to conceal anything from him. That made Kelly feel fleetingly guilty. She obviously trusted him rather more than he did her.

None the less he was determined. On the appointed day, as far as Kelly knew, Angel left for London as planned early in the afternoon. But Kelly waited until almost midnight before setting off for Maythorpe. He was being careful. Angel was unpredictable and he certainly didn't want to confront Mrs Nott during the day.

He drove straight up to the gates and, as he had done so many times now, tapped in the security code Angel had supplied him with. The gates opened in their usual smoothly magical fashion. At the front door he rang the door bell pull, just in case. There was no response. He did so a second time, to make sure. Then he inserted his stolen key in the lock. It turned easily. Once inside he dealt with the burglar alarm, then called Angel's name, just to make doubly sure. You really never knew what she was up to. She could have changed her mind, not gone to London at all and failed to bother to tell him, and he wouldn't have liked to have been forced to explain his acquisition of the door key to her or to anybody. But there was no response to his call.

When he was as sure as he possibly could be that he was alone in the big house, he headed straight for the library. He'd noted the shape, size and position of the books which Angel had removed when she'd opened the entrance to the priest's hole. They turned out to be a leather-bound edition of Mark Twain. Neat, pristine, and you could tell when you handled them that, as he had always suspected, they had probably never been opened, let alone read, Kelly noted as he lifted several of them off their shelf and piled them neatly on the floor. The wood-panelled wall behind them seemed quite smooth. There was no obvious recess or knob that might be used to open up the priest's hole in the way Kelly had seen. He ran his right hand slowly over the panelling, using his fingers to push and prod. Eventually he found it. A small section of panelling, which had looked no different at all to the rest, popped open on hinges at his touch. Kelly was momentarily elated, but he just hoped he'd be able to repeat the procedure in reverse, because he wasn't sure exactly what he had done to move the section of wood, thus revealing a small hollow in the wall and a handle within. Kelly turned the handle. The mechanism seemed well oiled. The section of wall, shelves of books still attached, which Kelly had seen move when Angel had gone into the priest's hole, slid smoothly out of the way.

With his heart beating considerably faster than usual Kelly stepped forward and peered inside. He could see nothing. Just blackness. He guessed there must be a light switch somewhere, there almost certainly was if he had guessed correctly and the priest's hole was in constant use as a secret hideaway storeroom. He reached a hand inside the opening and felt all around it. His hunch was correct, he found a switch, flipped it down, and the priest's hole was flooded with light.

Kelly gave an involuntary gasp. What he saw exceeded even his wildest expectations. The light revealed an irregularly shaped little room, probably six feet by three feet, and barely tall enough to stand in, every inch of its wall space lined with shelves on which were stacked video tapes. Right by the door was a wooden box. Kelly looked in the box first. It contained a largish bag of white powder. He didn't bother to taste it, but guessed that it was coke, and around four ounces or so of it. That was quite a supply, even for a heavy user, and would have a street value of more than £5,000. No wonder Angel never seemed to run out. There were also three or four ounces of cannabis resin in the box, and a small bag of grass.

Kelly resisted the temptation to help himself to a little. Apart from anything else, he had already told himself that as long as he only smoked dope or snorted coke when he was with Angel he'd be able to control it and not do himself any lasting harm. He didn't really even want to think that he might be becoming drug dependent again. Instead he turned his attention to the tapes. They seemed to be quite meticulously labelled and in order. In spite of Angel's perpetual disorder in other areas, Kelly was not surprised by that. Angel and Scott's music collection was much the same. They were people whose lives together had centred around the media, in more ways than one, thought Kelly. There must have been four or five hundred videos on the closely stacked shelves within the priest's hole. He was familiar enough with Angel's vigorous appetite for sex, but could these really all be blue home movies? He began to study the labels. It was extraordinary. Each one was neatly labelled with a date and a number, nothing else, and they were stored chronologically – which was almost too good to be true.

Kelly moved further into the priest's hole, bending over as he did so in order not to bang his head against its uneven ceiling, and ran his eye along the lines of tapes. A video labelled 12 November 2001 was in its correct place on the shelves. There it was. Just like that. It existed. But could it really be what Kelly suspected? He took the tape off the shelf and shifted the rest in the row just a little to cover the gap he had made. He was eager now to watch it, but first he had to close up the priest's hole behind him, and that took him several anxious minutes. At one point he really did begin to fear that he was just not going to be able to do so, and that on her return Angel would be confronted by almost irrefutable evidence of his night-time escapade. Eventually, however, and probably as much by luck as judgement, he managed to get the mechanism to work.

Once he had closed the priest's hole he stood for a moment or two checking that everything was in place and wondering exactly what he should do next. He was so eager to watch the video that he was extremely tempted to go into the living room and look at it straight away on Angel's TV there. At least he could return the tape then right after he'd seen it. But he had already shut up the priest's hole and, in any case, it would be far safer to stick to his original plan. He reminded himself that he had no real idea when Angel might return. He reminded himself again of her unpredictability, and decided to take no further risks, but to return to his own territory while he had the chance.

On the drive back to Torquay Kelly's mind was buzzing. The adrenalin was flowing like he hadn't experienced since he'd been in a war zone. The sense of danger was almost that great in a way. Kelly was so afraid of what the tape might reveal. But at the same time he couldn't wait to know.

Sixteen

When he got home, Kelly hastily locked the front door and ran up the stairs to his bedroom. Without even bothering to remove his coat he slotted the tape into his little portable TV's built-in video machine.

The first part of his hunch immediately proved itself to be correct. The film featured Scott and Angel having sex together. She had indeed told the truth, it seemed, about their relationship in that respect. Whatever the exact nature of his affair with Bridget Summers, which even Angel admitted had happened, Scott's continued enthusiasm for shafting his wife could not be in doubt. And Kelly couldn't help noticing how well-endowed the rock star was. Did Angel find him inadequate by comparison, he wondered. Then he gave himself a mental telling off. The purpose of having stolen the tape was not to compare himself sexually with Scott Silver or anyone else. Neither was it to become aroused. In spite of everything, and in spite of his instinctive distaste at seeing Angel with another man, even her husband, he began to feel unwanted surges of sexual excitement as images he could not help finding highly erotic unfolded on screen.

Scott and Angel were doing together all the things that he and Angel did. Only better, he thought fleetingly. Then kicked himself again. For a good thirty minutes it went on like that. Thirty minutes of earthy sex. He was beginning to get quite turned on in spite of himself when a tall heavily built man appeared in shot. Kelly's arousal vanished, and he felt himself break out in a cold sweat. He was so afraid of what might happen next. He peered closely at the screen. The man's back was to the camera but Kelly knew this must be Terry James. He could see no knife. However, James's right hand was not visible. For a few seconds James stood absolutely still, facing the bed. Kelly remained unable to see his face but guessed that he had been momentarily at least arrested by the sexual activity going on there. Then, quite abruptly, Scott Silver looked up, as if he had heard a sound, and spotted the intruder. He screamed something Kelly could not hear and, with impressive agility, literally leaped out of bed and threw himself at James, who, although he was so much bigger than Scott, seemed to be at first knocked off balance by the speed and force of the unexpected attack. But James, seasoned street fighter that he was, made a quick recovery, and wrapped his left arm round Scott's neck, the forearm pressing on the rock star's larynx. There was still no sign of a knife, but James's right hand remained concealed. The two entangled men half fell to the floor, and, struggling violently, rolled out of shot. Angel then climbed out of bed and half ran towards her husband and James until she was out of shot too. There were more screams and shouts, then a particularly blood-curdling scream – the moment when Scott was stabbed, Kelly guessed.

A few seconds later Terry James appeared on screen again. He was covered in blood, walking backwards, eyes wide with horror, jaw slack. He seemed to be in shock. Still no knife was visible. Then Angel reappeared. She too was bloody. Dripping blood. And she was holding a lethal-looking knife. It was a large kitchen knife, which Kelly was sure he had seen before in court during Angel's trial, and which had presumably already been responsible for the death of her husband.

Angel walked purposefully towards James, as she did so lifting the knife so that it was level almost with her shoulders, and pointed at James's body just above his waist. The big man, still looking dazed, continued to walk backwards until Angel lurched suddenly towards him and plunged the knife into his gut. James gave a little grunt, almost more in surprise than pain it seemed to Kelly, then stretched out his hands as if trying to push Angel away. She stepped back then, withdrawing the knife as she did so, which made a kind of sucking noise as it was pulled free of James's flesh. He went down at once, dropping heavily to the floor like a length of felled lumber. As he fell Angel stepped towards him again and continued to stab him, thrusting the knife into his body repeatedly. James made no further sound. Blood spouted from him like fizzy lemonade from a pierced can. Thick and red. Angel lashed out at him again and again. And when she finally stopped she stood over him, eyes unnaturally bright, lips parted, breathing deeply, looking, in fact, much the same way she did when she had sex.

Kelly was mesmerised, and shocked to the core. The events of that dreadful night had been filmed, preserved for posterity on a video tape which Angel obviously hadn't been able to resist keeping. He'd half expected that, hadn't he? But she'd kept it even though it barely seemed to tally at all with the version of events she'd given to the police and in court.

He wound the tape back and played it again. Then several times more. His head ached. He wished he hadn't been so darned sanctimonious and had helped himself to a little of Angel's stash of dope and coke. He could do with some mind-altering substances. This was turning into an extraordinary and quite terrifying night. Kelly desperately needed something to settle his shattered nerves, to restore some sense of wellbeing, in spite of everything. Maybe he was getting hooked again. It made no difference on this occasion as he had nothing to take. Instead he tried to concentrate on what he was going to do with the tape. He knew what he should do. He should hightail it round to Karen Meadows first thing in the morning. He also knew that he wasn't going to do that. He wasn't going to do anything until he had a chance at least to talk to Angel. But he had no idea where she was. London was a big place, and she had always avoided telling him not only where she was staying but also whom she might be with. Neither did he know for certain when she would be home. A couple of days, she'd said. He was well aware already that that could mean almost anything from twenty-four hours to a week or more. He would just have to be patient, which was hard, because he was desperate to get it over with now. Confronting her with what he'd discovered was not going to be a pleasant experience, he was sure of that

– for a start it would be pretty clear that he had broken into her home in her absence – but that is what he intended to do.

He switched off the light, undressed and climbed into bed, burying his head in the pillows, desperately seeking the release of sleep. It was hopeless. His brain was racing. His headache was getting worse. Eventually he hauled himself out of bed and paddled downstairs to the kitchen where he scrabbled in the drawer next to the cooker for the plastic drum of aspirin he knew was there somewhere. His fingers eventually located it, right at the back, of course, jammed behind a roll of bin liners, a box of sticking plaster and a packet of dishcloths. Thankfully he thrust three of the small white tablets into his mouth, filled a mug that had been upside down on the draining board with tap water and washed the aspirin down with one gulp.

He put the mug down again and turned away. Then he paused, turned back and picked up the mug once more. He was well enough aware that in the cupboard above him were a two-thirds-full bottle of whisky and two bottles of wine. When he had first come off the booze and the drugs all those years ago he hadn't been able to stand having drink in the house, and hadn't been able to cope with going into a pub because the temptation was just too great. But he had simply learned to steel himself. Moira drank. Nick drank, albeit very moderately. His friends drank. For years Kelly had been able to keep alcohol in his home in order to offer a drink to others without being worried by it, and certainly without even thinking about drinking it himself when he was alone. Tonight was different, he told himself.

He reached up, opened the cupboard door, removed the whisky and poured himself a hefty slug into the same mug. Then he paused. It was well over twelve years since he'd touched a drop. He tried to convince himself he could handle it, that he was never going to go under again, so what harm could a drop of whisky do? Anyway, he needed something. He really did. And the whisky was there. To hell with it, thought Kelly. With one hand he replaced the bottle in the cupboard and with the other he raised the mug to his lips and took a tentative sip.

First he felt the spirit hit the back of his throat, then that still familiar burning sensation, followed almost instantly by the glow of it coursing through his veins. For a true drinker there was nothing, absolutely nothing, like neat whisky. Except perhaps Eastern European vodka, although that didn't quite have the taste. Both provided instantaneous fixes. Just about the nearest you could get to main-lining out of a bottle. Kelly shut his eyes, savouring the moment. Twelve years without this, he thought. By God, it was good. He took another longer, deeper drink, rolling the whisky around his mouth with his tongue.

For a moment or two he stood there, just enjoying it. Then he reached up to the cupboard again, removed the bottle of Scotch, and headed back to bed, mug in one hand, bottle in the other.

The next morning he woke feeling terrible. He might not have forgotten how good whisky tasted, but he had forgotten what a whisky hangover was like. Selective memory, he supposed, the way most people so frequently look back at the past. On the other hand, he didn't have much recollection of having suffered from hangovers at all in the old days. The amount of booze he had put away with such regularity quite probably meant that he hadn't suffered from them much, that his body had gone past even reacting in that way.

Kelly lay very still. His mouth felt like the inside of a stale wash-bag. He might even be growing green mould in there, he thought wryly as he ran his tongue tentatively over furry teeth. His head ached even worse than it had the night before and his gut was periodically contracting with vague spasms of nausea. Perhaps he'd better go to the bathroom. Cautiously he propped himself up on one elbow and attempted to swing his legs out of bed. The room spun.

It was a while before he was able to move without minor disaster, and even then it took him some time to get his act together – brush teeth, shave, dress, all the routine things which were not normally a problem. But they were today.

Then he made his way painfully down to the kitchen,

brewed tea, took some more aspirin, and waited hopefully for his headache to fade away and his brain to clear.

It was the best part of an hour before he felt even marginally better. But his head still ached dully and his thought processes were definitely operating on an auxiliary engine. And not a very powerful one, either. The clock on the wall told him that it was 9.30 a.m. already. Kelly should have been in the office at 7.30. He groaned to himself and decided that it would be better to phone in sick than to turn up at his evening paper halfway through the working day.

Deliberately avoiding a direct call to any of his bosses, he succeeded eventually in managing to speak to Phyllis, the front desk receptionist. That alone was quite an achievement, particularly for a man in Kelly's condition, as, in keeping with the era of voice mail and computer technology, you had to work really hard to get through to the human being behind the piped music and various assorted bleeps of the *Argus* telephone system. Phyllis, however, was a good sort who had always given the impression of being quite fond of Kelly. He thought she'd do her best for him.

When he had finished spinning an entirely predictable yarn about a stomach upset, food poisoning, terrible cramps, and so on, Kelly poured himself more tea and tried to phone Angel. Situation normal. The landline phone to Maythorpe was switched to automatic answering mode, naturally, and there was no reply from her mobile. Did she *ever* switch the darned thing on, he wondered wearily.

None the less he called the mobile several times before finally admitting defeat. Then he went back to bed. He was unable to sleep much, but it still seemed to help a bit. Every time he woke up he attempted to phone Angel again, and then, in the late afternoon, he took a run out to Maythorpe just in case she had returned already. The house was deserted.

On the way back to Torquay he stopped at the Fitzroy Arms on the outskirts of town, a pub which he had never frequented before, and ordered a pint of bitter. Kelly had always been a beer man. Whisky gave you the instant hit, beer the slow soothing satisfaction. And there was, of course, nothing like a pint if you'd had a skinful the night before. He ordered a second pint, then a third, and gave serious thought to a Scotch chaser. Probably only the MG parked outside saved him from starting on the whisky again. He really couldn't afford to risk losing his licence. At least he still had some sense, he thought wryly, as he finished the third pint and headed for the door.

When he got home Nick was waiting for him, sitting in his car parked outside Kelly's house.

'Shit,' Kelly muttered to himself as he slotted the MG into a space right behind Nick's Porsche. He just hoped Nick wouldn't pick up the smell of beer on his breath.

Kelly and Nick climbed out of their cars and met rather awkwardly in the middle of the pavement.

'What a surprise,' said Kelly, with a forced brightness he certainly did not feel.

Nick did smell the beer on his father's breath, of course, and his heart sank. His childhood memories of what had happened when drink had almost destroyed his father remained so vivid, and what he couldn't remember his mother had always been more than happy to remind him of.

Nick felt afraid – for his father, and for the relationship he had with him, which he so valued. He struggled not to show his feelings. Not yet, anyway.

'Just wanted to make sure you were all right, Dad,' he said. 'Why haven't you replied to any of my messages?'

'I've been busy, that's all,' Kelly replied. 'I'm absolutely fine. C'mon in.'

Nick followed him into the house, and didn't speak again until they were inside. He studied his father for a moment or two. Kelly looked sheepish, as well he might, thought Nick. And that sheepish look was another unwelcome boyhood memory.

'You've been drinking, Dad, haven't you?' he remarked eventually.

'Oh, only a couple of beers,' said Kelly, with that same forced brightness. 'Nothing to worry about. I can handle it OK now.'

Nick doubted that very much. And he also doubted that his father could handle Angel Silver. He knew that Moira thought Kelly was under the woman's spell, and so did Nick. He wondered just how far things had gone between the two. He felt sure, somehow, that if any kind of relationship had developed between Kelly and Angel it would be one that could only do his father harm. And that meant Nick would be harmed too.

Nick was worried, very worried, and nothing his father was likely to say would alter that. But he decided not to go for further confrontation. Not yet, anyway.

To Kelly's relief Nick had to leave early the next morning to return to London. Their evening together had passed pleasantly and innocuously enough after Nick's early remark about Kelly drinking, but Kelly just did not feel comfortable with his son. He was harbouring too many secrets, for a start.

He decided again to give the office a miss and went through the fruitless process of continuing to call Angel repeatedly. He also once more took a trek out to Maythorpe, and afterwards visited the same pub. On the way home in the early evening he gave in to temptation, predictable by then, and stopped at an off-licence to buy a bottle of Scotch. In the safe seclusion of his kitchen he poured himself half a tumbler of the stuff, topped up with water, which he downed almost in one go. Then, perhaps curiously, perhaps not, he wasn't sure, after just that one big glass of the stuff he felt an overwhelming urge to see Moira. He was consumed by the need for the comfort of her, for the familiarity, for the common sense. He knew better than to attempt to drive, but fortunately she lived close enough for him not to need to. Kelly grabbed his coat and took off at a trot for Moira's house in Galleon Road.

If he hadn't been drinking, of course, he probably would not have had the gall under the circumstances even to contact her, let alone turn up unannounced. Indeed, it was just luck that she was off duty and at home, because he no longer had any idea what her rota was. Kelly was not yet drunk exactly, but Moira noticed at once that he had been drinking. After all, he hadn't drunk alcohol in all the time she had known him.

'Just a couple of pints,' he answered her swiftly voiced query, though even if it had been only a couple of pints they both knew how dangerous even that could be to him.

'John, what's happening to you?' Moira asked rather sorrowfully. She stood in the hallway, looking at him, making no move to stand aside, to gesture him in, instead keeping him outside on the doorstep.

'Please can I come in?' he asked by way of reply. He thought he sounded pitiful, he knew he felt it. Anyway, at least she took pity.

Moira invited him in then, sat him down at the kitchen table and promptly made him an omelette, without much further comment. Her daughter Jennifer came in from somewhere or other and gave him a big hug. Kelly liked Jennifer, who had always seemed to return the feeling. But he wasn't capable of taking any interest in her that evening. He barely even hugged her back. Jennifer retreated looking vaguely puzzled. Apart from anything else, Kelly assumed she had smelled his breath. Like her mother, Jennifer knew his history well enough.

Moira studied him unenthusiastically as he ate his omelette gratefully but quickly and without enjoyment, just out of the need for food. He couldn't remember when he had last eaten a proper meal. He hoped it would help him feel better. As it was, one way and another he barely felt capable of proper conversation.

Moira sighed. 'I don't even know what you want from me any more,' she said eventually.

'I just want to be with you, I suppose,' he reasoned lamely.

'Well, that makes a change, anyway,' she replied. 'Your girlfriend away somewhere, is she?'

Kelly looked down at his plate. Ashamed. Moira got the message.

'Why am I not surprised? You're making a complete fool of yourself, John, you know that, don't you?'

He managed an awkward, uncertain smile. 'I'm just a bit confused, that's all . . .'

'*You're* confused, John? What about me? I thought we had something good going. Now I don't know what to think. And you're drinking again, after all that you've told me, all that it did to you before . . .'

He looked sheepish; tried to wriggle. 'Look, I said, just a couple of pints –'

'And the rest,' she interrupted sharply. 'In any case, John, what difference does it make how much you've drunk? All the years I've known you now I've never seen you touch a drop. You've always said that you couldn't, that if you did you'd be gone again –'

'Well, maybe I exaggerated.'

He didn't believe that, of course. Not really. He felt terrible. Maybe he was slightly drunk, after all. He supposed he must be after downing all that Scotch. He no longer understood why he had done so. He had some tough thinking to do, and one thing was certain: whisky wouldn't help. The bloody headache was back as well. He asked Moira if she had any aspirin. She left the room and returned with some, handing them silently to him.

'Can I stay?' he asked eventually.

'You've got a bloody cheek, John Kelly,' she replied.

But she did let him stay. And, slightly to his surprise, she let him make love to her. He was also half surprised both that he wanted to, and that he could. But he did. The sex was warm and nice and loving and familiar. And normal, he thought. He knew that everybody's definition of normality in sex was different, but he also knew that the sex he had with Angel far exceeded his definition of normality. When the excitement died down, when it was all over, he didn't even like to think about some of what they did together, and yet he was completely hooked on it, even though he never felt afterwards the peace that he felt after making love with Moira. That gave him a deep peace. Even that night. Even with all that was happening. He wished he had valued it more before he had in a way defiled it, for himself, anyway. However, he fell quickly into a sound sleep, something that had evaded him for days, and as he did so he was only vaguely aware that Moira was lying there next to him wide awake, just watching him.

In the morning he was grateful but sheepish. He knew, and Moira knew, that in spite of how good it had been to be together again, nothing would stop him going to Angel as soon as he had the opportunity. And Moira, of course, didn't know the half of it.

'Thank you,' he said to her.

She smiled ironically. 'I would say you're welcome, but I'm not sure you really are any more.'

He nodded in understanding. 'To be honest I'm surprised that you did, well, you know, that you would . . .' he stumbled inarticulately.

'Old habits die hard, maybe,' she replied caustically.

He didn't know quite what to make of that, but he was just relieved, really, that Moira hadn't tried to lecture him. Maybe she didn't see the point any more.

He made it into the office that day, only half an hour or so late. Nobody passed any comment on his two days' sickness, but he was well aware that he was no longer the most popular boy in class. There were plenty of sideways looks from his colleagues, and conversations seemed inclined to dwindle away whenever he passed by. Well, he supposed he would have been rather surprised if there hadn't been a deal of gossip around about his relationship with Angel, and already probably about his pub drinking bouts, brief though they had so far been. Torquay was a small town. His beat was a local evening paper, and if the guys he worked with hadn't already picked up on his antics they shouldn't have their jobs, Kelly thought to himself. He would have done so in their shoes, that was for certain.

Over the next couple of days Kelly only just managed to function without going under, either to the newly rediscovered oblivion of alcohol or to his various neuroses about Angel, or to all of that at once. He continued to phone Angel repeatedly, succeeding in neither catching her mobile nor gaining any reply from Maythorpe. Each day he took at least one run out to the house to check if she had returned. Also each day, he found himself drinking at some stage or another. What with that and his preoccupation with Angel and what he had seen on the videotape, on the third day he again didn't go to work at all. Neither did he bother to call in this time. He received at least three or four calls from Kit Hansford, which he managed successfully to avoid, as both his mobile and his digital phone at home obligingly told him who was calling.

At home on the evening of that third day his phone rang for the umpteenth time and he saw Angel's number flash on to the display panel. His heart leaped. He was so suspicious of everything about her, he had determined that he would give her a seriously hard time. He had even considered taking the incriminating tape to the police, hadn't he? Well, he kidded himself that he had, anyway. But he still couldn't help reacting the way he did, just to know that she was on the other end of a telephone.

'Are you coming over or what?' she enquired. Only it wasn't an enquiry, more of an order as usual. It was absurd. She had been away for four days, had not contacted him at all, and had been vague to him about her whereabouts, yet she made it sound as if he had been giving her the run-around. He knew he should tell her where to get off. Instead he obediently set off for Maythorpe Manor within minutes of being summoned.

He had drunk several whiskies, while desolately half watching something totally forgettable on TV. He knew he shouldn't be driving. But that didn't stop him. Not any more. His common sense seemed to be deserting him in spades. Nothing could have stopped him. He doubted an army would have stopped him. The mood he was in he reckoned he would have found a way round them. That was just how things were, and there didn't seem to be anything he could do about it.

When she opened the door to him she was wearing men's pyjamas several sizes too big for her. An old pair of Scott's perhaps? But he couldn't imagine Scott Silver in pyjamas of any sort, let alone the ones Angel had on. They were old-fashioned stripy cotton ones. The trousers were so long they draped over her feet in great folds. The bottom of the jacket reached almost to her knees. The left sleeve completely covered her hand and, in fact, the hem hung two or three inches below her fingers. She had rolled up the right sleeve several times so that it ended at wrist level, and in her right hand she held a large joint.

Her violet eyes were slightly glazed. Her face was pale as ever, the vermilion lipstick a little askew. She swayed gently as if being blown by a breeze that affected only her, and reached out with her left arm towards him. He could see the shape of her fingers inside the huge pyjama jacket sleeve as she struggled to free her hand from the material.

She looked so vulnerable. Kelly felt the usual almost unassailable desire to take her in his arms and protect her. And, of course, he also felt the usual desire to feel and taste her body, to enter her in every possible way. All the ways he had never experienced with anyone else.

Judging from her reaction it showed in his eyes, in his entire body language probably.

'Take me to bed,' she said huskily. Another command. But dope always seemed to make her even more randy. And he wondered – as he had done many times before, although he preferred not to think about it – just how much all the various drugs she hardly ever seemed to be totally free of were responsible for her extraordinary level of sexuality.

He took a step towards her. Such was the effect she had on him that only then did he remember why he had wanted to see her so much. And it wasn't, for once, to fuck her. It was to tell her about the tape, to confront her with what he had seen, what he had learned. He just had to do that. He realised at the same time that all he wanted was for her to come up with some plausible explanation, yet again. And the last thing in the world he wanted to do was to prove that Angel Silver had committed any crime at all, indeed done anything even morally wrong, let alone legally. Yet he always seemed to be trying to catch her out, which was why he had searched for that tape in the first place. It was quite paradoxical behaviour. He knew that. But he had to do it, he had to put it to her. Now that he had seen that videotape, he had no choice.

'Angel, we need to talk,' he told her quietly.

'Do we? How deeply boring,' she said, and started to undo the buttons of her pyjama jacket.

'No, Angel, I mean it,' he insisted. And she was probably so surprised that he should demur at anything she said or did that she allowed herself to be led, without dissension and without undoing any more buttons, into the living room.

He sat her down on the big sofa and drew up a more upright chair, slightly higher, so that he was facing her directly just a couple of feet away. He'd always known the psychological advantage of being able to look slightly down on someone you wanted to get to tell you something they might not wish to tell you. There was just a suggestion of intimidation in it.

'I've seen the video, Angel,' he said.

He thought there was a flicker of something in her eyes, as if she knew already, without further explanation, exactly which tape he meant. But if that was so then she made a very fast recovery.

'What video?' she asked ingenuously, eyes very wide, lips slightly apart, a picture of innocence.

'The video of what happened the night Scott was killed, the night you killed Terry James.' Kelly spoke very deliberately, almost spelling the words out, even though he strongly suspected it was not really necessary to do so.

'Oh, and how did you get hold of that then?' The violet eyes definitely flickered then. Angel's voice was calm, but there was just a touch of menace. Trust Angel to switch into attack mode like that, he thought.

'I expect you can guess how, can't you?'

'You haven't been snooping around here while I've been away by any chance, have you, John Kelly?' she asked, a hint of banter in her voice now as well as the menace.

'I wouldn't put it quite like that –'

'Well, I bloody would,' she interrupted him.

He sighed. 'Angel, it doesn't actually matter how I got hold of that tape, it doesn't actually matter whether you reckon I was snooping, it doesn't matter how out of order you think I've been. What matters is that I did find it and I have watched it. If the police had found it I doubt we'd be sitting here now on fancy fucking chairs in your great big opulent sitting room. I reckon you'd be banged up in jail where you might well belong. It's totally incriminating, Angel –'

She interrupted again. 'What do you mean, incriminating? I don't see what's incriminating about it.'

'Don't you? So why didn't you just hand it over to the police, then? You're not stupid, Angel – all sorts of things, but never stupid. I think you see very well. You didn't kill Terry James in self-defence. He was trying to get away from you. You went after him with the knife.'

Her face was expressionless at first. Then she lowered her eyelids as if offended but trying not to show it.

'Is that how it looks?' she enquired. She was cool, very cool. Impressively so. Her voice was still calm. But he could see that the hand protruding from the rolled-up right sleeve of the pyjamas was tightly clenched, the joint squashed carelessly between her fore and middle fingers.

'Yes it is,' he replied bluntly.

She couldn't keep it up then, her pretence of lack of concern.

'I was terrified out of my mind, for fuck's sake,' she yelled at him. 'Yes, I had the knife. The bastard dropped it after he killed Scott. For a second or two he looked almost as frightened as me, and that was even scarier. Terry James was a huge man, John. What was I supposed to do? Wait for him to pick the bloody knife up and use it on me? No! I grabbed it. Somehow or other I managed to react more quickly than he did. And once I had the knife, what was I supposed to do then? Wait again, for him to take it from me. If I hadn't got a blow in first he could have got it from me so easily. Like taking candy from a baby it would have been for a man his size. And I'd just watched him commit a murder. Do you honestly think he was going to let me live to tell the tale?'

'He was walking away, though –' Kelly began lamely, his voice uncertain.

'Taking a step or two backwards, nothing more. After all, I did have the knife,' she interrupted. 'But he wasn't going anywhere. He was going to come for me and he was going to kill me. I was absolutely sure of it. Tape or no tape, you couldn't see his eyes like I did. You should have seen his eyes, John. I didn't have a second's doubt. He was going to kill me. I had just one chance to kill him first. And I took it.'

Kelly tried to think clearly, to be dispassionate and rational, to look at things logically. He wished he hadn't drunk so much whisky. Angel might be doped up, but as ever it didn't seem to affect her ability to function. He suspected that if he had smoked half as much as she already had that day he would be unable to speak, let alone think. He concentrated hard.

'So, if that's what you honestly believe, I'll ask you again, why didn't you give that tape to the police?'

'You have to be joking! I didn't give it to them because they wouldn't have understood, would they? Wouldn't have wanted to, either. If you can behave the way you are having seen the bloody thing, what hope would I have with the Devon and Cornwall Constabulary, for fuck's sake? I'm telling you God's truth, John. You must know that, surely.'

He didn't know. It was terrible. He was in love with her. He hated putting that into words, even inside his head, but that was how it was. He was passionate about her. He was besotted by her. But he had no idea whether she was telling him the truth or not. It occurred to him that he never had had any idea whether she was telling him the truth or not. Not from the beginning. Not about anything.

'I don't know what I believe with you, Angel,' he told her, not for the first time.

'Well then, you should –' She stopped in her tracks, a look of panic setting in. 'John, you wouldn't give that tape to the police, would you?'

For a moment he felt the weight of the world on his shoulders. He sighed. 'Why on earth did you keep the bloody thing, Angel?' he asked.

'I don't know. Stupid of me, wasn't it? Habit, I suppose. We kept all the bonking tapes, it was like our own library of blue movies.' She laughed bitterly.

'Angel, this isn't a blue movie, it's a fucking snuff movie, and you're the only fucking killer it shows. How sick are you, for Christ's sake?'

She flinched away from him. 'Sick? You think I'm sick, d'you?' Her voice was suddenly very small.

He knew that was probably just another of her tricks. None the less, he hesitated before saying, 'Sometimes I do, yes.'

'But not when you're in bed with me, not then. You don't think at all then, do you?'

She was quick, very quick, and she was right, of course.

'No, not then, but don't imagine for one moment that makes me proud,' he snapped.

Her lower lip trembled. Her mood swings never ceased to amaze him. 'You sound as if you hate me,' she whispered.

'Hate you? I could never hate you. Sometimes I wish I didn't love you as much, that's all.'

'Please, John, I'm begging you, you won't go to the police with the tape, will you? Please tell me you won't. Please.' To his astonishment he saw that she had started to cry. He realised it was the only time that he had seen her weep since that first interview he did with her before her trial.

She reached out for him with both arms, one hand completely concealed in the pyjama jacket, the other still clutching her joint, which, unsurprisingly considering the treatment it had received, seemed to have gone out. The tears were pouring down her cheeks.

'I'm at your mercy, John,' she said. 'Please don't do it.'

Half of him knew it was manipulative nonsense. But he could not resist, of course. She seemed to him to be more vulnerable, more fragile than ever. He was, as usual, lost.

'I suppose not –' he began.

She gave him no chance to finish the sentence. She clamped her mouth on his mouth. The tears from her face ran on to his tongue. He tasted the salt. Her nose was pressed close to his. He breathed in her breath. Her tongue forced his lips apart and then pushed his tongue back, heading for his throat. Her hands pulled at his shirt front and the fastenings to his trousers.

That was the beginning. After that it was all so inevitable.

She carried him with her on a roller coaster of sensations, a frantic night-long seeking for the heights of sexual pleasure. It was dangerous, he knew that. To Kelly it was almost depraved. He actually felt that, even as it was happening, but he couldn't stop. Sometimes, he feared he would never be able to stop.

Kelly didn't go home for two days. Neither did he go to work, even though he knew he was already skating on very thin ice as far as his job was concerned. Neither did he contact anyone in his office to attempt to explain his absence. Not even Phyllis. Neither did he contact Moira. For two whole days and two nights he existed only with Angel on a high of sex, booze and drugs.

He was still kidding himself that he could handle it, all of it, but one half of him knew that he was kidding himself.

And when he did go home he was aware that it was probably only because he couldn't take any more.

None the less, the first thing he did was to play that tape again. Several times he watched it. And all he could ever see in Terry James's eyes was cold fear.

Seventeen

Later that evening Kelly walked to the nearest off-licence to buy a bottle of Scotch. He hadn't intended to do so, but he couldn't stop himself. The phone rang as he returned to his house. He ran to check the display, to see if it was Angel. It wasn't. It was Nick. Kelly couldn't face his son. He knew he was letting Nick down yet again, and he couldn't stop. It was the same as before. Once Kelly began drinking, drink took him over. That and Angel Silver. There was no room in his head for anyone else.

He ignored the phone, locked the front door and retreated to bed with the whisky. Again he kept watching the videotape. It was a kind of morbid fascination, another sort of obsession.

He set the video machine on auto play. When the tape reached its end it automatically rewound itself and started playing again, and would do so until he programmed it to stop. Each time he watched it he kept looking for some new clue to what had really happened, and, if he was truthful, some new way of vindicating Angel. That was all he really wanted to do.

He consumed the whisky steadily. Already he had started not to bother with a glass, instead drinking it straight from the bottle. Just like the old days, he had to admit, then dismissed the thought. It was not like the old days, he tried to reassure himself, it really wasn't, and he'd never let it be. Not again. Then he took another deep drink.

At some stage he must have fallen asleep. Something woke him, he had no idea how much later. He felt terrible, physically and mentally, slightly nauseous and very uneasy. The video was still playing. On the TV screen before him Scott and Angel were indulging in their lurid sex games. She was kneeling on the edge of the bed. Scott was standing behind her, looking at her, holding his huge dick casually in one hand. Kelly knew exactly what was going to happen next. He had seen it often enough. And the truth was that he liked watching that part of the movie, liked it a lot, even though he also knew well enough the horror which came later.

Then suddenly he became aware of movement in the room. Startled, Kelly turned his attention away from the screen and looked round. Moira was standing in the doorway, an expression of disgust on her face, her eyes fixed on the TV. Suddenly she gave a little gasp of horror. Kelly turned back to look at the screen just in time to see Scott entering Angel in the way he knew so well.

Frantically he scrabbled among the bedclothes for the remote control. He couldn't find the darned thing. Finally he hauled himself up from the bed, launched himself at the TV and fumbled for the off button. Eventually the images which he didn't want Moira to see faded away. At least he had managed to switch the darned thing off before Terry James appeared on the scene.

But what she had seen seemed to have done an effective enough job of shocking Moira.

'What kind of pervert are you turning into?' she asked him, her voice incredulous.

'I didn't want you to see that,' he replied lamely.

'I'm bloody sure you didn't, John,' she said. 'What else don't you want me to see? Have you also got videos of yourself in bed with that bitch, as well as her and her dead husband? And what sort of filthy perverted things do you two do together?'

Kelly made no reply. He couldn't look Moira in the eye. He really didn't know what to say to her.

'Maybe she brings out the real you, John,' Moira continued, slightly sarcastic now, but not convincingly so. Not like bloody Angel, that was for sure, he thought. Angel was the mistress of sarcasm.

'I'm off. I can't compete with that.' Moira cocked her thumb at the TV before continuing with some disdain: 'And I wouldn't want to either.'

Kelly felt cornered, put at a disadvantage. Unfairly so. This was nothing to do with Moira. She didn't understand what the tape was about. She didn't know what he was trying to do. Mind you, he wasn't entirely sure that he knew himself. Still, he decided to go on the attack.

'I didn't ask you to come here,' he told Moira nastily. 'I haven't invited you into my house. What are you doing in my house? And how did you get in?'

She looked hurt as well as angry.

'I used the key you gave me in the days when you were still a decent human being,' she snapped. 'And I only came round because I was worried about you. Nick's been trying to get hold of you – he's been worried too, and they're going mad at the paper. Joe Robertson phoned me. He's been trying to get in touch with you for days. He wants to know if you're ill. He said he'd been told you'd been seen hitting the booze in a pub. He wanted to know if it was true. That man stood by you, gave you a job when nobody else would touch you, John. Is this the way to reward him?'

Kelly shrugged his shoulders and sat down on the bed again. He didn't have the energy for any of this, he really didn't. He made no reply.

Moira came towards him, stood in front of him, put a hand on both his shoulders and, albeit quite gently, shook him.

'John, John, I just don't know what to say to you. You're destroying yourself again, I can see it happening.'

He pushed her hands away.

'Leave me alone, Moira. It's none of your business.'

'Isn't it? I've shared my life with you for seven years, John. That's a long time. We've been good together. We both had pasts we needed to get away from. We both needed to rebuild our lives, and we did it together. We worked things out, got something worthwhile going. I loved you. I still love you, damn it. And I thought you felt the same.'

Kelly shrugged again and looked away. It wasn't that he didn't care. He just couldn't cope.

Moira stepped back then. He could feel the intensity of her stare. His eyes were drawn to hers. He saw pity and disappointment. She had the look of someone who reckoned she had done all she could, a look that said she was about ready to give up on him. And that, it seemed, was exactly what she planned to do.

Abruptly she tossed his front door key on to the bed beside him.

'I'm not going to beg you, John. It's your life,' she said. 'If you want to throw it away, then do so. You're behaving like you're out of control. You do know you're making a complete fool of yourself in every possible way, don't you?'

'Just go away, Moira, just go away.' Kelly's voice was full of weariness. It wasn't what he wanted, not really, only that he didn't know what to say to her. She was right, of course, which made it worse. If he wasn't quite out of control he was damned near it. And he couldn't put a halt to it, not any of it. The suspicions he harboured about Angel just made his behaviour all the crazier.

He reached for the whisky bottle, which was on the floor beside the bed. There was just a dribble left. No wonder he felt awful. He'd drunk damned near a whole bottle already without even really realising it. He unscrewed the cap and drained the last dregs from the bottle straight into his upturned mouth.

Moira was still watching him.

'Just go away, please,' he said again. He didn't look at her. He couldn't. He had a sudden flashback inside his befuddled head of how it had been before when he'd been drinking seriously. If anybody had tried to help him he'd just kick them in the teeth.

'I'm going, don't worry,' she said, the hurt and disappointment as clear in her voice as it was in her eyes.

He sensed her move to the door, heard the familiar creak of the loose floorboard in the bedroom doorway. Still he didn't look up. But he knew somehow that she hadn't stepped out on to the landing yet, that she was still there, staring at him.

'What do you want me to tell Joe?' she enquired.

'Tell him what the fuck you like.'

There was no reply. The floorboard creaked again. Then he heard her footsteps on the stairs and the bang as she slammed the front door.

'Damn,' he muttered to himself through dry lips. 'Damn and damn again.'

He'd resolved to stay away from Angel for a few days, to try to clear his head, although he had just about enough sense left to realise that there was little chance of that now that he'd started to drink again. He couldn't stay away, though.

He picked up the phone to call her, to tell her he was coming round. Then he replaced the receiver. There was little point. In the first place she almost certainly wouldn't answer the phone – she hardly ever did – and in the second place he was afraid of giving her even the chance of saying that she didn't want to see him. He'd just go round unannounced. Surely they had reached the stage now where he could do that?

He pulled on his shoes, ran a hand over his stubbled chin, thought about shaving, then dismissed the idea. He held his hands in front of him. They were shaking quite violently. Whether that was as a result of the alcohol he had drunk or his nervous condition, he wasn't sure. One thing was certain, if he tried to shave he'd probably cut himself to ribbons.

He knew darned well he shouldn't be driving either. His head ached and he couldn't focus his eyes properly. He didn't know whether he was drunk exactly, didn't really think that he was, in fact. He'd slept for some time since drinking the bulk of the whisky, but he knew enough about the effects of alcohol to be well aware that it would be hours before his system had disgorged the alcoholic content of a bottle of the stuff.

However, he seemed to be past caring about anything except Angel.

She came to the door before he rang the bell. She was wearing a dress made of something flimsy in an orangy colour with big blue flowers on it. There were lavish frills at the neck and on the short, slightly puffed sleeves. The hem to the skirt, several inches above her knees, was ruffed. Angel had to be the only forty-year-old woman in the world who could get away with a dress like that, he thought, as he so often did about her clothes. But get away with it she did, as always.

She smiled at him wanly, stretched upwards on barefooted toes and pecked him quickly on the cheek. The violet eyes looked tired. For once there was no sign of the unnatural brightness which he always suspected came primarily with the effects of the cocaine she was so fond of. Her hair was slightly ruffled and looked squeaky clean. He thought she might have just had a bath or a shower. She smelled of soap. She was wearing no makeup. There were, as usual, deep shadows beneath her eyes, black flaws in pure porcelain. God, he thought, she's even paler than ever.

She stepped back to let him enter the house and shut the door behind him. Then she just stood there, very still, very fragile. And vulnerable. As always it was the vulnerability which got to him.

'I'm glad you've come,' she said. 'I've been worried, John.'

'Yes, so have I,' he said.

Neither needed to spell out what they were worried about. Obliquely he was suddenly very aware of his unshaven state, of eyes that he knew were red and bleary, of his crumpled shirt and trousers. Compared to her he felt so big, so dirty, so clumsy. He was sweating too. It seemed very warm in the house. He removed his leather jacket and stood holding it awkwardly for a moment. She took it from him, folded it and put it on the chair behind the door. Her hands were trembling slightly, like his, he thought. Only his was more than a slight tremble. Her nails were painted the same vermilion shade as the lipstick she usually wore, and the varnish on at least a couple of them was chipped. Her hands were very white and very thin, like the rest of her. Her fingers were twiglike, so narrow it seemed they must break if she undertook even the simplest of tasks with them. He felt the usual urge to protect her, to keep her safe.

And yet he needed reassurance too. It was as if, and not for the first time, she was able to read his mind.

'Look, John, I've told you everything, I've told you the truth. I just don't know whether you believe me or not. And if you don't, who else would? Please, John, I couldn't face another trial. I couldn't get through that, really I couldn't. You've no idea what the last trial did to me. You have to remember I was brought up never to let the act drop. Just because I don't wear my heart on my sleeve doesn't mean I didn't suffer. I went through hell, John. Please don't let that happen again.'

He could see the tears welling up in her eyes.

'Hold on, Angel. Calm down, darling,' he said. 'It isn't going to come to that.'

'It could if the police ever get hold of that bloody video, you know it could.' Her eyes were very wide. 'John, I might go to prison. I'm begging you, John. What would happen to me in prison? That would be the end of me, wouldn't it?'

She looked up at him, tears streaming down her cheeks now, lips trembling. 'That would be the end of everything.'

Yes it would, he thought. He would not be able to hold her close if she went to jail, he would not be able to spend all night with her in the big bed, he would lose her. He had no idea what the police would make of the video. He doubted that it would actually give them grounds to open another prosecution case, but it would certainly open a whole new can of worms.

'I do love you, John Kelly, you know that, don't you?' Angel continued.

He didn't. He loved her. And he'd told her so. She'd certainly never told him it before. And even as she said the words he still wasn't convinced. But, by God, he liked the sound of it. He ached for the woman. In spite of all his doubts he felt himself wavering.

She pushed closer to him.

'I really do, John, I really love you. I just do.'

He was lost. Totally lost. It was, of course, inevitable. Maybe he had only decided to come to her again in the way that he had because he wanted this to happen. He wanted to believe that she loved him, more, probably, than anything in the world. He was beguiled by her. He suppose he had always known that he could never betray her.

He reached out his arms for her and she half fell into them.

'I won't let that happen, Angel, I promise you, my darling,' he whispered. His mouth was furry and tasted of stale whisky. The inside of his head felt much the same. It was throbbing dully, and even without struggling to deal with the after-effects of what he had drunk, he knew he had no chance of thinking straight when he was with this woman. Sometimes it was as if that was what he wanted to happen. He just didn't want to think any more.

'So will you give me back the tape? Will you, John? Will you? Nobody else must see it, you know that, don't you?'

He was already lost. As always with her, he was totally lost.

'Yes, Angel, I'll give you back the tape. I'll not do anything to hurt you, you know that.'

In some ways Kelly could hardly believe what he heard himself saying. He was certainly aware that he must sound quite pathetic. He was also aware of how much he was under Angel's spell again, and that he was doing the wrong thing once more, going against all his best instincts. It didn't matter. He was a lost soul.

She reached up and kissed him passionately on the lips, pushing her breasts against his shirt front. Desire welled up in him – in spite of his weariness, in spite of the booze.

'Oh, John, oh, John, I knew you'd never let me down,' she whispered, her voice husky as she started kissing him again. Then, abruptly, she drew away.

'We must destroy the tape, that's what we have to do. It's the only way I'll feel safe now,' she said, and he knew she must be wishing that she'd done just that in the first place.

'All right,' he said, wanting only to keep her happy. 'I'll do it when I go home.'

'No,' she responded quickly, her voice sharp. Then more softly, she continued: 'No, John, bring it here. Let's do it together, then I'll know it's gone. Then I'll know it's not a threat any more. I'm so frightened.'

She pressed herself closer to him, stretching her face up towards his. He could feel her breath on his neck. It was almost like steam against his flesh.

'I'll do it tomorrow.' His attention had after all been most effectively diverted away from the videotape, as he'd probably always known that it would be.

'No!' Her voice was urgent and loud. 'No, John! Let's do

it now. Go and get it now, and bring it back to me. I won't be able to relax until it's done.'

In the end he gave in to her demands. When did he not, he wondered wearily as he turned into his St Marychurch street. In the hallway of his house he paused for a moment. The place felt cold and empty, almost as if it too were disapproving of his behaviour. He shrugged such absurd thoughts out of his mind, although he still believed houses could talk to you if you bothered to listen. He climbed the stairs to his bedroom, removed the videotape from under the mattress where he had stowed it in a vague attempt at some kind of security, and immediately left again, once more ignoring the telephone answering machine.

Back at Maythorpe Manor, Angel greeted him enthusiastically. There was something about her that led him to think she might have been at the coke again while he had been away.

'Have you got it? Good. Come with me then.'

She led him to a door beneath the stairs which he had previously assumed was just a cupboard. However, there was another staircase inside, leading down to a cellar he had not known existed. No wonder the house seemed so unusually hot. A huge cast-iron boiler was roaring away in the middle of a cavernous basement room.

He studied it in some surprise. Surely he'd noticed a modern oil boiler in the kitchen.

'That's the old solid-fuel boiler. It was here when Scott and I moved in,' explained Angel. 'We didn't want to rely on having to stoke up some ancient boiler every day so we installed a new state-of-the-art heating system, but we kept this as a standby in case of a problem with the other one.' She grinned. 'Jolly useful for disposing of things,' she added.

He glanced at her, wondering suddenly what else she might have disposed of in the boiler. Using a big pair of pliers she wrenched open the boiler's feed door. Not for the first time he thought how surprisingly strong she was for someone so small, who gave every appearance of fragility.

Once the iron door was open the heat of the fire became almost overpowering.

'Go on, throw the video in,' she commanded.

He hesitated only for a second or so before he did so, allowing himself to give no further thought to the immensity of what he was doing. The flames engulfed the black tape. It disappeared instantly into the white-hot molten mass within the boiler.

Angel closed the door to it at once and turned to him.

'I suppose that was the only copy,' she said, a sly note creeping into her voice.

'Of course.'

'Why of course? I'd have made another copy if I'd been you.'

Yes, thought Kelly, I bet you would. But all he said was: 'Well, you're not me, are you?'

'You really didn't copy it?'

'No.' And that was the truth. Extraordinary really, thought Kelly. He didn't quite know why he hadn't copied the tape. He only had one video recorder in his house, the one in his bedroom, but that was just a technicality. He had not even considered it. Of course, he'd been drinking so heavily over the last few days that he had lost his impetus to do anything much. But the truth was that all he had ever wanted, once he had acquired the tape and watched it, was for Angel to explain away what he had seen on it.

Which she had done. Or had she? Kelly didn't really know. More than anything he wished his head would stop aching, but that seemed to be an almost permanent state nowadays.

They climbed up the stairs again to the ground floor. As they passed the library he glanced in through the open door. The false wall which concealed the priest's hole was open.

He jerked his head towards Angel and looked at her questioningly. He had a feeling she had not lit that huge boiler just to burn one tape.

'I thought it was time for all the tapes to go,' she replied to his silent query. 'They were too dangerous. And, anyway, now that Scott's dead, well, it's not the same . . .'

No, thought Kelly. Was he then such a poor substitute? Oh God, he wondered, why was he so obsessed with his sexual prowess, or lack of it, when he was with Angel?

Unexpectedly her face broke into a big grin. 'We can start a whole new video library, if you like, John,' she said.

Kelly shook his head. He didn't particularly enjoy being reminded of that side of their sex life, although he could hardly deny the kick he got out of watching the two of them in bed together.

'Did you mean what you said earlier?'

'What was that?' She looked quite ingenuous. Had the words meant so little to her?

'That you loved me,' he replied flatly.

Her eyes were very wide open and quite unfathomable as usual.

'Absolutely,' she told him.

Eighteen

They went to bed, their activities aided as usual by a heady mixture of dope and coke. Kelly got an almost desperate relief from being in bed with her again. She was as passionate as ever. Not for the first time he told himself she could not give so totally if she didn't care about him. But he knew really that the sex they indulged in together was not about caring. It was the most torrid he had ever known, and he remained thrilled by it. Yet as he lay back on the bed afterwards he was aware that he felt sated rather than satisfied. Certainly there was no peace.

Then just before midnight Angel suddenly announced that she wanted to go clubbing. Kelly was surprised. They had never gone out anywhere together.

'I'm bored,' she said.

Kelly studied her wearily. He should be used to her mood changes by now, he supposed, but she did have the knack of never ceasing to surprise him.

'I'm tired, Angel,' he responded.

She pouted at him sulkily. 'Scott and I used to go out all the time.'

Kelly didn't think that was true. Not in Torquay, anyway. He'd have heard. In any case he really was tired. Bone tired. He just wanted to go to sleep. He felt emotionally drained, and the soporific aftermath of the whisky he had drunk, not to mention the joint he had shared with Angel, seemed stronger than the rush of nervous energy he would expect to have been generated by the cocaine he had snorted, but he had only taken one small line.

'Not now, Angel, surely,' he protested lamely.

'Why not?' she enquired, adding mischievously, 'Are you ashamed to be seen out with me?'

Nothing, of course, could have been further from the truth. He loved the idea of being seen around town with Angel Silver on his arm. She was a widow and he was single – well, not living with anyone. Though that had, until recently anyway, not been true in spirit, as he knew very well. He was aware, even half stoned, that he had betrayed Moira and was continuing to do so.

There was nothing he could do about that now, he told himself. He had blown that relationship for good, and when he was with Angel, of course, he didn't even care. So far his liaison with Angel had been conducted as if it were a clandestine affair, with him often turning up in the middle of the night, lying to Moira and his friends and colleagues. The prospect of them going public had never been raised. They had never even been to the pub together, never been out for a meal in a restaurant. In fact they hardly ever ate. Kelly pulled himself up into a sitting position and looked disconsolately down over his body. You would have thought that at least one good thing to have come out of all this would have been that he might have lost his paunch. He hadn't. It didn't seem to have diminished at all. He supposed that was the booze.

He turned to look at Angel, who was lying naked on the bed beside him. If only he could give her a few of his excess pounds. She remained so painfully thin, and so beautiful, he thought yet again. Even through the haze of the alcohol and assorted drugs which were fighting each other inside his head, he experienced that familiar, almost painful pang of deep tenderness for her, a tenderness he had become resigned to never being returned.

Of course, Kelly realised, life with Angel Silver was always going to be different from anything he had experienced before. And if they started going out together he would have to get used to the likelihood of her being recognised wherever they went. Any kind of outing for him and her was bound to be more than just a night on the town. It would be a statement. He battled with his weariness.

'Ashamed to be seen out with you? You've got to be kidding,' he replied, then added with a grin, 'I'm just not sure

I have the energy, that's all. You're an exhausting woman, you know.'

She smiled her Mona Lisa smile. 'C'mon,' she said. 'Do another line.'

Obediently he complied, this time snorting up a much larger amount of the fine white powder through the rolled-up tenner that she passed to him. And this time it hit the spot instantly. The lethargy of the whisky and the joint he had smoked earlier just disappeared.

His brain was buzzing. Suddenly he felt a hundred per cent alive and awake. He could conquer the world probably. He could certainly do the town.

'Right,' he said, almost jumping out of bed. 'What are you waiting for, my darling?'

It took Angel only seconds to pull on a skimpy black dress. All he had was the jeans and sweater he had arrived in earlier, plus his trusty leather jacket. She didn't seem to mind. Neither of them had showered. He guessed they must both smell of sex. He pulled her close to him, buried his face in her neck, in her hair, in the tantalising cleavage at the low-cut neckline of her dress. He was right, she did smell of sex. Strongly. And how he liked that. He felt his cock stir, pulled her still closer to him. God, he felt good. He was sure he could fuck her all night. Maybe he wouldn't let her persuade him to take her out after all.

She pushed him gently away. 'Later,' she said, brushing her right hand lightly over his crotch, then grabbing his hand and pulling him towards the door.

'Oh, all right,' he responded grudgingly. Then a thought occurred to him. He hadn't a clue where to take her. Late-night clubs were hardly his scene.

'Where are we going anyway?' he asked.

'Valbonnes, of course,' she said.

He'd heard of it, and knew where the place was in Upper Union Street, close to the town centre, but had never been there. It was hardly Tramp or Annabel's, but, knowing Angel, probably the nearest Torquay got to either of those.

He tripped over the first wide step outside the house, and was only prevented from falling by Angel's grip on his hand.

They started to giggle. They were still giggling when they climbed unsteadily into the MG.

Afterwards Kelly had no idea why they hadn't called a taxi. No idea why he had not even considered whether he was fit to drive. That, of course, was what coke did to you – made you believe you were indestructible, above the law, above pain, superior, sharper, invincible.

They never got to Valbonnes. They never even got to Torquay. At the road junction between Rock Lane and the main road into town, Kelly drove straight out without pausing to look. Or at least he attempted to. Inside his coked-up head he had seen no reason to stop. It was partly as if he believed the rest of the world would get out of his way. Partly that he no longer knew what he was doing. He smashed straight into the side of small saloon car travelling law-abidingly along the road at right angles to him.

Kelly couldn't get out of the car. His first coherent thought after the accident was that he was trapped. The driver's door wouldn't open. It had been buckled by the force of the collision. His second realisation was of a sharp stabbing pain in his abdomen and that his head felt seriously woozy now. In fact, it felt rather as if it didn't belong to him at all. He was vaguely aware that he had been drinking and that he taken coke, so it could just be that which was making his head feel so strange. He reached up a hand. There was already a swelling forming on his right temple. Somehow or other he'd managed to bump his head, it seemed, although, miraculously, he was wearing a seat belt. He had a vague feeling that he might have been knocked unconscious for a minute or two. He wasn't sure. His brain just wouldn't work properly. He wasn't sure of anything.

The front of the MG had caved in. The bonnet was buckled and the remains of the engine was spouting steam. There seemed to be a lot of noise in the road around Kelly, mostly screaming and shouting. He realised that the screaming came from the car with which he'd obviously collided. The MG's windscreen had smashed and he could see very little of anything that might be happening in front of him. He became aware of someone tugging on the handle of the driver's door from the outside. It still wouldn't budge.

He felt terrible. He really had no comprehension of what had happened. Angel. Angel was with him. Was she all right? He turned towards her anxiously. She wasn't there.

He tried to look out of the driver's side window, peering into the darkness, which was punctuated now by the lights of other vehicles and one much smaller light which was moving erratically. For a moment he was puzzled by that and then a brief flash of clarity entered his spinning head. It was a torch, of course. He could see figures moving but they were just black shapes. He had no idea whether or not one of them was Angel.

The soft top of the little car had snapped open like a big gaping black mouth. Kelly tried to push it further back so that he could climb out, over the boot or the bonnet perhaps, but it too had jammed somehow. As he pushed, though, he strained himself upwards and over the MG's shattered windscreen and could see the car he had hit. The near side of it had caved right in and the force of the impact had jammed the car against a wall on the far side of the main road. Kelly's headlights no longer even existed, but there was a motel on the other side of the road, and its lights cast enough illumination for him to make out two figures trapped inside and to see that the one nearest him, in the remains of the passenger seat, a woman he was almost sure, was slumped back, unmoving, with blood pouring out of the side of her head. He could also see the mouth of the figure in the driver's seat opening and shutting. That was the person doing the screaming, the quite awful nerve-shattering screaming, he realised. It was like a horror movie unfolding before his eyes.

Panic as well as pain engulfed him. He had to get out, had to get away. Even above the clamour and the dreadful screaming he could hear the beat of his own heart, pumping, pumping, far too fast. He was hyperventilating. He felt as if no breath at all was getting into his lungs. He had to free himself from the smashed vehicle. He just had to. Suddenly he noticed that the MG's passenger door was slightly ajar. He had no idea why he had not seen that before, but then he was barely functioning. He felt very peculiar and it occurred to him obliquely that he might be quite badly hurt. He began to manoeuvre himself over the arm rest and gear lever system between the car's two seats, pushing himself upwards with his feet and trying to crawl across towards the open door. But the shooting pains in his abdomen immediately became agonising. It felt as if he was being stabbed repeatedly by something jagged like a piece of broken glass – and that thought brought unwelcome images into his mind too. He cried out with the pain and collapsed across the seats, unable to push himself any further. For a few seconds the stabbing sensation, the unnerving thump thump thump of his heart and his inability to breathe properly were all he was aware of. Then the door of the MG opened fully, strong arms reached through it, and he was half pulled, half lifted out on to the street.

There was a powerful smell of oil and petrol. Kelly's car was still hissing steam. He could feel his legs buckling beneath him. The arms lowered him gently to the ground at the roadside. For a moment he just slumped there, only vaguely aware of the commotion which now seemed to be all around him. Then he hoisted himself on to one elbow.

'Angel,' he called. 'Angel, where are you?'

He tried to stand up, but he just fell down again.

Someone, he had no idea who, put a restraining hand on his shoulder.

'Steady, now, mate. Take it easy . . .'

He could hear the words clearly enough, but it was as if they were somewhere in the distance.

'Where's Angel?' he asked. 'Where's . . . where's . . .'

He couldn't quite get the words out, even though he knew exactly what he was trying to say. Eventually he managed it.

'The woman I was with, w-where is she? Is she all right?'

'I didn't see no one with you, mate.' It was the same voice, a man's voice. The man who had pulled him out of the car and then tried to reassure him. 'And I was first on the scene . . .'

'But she was there. What's happened to her?'

'Anybody see a woman in the MG?' The man raised his

voice. There seemed to be a number of people around now, mostly surrounding the other vehicle, and there were a few mumbled responses, but Kelly couldn't quite make them out. He could hear the wail of sirens. Vehicles with flashing lights were approaching at speed. He realised, even in his befuddled state, that these were ambulances and police cars arriving. It occurred to him vaguely that he might be in serious trouble as well as injured.

'No, mate, nobody's seen no woman,' the same male voice continued. 'You was on your tod in the car, time I got here. Maybe you're just mixed up, aye?'

Kelly tried again to get to his feet. Where the hell was Angel? Had she just gone off and left him to face the music, just walked away, not even bothering to find out how badly hurt he was? Surely she wouldn't have done that. The thoughts were all jumbled up inside his head, which was really starting to swim.

The man who had been talking to him came closer, and put his hands on Kelly's shoulders in an attempt to stop him from trying to move. Kelly couldn't even see him. There was only blackness in front of his eyes now. He realised he was about to pass out. Maybe for the second time.

The last words he heard before he did so, were: 'Jesus Christ, he's drunk. That's what's wrong with the bastard. He's drunk as a skunk.'

Kelly came to in Torbay Hospital to find Moira sitting by his bedside. Instinctively he raised a hand to his forehead, which was throbbing for England, and as he did so the movement caused shooting pains in his abdomen. He grunted involuntarily.

Moira passed no comment on his obvious discomfort. Her face looked pinched and sad.

'I don't know what I'm doing here,' she said. She looked fed up, totally exasperated, angry, perhaps as much at herself as at him. 'I spend quite enough time in this place without coming back in when I'm off duty to see someone who's behaved like a raving lunatic.'

'Well, thanks anyway.' Kelly was desperately trying to

remember through the pain what had put him in hospital in the first place, what his latest felony had been. But when he did begin to remember he wasn't sure that he wanted to.

Moira was continuing to speak. 'They called me from casualty soon after you were brought in. But to be perfectly honest, John, I'm inclined to wish they hadn't. And I really wish they hadn't known that you were the man I shared my life with. Or used to!'

She put a sharp emphasis on the last three words. Kelly winced.

'You know what gossip's like in this place. Everyone knows the state you were in and what you've done, which is really absolutely terrific.'

'I'm sorry,' said Kelly.

'You're going to be,' said Moira feistily. 'You know you're going to be done, don't you? Drink driving at the very least. Quite probably something much more serious . . .'

Her voice tailed off. Kelly thought, in as much as he could think, that he already knew well enough what she was getting at. He could suddenly see all over again the awful tableau that had unfolded in front of him when he had peered out of the battered MG.

'The people in the other car . . .?' he began, afraid to finish the query.

She knew what he meant. 'The passenger was badly hurt, a woman, I have no idea how badly.'

'B-but she'll be all right, will she?'

'I've no idea, John. You'll have to ask the police. There were a couple of constables here earlier. No doubt they'll be back.'

Kelly nodded his head, which was a mistake. It ached dreadfully. Not the dull ache caused by getting stoned and having too little sleep, which he had been becoming used to, but a quite viciously acute ache. No doubt they would, he thought, gritting his teeth and trying not to show how much pain he was in.

'I was afraid somebody might have died . . .' His voice tailed off again.

'They might still, for all I know,' said Moira. She was

angry, and it showed. She was certainly making no attempt to be gentle with him, and he didn't blame her.

Kelly started to imagine himself facing prosecution for causing death by dangerous driving as well as a drink driving charge. He supposed there could be drug charges too. Christ, they'd lock him up and throw away the key, he thought. Then fleetingly he was ashamed of himself. Not only had he almost certainly caused a terrible accident but he was already more concerned about what would happen to him than the state of the people in the other car.

Then another thought overcame him.

'Angel?' he queried. 'Is she all right? Has anyone seen her?'

Moira stiffened. She brushed her blonde fringe back off her forehead, not once but several times. It was a gesture Kelly had seen her make before, invariably when she was upset or angry.

'What has that woman got to do with anything?'

'She was in the car with me. I d-don't know what happened to her.'

Moira gave a little sigh. 'Well, if she was in the car with you that's the first I've heard of it. The police certainly don't think there was anyone else in the car.'

Kelly really wasn't thinking straight. 'She was, I'm sure she was . . .'

Only suddenly he wasn't quite so sure any more – not of anything except that he knew his head was in a mess. And his gut. Just the effort of talking caused his abdomen to remind him of its injuries, whatever they might be. He didn't even know what damage he had done to himself yet. He tried desperately to concentrate. Maybe Angel hadn't been in the car. She had, though, hadn't she? And in that case, she really must just have run off . . .

Moira was studying him, looking as if she could read his mind. She shook her head.

'I was hoping this might have brought you to your senses, John,' she said. 'It hasn't, though, has it? I can see that in you.'

He did not reply.

*

Moira was right, of course. As she all too often was.

As soon as he was told he could leave hospital Kelly had two aims in mind. He wanted a drink – he knew that was asking for further even bigger trouble but he couldn't help it any more – and he wanted to find Angel. The first was easily accomplished at a pub just around the corner from the hospital. A pint of bitter and two large whisky chasers made him feel slightly better. He had giving up even kidding himself about drinking. His alcohol dependency had returned with a vengeance, and he knew it.

He had been lucky in one respect, at any rate. The injuries to the woman passenger in the car he had hit were not quite as severe as he had feared. She had a broken leg, but the gash on her head, which had looked so awful to Kelly and had spouted so much blood, had proved to be merely superficial.

None the less, he had been charged with dangerous driving in addition to the drink driving charge. As was routine with drink driving offences, it would be fast-tracked through the local magistrates' court within a couple of weeks. His beloved MG, not surprisingly, was a write-off.

Kelly's own injuries, although painful, had also proven not to be too serious. He had three cracked ribs in addition to the bump on his head which had caused him to black out. He looked terrible, however. His head injury had resulted in two black eyes and the pain from his damaged ribs meant that he could not stand fully upright, instead walking with a pronounced stoop. In the pub he was aware of people staring at him curiously.

Predictably enough, Kelly's second aim, to find Angel, proved more difficult. He took a taxi out to Maidencombe but he somehow knew as soon as he arrived at Maythorpe Manor that Angel was not there. It was strange how he could tell just from looking at the house that it was empty. The sun was shining brightly over the sea, which you could just glimpse through the trees beyond the big house. It was a beautiful day. Kelly didn't even notice.

He asked the taxi driver to park outside the gates. Then he pumped the security code into the electronic system. Nothing happened. Had she changed the code? For a dreadful moment he thought that she must have done, and that she was shutting him out. He had driven his car while stoned half out of his mind and he had nearly killed innocent people. Yet all he could think about was Angel. Could she really have been so uncaring not only to have left him at the scene of the crash, but just to have disappeared? He tried the code again. There was a beep and a click. The big gates opened soundlessly. He must have keyed in the numbers wrongly. He glanced down at his hands. They were trembling.

He tried the front door. Locked. Which was probably another indication that Angel was not inside as she continued hardly ever to seem to bother to lock the door when she was. In his pocket he still had the stolen key she had never demanded back. The door unlocked as smoothly as ever, though the small amount of physical effort required caused him to double up slightly with the pain from his damaged ribs. As he stepped into the hallway he called her name. He knew it was pointless but did so all the same. There was no reply. He walked slowly through the house, checking every room. There was no sign of her.

Disconsolately he left the mansion, slamming the door shut behind him, and made his way out through the gates and back in the taxi. He gave the driver his home address. On the way he tried Angel's mobile number yet again. One last time, he told himself. He would walk away from her, he really would. He would rebuild his life yet again. He would patch things up with Moira. He really would.

He expected to receive no reply from Angel's mobile, but on the second ring she answered. He was momentarily taken aback. He had got used to having virtually no contact with her except when she orchestrated it.

'Hello?'

'Is that you, Angel?'

'No, my mobile is public property. I rent it out, didn't you know?'

Sarcasm again. Perhaps it was a defence mechanism with her, he didn't know. He did know he was tired of it, but he decided not to allow himself the luxury of reacting.

'I – I've been looking for you,' he stumbled.

'I thought it might be a good idea to go away for a bit.' She sounded unhurried, languid – no, beyond languid, sleepy. As if she were in bed, he thought suddenly, and had just been awakened by the call. He checked his watch: 5 p.m. Why should she be in bed at 5 p.m.? His heart sank. His imagination began to run riot. This was ridiculous. He struggled to get a grip.

'So you just left me in the car? Just like that? I've been charged with dangerous driving. I was three times over the alcohol limit. I could go to jail.'

He sensed a shrug at the other end of the phone.

'It would have been even worse if I'd stayed around. Think of the publicity.'

'I can't believe you just went.'

'You were driving, John.'

'And whose idea was it to go clubbing in the first place?'

'Don't be a baby, John. If you play with fire sometimes you get burned.'

'God, you can be a bitch, Angel.'

'Really?' She sounded cool, amused even. 'In that case you won't want to talk to me, will you? I'll just say goodbye then.'

'Wait, wait. Angel, when are you coming back here? Or can I come to you? I need to see you.'

After a bit he realised he was talking to an empty phone. He kicked himself mentally. Even with all that had happened, the way she continued to treat him, he had ended up begging to see her, or damned near. And what he had said was absolutely right: he did need her. Yet, knowing as she must that he had been injured in the smash, she hadn't even asked how he was.

The taxi driver was very quiet. Kelly realised he would have been listening to every word. He knew he should care, but he didn't. He wrapped his arms round his damaged ribcage. All he wanted to do now was to kill the pain, both emotionally and physically.

'Change of plan, mate,' he said. 'Take me to the Fitzroy Arms.'

*

They found him three days later slumped in the middle of Castle Circus roundabout. Unshaven and filthy, he was lying in his own urine and vomit. As well as the bump on his forehead, which he had received in the car crash, Kelly now had a bloodied nose and a cut on one cheek. The black eyes that had resulted from the earlier incident had started to fade, but one of them at least appeared to have received a further blow. It was badly swollen and the lids looked as if they were glued together. Kelly was lying awkwardly and his breathing was shallow.

PC Perkins, the young constable who found him, also noticed that his lower left arm looked twisted and wondered if it had been broken. He thought that Kelly might have other, unseen injuries too. There was little doubt that he had been badly beaten up.

It was early morning, about 5.30 a.m., and it seemed obvious to PC Perkins that Kelly had spent the night at Castle Circus in a more or less unconscious state. It was only mid-April but, luckily for Kelly, the night had been dry and unseasonably warm. His wallet and two empty bottles of whisky were by his side. PC Perkins carefully checked the wallet and was unsurprised to find that it contained no money. Not any more, he thought. He did, however, find Kelly's press card, which he reported as soon as he called in.

The duty sergeant, Stanley Smith, was a long-serving officer who always liked to cover his back. He called DCI Meadows as soon as he had spoken to PC Perkins. Like almost every police officer in the region Stan Smith knew of Karen Meadows' friendship with the reporter, which was a constant topic of station banter with much ribald speculation about how it had all started.

The DCI was just stepping out of the shower when she took the call. For two or three minutes she listened in weary silence while Sergeant Smith related the night's events.

'I'm sorry to bother you, ma'am, but I thought you'd like to know.'

Karen wrapped an inadequate towel tightly round herself. She was still wet and she was shivering with the cold. She was also upset and angered by the news she had heard. What was

Kelly thinking about? As if she didn't have a bloody good idea.

'I'm not sure that *like* is quite the right word, Stan,' she said. 'But thanks anyway.'

Karen rubbed herself dry and dressed quickly. She moved into the kitchen, made a cup of tea and sat at the table by the window, looking out over the bay. Sophie immediately jumped on her lap. Absently she scratched the cat's head. The early morning had been bright and sunny, but the sky had darkened and it was just starting to rain. The sea was getting up too. Kelly really had been lucky, with the weather at least, she thought. As for anything else, Karen was not sure that she wanted to know any more. Kelly was becoming an embarrassment, professionally and personally, and Karen still had this niggling feeling that the Scott Silver case, in which she had reason to believe Kelly had become deeply embroiled, was far from over. The sensible thing would be for her to end her friendship with Kelly once and for all. She had always known that he was potentially a loose cannon, but she had never thought he would get himself into this mess. Not again.

He was not only facing a serious criminal charge, he seemed to have pushed the familiar old self-destruct button in all directions. She had been well aware that he was drinking again even before the accident, and she had known him before when his drinking had got out of control. She was also familiar with the rumours about Angel Silver. If they were true, and she believed that they were, she still found the concept of some kind of affair between the rock star's widow and the veteran journalist extremely puzzling. Perhaps disloyally she was unable to grasp why Angel would get involved with Kelly. He really didn't seem to be the type who would hold much attraction for the likes of her. The DCI could see clearly enough the attraction Angel would have for Kelly. Every man who came into contact with the bloody woman seemed to fall under her spell. But Karen really would have thought that Kelly, soft touch though she knew he could be, was old enough and streetwise enough to have avoided getting entangled. He *had* got entangled, though, there was no doubt about that. And he had allowed himself to become involved in the murky word of mind-altering drugs, which she had always suspected Angel Silver was into.

As Karen finished her tea and prepared to leave for the station her phone rang again. It was Moira, calling from the hospital.

'Look, do you know about John?' she asked bluntly.

Karen said that she did.

'They brought him in an hour ago,' Moira related. 'I was still on duty. The word got to me in no time. Typical of this place . . .'

Her voice tailed off. Karen didn't know what to say. She hadn't even known that Moira had her home phone number. She'd certainly never called before.

'I can't believe the state he's in,' Moira continued. 'I was hoping you might be able to tell me what happened.'

'Yes, of course,' said Karen. 'Well, as much as we know, anyway, which I'm sure isn't everything.'

She liked Moira a lot. And she still liked John Kelly, in spite of everything. Half of her wanted to help all she could. The other half wanted to keep out of it. Protect herself. She did have her career to think about, after all. And the part Kelly had played in her past was now a very long time ago.

Moira picked up on her lack of enthusiasm.

'Look, I'm sorry to call you at home like this. I got your number from John's diary. He still had that in his trouser pocket. It's just that I've been trying to find him for days, you see. I knew he hadn't been in to work and I didn't think he'd been home either. I was planning to report him missing today. If only I could find out exactly what's been going on maybe I could make some sense of things. I try not to care, I really do. But, well, you know how it is . . .'

Karen relented, as she might have known she would. She did know how it was. There was something about Kelly that had always drawn Karen towards him. There had been times, in her mind anyway, when their friendship could perhaps have developed into something else. She certainly understood Moira's feelings for him. She also had a pretty good idea of how Kelly had been behaving lately, how he must have been treating Moira, who really did not deserve the shit she was having to deal with.

And so Karen told Moira all about how and where Kelly had been found, and how he had apparently been beaten up and robbed.

'But what happened before that?' asked Moira. 'Where was he for all that time and who would do such a thing to him?'

Karen sighed. This was just the sort of area she didn't want to enter into.

'It seems likely that he'd been on a bender more or less since he came out of hospital the last time,' she said. 'We don't know who beat him up. It could just have been a chance thing, thugs having a go at a drunk to get his wallet. Or it could have been something else, we just don't know yet.'

'What do you mean, something else?' Moira asked sharply. 'Something to do with Angel Silver, I suppose.'

'Well, indirectly, yes,' replied Karen cautiously.

The thought had occurred to her, of course, that Ken James or other members of the James family could well have been responsible for giving Kelly a hiding. But she had no proof. She also had little doubt from Moira's tone of voice that the other woman was well aware of Kelly's liaison with Angel Silver, and that was something she really didn't want to discuss either. She was relieved when Moira didn't push her on that issue.

Instead Moira merely enquired, 'Was John alone when he was found?'

But Karen immediately knew what she was getting at. However, the very thought of Angel Silver spending the night on the Castle Circus roundabout was so ludicrously wonderful that it actually made Karen Meadows smile in spite of everything. Although Karen was well aware of Angel's turbulent past, and was growing increasingly uneasy, following the albeit unsubstantiated rantings of Bridget Summers, about the events of the night when Scott Silver and Terry James had died, she remained quite sure that Angel Silver was the type who hardly ever lost control. Unlike Kelly.

Karen Meadows could still remember very clearly the first time John Kelly had pushed the self-destruct button. It saddened her that he had done so again, but did not particularly surprise her. He had always been that kind of man.

It also saddened her that she really could not help him any more.

'He was quite alone apart from two empty bottles,' she told Moira.

Nineteen

Kelly woke up in a hospital bed again. It was beginning to become a habit.

He ached all over. He didn't think he could move, and, in any case, he didn't dare. His left arm appeared to be in a sling. He had no idea whether it was broken or not. His ribs hurt even more than they had first time round. His stomach felt empty, yet it was all he could do not to retch. He was afraid that if he did his ribcage would just fall apart. There was an acrid taste of bile at the back of his throat. His whole face was sore. His mouth hurt particularly badly and there was a throbbing pain behind his eyes which felt as if they were glued together.

He couldn't remember, of course, exactly what had happened to him or how he came to be in hospital again in such a state. But he knew he'd been on a terrific drinking bout. He had a vague memory of a succession of pubs and clubs, and of kipping on some itinerant drinking companion's sofa at some stage, and then he recalled being very cold, and aware that he was lying on the ground somewhere outdoors after dark. There had been a road. No, a roundabout. Or had there? It was all so hazy. After that all he could remember was pain. He winced. Yes, somebody, more than one somebody he thought, had used him as a punch bag. He had no idea whether or not it had been somebody he knew. No idea at all.

Very slowly and carefully Kelly attempted to open his eyes, or at least to do so as best he could. There was someone sitting on a chair by the bedside again. At first he couldn't even make out who it was, then his vision began to clear a little. Moira? No. It wasn't Moira. Not this time. No. It was Nick. And the expression on his son's face said it all. One of

Kelly's eyes wouldn't open at all and the other wasn't focusing properly. But he could see Nick quite well enough. Nick's eyes were red-rimmed and full of reproach. Kelly could think of nothing to say. Then Nick lowered his head, and cast his gaze down at the ground as if he did not really want to see his father at all. Kelly didn't blame him.

For two or three minutes there was total silence in the room. Nick made no attempt to speak at all.

'Hello, son,' Kelly managed eventually. It was a big effort to move his lips, which were obviously quite badly bruised and swollen. His tongue found a broken tooth. He could taste blood.

Nick didn't reply, but he raised his eyes again and looked his father full in the face. Kelly could feel his son's disappointment and he was ashamed. But the only way he knew of coping with his shame was to hide it as best he could.

'I didn't know you were about,' he remarked, struggling for normality, trying to pretend that it was perfectly normal for a middle-aged professional man to go on a three-day bender and be found half unconscious in the middle of a roundabout, having been punched silly and probably robbed, if his memory was even partly working, Kelly thought.

'Moira called me,' said Nick flatly.

'Ah.' Kelly slumped back on the pillows. He didn't know what else to say. He knew what he needed – a very large drink. His throat was parched. The old familiar craving for alcohol nagged at the core of him. He could hardly believe he had reached that stage so quickly, but he knew that he had.

Suddenly Nick stood up, eyes blazing. 'You're a fucking disgrace, Dad, you know that, don't you?' he shouted.

'I guess,' said Kelly.

'It's that bloody Silver woman, isn't it?' Nick continued, still shouting. 'You're under her spell, aren't you, you stupid bastard? And I didn't need Moira to tell me that. I could work it out for myself.'

Kelly didn't reply. He had nothing to say.

'I was just a kid when you did this before, when you just walked out on Mum and me, and I've spent the rest of my life fucking well making excuses for you,' Nick went on.

'Sorry,' said Kelly lamely.

'I've heard that before, Dad, and all I'm here for today is to tell you that I never want to do that again. Not as long as I live. There are no excuses for you any more, there really aren't. I just don't want to see you again, do you understand that?'

'I understand,' muttered Kelly, trying desperately to clear his fuddled brain. 'But I want to see you, you know that.'

'Do you?' stormed Nick. 'Well, tough shit. I don't think you give a fuck, in any case. You might kid yourself that you do, but you don't. You never did in my opinion. Not about me or Mum, not ever, and now I don't think you do about Moira. She doesn't fucking well deserve you, in fact nobody fucking deserves you. The only person you ever seem to have cared about is that flash bitch Angel Silver, and she's probably the only one who treats you the way you should be treated. Like the scum that you are.'

Kelly recoiled on to the pillows, almost as if Nick had punched him. He had never heard his son swear like that before, never seen him lose his temper, rarely heard him raise his voice. He had often congratulated himself on the well-adjusted, even-tempered son he had somehow managed to produce, a young man so very different from his father, Kelly had thought.

But this was a new kind of Nick. Neither had realised that Kelly's behaviour could give rise to that level of emotion in Nick.

'Look, I'm sorry,' Kelly began again, not sure at all where he was going from there.

He didn't need to worry. His son appeared to have no intention of letting him go anywhere. Nick's eyes narrowed. There was a steeliness in them which Kelly had never noticed before.

'Save it,' he said in an icy-cold voice that somehow indicated the depth of his anger far more than when he had shouted earlier. 'You're on your own now as far as I'm concerned. The biggest pity is that you didn't manage to get yourself killed last night.'

Again Kelly felt he couldn't argue. He did not attempt to

reply. Nick got up from his chair and stood by his father's bedside for a minute or two just looking through those narrowed eyes. Then he shook his head dismissively, turned on his heel and left, disappearing through the curtain screen into the main ward.

Outside the ward in the corridor Nick paused for a moment, leaned against the wall, closed his eyes, and struggled to regain control. Nick didn't like losing control. Unlike his father he was naturally a very controlled man. And his army training had made him even more so.

He realised that his fists were tightly closed and it was only with some difficulty that he managed to prise them open. He really had wanted to punch some sense into his father.

The problem was that he didn't know what to do, how to help, if indeed there was a way of helping.

He had blamed Angel Silver, and he still blamed Angel. But his father had displayed that tragically weak side of his nature yet again.

Perhaps Nick had only been kidding himself that Kelly had ever really changed. It seemed that Kelly had once more displayed a complete lack of strength of character.

Kelly was relieved to see the back of Nick. Confrontation was beyond him at that moment. He sank deeper into the pillows. Nick was probably right. He certainly couldn't argue with him. It might well be better if he had got himself killed. His son had accepted so much that his father had done. Kelly had been forgiven and loved by a young man who had every reason to bear a grudge. But somehow or other Nick never had – not previously, anyway, or not as far as Kelly knew. Now Kelly had gone and done it again, and this time he'd well and truly blown it.

He closed his eyes, hoping for oblivion, but it never came. And when eventually he did manage to drift into fitful sleep an unwelcome dream enveloped him in such a way that he felt that he was still awake. Angel stood in front of him. She was wearing black leather – not motorbike gear, more the sort that's sold in Soho sex shops. Knee-high stiletto-heeled boots, a micro-skirt and a tight bodice, laced down the front, exposing the tantalising swell of her breasts. She had a mocking smile on her face, yet at the same time she was beckoning him towards her.

Kelly stepped forward and hit some kind of invisible barrier; maybe it was glass. He leaned into it, pushed against it. Nothing made any difference. He could not reach her. But he could hear her voice, husky, slightly slurred, the way it all too often was.

'What's the matter, John? Don't you want me any more?' She kept on beckoning him. 'Come to me, John, come to me. I need you. I want you . . .'

He lurched towards her, reaching out to her, trying to speak. The words wouldn't come, but he stretched out his arms to her. Only when he sought to grasp hold of her there was nothing there. He felt himself crashing to the ground. His head hit something sharp. He couldn't even see her any more. There was only blackness in front of his eyes again.

He could hear other, new voices.

'Should we get help, Moira?'

'I am the bloody help. I'm a nurse, remember.'

Moira's voice was hard, but then Kelly felt a soft hand round his wrist. Fingertips gently lifted an eyelid.

'No, I think he's all right. Maybe he had a dream. He's waking up, look. Let's just help him back into bed.'

Moira was right. Kelly was waking up. His dream had been so vivid that he glanced over towards the window to see if Angel was still there. She wasn't. It was only then that he realised that he must have been dreaming and, although Kelly knew it was madness, with that realisation came a quite terrible disappointment.

He forced himself to concentrate on what passed for reality. But the struggle to get his faculties working again was a tough one. Moira was there. He'd heard her name used, and in any case he knew her voice well enough – as indeed he did the male voice, but none the less it took him a little while to put it together with a face he could see only hazily. His vision still wasn't good but recognition came to him suddenly. Joe Robertson. Joe and Moira. It was Moira who still had one hand round his wrist, checking his pulse rate, and he could see that she looked concerned. He was just about together enough to wonder that she could still feel any concern for him.

Joe Robertson did not look concerned. Instead he looked plain furious. Kelly had only very rarely seen Joe angry, but his normally genial face was now as black as thunder. And the big man seemed to be looming over him.

It was then that Kelly realised that he was on the floor. So that was what they meant about helping him back to bed. He struggled to raise himself, tucking one leg under his body, reaching out a hand. Vicious stabs of pain immediately shot though his battered torso. He felt himself falling again. He grabbed something and tried to hold on. It was the bedside cabinet which, it seemed, was on wheels. A very dangerous piece of furniture to a man in his condition. It swung towards him as he pulled on it. Moira, still crouched next to him, just managed to get out of the way but the cabinet hit Kelly full in the chest. His leg gave way beneath him and he slumped full length on to the floor once more.

'For God's sake,' boomed Joe.

Then Kelly felt hands tuck under his armpits and strong arms raise him and hoist him none too gently on to the bed.

'Th-thanks,' he murmured.

'Don't thank me yet, you waste of space,' stormed Joe. 'I'm here to give you the bollocking of your life.'

Kelly glanced weakly at Moira, then at the clock on the wall. It was just gone noon. He knew that Moira always came off duty by 7.30, but she was still in uniform. He could only assume that, in spite of her justifiably acerbic manner towards him, she had stayed on at the hospital because of him. And he knew that he didn't deserve that.

'You needn't look to me for support,' she told him sharply. 'I'm telling you now, you've got one chance left to sort yourself out, and you can think yourself bloody lucky you're being given that. The alternative is the gutter again. Even you must be able to grasp that. You've been there before, after all.'

'W-what?' stumbled Kelly.

'It's quite simple,' said Joe. 'You go into rehab now. As soon as they let you out of here. You get yourself sorted out. If you don't you lose your job. I would have no compunction whatsoever about sacking you. In fact it's only because of how far we go back, you raving lunatic, that I'm not sacking you now. And along with your job you'd lose your home and everything else. You've already lost your son, from what I hear, and what Moira is doing here, God knows . . .'

'Habit, I think,' said Moira grimly. Obliquely Kelly remembered when she had told him that before, the last time they had made love. 'I'm not hanging about, I can tell you now, John,' she went on. 'Enough's enough.'

'Right,' said Joe Robertson. 'If you are going to have any chance at all of rebuilding your life, for the umpteenth fucking time, John Kelly, you do as I tell you. You go into rehab. I will help you get all the help there is and I'm even prepared to get the *Argus* to finance it, though God knows why. We still have a management with a certain limited tolerance of talented boozers. But it is limited, John. And even as things are, I don't know how I'm going to square it when your court case comes up. The management don't know about the coke yet, and it'll be public knowledge after you go to court. You're firmly in last chance saloon. Mess this is up, and it's all over. The choice is yours, but I want your answer now.'

Kelly really didn't care, but neither did he have the strength to argue. 'Whatever you say,' he responded lamely.

'And I suppose that's your way of saying thank you, is it?'

Kelly gritted his teeth. Which hurt a lot. 'I'll do it,' he said weakly. 'I feel too bloody awful to make a speech.'

Joe glowered at him. 'If you let me down I'll kill you,' he said.

Kelly groaned.

'You won't need to,' said Moira. 'He'll kill himself.'

Kelly groaned again.

'We'll be back,' said Joe, making it sound like a threat, as he and Moira headed for the curtain screen.

Joe pulled the curtain to one side and then turned once more to study Kelly in silence for just a moment or two.

When he eventually spoke his voice was much quieter, resigned, almost sad.

'It's true, John,' he said. 'Anybody but you I'd have sacked already. Thing is, I remember the man you almost were.'

Suddenly Kelly felt tears pricking.

'I am sorry, Joe,' he said, meaning it at that moment at least. 'And I will try not to let you down.'

Joe Robertson's features softened, just a bit. Moira, standing to one side of the editor, still looked betrayed. However, Joe gave a small smile. His usual good humour had yet to be restored but at least his fury seemed to have abated, thought Kelly.

'It's for your own sake, John,' Joe said.

They booked him into a rehab centre on the outskirts of Newton Abbot. And four days later, early in the morning, Joe Robertson came to pick him up from hospital and drove him there.

Kelly was contrite, so much so that he was almost surprised at himself. But then he, more than anyone, knew the path along which he was travelling and where it would lead. He was also physically weak and battered, which made him all the more compliant. He could walk unaided, in spite of his cracked ribs, which had indeed been further damaged when he was beaten up, and his arm had not been broken in the fracas, rather his wrist had been badly strained. But everything hurt, particularly, still, his face and head.

Joe carried Kelly's small bag into the hall of the big Victorian villa known as Plumpton House, and rather pointedly did not leave until Kelly was safely handed into the care of a senior helper.

'Right then,' said Joe in what sounded like a deliberate attempt to be brusque and businesslike. 'You're in the hands of the experts now. Just do what you're told and they'll get you sorted, I'm sure of it.'

Kelly hoped so. But only he knew the mess his head was in. However, he resolved to do his best. He recognised the faces of the other people at the rehab centre as he was led through the public rooms on the ground floor and then upstairs to his bedroom. He didn't know any of them, but, by God, he knew the look in their eyes.

It was fear.

Kelly was afraid too – more afraid than he had been for a long time. He hadn't really needed Joe to tell him he was in last chance saloon. He been aware of that, even before he was mugged and left to rot in the middle of Castle Circus, which he now understood to be where he had been found in such a sorry state. He had known that he was en route to self-destruction. He just hadn't been prepared even to think about it. He'd been on a roller coaster ride and he hadn't known how to get off.

Kelly's bags were searched thoroughly when he got to his room. The clothes he was wearing were checked and he was asked to turn out his pockets. It was a bit like arriving for your first term at a particularly strict boarding school, he thought obliquely, but he understood perfectly what was going on. The staff were looking for concealed alcohol. When so many of the inmates were only there because their employers or relatives persuaded them or even bullied them into it, smuggling in supplies of booze was common. The sheer terror of not being able to get a drink could never quite be understood by anyone who was not an alcoholic. Kelly understood.

Kelly, however, was clean. It was not his intention either deliberately to waste the *Argus*' money, or to slide any further down the slippery slope he knew he was on.

He felt close to despair as he sat on the narrow bed he had been allocated in a room which also contained three other beds and very little else. He had yet even to meet the men he would be sleeping alongside, and Kelly couldn't remember when he had last shared a room with anyone other than a woman.

He was not given long to dwell on his misery. Plumpton House operated a strict and relentless regime. It was only just before 10 a.m. when he was taken to his first therapy session, but he was told that had begun at 8.30. All day he attended lectures and therapy of one kind or another. And in the evening he and the other residents were bussed to an

Alcoholics Anonymous meeting nearby. Kelly had no time to himself at all until after 10.30, when he half threw himself, exhausted, face down on his bed.

Plumpton kept the same routine going from 8.30 a.m. to 10.30 p.m. every day, seven days a week. And Kelly, like most of the others, had agreed to complete a four-week course.

At first, perhaps because of his weak physical condition, Kelly really did find the regime gruelling. But he continued to do his best. He arrived punctually for his lectures and therapy sessions, and really tried to immerse himself into the Plumpton House programme. At least he was accepting help, he told himself, and it was always said that was the first step to recovery. Kelly vowed to others and to himself that he would stay off the booze, and he meant it. He also made a promise to himself that this time, even after coming out of rehab, he would persevere with the AA meetings, by which Plumpton House, like most rehabilitation centres, put so much store.

Joe visited and so did Moira, which Kelly knew was more than he deserved.

Then, after he had been at Plumpton for two weeks, on a glorious spring afternoon, Nick turned up. Kelly was overcome. He had believed his son when he'd told him he wanted no more of him. He had believed it because he had come near to destroying the boy's life once many years previously, and he more than understood that Nick was not prepared even to give him the chance of doing it again.

But Nick's visit proved to be a pleasant surprise. He was standing looking out over the garden with his back to the room when Kelly walked into the big old conservatory where the residents habitually received their visitors.

Hearing his footsteps perhaps, Nick turned round at once to face his father. The sun glinted on his sandy hair and his face looked tanned. Nick almost always looked tanned. And very handsome, Kelly thought. And Nick was smiling at him. Hope rose inside Kelly like the dawning of a new day. Perhaps he had not lost his son after all. Nick was definitely smiling, albeit a little tentatively.

'I didn't mean what I said, Dad,' he told his father.
'You had every right to,' replied Kelly.
'Yeah.' Nick stopped smiling and his voice was serious when he spoke again. 'That's not what it's about, though, is it?'
'Isn't it?' responded Kelly. 'All I've ever done is let you down, Nick. You told me that yourself, and you were right.'
Nick nodded. 'Yes, that's true too. But you're my father and I love you. I can't change that. I wish I could sometimes, but there it is.'
'I bet you wish you could,' said Kelly. And he had felt quite swelled with love and pride.
'Just don't mess up, Dad, will you? Not this time. Not again.'
'I won't,' Kelly promised him.
'I've got to go abroad, just for a few days, and then I'll come down again as soon as I can.'
'Where are you going?' asked Kelly, pleased to be able to concentrate on somebody else's life for a moment instead of the mess his own was in.
'Munich,' responded Nick shortly.
'Anything interesting?' Kelly enquired without a lot of hope of much reply. Nick had never given a lot away about his work and Kelly still didn't fully understand exactly what his business had been since he left the army.
'Deeply boring,' replied Nick. 'Like everything about computers, unless you're a geek like me.'
Kelly smiled at that. Anyone less like a geek than this fit and handsome son of his, who still looked every inch the soldier he had once been, was difficult to imagine.

A few days later, while he was still living at Plumpton House, Kelly's case came up at Torquay Magistrates' Court. Kelly had spent plenty of time in courts at all levels, but he had never stood in the dock before. He found that he did not like it at all.
He was, however, lucky. Joe spoke up for him. The chairman of the magistrates did not seem so vehement about

drink driving offences as most of his ilk, and in fact must have been a particularly tolerant man, as even the revelation that drugs had been involved didn't send him totally apoplectic. Kelly was given a six-month jail sentence suspended for two years. He was extremely lucky. He could easily have gone to jail, and he knew it.

Because of his narrow escape, because of Nick, because of Joe, and yes, because of Moira, Kelly became even more determined to keep his promise to himself, to finish his course at Plumpton, and totally to clean up his act. He was also determined that he would walk away from Angel, and make it up with Moira, if she'd let him. After all, Angel had been the cause of most of what had gone wrong. But Kelly knew that wasn't entirely fair. It was his own obsession that had contributed so much to landing him in this mess. He had had choices. And he'd known with devastating clarity at every step what he was getting into. With his background he had known more than most. To get involved again with drinking and doing drugs had been the ultimate stupidity. But, once he had started, and with Angel to share those various seductive mind-altering substances with him in such exciting ways, he hadn't been able to stop. Which, of course, had been more or less the story of his life.

He was going to stop now, though, he really was.

And yet, and yet, Kelly wasn't able to stop himself calling Angel. From the very day he arrived at Plumpton House, he kept trying her repeatedly, at the same time swearing to himself that he would let go of her. That he wanted just to speak to her one more time.

He called her mobile without any success. He kept phoning Maythorpe Manor, getting only the answering machine as usual. Eventually one night, at around midnight, she answered. She sounded high and he thought he could hear a male voice in the background.

'I can't talk to you, John,' she said. 'I'm knackered and you've just woken me up. Call again in the morning, will you?'

He was quite sure that she was lying, and also that if he called in the morning he would get only a recorded message again. He proved to be right, but kept trying. He told himself that he was in any case only calling to end it.

It was early evening, already dark after a damp, grey day, when Kelly was eventually discharged from Plumpton House, physically more or less mended and very, very sober. But emotionally he was not nearly as together as he had hoped. And so, instead of calling Moira or even Joe to collect him, he did exactly what he had told himself he wouldn't do. A taxi had been booked to take him first to an AA meeting near his St Marychurch home. But as soon as he climbed aboard Kelly redirected the driver. He asked to be taken straight out to Maidencombe, to Maythorpe Manor.

As the taxi approached the big old house he could see a light on in the bedroom. He could also see shapes behind the curtains. More than one shape? He got out of the taxi outside the gates of Maythorpe and asked the driver to wait for him there in Rock Lane. As if bent on torturing himself, he decided to try to enter the house surreptitiously. Feeling quite nervous he walked to the gates and pumped the security code into the gizmo to one side. The gates swung silently open.

Kelly made his way carefully across the gravelled courtyard, trying to make as little noise as he could as his feet crunched on the little stones, and wondered if his key would still work. But he did not even have to use it. When he tried the front door he found that it was unlocked. Typical, he thought, as he opened it and slipped inside. Angel's idea of security remained as erratic as ever, it seemed.

He closed the door as quietly as he could behind him and climbed the stairs cautiously. The bedroom door was ajar. He stopped in the doorway, looking in at a scene which he had somehow half expected, but that made no difference. It was still a shock.

Angel was in bed with two young men. She was sitting astride one of them, while the other had entered her from behind. Kelly's first bizarre thought was that she looked like the filling in a rather outlandish sandwich. He watched in a kind of morbid fascination for a few moments. The bedroom he had spent so much time in smelled like a cross between a brothel and an opium den. There was little doubt that all three people on the bed were doped to the eyeballs. Kelly had no idea who they were, and suspected Angel probably didn't know them very well either. She had often teased him with stories about having sex with strangers. But she was so high profile Kelly was still surprised that she would stage a mini orgy like this in her own home.

Kelly's feet felt as if they were nailed to the floorboards. He didn't want to watch, but neither could he move. Eventually Angel glanced over her shoulder and saw him. She was moving in rhythm with the two young men and she didn't pause for an instant. Her eyes were glazed and puffy. Her mouth hung open. She pulled her lips into the familiar mocking smile.

'Why don't you come and join us, John?' she invited him, her voice deep and husky.

For once he didn't think she looked beautiful. In fact he thought she looked quite ugly. And her words somehow brought the life back into his legs. He did not reply. He had no reply. Instead he just turned round and fled. He took the stairs in leaps and bounds, hurried out of the house and half ran across the courtyard. There he had to pause because the big gates had automatically closed behind him earlier. With trembling fingers he punched in the security number to open them again, getting it right only at the third attempt. He could not stop himself looking back at the bedroom window. The shapes were still moving behind the curtains. He didn't want to think about what she was doing, what was being done to her, but he couldn't help it.

The window was almost hypnotic to him. It took a huge effort of will for him to look away and walk out through the gates to his waiting taxi. In the back of the car he felt the tears begin to roll down his face. He tried to wipe them away with the side of his hand. They wouldn't stop. He hoped the driver wouldn't notice, but he was beyond caring all that much.

A car Kelly would have recognised had he seen it was parked in the entrance to another big house just a short distance up Rock Lane from Maythorpe. Its lights were switched off, but in any case Kelly was in far too much of a state to notice anything.

He was still crying when he arrived home in St Marychurch. He wanted a drink, but he kept that resolve at least. He did not have one even though he thought there might still be booze in the kitchen cupboard. Instead he found some sleeping pills and took three.

He sought oblivion and he found it after a fashion. But when he woke suddenly several hours later with a headache and a fuzzy mouth, his cheeks were still wet with tears.

Twenty

The telephone was ringing. That was what must have woken him up so abruptly, Kelly realised. He opened his eyes blearily and hoisted himself into a half-sitting position. For just a moment he wasn't even sure where he was. The phone continued to ring. Eventually he reached for it, rubbing his eyes to wipe the tears away.

'So you're there, are you?' said Moira rather tetchily.

Kelly heard himself mumble a reply.

'Are you all right?' Moira's voice was sharp.

Kelly knew what she was thinking at once. Those sleeping pills had really knocked him out. She was probably afraid that he had already started drinking again.

He struggled to pull himself together and clear his head.

'Yes, it's OK,' he said. 'I couldn't sleep so I took some pills. One more than I should have done, probably.'

'Oh.' Moira did not sound entirely convinced. Kelly couldn't blame her.

'I didn't realise you were leaving Plumpton last night,' she went on. 'We didn't expect you to be released till today. I only found out this morning. You should have called. I'd have picked you up.'

'I didn't want to bother you. I just got a cab to take me to an AA meeting and then home,' Kelly responded, wondering if the day would ever come again when he didn't seem to be lying to everyone. 'My last therapy session was late yesterday afternoon and afterwards they said I didn't have to stay the night unless I wanted to.'

'What are you going to do today?'

'I don't know yet.' That at least was the truth.

'Well, I think you should call Joe and talk to him about when you can get back to work. He's performed miracles keeping your job open for you. He deserves a big thank you.'

'I know he does,' said Kelly. 'And so do you.'

'Forget it,' said Moira, and rang off.

Kelly felt that she was probably making a conscious effort not to get too involved again. And he didn't blame her for that either.

Miserably he dragged himself out of bed and made his way downstairs to the kitchen. He brewed a strong pot of tea and sat at the kitchen table to drink it. As the hot brown liquid hit the back of his throat, somewhere inside the fuzziness of his head his brain began to clear just a little.

He looked around him, taking in the surroundings of his home for the first time. There had been fresh milk in the fridge and a packet of sliced bread lay on the worktop by the cooker. The kitchen was immaculate. In fact the whole house was neat and tidy, and he was pretty damned sure he hadn't left it that way. Moira, he thought. And it was typical of her. Only she could have been in and cleaned the place so thoroughly. Obliquely he wondered where she'd got a key from. He remembered her almost throwing her own set back at him. Nick had keys, of course, and she might even have borrowed Kelly's own which had only been handed back to him at Plumpton House the previous day.

Either way, that was another thank you he owed Moira. He also felt guilty. Moira certainly would not approve of the thoughts which were beginning to form in his mind as he poured himself a second mug of tea.

A course of action was starting to frame itself and, although he was unsure that it was the right one, it seemed to him to be the only one. The truth, the whole truth about everything, he was convinced, was all that could exorcise the demon that his obsession with Angel had become. Suddenly he was determined that he would make Angel tell him everything, and that he just had to do that in order to preserve any of his sanity. He wanted to know the absolute truth, not only about the deaths of Scott Silver and Terry James, but also the truth about Angel's feelings for him. In Kelly's mind the two were inextricably linked.

Kelly's stomach lurched queasily. He considered making himself some toast, but couldn't quite be bothered. The last little vestige of his common sense was hanging on in there grimly, warning him that he might not like the truth very much, and also sending him the message that if he didn't know what Angel's feelings for him were after the way she had treated him, and after what he had seen last night, then he really was a seriously sad case.

Kelly managed a small smile. Sad or not, at least he had reached a decision. He had no particular game plan, but he convinced himself that if he confronted Angel in the right way she would tell him the truth for two reasons. First, she had seen him destroy the tape in front of her and believed, almost certainly correctly, that there was no evidence against her. Secondly, and probably most importantly, for the first time since it had all begun he really did want the truth.

Previously when he had confronted Angel he had always been looking primarily for reassurance. He had really only ever wanted things to continue the way they were while he buried his head in the sand. And he suspected that she had always been well aware of that.

This time it was going to be different.

He drained the last of the tea from the pot into his mug and checked the time. He had slept, albeit fitfully, for almost ten hours. It was now nearly 1 p.m. Surely Angel and her young men were out of bed by now, he thought. Anyway, he wasn't sure that he cared. He was feeling surprisingly bullish. He'd drag her out of bed and make her talk to him, if he had to.

Then he thought again. She was hopeless early in the day, and 1 p.m. was still early for Angel Silver. In any case there was no point in provoking her for all the wrong reasons. He'd wait until the evening. That was also likely to be when she would be at her most lucid, recovered as much as ever from the excesses of the previous night and hopefully not yet totally stoned again.

He passed the day and early evening watching TV and psyching himself up for what he intended to do. When it came to it, however, he started to get nervous about his plan and kept coming up with reasons for putting off leaving the house. Ultimately it was almost 11 p.m. before, cursing the fact that he was off the road and would be for a very long time, he finally called a taxi to go out to Maidencombe. Repeating his process of the previous night, he asked the driver to park and wait outside the perimeter walls, opened the electronic gates and made his own way into the house. He didn't ring the bell and wait for her to answer it, because, once again, although for different reasons, he wanted to take Angel by surprise. He didn't want to give her time to erect her defences, something she did so well and with such alacrity.

He found her in the kitchen. She was standing by the worktop watching the kettle boil. From the doorway he saw her reach for a mug and then a spoon, trembling hands protruding from the sleeves of a grubby towelling dressing gown which had probably once been white.

Just like the night before she sensed his eyes on her and turned to face him. Her hair was a mess, platinum strands hanging lankly from distinctly dark roots, and her skin looked pale and blotchy. Her eyes were still surrounded by the black smudges of yesterday's mascara, which blended with the heavy shadows beneath them. It looked like she had been through a long night, which had probably gone on right through the day as well. Kelly thought he had made the right decision not to confront her earlier. He doubted it would have got him anywhere.

There was an ugly bruise on her forehead which hadn't been there yesterday, and Kelly felt that sudden dart of the familiar compassion and protectiveness which she always brought out in him. Then he looked again. Yes, Angel was still the little girl lost. There was also something pathetic about her. And he realised again that he didn't find her beautiful any more. Indeed, he wondered how it was that he had never before noticed the ugliness that there was about her.

Her mouth set in a thin hard line when she saw him. 'Are you going to make a habit of sneaking into my house?' she asked.

He made no direct response. 'I didn't like what I saw last night,' he said instead. He spoke mildly enough but he knew that she would see his remark as a challenge he had no right to make. That was Angel. And he wasn't wrong.

'What makes you think I give a damn about what you think, you sad bastard?' she rounded on him.

It still hurt that she could be so openly contemptuous of him, just the way she had been before he had found the incriminating video. And she was so arrogant. He was just about reasoned enough to wonder how she could be, or at the very least give the impression that she was, so sure of herself, and even that she had the nerve to call him sad. Did she never look in a mirror?

'You told me that you loved me once,' he said, as calmly as he could.

'Yeah, well, I had a reason for that, didn't I? Oh, and by the way, you're arguably the worst fuck I've ever had. I only went with you in the first place to stop you being so bloody nosy.'

Kelly had always suspected that too, really. None the less he was rocked by her words. Not for the first time he couldn't understand why she was quite so vitriolic towards him, couldn't work out why she seemed to have so much contempt for him. Maybe it was about control, and that once Angel had gained control, as she most certainly had of him, with it came the contempt for anyone weak enough and compliant enough to succumb to her. He'd often wondered why she had gone to bed with him at all. Well, she'd told him now, hadn't she? But was it the truth? You could never tell with Angel.

Once again he avoided responding directly to her remarks. 'I could still go to the police,' he told her instead.

'Really? But you destroyed the evidence. I saw you do it. You'd do anything for me, wouldn't you?'

Kelly felt sickened. By himself as much as anything.

'I may have a copy,' he said, as sharply as he could manage.

'No you don't,' she replied, almost smugly. 'You told me you hadn't made one.'

'And you believed me?'

'Oh yes.'

She smiled at him with absolute certainty. She believed him and was right to do so. Kelly was infuriated by his own stupidity, by the way he always seemed to play into her hands.

'Will you just tell me the truth?' he asked.

'You've never wanted the truth before, have you, you pathetic bastard?'

She was dead right again, of course. As astute as ever. And cruel.

'Tell me what really happened the night Scott and Terry James died. Tell me the truth, and I'll get out of your life.'

'I don't actually care whether you do or not.'

That, he was sure, was absolutely the truth. He didn't reply.

Angel was on a roll, on a high.

'What do you think happened, anyway, John? What wonderful theory has your great investigative journalist's brain come up with?'

Kelly shrugged; tried to sound detached. 'I think maybe somebody had a hidden agenda,' he said. 'I think it is possible you took advantage of a heaven-sent opportunity to sort out a marriage that had turned sour.'

'Really. And what does that mean?'

'I think maybe you did kill Scott, as well as Terry James. That's certainly what it looked like to me on that video.'

'Is it indeed? What a pity you let me burn it then.'

'Yes, maybe it is. But it does mean you can tell me the truth without putting yourself in too much danger, doesn't it?'

She laughed briefly. 'Why is the truth so important to you?'

'Because I can't believe that I fell in love with someone who's as evil a bitch as I think you might be.'

She smiled, as if taking the remark as a compliment. 'Really?' she queried. 'So it would make you feel better to be able to believe that I really am innocent of everything except trying to defend myself and my husband, would it?'

'Yes, it would.'

'Because of what it would otherwise make you?'

'Maybe.'

'Well, I have bad news for you, John Kelly. You're on the right track, for once in your life.'

Kelly felt his heart begin to beat faster. She couldn't really be about to tell him what he feared that she was, could she? He didn't want to be right, he really didn't. He said nothing more, instead waited for her to speak again.

Angel's mouth, still surrounded by smudges of dark lipstick, hung open in a kind of leer.

'Yes, I killed Scott,' she said abruptly. 'And God knows, the bastard had it coming.' She spoke with a kind of studied casualness. Blurted the words out just like that. No build-up. She could have been making a dinner date or telling him about a football match.

Kelly was shocked rigid, not just by the confession Angel had thrown at him so casually, but also by the speed of it. He had psyched himself up for a long verbal tussle with her. He had banked on her arrogance, on her belief that neither he nor anyone else could prove anything any more, to make her almost want to tell the truth if he pressed her. But he hadn't expected it to come so quickly, so easily.

Often he had no idea what kind of game Angel might be playing. But this time he was horribly sure that she had told him the simple unadorned truth. And, of course, all along he had made himself believe in her innocence. If he had done any other he would not have been able to justify, even to himself, his own behaviour.

Kelly felt physically ill. His head hurt. It was probably partly still the lurking aftereffects of the physical battering he had taken lately, and partly a kind of hangover from those sleeping pills. But that wasn't all. This was the final blow. Kelly was quite desolate.

Angel continued to speak. Somewhere in the distance he could hear her voice. His beleaguered brain began to decipher the words. Words he didn't want to hear.

She sounded quite conversational. As she talked she put a tea bag in the mug in front of her and poured in hot water.

Rather conspicuously she failed to offer him a cup of tea, or anything else, for that matter.

'It was the One God, One People sect which caused the problem,' she remarked. 'Everything was all right until then. Scott really did discover God in a big, big way. I never knew which came first, that little slag he was shagging or the born-again Christian crap. And I never worked out quite how he reconciled the two, but he did. Scott was good at justifying his actions. Always had been. Anyway, it took him over. Apart from fucking little Miss Preaching Boots he really cleaned up his act. Cut out the drinking and gave up the shit. He tried to make me do the same, but I told him to stuff it.

'Then I found out about that plain little mouse, Bridget, the dumb slag. It was all true what she said, you know. He fell for her all right. Head over fucking heels. You wouldn't believe it, would you? He preferred her to me, no doubt about it.'

Angel looked genuinely surprised at the thought. Her arrogance remained impressive. In another kind of situation Kelly might have been amused.

'None the less, he still wanted to fuck me all the time, which was bloody typical,' Angel continued. 'He said there was nothing wrong with that in the eyes of God, as long as I was his wife. I told you the sanctimonious sod was good at justifying his actions, didn't I? I knew that he was planning to divorce me, though. And we did have one of those fucking pre-nuptials, didn't we? I lied about it to you and everyone else, even though I knew that was a dangerous thing to do, because I didn't dare do any other. Also, the solicitor who drew the bloody thing up had died, so I figured it might not come to light that easily, with a bit of luck. But the dumb slag was right about it. I'd have had to leave this house and I'd have ended up with sweet FA. I had to do something about it.'

'Are you telling me you planned it all?' Kelly's forehead felt clammy. He had broken into a sweat and yet he could not stop his body trembling, as if with cold. At the very worst he had thought she might have been guilty of grasping a terrible opportunity, of committing an awful crime in the heat of the moment. He had never really seriously considered that she might have preplanned the whole thing.

'What do you think?'

Angel shot him another contemptuous look. 'Greedy young bastard, that idiot tea leaf. And he worshipped Scott. He was always out at the house genuflecting away every time Scott appeared in view. I took him on to help in the garden and do odd jobs so that I could get to know him. I made up a story about big financial trouble. I told him that he could help save Scott from bankruptcy if he staged a robbery. I told him it was all an insurance scam, didn't I? I gave him the combination to open the gates. I knew that wouldn't matter because Scott and I had done that with half the people who worked here. I said I'd make sure the alarm system for the house was switched off, and all he had to do was break a window to get it, then come into the bedroom. We'd all pretend to fight, exchange a few bruises, make it look good.'

Angel threw back her head and laughed hysterically – just as she had the first time she and Kelly had had sex. Kelly clenched his fists behind his back. He didn't want her to see how badly his hands were shaking. The trembling that had engulfed his entire body was almost out of control now.

'Terry James was part of the furniture. He hung around here so much, even when he wasn't working,' Angel went on. 'It was easy. I started to invite him in when Scott wasn't around, told him Scott was too shy to meet his fans, kept giving him bogus messages from Scott.'

Angel shot Kelly a sideways look. 'He liked to fuck, did young Tel, by the way. Oh, how he liked to fuck. He was hung like a donkey too. Just looking at his dick could bring me off. Made Scott look under-endowed.'

Kelly, remembering the video he had stolen, was well aware of how well equipped the rock star had been in that area. Angel knew that. She continued to look steadily at Kelly, half triumphant, half mocking.

'It gave him a real thrill to have Scott Silver's missus. Seriously turned him on – he could keep going for hours. How he squared that with his adoration of the great star I have no bloody idea. In the end he was just another fool who'd do anything for me.'

Had she any idea what she was saying and how she sounded? Did she believe the stuff she spewed out in that offensive fashion? Did she realise the effect she was having on him, and was that really her intention? Kelly had no idea really what she was trying to do or why.

Angel started laughing again. Kelly wondered if she was still high. Maybe that was it. When he had arrived she'd looked like somebody who had just come heavily down off a trip. Now he wasn't sure any more. He wasn't sure of anything.

Suddenly she began to take her clothes off – just like the first time, only she didn't stop laughing at all. In fact the laughter grew louder as she embarked on a kind of lewd parody of a stripper at work, sliding her dressing gown slowly down off her shoulders.

'So what difference does any of it make, John?' she hissed at him, her mouth leering even more grotesquely as she thrust her crotch towards him and began to make a show of playing with herself with one hand.

'This is what you want, isn't it, you pathetic bastard?' Her voice slipped down an octave or two. She began to use two hands on herself. 'This is all you want, isn't it?'

Her eyes were bright. Inside her open mouth he could see her tongue moving provocatively.

All Kelly really wanted at that moment was to go back in time. To be able at least to kid himself that he knew nothing of what she had just told him. And then to walk away, to leave Maythorpe Manor and Angel Silver behind him. For ever. But he felt rooted to the spot.

Angel stepped towards him, smiling rather unpleasantly. She put her hands on his shoulders as she raised a knee and pushed it into his genitals, quite hard.

'You'd do anything I want just to fuck me, wouldn't you, John, anything at all . . .?'

'Stop it,' he told her sharply. 'Just shut up.'

He could hear the strain in his own voice. He realised that he was near to breaking point. But Angel seemed to have no idea. She just wouldn't stop. Maybe she couldn't stop, he thought obliquely.

Her taunting was terrible to him. He had loved her, after all – maybe still did love her, in spite of knowing all along what madness it was. Kelly felt a numbness overwhelm him. He could still hear Angel mocking him, like some dreadful slow torture, but it was as if her voice were muffled and came from a long way off.

There was a kind of mist in front of his eyes. He could only barely see her face through it. And what he could see looked so ugly and distorted. This was not the Angel he had loved so much, albeit against his better judgement, it really wasn't. This was a woman capable of the vilest kind of murder in cold blood, capable of stabbing her own husband to death, without, it seemed, any regret. He pushed her away.

'Stop,' he ordered her again. 'Please stop.'

He tried to keep his voice quiet and authoritative. Again she would have none of it. She continued to leer at him, to mock. She stepped towards him again, groping at his trousers with one hand.

Kelly thought his head was going to burst. What she had told him, all of it, about the murder, and then the taunting of him, that and what she was trying to do, this kind of ritual humiliation she seemed to be indulging in, was just too much for him. His hands were shaking wildly. He could no longer control his trembling body at all.

He pushed her away again. This time she stood her ground in front of him, just looking at him with the so familiar contempt.

'What's the matter, John?' she asked. 'Don't you want to fuck me any more now you know I'm a murderess? Or maybe you just can't do it any more? Do you want me to invite the boys back? Then you could watch. You like to watch, don't you? Remember the videos?'

The videos. Those videos of him and Angel having sex, which, yes, he had loved to watch, and afterwards hated himself for. And finally a real life snuff video. For that's what he had seen. That's what he had destroyed in order to save Angel, because he had been besotted by her, because he had been obsessed with her, because he had been totally and utterly under her spell.

Suddenly he hated her. The bile rose from deep inside him. God, how he hated her. And how he just had to make her stop.

He took one hesitant step forward and then he lunged at her. Threw himself at her, his bulk overwhelming her, his arms flailing, striking out at her with all his might.

Yet he only wanted to make her stop. That was all. Just to stop . . .

Twenty-one

'They've found another body out at Maythorpe Manor,' DS Cooper blurted out excitedly as he burst into Karen Meadows' office. 'We've just had a 999 call, boss.'

Karen Meadows looked up at him. She had been sitting at her desk, dealing with a mountain of unwelcome paperwork. Almost involuntarily she jumped to her feet.

'Whose body, who is it?' she enquired.

'Angel Silver, almost certainly,' replied Cooper. 'It was her daily, Mrs Nott, who found her. The woman was half hysterical on the phone, apparently, but she kept saying that it was Mrs Silver. "Mrs Silver's been murdered." '

'Christ,' said Karen. 'I just knew this one wasn't going to go away. Did Mrs Nott say how she thought Angel had been killed?'

'No, just that there was a lot of blood everywhere.'

Karen grabbed her shoulder bag from her desk and headed for the door. There was no point in asking Phil Cooper any more questions. She needed to get to the scene of the crime fast to see it all for herself.

'C'mon Phil, let's get out there,' she said.

Angel Silver's body lay spread-eagled on the kitchen floor. Her eyes and mouth were wide open. Her face was bloodied, particularly around her nose and mouth, yet her expression was far more one of surprise than of fear, or even of pain.

One of her arms was lying at an impossible angle, almost certainly broken. The fresh bruise on her forehead, which Kelly had noticed and been disturbed by when he made his late-night visit, looked even more prominent in death, and Angel's grubby towelling dressing gown was heavily blood-stained.

Karen Meadows peered at the body, getting as close as she dare before the SOCOs arrived and sealed the crime scene. She could see no signs of a major wound.

'Is that more blood behind her head, Phil?' she asked DS Cooper.

The young detective sergeant leaned forward to study the black and cream tiled floor. There was a smattering of dark red spots on the shiny slabs.

'I reckon so, boss,' he said. 'There's blood in her hair too, I think.'

He pointed to a patch of Angel's hair protruding from behind one of the dead woman's ears. The DCI could see that it was also dark red and matted.

'Yes,' said Karen Meadows. 'Quite a bash on the head she's taken. How exactly? That's the question.'

'She could just have fallen and cracked her head on the worktop,' said Cooper. He gestured towards the granite surfaces. 'Hard as nails, this stuff, and the edges have got sharp corners too.'

DCI Meadows nodded. 'Thing is, was she pushed?' she asked almost rhetorically.

'Look at her eyes,' said Cooper. 'Pupils dilated. She was high as a kite when she died, I reckon.'

'They did teach you something at college, then, Phil?'

'Oh yeah, boss. I'm an expert on drug abuse, got really good at it.'

The young policeman grinned. Karen grinned back. She liked Phil Cooper's sense of humour. You needed things to be lightened sometimes in their job.

The SOCOs arrived swiftly, as did the region's Home Office pathologist. Karen had had a good relationship with his predecessor. She wasn't too sure of Audley Richards, a taciturn character as precise as his small neat moustache, who invariably didn't give an inch. But there was no doubt that he was darned good at his job.

Richards almost immediately made one pronouncement, which was a result in itself from a man who seemed to regard any form of educated guesswork or speculation in pathology as a crime equal almost in severity to murder itself.

Peering close to the body he said, 'I think all this blood might be deceptive. I think she might have had a nose bleed.'

Karen Meadows leaned closer. 'Caused by what?' she asked.

'Don't be ridiculous, Detective Chief Inspector. I'm a pathologist not a clairvoyant.'

Karen decided to resort to flattery. 'Oh, come on, Audley,' she said. 'You always know more than you want to let on. You're a seriously clever bastard. That's why we all love you.'

Richards turned to face her. 'The former I'm well aware of, so therefore it is vital that I protect my reputation when faced with impossible questions before I even have a chance to examine the corpse properly,' he said. 'The latter I can only assume is your idea of a joke, Karen.'

The use of her Christian name, in spite of the admonishment issued in an apparently frosty tone, was, Karen knew, a good sign. And indeed, it did seem that the flattery had worked, because Richards continued to speak and, considering that he had so far made only the briefest of preliminary examinations, proceeded to be unusually helpful.

'Look at the membranes between her nostrils,' he said. 'They're quite severely damaged. You wouldn't have had to give that nose much more than a tap to make it bleed. Coke, of course.'

'Christ,' said Karen, wondering suddenly why she and Phil Cooper hadn't themselves already noticed how paper thin the skin and tissue division which separated Angel's nostrils had become. 'I'm sure she wasn't like that when I last saw her.'

'It can happen quite suddenly after years of abuse.' Audley Richards looked thoughtful. 'This is quite an extreme case, too.'

'So the blood has no relevance to her death?'

'Hard to say.'

For a man who was famously reluctant to provide information at the scene of crime, Richards was being extremely co-operative, almost avuncular by his standards. Karen knew all too well how much he preferred to wait until he had examined a subject in his laboratory before giving anything away.

'It would seem most likely that she was attacked and that her attacker hit her in the face,' he went on. 'But there is some sign of bruising, which indicates that she didn't die straight after the blow to her face. I really can't say any more yet until the post mortem.'

'Time of death?' Karen enquired, adding quickly, in order not to antagonise the pathologist, 'Only approximately, of course.'

Richards grunted. 'Very approximately, some time around midnight, I would say.'

Karen nodded thoughtfully. So, just as she had already guessed, Angel had lain dead in her kitchen overnight until the arrival of her daily help, Mrs Nott, first thing that morning.

The DCI persisted in trying to extract as much information as possible from Audley Richards.

'Could that blow to the back of the head have been enough to kill her, Audley?' she asked, although pretty sure she wouldn't get a straight answer until Richards was able to do the job properly. She was quite correct, too.

'Hit the right spot and a tap can kill you, Karen,' he said tiredly. 'As you well know. So can three inches of water, half a peanut if you have that allergy, and an unexpected aneurysm without warning as you walk along the street. Doesn't mean a thing, does it?'

He wouldn't budge. The DCI would have to be patient, something she wasn't all that hot on if the truth be known.

Meanwhile she went into standard operating mode for the senior investigating officer at a suspicious death, which, she had to remind herself, was all that she had at the moment – although she was somehow pretty damned sure it was going to turn into a murder case pretty sharpish. A team was dispatched to ask questions in the neighbourhood about any comings and goings the night before.

Mrs Nott had been asked to wait in the living room, and Karen Meadows decided to talk to her herself, along with DS Cooper. The daily help could provide no hard information at all about who might have visited Angel Silver during the previous night, but she was willing, with little or no encouragement, to hazard a guess.

'That reporter feller on the *Argus*, he's always out here, snooping about,' she said. 'And he's been here upstairs sometimes, in her bedroom more than likely, when I haven't been supposed to know about it.'

Mrs Nott, making a quick recovery from her gruesome discovery, looked quite smug about that.

'So how did you know about it then?' Karen asked rather wearily.

'You couldn't miss that flashy little car of his, could you? He used to park it round the side of the house but there's nowhere here to hide it, and how many dark green open sports cars are there around? I ask you.'

Mrs Nott had sniffed derisively. Karen felt an unwelcome shiver of anticipation run down her spine.

'Do you know this reporter's name, Mrs Nott?' she enquired flatly, aware that it was a question she hardly needed to ask.

'Course I do. His name's been all over the papers, hasn't it, ever since this started. John Kelly, that's his name. And the papers isn't all he's been over, that's for sure.'

Karen felt irritated. The woman's sanctimonious superiority was a little hard to take.

'Did you see John Kelly at this house last night?' Karen asked sharply.

'Well, no, of course I didn't,' responded Mrs Nott quite chirpily, apparently blissfully unaware of the warning chill in Karen Meadows' voice. 'I go to bed at night, me, at a proper time, like decent folk.'

The DCI sighed. 'So have you any specific reason at all for suspecting that John Kelly may have been here last night?'

'Well, he's always sniffing around here, isn't he?' Mrs Nott repeated. 'Can't keep away. Well, he couldn't anyway . . .' The woman's voice tailed off, as if she was suddenly remembering again what she had seen that morning.

'Thank you, Mrs Nott. Doesn't look like you can help us at all, really, does it?' said Karen even more sharply. And this time Mrs Nott did at least have the grace to look a little

Until he met Angel Silver, she thought. Karen had fallen wildly in love with David Flanigan all those years ago and had totally lost any sense of judgement – a condition, she suspected, that was at the root of John Kelly's potentially disastrous behaviour.

Now it seemed that Kelly might have been driven to murder. Karen Meadows found herself suddenly overwhelmed with a terrible sadness, not to mention a sense of impending loss. The only way she knew to deal with it was simply to do her job.

'We'd better get Kelly in for questioning,' she said expressionlessly.

After he had returned home Kelly had sat up all night watching TV. Somehow he had not needed to sleep. And, in any case, he had known that he would not be able to. But at around 8 or 9 a.m. the exhaustion caught up with him and he did fall asleep in his armchair, TV still on, waking with a start just as the lunchtime news bulletin was starting.

'The body of a woman has been found at Maythorpe Manor, the Torbay home of the late rock star Scott Silver. It is believed that she may be Silver's widow, Angel . . .'

The shock ripped through Kelly's body like a flash of freak lightning. Could she really be dead? He supposed that he shouldn't be surprised. Well, not shocked, anyway.

It was over then. Angel was dead. His own life was in tatters. But at least it was over at last. And maybe it could only ever have ended with death, he thought.

He stood up and put on his old leather jacket, which looked even more battered than usual as he had spent most of the night and morning using it as a pillow.

The team sent by Karen Meadows to bring Kelly in arrived several minutes after he had already left his St Marychurch home. And by the time DC Burns had tracked down the taxi driver who was able to confirm that he had picked up Mr Kelly from his home in Crown Avenue, taken him to Maythorpe and waited for him for around forty-five minutes before driving him back, his evidence was not really needed.

Kelly was waiting at Torquay Police Station when Karen

Meadows returned from the crime scene. They had put him in an interview room and left him in the company of a uniformed constable. Kelly refused to talk to anybody except the DCI.

'I've come to give myself up for the murder of Angel Silver,' he told her simply.

Neither his voice nor his face gave anything away. Kelly had shut down his emotions. Cut himself off from his surroundings and his circumstances. It was almost as if he was talking about something which didn't concern him at all.

Twenty-two

Karen Meadows sat down with a bump in the chair opposite Kelly. She studied him thoughtfully for a moment or two. Her old friend was very still, his eyes met hers briefly, but his facial expression gave nothing away. There were a couple of angry red weals on his left cheek which could have been scratch marks. Karen's heart sank even further. She studied him carefully.

'Right then, John, you'd better tell us all about it, hadn't you, get it on the record,' she said eventually, and, glancing at the young detective sergeant standing alongside her, 'I'd like DS Cooper to do the interview –'

'No,' Kelly interrupted sharply. 'It's you or nobody, Karen. I've already said that.'

The DCI hesitated almost imperceptibly. She could understand well enough why Kelly was so insistent on talking only to her, to someone he knew and presumably trusted, as she always had him. But she really was not sure she was the right person at all to do the job. She didn't even want to listen to him confessing to a murder, if that really was what he was about to do, of which there seemed little doubt.

There was also the question of politics again. Media and public attention was about to be firmly focused on the activities of the Devon and Cornwall Constabulary once more, and Karen confidently expected to have the chief constable down on her like a ton of bricks at any moment.

Aloud she said, 'Fine. Let's do it properly then.'

She gestured to DS Cooper to switch on the double tape recorder on the table in front of Kelly.

'OK, John, so why don't you tell me exactly what happened?' Karen began, after first recording the obligatory formal introduction to the interview.

'I snapped,' said Kelly simply. 'I just flew at her. I hit her in the face. It was a moment of madness, I suppose. But, by God, she provoked me.'

'Start at the beginning, please.'

Kelly's expression changed then. His eyes darkened. Karen was unsure exactly what she could see there but she knew she didn't like it.

'The beginning?' he queried. 'You want the beginning? I wish I knew how it began, I really wish I did. I know I was obsessed with Angel. She took over my entire life. She was all I could ever think about. Most of the time I didn't even want it to be like that, but I never seemed able to do anything about it.'

He paused. Karen thought there were tears in his eyes now.

'I loved her, you see, like I'd never loved anyone before,' Kelly went on. 'She never returned that. She told me she did once, but I knew it wasn't true. I really did love her, though. A part of me still loves her, even after . . . after everything . . .' Tears began to run down Kelly's face then, yet he seemed quite unaware of them. 'She treated me like dirt half the time, and yet I couldn't stop loving her . . .' His voice tailed off. He sounded almost surprised at his own behaviour.

Karen did not speak. She did not feel she needed to. DS Cooper fidgeted slightly in his seat. He was not a man at ease with displays of emotion.

'There was the sex, of course. It was almost as if I'd never had sex before. There weren't any boundaries, you see. It went so far beyond anything I'd ever experienced. Yet I didn't even like an awful lot of what we did. Not afterwards, that is.' Kelly laughed briefly and without humour.

DS Cooper fidgeted all the more. Kelly seemed suddenly to become aware of the tears that were still running down his cheeks. He stopped talking and rubbed at his face ineffectually with the back of one hand. His fingers touched the weals on his left cheek, and he winced.

Karen thought he looked surprised, as if previously unaware even that his face had been injured. She waited for a few more seconds. It was almost as if Kelly had gone into some other world.

'So exactly what happened last night?' Karen asked, in an effort to bring him back into this one.

Kelly looked down at the table. 'I've never hit a woman before,' he said. 'Even when the drink's got to me, even when I hit rock bottom all those years ago, at least I never did that. But she just went too far. I couldn't stop myself.'

'Describe to me how you hit her exactly,' Karen asked. 'Did you punch her?'

'No, not that really.' Kelly leaned forward and put his head in his hands. Karen didn't think he was avoiding the question, just trying to think, to get things clear in his mind. After a good minute or so of silence, though, she decided another prompt was in order.

'So what did you do, John?'

'Well,' Kelly still seemed to be struggling with his thoughts, with his memory, 'I suppose it was more of a slap really. I lost control. It's hard to remember exactly what I did. I just hit out.' He moved his hands away from his face a few inches and studied them almost with a kind of curiosity, as if amazed by what they had been responsible for. 'I think I caught her with my palm. Her nose just seemed to explode. There was blood everywhere. She fell back against the kitchen worktop and then on to the floor.'

'So what did you do next, John?'

'I just took off. I was horrified by it all.'

'You didn't try to help her?'

'No, I was just desperate get out, to get away.' He paused again. 'In any case, it seems crazy now, but I didn't even think about helping her. I didn't think she'd want my help, for a start. She'd just spent some time explaining to me in detail how much contempt she had for me.'

'So you left her for dead?'

Kelly looked shocked. 'No, not that. I didn't think she was dead. Well, she wasn't, not when I left. She was half lying on the floor, just staring at me. I didn't think I'd hurt her that badly, not then. She looked, well, it sounds stupid but . . .'

Again a pause.

'She looked what, John?'

'She . . . she looked almost triumphant. As if she'd wanted me to hit her, as if she'd got her own way.'

'Did you use a weapon at all?'

Kelly looked puzzled.

'No, of course not,' he said. 'I just hit her.'

'In the face?'

'I told you so.'

'Not on the back of the head?'

'No, no, I don't think so.'

'You sound unsure.'

'Well, it all happened so fast. I know I just lashed out. But I think only that one blow really connected. I'm just not sure, I just can't tell you any more . . .'

'You have what looks like scratch marks on your face. Did Angel do that to you? Was there a struggle?'

'I don't know. I think she tried to push me away. It's so hard to remember exactly.'

'Angel Silver suffered a wound to the back of the head, which is what we think killed her,' Karen went on. 'Do you think you could have been responsible for that, John?'

'I must have been.' Kelly put his head in his hands again.

'But how, how could that have happened? Think, John, think.'

'I just don't know, I really don't.'

'All right.' Karen decided to change tack. 'There must have been something, something specific that happened that night which made you lash out like that, John.'

Kelly shrugged.

'C'mon,' the DCI prompted. 'Try to put it into words.'

Kelly smiled, again without humour, his eyes still full of tears.

'You wouldn't believe me if I told you.'

'Try me.'

'I had reason to suspect that Angel had killed her husband as well as Terry James. That the whole robbery thing was a put-up job. Good reason. I decided to confront her, to make her tell me the truth.'

'And did she?' Karen struggled to keep any expression out of her voice.

'Oh yes, I'm almost sure of it. That was the worst thing of all.'

He told her, then, exactly what Angel had told him, all about Scott and his affair with Bridget Summers and how he'd been planning to leave Angel, about the pre-nuptial agreement and how Angel had plotted to make sure both that she would keep all of Scott's wealth and never lose her man to another woman. How she had been prepared to kill her husband and another innocent man in order to do that.

'Her motive was a mixture of greed and pride, and passion too, because she did love Scott, like I loved her, I suppose,' said Kelly, sounding strangely detached. 'She was passionate enough about him to kill him, yet there was no way she'd let him leave her.'

Karen had already been given cause to have grave doubts over the events at Maythorpe Manor the night Scott and James had died, but hearing the words, just like that, from the person who had probably been closest to Angel following her husband's death, was, none the less, quite devastating. Even DS Cooper, watching her conduct the interview with her usual calm professionalism, would have had no idea of the effect Kelly's revelations were having on the DCI. She was actually quite stunned.

'So why did you suspect her so strongly, John?' she asked levelly.

'It was more than suspecting. There was evidence that pointed directly to her, only I chose to ignore it – well, as best I could . . .'

His voice tailed off again.

'What evidence, John? We didn't find anything.'

'No.' Again a brief humourless laugh.

Karen pressed the point until Kelly told her about the video film which had so clearly shown Angel killing Terry James, stabbing him repeatedly, and also all that the video had indicated to him about how Scott may also have died at her hands.

'So where is that video now?'

'We burned it.'

'We?'

'I confronted Angel with it and she asked me to destroy it. I did her bidding. I pretty darned well always did.'

Kelly was angry with himself, Karen thought. But not nearly as angry as she felt.

Karen rose from her chair.

'Interview terminated at twelve fifty-five p.m.,' she announced for the tape, then, without addressing Kelly further, turned on her heel and left the room, gesturing Cooper to follow her.

Once they were outside she turned to the sergeant.

'What a fucker, Phil,' she said. 'So much for Angel Silver as the brave little woman who only wanted to defend her husband.'

'She must have been a total monster, boss.'

'Yup. A lethal one too. And when it all comes out there's going to be hell to pay, you know that, don't you?'

Cooper nodded. 'They'll be looking for scapegoats, boss, won't they? Our brass, the press, the Home Office even. Anyone involved with the previous investigation and that apology for a trial will be heading the list.'

'You're not wrong about that, and no doubt I shall be right at the very top,' said Karen resignedly as she began to walk along the corridor, Cooper, quietly thoughtful, at her side. They arrived at the door to Karen's office at the same time as DC Burns, who came hurrying along from the direction of the incident room.

'The Chief Constable's Office has been on, boss,' said Michael Burns. 'Mr Tomlinson wants to talk to you straight away.'

'I'll bet he does,' muttered Karen. 'Who took the call?'

'I did, boss,' said Burns.

'And what did you tell them?'

'That you were interviewing the leading suspect and couldn't be disturbed, boss,' said Burns expressionlessly.

Karen shot him a sideways glance. Maybe there was more than there appeared to be to this big muscle-bound lad.

'Well done, Mike,' she said approvingly. 'And I think that

interview is going to have to go on for some time. I can't quite face the chief constable at the moment.'

She beckoned the two detectives to follow her into her office and slumped into the chair at her desk, brushing the remains of that morning's paperwork casually to one side. She certainly had no time for any of that.

Cooper, without waiting to be asked, sat down opposite her. Burns, still ill at ease with the more informal ways of CID, stood quite stiffly, almost to attention, by the door.

'For God's sake, Mike,' said the DCI, suddenly noticing his awkward stance. 'Sit down somewhere, will you? You look as if you're facing a court martial.'

'Heaven forbid, boss,' murmured Cooper with a wry smile.

Karen managed a very small smile back. 'Indeed,' she said. 'I can, however, see an internal inquiry and God knows what other shit looming unless we make a damned near miraculous recovery on this one, Phil.'

She leaned forward across her desk, fists clenched, her forehead creased into a frown of concentration.

'Right! Let's get at it. I know that Angel's death at least seems cut and dried. We have a confession and all the evidence seems to back that up. But I'm just not happy, and we certainly can't afford any more mistakes. I want a check on any other possible suspects. I'd like to talk to Bridget Summers and to Ken James.'

'I'll get on to it, boss.' Phil Cooper was quite serious now.

'Any word of Angel's mother, by the way? Do we know if the Met have broken the news to her yet?'

'Yes, they have, boss. I heard just before we went in to interview Kelly. Apparently she's on her way to Torquay and she wants to see you.'

Karen nodded. 'I want to see her too. Though God knows what light she can shed on any of it.'

'And Rachel Hobbs is no chicken, boss. She's bound to be in shock.'

'No doubt,' said Karen, thinking that Mrs Hobbs wasn't the only one.

*

It was, however, Rachel Hobbs who had coached her daughter in the old showbiz maxim of never letting the act drop.

Like Kelly all those months previously, Karen Meadows was surprised by the now seventy-one-year-old woman she had expected to have to treat so carefully.

Mrs Hobbs was immaculately turned out, in her own particular style, all bouffanted platinum-blonde hair, tight tailored suit and high-heeled shoes. If she had shed any tears at all at her daughter's death, it didn't show. Whatever her feelings were, she was keeping them to herself. This was no broken mother, rather she was a woman on a mission.

'My daughter was a very famous woman, the wife of a great star, and once upon a time, quite a star herself,' Rachel Hobbs announced. 'I need to know exactly what you think happened to her, and why. I know you've got John Kelly in custody, but I find it really hard to believe that he would have hurt Angel. I need to know what's going on, because my Angel had a certain image. She was somebody. That meant a lot to her, I know, and it meant a lot to me, Detective Chief Inspector. I intend to protect that image with my last breath if I need to. One thing is certain: I will not let her name be tarnished. That's why I am here.'

Karen listened in some amazement. This was not what she had expected at all. She studied Rachel Hobbs carefully.

Karen had, of course, absolutely no intention of revealing to her what Kelly had told her about her daughter, and how she now believed that Angel Silver had not killed an intruder in self-defence, but was, instead, a double murderer. Deep in thought, she let Mrs Hobbs' words wash over her.

'Have you any reason to think that Angel's name will be tarnished?' she asked eventually.

Rachel Hobbs looked startled. 'No, of course not. But you never know what will come out of something like this, do you?'

'A funeral perhaps?' Karen hadn't meant to be so sharp, but Rachel Hobbs had thrown her off kilter and she was always inclined to speak her mind.

Mrs Hobbs stared at her for fully half a minute before reacting, then she seemed to slump a little in her chair.

'You think I don't care . . .' The words faded away.

'No. I don't think about that at all. My job is to find out what happened at Maythorpe Manor and to bring your daughter's killer to justice.'

Karen could see Mrs Hobbs making a conscious effort to pull herself together again. 'So, do you think you have found him? Is it really John Kelly? And if so, why? Why on earth would John Kelly harm Angel? He always adored her.'

Karen wondered if the woman had any idea that her daughter had been having a torrid affair with Kelly. She thought not.

'I don't know the answer to any of those questions, Mrs Hobbs,' she said. 'But I do intend to find out.'

During the next twenty minutes or so she gave Rachel Hobbs all the information she was prepared to about Angel's death, which wasn't actually that much, and also asked a few questions of her own. But it quickly became apparent that Mrs Hobbs could be of little help in the investigation.

'I only saw Angel a couple of times after Scott was killed, and that was quite early on,' she said. 'We hardly talked about that night at all. Angel didn't want to. To be honest, I didn't think she could. She had always visited me quite often, but after Scott's death she seemed to pull away. There were phone calls, but that's not the same, is it? And she made it quite clear that she didn't want me to come to Maythorpe. I was hurt, to tell the truth. I wanted to support her, and she wouldn't let me. But that was my Angel. You could never second-guess how she would react to anything.'

That, certainly, was true enough, thought Karen. And another certainty seemed to be that Mrs Hobbs knew virtually nothing at all about anything that might have led to Angel's death.

Karen found herself relieved when she was finally able to show the woman out of her office.

But at the door Rachel Hobbs turned round to face her again. 'Don't think I'm not devastated by my daughter's death, Detective Chief Inspector,' Mrs Hobbs announced. 'She was my only child and I loved her to bits.'

Now, finally, Karen saw that her eyes were filled with tears and her lips trembled when she spoke.

'I try not to think about what I've lost, that's how I cope,' she said very quietly. 'That and by carrying on doing what I've always done, I suppose. Trying to fix things for Angel . . . trying to look after her, even though she's not here any more . . .'

Mrs Hobbs abruptly swung away and hurried off down the corridor. Karen could see that her shoulders were shaking. Even the likes of Rachel Hobbs can't always keep the act up, she thought.

Alone in her office later, Karen went over in her mind for the umpteenth time the events of the last week. She had genuine doubts about Kelly's guilt, in spite of his confession, but she needed to be able to convince herself that these had nothing to do with their shared history and her personal feelings for him. She needed to seriously think it through.

There was no doubt that Kelly had gone to Maythorpe that night and that he had physically attacked Angel, hitting her in the face and causing her nose to bleed – something which had not called for a huge blow exactly, reflected Karen. None the less, Kelly's version of events to that extent was backed up by almost irrefutable evidence. But Kelly still denied any recollection of having used a weapon on Angel, although he was so uncertain and vague it was difficult to judge the credibility of some of his evidence, even if you accepted that he was being as honest as he could be. His return to drink and drugs might seriously have addled his brain this time, Karen feared. That and an unhealthy obsession which seemed to have totally blinded him to reality.

On an impulse she put in a call to Audley Richards, even though she suspected that the Home Office pathologist might not be overjoyed to hear from her again. And she was right about that.

'Look, Audley, I just wanted to go over it again. Are you sure the blow to Angel's head couldn't have been caused by her hitting the back of her head either on the worktop or on the floor after she'd been hit in the face?'

'Karen, this is the third time you've phoned on this. I can't tell you any more than I have already. I am ninety-nine per cent certain that Angel Silver's fatal injury was caused by a blow to the head administered by a blunt instrument. However many more times you call me, nothing will change that.'

Karen ended the call, leaned back in her chair and tried to sort it out inside her head. The logical solution was that Kelly had used some sort of weapon on Angel and had either blanked it out or was deliberately denying it, knowing that his lawyers would probably attempt to have his charge reduced to manslaughter.

Audley Richards said ninety-nine per cent. That one per cent doubt, plus no murder weapon having been found, made it likely that a manslaughter plea would be accepted. Kelly would plead guilty to that and probably end up with just a few years in a low-grade prison.

Yet there were enough unanswered questions to make the DCI feel extremely uneasy. Then, just as she was contemplating attempting another interview with Kelly, her telephone rang. It was the chief constable. She had known she could not avoid him indefinitely. The call was, however, extremely unwelcome.

Harry Tomlinson didn't even attempt his cheerful act.

'I have been trying to get to speak to you for almost half a day, Detective Chief Inspector. Have you been deliberately avoiding me?'

Karen took a deep breath. She knew that it was a very bad sign when the chief constable addressed you by your rank. The bloody man prided himself on his chumminess.

'Of course not, sir. It's been a very busy day, that's all. I've been in the interview room most of the time.'

Tomlinson grunted unenthusiastically. 'And with any constructive results, may I ask?'

'To be perfectly honest, I'm not sure, sir –'

'Are you not, DCI Meadows? Well, you should know I have managed to obtain reports from other officers less elusive than yourself.' He paused to allow that one to sink in. Karen refused to let herself rise to the bait.

'I understand that there is a clear-cut case against John Kelly, that he has confessed and that forensic and DNA evidence is likely to back up that confession. Is that not so, Detective Chief Inspector?'

'Well, that's one way of looking at it, sir –'

'One way of looking at it?' Tomlinson's voice had risen several octaves. He was virtually shouting down the phone. 'I'll have you know, DCI Meadows, that it's my way of looking at it, and I have little doubt the way of any decent police officer. I just hope you are not allowing any personal prejudices to get in the way of your judgement on Kelly.'

The chief constable had put extra emphasis on his last remark. Oh shit, thought Karen. So he too thought she'd had an affair with John Kelly. Well, there was nothing she could do about that. She certainly wasn't going to deny something Harry Tomlinson would never dare put into words.

'I can assure you, sir –' she began. But Tomlinson interrupted her before she could even put a sentence together.

'The only assurance I want from you is that you're going to charge John Kelly with the murder of Angel Silver, and fast. We need somebody in the frame. We've got the man, and I don't want him slipping through our fingers. God knows what will come out in court about the bloody mess we seem to have made of the whole Silver case so far, but we'll just have to weather that one when it happens. I'm talking about damage limitation, DCI Meadows, and you, I may remind you, have a hell of a lot of damage to put a limit on.'

'Yes, sir,' said Karen.

She couldn't think of anything else to say, but, in any case, it didn't matter much. By the time she had muttered even those two words she was already speaking into a buzzing receiver. Harry Tomlinson had hung up.

Cooper came into Karen's office then, just in time to see her looking quizzically at the telephone receiver in her hand. She put it down at once.

'Yes, Phil?'

Karen did not intend to tell anyone about her conversation

with the chief constable, not even Cooper. The political machinations of Harry Tomlinson were her problem.

'The team we sent round to Bridget Summers' place in Exeter have just reported back, boss,' Cooper told her. 'Apparently the house is all shut up, and the neighbours say they haven't seen her for weeks. We're still checking it out.'

'And Ken James?'

'Not around either, according to his mother, anyway. She claims he took off up north several days ago to work on some building job. That is what he does, boss. Kips in his van most of the time, I understand, and picks up a whole bundle of black money.'

Karen grunted, unconvinced. 'And no doubt his mother has no idea of his exact whereabouts?'

'Naturally not,' said Cooper.

'Keep the guys on to that, Phil.'

'Sure, boss.'

'They're a vengeful lot, you know, those Jameses.'

'I know. There's never really been much doubt that it was Ken James who chucked that brick through Kelly's window, has there?'

'Nope. And then when Angel was charged with his brother's murder Ken's anger was redirected at her. We know well enough how he was in court and then out at the house after Angel was cleared.'

'So perhaps young Kenny's managed to do for both Angel and Kelly as well in a way. Is that what you're getting at, boss?'

'God knows, Phil. I just don't want anything left to chance, that's all.'

However, during the next twenty-four hours little progress was made. The team seeking Bridget Summers found out that she was in America at the Kansas headquarters of the One God, One People sect, and were able to confirm that she had been there for almost two months. That put her beyond suspicion.

Further inquiries failed to unearth Ken James, against whom there was in any case no evidence.

Meanwhile, Karen, as well as everything else under orders from her chief constable to charge Kelly, ultimately had no choice but to do so.

She didn't like pressure from above, but even without that she knew that there really wasn't an alternative. Logic dictated that Kelly was guilty of the murder he had indeed confessed to.

The post mortem showed almost beyond doubt that Angel had been killed by a single blow to the back of the head administered by a blunt instrument. A police search of Kelly's home unearthed no further evidence and there was no sign of a murder weapon, but Kelly's fingerprints were found all over Maythorpe Manor, as DS Cooper had predicted. Also particles of skin were discovered lodged behind Angel's fingernails, which the police confidently expected DNA tests to later prove to be Kelly's, probably gouged from his injured cheek by a frantic Angel fighting for her life. In addition, tiny drops of blood, almost certainly from Angel, and spattered when her nose had bled, were found on Kelly's clothing.

Based on all of that, his own confession, and the evidence of the taxi driver who had driven him to Maythorpe Manor, John Kelly was duly charged with the murder of Angel Silver and remanded in custody.

The call came two days later. 'Check out Kenny James before you make fools of yourself again,' said a husky, slightly distorted voice.

'Who's that?' the DCI asked quickly.

'Never mind who I am. Just check James out. He wanted revenge for his brother, didn't he? Have a look in the back of his van.'

'Who is that?' the DCI repeated. But the line just went dead.

Karen immediately dialled 1471 and was mildly surprised to be given a number at all. But it turned out merely to be a call box in Exeter, a result unlikely to take the inquiries any further.

Karen hated anonymous tips, but once again had little

choice. She knew she must follow this one through. It was time to go heavy on the James family, she reckoned. First she obtained a search warrant and then, along with DS Cooper and a couple of uniformed boys, set off to Paignton.

Ken James's mother answered the door of number 24 Fore Street none too enthusiastically and stood forbiddingly in the doorway.

'Are you going to do this the hard way or the easy way?' enquired Karen mildly, holding up the search warrant in one hand.

With obvious reluctance Mrs James stood aside then.

'Why don't you leave us alone?' she snapped as she escorted them into her living room. 'You're persecuting us, that's what you're doing. My Terry was murdered, that's what happened to my Terry, and you lot did nothing about that at all.'

It now seemed that Mrs James might be absolutely right, thought Karen glumly, but this was not the moment to share that with the woman.

'I just want to talk to Ken,' she told her instead.

'Well, you can't. I told you, I've no idea where he is.'

'I think you have, Mrs James.' Karen looked around the plushly appointed room. 'And if you don't start remembering pretty darned fast I'm going to throw the book at you.'

She turned to DS Cooper and gestured at the state-of-the-art music system in one corner. 'Get the serial number of that and all the other electrical goods in this house,' she ordered. 'I have reason to believe that Mrs James is guilty of receiving stolen goods.'

The older woman paled visibly. The James family matriarch had, somehow or other, so far avoided ever being charged with a criminal offence of any kind, which was something of a miracle for anyone in that household, Karen reckoned.

'They were all gifts,' Mrs James blurted out. 'I don't know where they came from, do I?'

'Tough,' said Karen, and then, lowering her voice, she added, 'You should know that this is not just a very serious murder inquiry, it's my arse on the line. I don't intend to stop at anything in order to get to the truth.'

Mrs James's face puckered up into an expression of peeved resignation. She was a woman who instinctively understood how this kind of game was played.

'Oh, all right, all right. Kenny's holed up in our caravan on that site over by the holiday camp. When we heard that Angel Silver'd been killed I knew you lot would come looking for him, so I told him to lie low for a bit. Keep out the way.'

Karen nodded. 'Thank you so much, Mrs James,' she said in her most charming way.

The older woman scowled.

'He didn't do it, not that you lot care, and, anyway, you'll waste your time going over there now,' she said, sounding almost triumphant. 'He's gone to Birmingham for that football match tonight. God knows why he still supports Torquay after the way they've performed lately, but he does. He's a loyal boy, my Kenny. All my kids are loyal.'

Yes, thought Karen, that was probably true and was also half the point. The James family did not rest easily until they had avenged any perceived grievances against members of their clan. And murder was a very big grievance indeed.

'Has he taken his van?'

Mrs James nodded. 'Course he has. Who can afford train fares nowadays? Even if the bloody things are running.'

They searched the house then.

Ken James's bedroom was almost as interesting as Terry James's room had been all that time before. The walls were pasted with newspaper cuttings of the killing of Scott Silver and Terry James at Maythorpe Manor, and of Angel's trial for the manslaughter of Terry. There were also a selection of photographs of Angel, some with Scott, which Karen thought may have earlier adorned Terry James's bedroom. All the pictures of Angel had something in common. They had each been grossly defaced. In some her face had merely been obliterated with what looked like marker pen in various colours, primarily black or red. Others had been drawn over obscenely, with the addition of unpleasantly distorted breasts and sexual organs. Several had 'Die, you bitch' written across them.

The DCI and DS Cooper exchanged glances.

'Right,' said Karen. 'Let's get on to Birmingham. We need to find Kenny James and that van of his, smartish.'

Less than a couple of hours later the West Midland Constabulary called to say that they'd found Ken James, a quicker result than anybody had realistically expected. But it seemed that his details had already been logged when the West Midlands received the call for help from Torquay.

Ken had apparently been involved in a pre-match pub brawl. His neck had been broken and he was in hospital in a coma. His van had been parked outside the pub and a preliminary search had revealed a lump hammer wrapped in a pair of bloodstained combat trousers.

Twenty-three

Eventually even the Chief Constable agreed that the murder charge against Kelly had to be dropped in view of the fresh evidence. He didn't like it, though.

'Basically, Karen, you're telling me now we haven't got enough on Kelly, even with his confession, and yet we haven't got anyone else realistically in the frame either,' he told the DCI irritably.

Karen, summoned yet again to Harry Tomlinson's office at headquarters in Exeter, forced herself to remain cool.

'We now have the murder weapon, there's little doubt about that, sir,' she began. 'Kelly confessed to attacking Angel Silver but he absolutely denies using any kind of weapon. The PPS reckon there are too many grey areas and that any defence brief worth his salt would have a field day with the weapon line. It was found in Ken James's van, and Ken James had motive in spades. He has made no secret of the bitter grudge he holds against Angel. Manslaughter or murder, it's never made much difference to Ken. Angel killed his brother. Circumstantial stuff, I know, but the PPS reckon we've little or no chance of getting the charge against Kelly to stick.

'His solicitor has already told me that he has advised Kelly to plead not guilty, in spite of his confession, and I've no doubt he'll just do that. Kelly confessed on the spur of the moment because he was frightened and confused. And we all know how those kind of confessions go down in court. He'll have plenty of time to think things through, too, before his case comes up at Crown Court, and his brief's going to be able to drive a truck through our case. That's what the PPS say, anyway.'

Harry Tomlinson grunted. 'But we don't have any chance of getting a charge against James to stick either,' he responded.

'Well, no, certainly not as long as Ken James is unconscious.'

'And if he comes round? You reckon he'd confess?'

'I've no idea, sir,' said Karen non-comittally, although she actually thought it was about as likely as James emerging from his coma and announcing he wanted to join the Salvation Army.

'So, we've no result, nor likely to get one, Detective Chief Inspector. Is that what you're telling me?'

Karen winced at that dangerously formal use of her rank again. She decided to attempt the political card.

'Not at the moment, sir. But, don't forget, if Kelly had gone to trial all that stuff about Angel allegedly telling him she had killed both men and planned to do so would have been bound to come out. It was what caused Kelly to strike at her, after all. So we may have got a result of sorts, sir, within the force, anyway. This way that won't happen, and the public may never know how wrong we got the original investigation.'

As she spoke Karen realised that her final remark was a mistake.

'How wrong *you* got it, Detective Chief Inspector,' snapped Tomlinson.

But then he appeared to think about the rest of what she had said.

'Mind you, I suppose you're right up to a point,' he remarked eventually. 'Some things are better kept away from public knowledge.'

Karen arrived back in Torquay just in time to see Kelly, whose reprieve had come before his planned transfer to the County Jail, off the station premises.

'Thanks for everything, Karen,' he said when the DCI told him he was free to go.

'If you want to thank me, John, just stay away from me for the foreseeable future,' Karen replied tetchily. 'This case has come very close to bringing me down, and not least of that has been your involvement in it and our so-called friendship.'

Kelly merely shrugged an apology. 'Don't worry, all I want to do is keep out of trouble from now on,' he said.

Karen sighed wearily. Well, there was a first time for everything, she supposed.

In her office she went over and over it all in her mind for the umpteenth time. The new evidence was certainly circumstantial, and there were no fingerprints on the hammer – but Karen and her team had never been very optimistic on that score. Ken James was far too streetwise to leave prints anywhere. But also the combat trousers were virtually brand new and seemed to have been worn over leggings so there was little chance of coming up with any hair or skin particles which could provide DNA confirmation that they had been worn by James.

The chief constable was right enough, she thought. Unless James confessed there was probably even less likelihood of getting a conviction against him than there would be against Kelly.

'I'd still like to know who made that anonymous phone call, though, boss,' remarked DS Cooper a little later.

'And I'd like to talk to Ken James,' responded DCI Meadows. 'But who knows if we will ever get the chance.'

'Even if he does come out of his coma OK, he'll deny all knowledge,' said the detective sergeant echoing Karen's own thoughts on the matter. 'I've never known a James confess to anything yet.'

Karen Meadows pulled a long-suffering face. 'So unless something else new, and something bloody good, turns up again, we've had it, Phil,' she said. 'The only evidence we have against anyone is conflicting and insubstantial and we've got little or no chance of any sort of result, as our own dear chief constable has already pointed out to me.'

The DS muttered his agreement. Angel Silver was dead and could not in any case have been tried for Terry James's murder, having already been cleared of his manslaughter. And there was no evidence to point to that either, nor to prove that she had murdered her husband in the way Kelly had described.

Kelly had destroyed the videotape. All Karen could do was

put the case on file. Along with a pending assault case against Kelly, which would almost certainly never be proceeded with, either.

Karen was, however, not quite as unhappy as she maybe felt she should be. There was that one advantage of this lack of action against Kelly – that Angel's confession to the reporter so shortly before her own death might well not ever come to light now. Karen supposed Kelly could still write the story, but she had a feeling it was the last thing he would want to do. Even if he did, she wondered if anyone would print it. John Kelly had been pretty well discredited, after all, particularly as far as the Silver case was concerned.

And if what Karen sincerely believed now to be the truth – that Angel Silver murdered her husband and then Terry James – was never publicly revealed, then both Karen and her chief constable would probably keep their heads after all. As she had inferred to Harry Tomlinson as directly as she had dared.

Of course, Karen would always have bet on Tomlinson keeping his head. Her own had been another matter. She'd felt sure from the moment things started to go pear-shaped that she was the most likely scapegoat.

'But do you really think James did it, boss?' asked DS Cooper. He still thought like a proper policeman, Karen reflected wryly. He'd never get on in the modern force.

However, all she said was, 'I think I do, Phil.' And she just hoped she was telling the truth. 'Either that or there's been some seriously elaborate frame-up. It's James's style, isn't it, anyway? To be honest, I'm kicking myself. We should have searched his gaff before charging Kelly, confession or no confession. That was a mistake.'

Phil was less self-admonitory. 'I guess so. But what with the taxi driver and everything why should we have doubted Kelly? You can't just dismiss a confession. It all added up. Why on earth should we have doubted anything?'

The DCI grunted, unconvinced, dissatisfied with herself. 'Check every angle. That's always been my rule of policing. We fell down on it. Crazy thing is, I was somehow never quite convinced about John Kelly, even without the new angle, and

I'm not at all sure I didn't compensate for my own feelings of friendship towards him when I had him charged so quickly. Tomlinson was down on us, but I've fended him off before; I should have done so this time.'

DS Cooper shook his head. 'You're beating yourself up, boss. Look, we even had DNA evidence which we were damned sure from the start was going to match up. In fact, if you want to know, I reckon there still has to be doubt about Ken James. How the fuck did Kenny get in and out of Maythorpe, for a start?'

Karen shrugged. 'They're a bunch of Houdinis, that James lot. In any case, Terry James and God knows who else seem to have had the security code. Maybe Terry passed it on to his brother. Or maybe Ken got it from someone else.'

'But didn't Angel change it? She must have been advised to, surely.'

'Who knows what that woman did. If Kelly's theory is right, and I bet it is, she knew she wasn't in any danger, didn't she? And she was, in any case, a law unto herself, that one. Anyway, there's bugger all we can do about any of it now.'

'So it's over, boss?'

'I guess so, Phil,' responded Karen Meadows. 'Fucking frustrating, though, isn't it?'

Later that day Karen called Rachel Hobbs. She had, after all, promised to keep Angel's mother informed.

Rachel listened carefully as Karen gave her a précised account of events, deliberately leaving out her own feelings on the matter and, of course, everything that Kelly had told her about Angel's confession to him.

'So it really looks as if Ken James killed Angel simply in revenge for his brother's death?' Mrs Hobbs enquired.

'That's right.'

'And how long is he likely to be in a coma for?'

'Hard to say. It's quite possible he may never come out of it, I understand.'

Karen considered again the implications of her last few words. She really was becoming more and more convinced that it would be all for the best if Ken James didn't come round. She didn't like herself for that, but it wasn't only the chief constable who understood about damage limitation.

Karen's imminent promotion to detective superintendent was still on course, she had been told, and that was a real result under the circumstances.

There was all too much in this case that nobody involved wanted to become public knowledge. Including her, she now had to admit. And she hadn't just been spinning the chief constable a yarn when she had set him thinking that way.

Karen had once believed unfalteringly that a police officer should always seek the truth, regardless of the consequences. But the more senior she became in the force, the more she had learned to accept grim reality. All too often the discovery of truth was neither wise nor desirable.

And there were some cases it was actually preferable never to solve.

When Kelly arrived home in a police squad car Moira opened his own front door to him.

'God, I'm glad to see you,' he said, and he meant it.

Kelly was completely washed out. At one point he had quite convinced himself that he really was a murderer. He was now beginning to realise that, at least as far as Angel Silver's violent death was concerned, he had merely been a victim of circumstances and of coincidence. But it took a bit of getting used to.

His own company had not been an inviting prospect.

Kelly could smell cooking in the kitchen, and he could hardly believe his luck.

He sniffed the air appreciatively. 'I know I don't deserve this,' he said. 'And I certainly don't deserve you.'

'No, you don't,' said Moira.

Kelly reached out a hand tentatively and stroked her hair.

'Love is nothing to do with what people deserve, is it?' she continued. 'You can't just switch it off. I tried and it didn't work.'

'It certainly isn't,' said Kelly, reflecting on the madness of his feelings for Angel, and what it had led to.

Suddenly he leaned forward and pecked Moira on the cheek. He half expected her to resist even that, but she didn't, although neither did she respond.

'At least I know I'm not a murderer now,' he said. 'I don't think I could have lived with that under any circumstances.

'I really did think I'd done it, you know, Moira. I was so confused when I heard Angel was dead, and I'd been so bloody angry. My head just wasn't working. I didn't know what I might have done for a bit. But all I did was push her, it seems. I'm not even sure I ever hit her properly. Apparently her nose was shot to hell, that's why it bled so quickly and so much.'

Moira didn't know any of what Angel had told him about the night that her husband and Terry James had died, about how she had murdered both of them in cold blood. And Kelly didn't intend to tell her. Not unless he ever thought she might learn about it from some other source.

But, like Karen Meadows, he reckoned the whole thing might stay under wraps now. And like the DCI, although for very different reasons, he thought that would be, by and large, the best thing.

Kelly's folly was already great enough in Moira's eyes, he was sure, as it indeed was in his own. He didn't see the need to reveal that the woman he had been so obsessed with, the woman with whom he had so recklessly joined on the road to self-destruction, was also a double murderer.

Abruptly, Moira stepped away from him, held him at arm's length and studied him quizzically.

'You were a bloody fool, weren't you?' she remarked.

'I certainly was,' he agreed.

'You do know that now, don't you?'

'I do. Yes.'

Moira nodded. And there was real aggression in her voice when she spoke again. 'I'll tell you one thing,' she said. 'Whatever you say, I wouldn't have blamed you for killing that bitch. I could have done so myself, for two pins.'

'No you couldn't,' said Kelly mildly. 'Oh no, you couldn't.'

But Angel Silver could kill, he thought. Just like that. He

would carry the terrible truth about her around with him for the rest of his life, and it would be a burden like no other he had ever had experience of. There was another terrible truth too. He hadn't attacked Angel because she'd told him about the murders she'd committed, as much as because of the contempt she'd shown him. He had still been in love with her in spite of everything. Maybe a bit of him always would be. He had just no longer been able to stand the way she had tormented him.

He avoided Moira's gaze. At that moment he didn't dare look her in the eye.

'We've got a lot to talk about,' she said, and he hoped she hadn't been reading his mind.

'Yes,' said Kelly quietly. And a lot we won't ever talk about, he thought.

'But not now, not tonight.'

As if on cue the doorbell rang. Moira reached past Kelly and opened it. Nick stood on the doorstep, his smile more uncertain than Moira's – but at least he was still smiling, thought Kelly.

'Hi, Dad,' he said.

'It's very good to see you,' replied Kelly, feeling the tears well up.

'I called Nick on his mobile as soon as I knew you were being released,' said Moira. 'He said he'd come straight away. But I didn't think he'd be this quick.'

She shot Nick an affectionate glance.

'I wasn't so far away. I was on a business trip to Bristol. Lucky coincidence. Just wanted to welcome you home, that's all, Dad.'

'Luckiest thing around here is that I've still got you two,' said Kelly. And he found that, at least for a while, he was able to stop thinking about the turmoil of his recent past.

'Just hold it together this time, Dad. Keep off the hooch and any other crap that's around, will you?'

'Yes. I promise.'

'And stay way from loose women too.' Nick grinned.

Kelly was not very amused, although he managed a weak grin back. 'I promise that as well,' he said automatically.

But all he could think of was that neither Nick nor Moira really had a clue about his feelings for Angel and the strange power she had had over him.

He supposed it really was over now. Angel was dead, after all, and he couldn't say he was sorry about that any more. Actually, he wasn't sorry. In fact, in spite of the fact that he probably still loved her, he was almost glad. It was, as he had known from the moment he had first heard of her death on the TV news, the only way any of it could ever be over for him. He was also glad that he hadn't killed her. That would have been too much to cope with.

He could rebuild his life now. He would rebuild his relationship with Moira too, if she'd let him, and every indication, somewhat miraculously, was that she would. Eventually. He would stay off the drink. And the drugs. If he'd ever harboured the notion that enough time had passed since he'd hit the bottom of the pile and that he could cope with either of them, then he'd learned that lesson the hard way.

In the morning he'd phone Joe Robertson and see if his job was still there for him. He had no idea whether it would be or not, but if there was anyone in the world who would stand by him in spite of everything, after Moira and Nick, of course, it was Joe.

Kelly was being handed another chance again. He knew it, was grateful for it, and he genuinely intended to make the most of it.

He also knew, however, that if Angel were still alive, none of that rebuilding would be possible. Because as long as she were there, somewhere, almost anywhere, Kelly would not be able to stay away. His obsession was something he still couldn't explain, even to himself. It was not something he liked. It was not something he had ever liked much really, not something he had enjoyed most of the time. It had been completely beyond his control. Angel's power over him had been frightening and total. He didn't suppose he would ever have been able to overcome it. Not if she had lived.

Her death had freed him.

He put an arm round both Nick and Moira and the three

of them moved together into the dining room. They were his future now. And at least Kelly realised how extraordinarily lucky he was to have any kind of future at all.

Moira had roasted a chicken, the traditional way with sage and onion stuffing.

Nick liked roast chicken. He liked Moira too, and thought, as he had so many times before, how good she was to and for his father.

He would, of course, have preferred his father to have stayed with his mother and to have been the dad he had always wanted, both in his childhood and throughout his life. But even Nick had sometimes to accept that you couldn't have everything. He certainly didn't resent Moira. She had arrived on the scene far too long after his father had messed up the first time round, and abandoned him and his mother, to be resented in any way. In fact, one of the reasons he liked Moira so much was that she had been instrumental in giving him back his father. Moira had kept Kelly on the straight and narrow, Moira had provided the kind of family environment that Nick had never thought his father would attain again. Nick liked that. He'd liked it a lot until Angel Silver had come along and spoiled it all.

Nick hadn't liked it being spoiled. And he hadn't wanted to lose the father he had so recently regained. Indeed, he had ultimately decided to make sure that he wouldn't lose him.

People didn't realise, thought Nick as he leaned back in his chair and watched Kelly and Moira mend bridges, just how much it meant to have a father. To be honest, he thought, he himself had been surprised by the strength of his feelings for a man he had barely known until a few years ago. A man he could have felt just the opposite about, except that John Kelly was the only father Nick had, and that mattered to Nick more than he would have thought possible.

The kind of father-son relationship that, it seemed to Nick, almost everybody else in the world had, came to him late. But he had eventually found it. And it had genuinely destroyed him to see Kelly lying in a hospital bed, bashed and battered and damn near down and out. Nick had quite a lot in common with the James clan, really. He was fiercely loyal to his family, even though, unlike the Jameses, Nick had never really had a family. However, that seemed only to make his feelings for his father more intense once he had been reunited with him.

Although it was Nick's nature to take action when he or anything that he wanted or revered in life was threatened, he had never intended to do anything about his father's situation except offer his support. He really hadn't . . .

'Nick, Nick.'

His father's voice, somewhere in the distance, interrupted Nick's thoughts.

'Sorry, Dad. I was miles away.'

'Could see that. Look, there's an AA meeting in town tonight. I don't want to go. But everyone tells me how important it is, and I reckon I ought to start how I mean to go on.'

'Sure, Dad.' Nick liked the sound of that, saw it as an indication of just how serious his father was this time.

'It's down in Union Street and I was wondering if you might drive me there. I shan't be driving myself for a bit, as you know,' Kelly finished wryly.

It was when they swung into Union Street, just by the magistrates' court, that Kelly was suddenly overwhelmed with unwelcome memories.

It was there that he had watched Angel first plead not guilty to manslaughter. There that he had sat in the press bench and been overwhelmed by her beauty and her composure.

Kelly found himself staring at the old courtroom building, turning his head round for a further look at it over his shoulder.

He was aware of Nick shooting him a quick glance. They were close, father and son, surprisingly so considering how long they had been separated. Kelly was fairly sure that Nick knew what he was thinking. And he seemed to be right.

'You are going to be able to put all this behind you, Dad, aren't you?' Nick asked, a note of tension evident in his voice.

'I promise you, Nick,' Kelly said.

Nick made no reply as he drew the Porsche to a halt a hundred yards or so further on down the street, outside the venue for the AA meeting.

Then, just as his father was getting out of the car, he asked testily, 'For Christ's sake, Dad, how did you come under that woman's spell the way you did? What the hell was it?'

Kelly was taken aback. The outburst was completely unexpected.

'I don't know exactly,' he answered honestly. Then he smiled. 'She was very beautiful, you know.'

'Beautiful?' Nick shouted the word, his handsome features suddenly contorted. 'She was a slag, for Christ's sake. A filthy slag. Rich, famous, and a slag. Nose shot to hell by what she stuffed up it. Old makeup smudged all over her face and a filthy stinking old dressing gown. That was her style. That's how she was when she died and that's how she was when she lived.'

Abruptly Nick reached out for the car door which his father was still holding open and slammed it shut, almost trapping Kelly's fingers.

Kelly was both disturbed and thoughtful as he watched his son roar off. He was shocked by the level of Nick's anger, and he was also puzzled.

He didn't think that a detailed description of the state Angel had been in when she was killed had ever been released by the police. Even the stuff about her wrecked nose wouldn't become public knowledge until the inquest into her death, which had yet to be heard.

Kelly stood quite still on the pavement as the Porsche disappeared into the distance, concentrating very hard, forcing himself to remember everything.

Nick had even known about the grubby dressing gown Angel had been wearing when she was killed.

Kelly shook his head, partly to clear it, and partly in denial of the unthinkable.

Nick took deliberately measured long deep breaths as he drove far too fast through the town.

This would never do. He was usually so controlled. But this entire business between his father and that bloody woman had caused him to lose it more than anything else, ever.

He really would have to be more careful. Not that he regretted what he'd done, of course. Not for a moment. He just realised that he might well have said too much, and could only hope that Kelly had not taken in the significance of his angry remarks.

He stopped the car down by the seafront, deciding to wait there for the hour or so his father would be at the AA meeting, rather than return to St Marychurch, where he would be expected to talk to Moira.

It was a clear moonlit night. Nick wound down a window and gratefully drank in the cool fresh air.

It had all begun for him on the night before Angel Silver's death, the day his father was discharged from Plumpton House. What Nick witnessed that night changed everything. Before that he really hadn't intended to do anything.

Under the impression, like Moira, that Kelly was not being released until the next day, Nick had arrived unexpectedly at Plumpton just as Kelly was leaving. The taxi carrying his father had passed Nick as he'd pulled off the main road into the lane leading to the rehabilitation centre. Kelly had been using his mobile phone, and had not noticed his son or his distinctive car. Nick had been about to blow his horn and flash his lights, but something stopped him. He decided instead to turn the Porsche round and follow the taxi at a discreet distance.

It was already dark and Nick was good at surveillance. He had, after all, been trained in it. And somehow, he wasn't altogether surprised when the taxi swung off the main Torquay drag into the road, past the hospital and the *Argus* offices, which led to Maidencombe. As Nick by then expected, the taxi had turned into Rock Lane and proceeded down the hill to Maythorpe Manor. Nick switched off his headlights and coasted into the entrance of another house just up the lane, hoping that nobody would want to come in or out. He watched his father get out of the taxi and open the electronic gates to Maythorpe, unsurprised that he seemed familiar with the appropriate combination number.

Then, during the brief time that Kelly was inside the old manor house, Nick sat and thought about exactly what he was witnessing.

Nick knew that his father was a weak man, but he blamed Angel Silver for Kelly's fall from grace even more than Kelly himself.

And suddenly, rather in the way his father had later realised it when he heard the radio report of Angel's death, it had struck Nick with devastating clarity that as long as Angel Silver was alive, John Kelly would never be able to extricate himself from her. He would be under her spell always. He would almost certainly start drinking and doing all manner of drugs all over again, because of her.

If that was allowed to happen then Nick would lose his father again.

It was then that he made a decision. Nick was good at decisions. And he was extremely well equipped to carry out the decision he had made.

Nick was indeed a computer expert, but of a very special kind. He was an expert at overcoming security systems, and his special talents, plus his all-round exceptional ability as a soldier, had led to him being seconded to the SAS, a regiment well suited to his nature, which was both daring and devious.

But Nick had always liked the good life, something he had inherited from his father, he thought wryly, although Kelly, of course, had had seriously to downsize his expectations in that direction.

As a lucrative sideline Nick had farmed out his knowledge, and even some of his equipment, to various freelance operations of the kind that the British army could never approve of. More often than not some dodgy mercenary outfit.

Nobody outside his regiment knew, least of all his father, but Nick's days in the army had ended abruptly when one of his extra-mural activities had been discovered. Nick had not been thrown out. That would not have been good either for army morale or regimental reputation. Instead, he was discreetly asked to leave, and always being one to know when the game was up, unlike his father on most occasions, Nick had done so promptly and discreetly.

Now he just continued out of uniform what he had started while in it. He lent his expertise to almost anyone who had a security system to breach. Often, because of his army background, there was a military connection. Sometimes the operations he took part in were criminal. Nick didn't care a lot. He loved adventure and did not understand morality very much. He knew what he wanted and how to ensure that he got it.

The striking of a clock somewhere in the town interrupted his thoughts. Nick checked his watch. It was time to collect his father. He started up the Porsche and motored slowly along Union Street. Kelly was just stepping out on to the pavement as he approached.

Kelly was apprehensive. He had been preoccupied throughout the AA meeting. Unwelcome speculation filled his head.

'Hi, Dad,' said Nick cheerily. Kelly looked him up and down. Nick was smiling and seemed absolutely calm and controlled, the way he usually did.

'You all right?' Kelly enquired casually.

'Sure, Dad. Sorry about earlier. It really shook me up, you know, you going back on the hooch and then being charged with murder, for God's sake!'

'Yeah, I know.'

Kelly did, too. Of course it was perfectly natural for Nick to show his anger occasionally. It was Kelly who'd behaved like a prat, not his son, he reminded himself.

He opened his mouth to ask Nick how he knew so much detail about the way Angel was when she had died. Then he thought better of it. It could only antagonise Nick. There would be a simple explanation. For a start, Kelly had not seen all the papers when he'd been locked up. More than likely some journo somewhere had got hold of more than the official line.

Nick put his toe down as they hit the hill leading up to St

Marychurch. Like his father, he was inclined to drive far too fast.

Kelly studied him affectionately.

He couldn't even allow himself to think along the lines he had been earlier. It was total nonsense even to consider that Nick could be involved in any way.

Kelly would just put that out of his head, along with so much else.

Nick was relieved. He'd got away with it again. His father obviously didn't suspect a thing.

He smiled to himself, thinking back over the smooth operation he had conducted.

He hadn't wanted to follow his father into Maythorpe Manor that night, and possibly allow suspicion to fall on Kelly, so he'd decided that he would return the next night, which would also give him time to sort out the necessary equipment.

And so, just before midnight the following day, Nick had driven out towards Maidencombe, parked his Porsche in a concealed lay-by a mile or so away, and walked across the fields to Rock Lane. He wore dark camouflage gear, combat trousers and jacket, and had pulled a black balaclava over his head. A small rucksack on his back had contained all that he needed. He climbed over a gate into the lane, as near as he could to Maythorpe, and kept close to the tall hedges until he reached the wall which surrounded the old manor house. No vehicle passed him. Had one done so Nick, in his camouflage gear, would have literally thrown himself into the hedge almost certainly out of sight. He knew how to avoid detection.

The defences of Maythorpe Manor, sophisticated as they might seem to civilians, presented him with no more problems than he had expected.

His natural athleticism, plus the grappling equipment he had brought with him, meant that he did not find it difficult at all to scale the tall wall. And it didn't take him long to disable the system of alarmed cable at the top of the wall in such a way that the security company to which it was connected by telephone link was not alerted. Nick had, after all, been trained by arguably the best in the world to do just that.

He knew all about creating an alternative circuit so that there would be no alert when he cut through the sensitive original wire. Nick was an expert. And when he had entered the house he had done so with admirable stealth.

He found Angel Silver in the kitchen. And it was there that he killed her.

She had had her back to him as he entered the room and had not even known he was there, silently closing in behind her, until he had swung the lump hammer into her skull and smashed the life out of her.

It was only when she fell to the ground that he realised that her nose had been bleeding and that she had been standing over the sink trying to stem the flow. As she fell, some of the blood splashed on to his dark combat trousers. He didn't need to check that she was dead. Nick had also been trained to kill with one blow. He turned away almost as she hit the ground.

Then he had simply exited swiftly in the way that he had entered, repairing the security circuit behind him in such a way that only the most minute of examinations could ever have discovered it.

It was only when his father had been arrested and charged that Nick had realised that John Kelly must have been at Maythorpe Manor earlier that night – indeed, by unfortunate coincidence, only minutes earlier, Nick later learned.

Nick then made another decision. He had to take further action to protect the father he did not intend to lose.

Fortunately the lump hammer and his bloodstained trousers had still been in the boot of the Porsche. After all, Nick was not even remotely under suspicion and he had had a strange feeling that sooner or later both might come in useful. His plan had once again been very simple. Nobody had a bigger grudge against Angel Silver than Ken James, who Nick knew had actually publicly threatened her. So Nick staked out the Jameses' house, followed Mrs James to the seaside caravan site where he found Ken James's van.

He planted the lump hammer, wrapped in the trousers, in the back of it, later calling Karen Meadows anonymously to tip her off.

Very straightforward. And it had all worked extremely well. Of course, Ken James getting his neck broken in a pub brawl had been an added bonus. A real stroke of luck. But then, Nick reckoned you made your own luck in the world. And he should know, the way he'd been brought up.

It had meant nothing to Nick to kill Angel Silver.

Nick didn't have a great deal of respect for human life. Much of it deserved to be snuffed out, in his opinion. The due process of law took far too long to satisfy him. And Angel had been a prime example of a human being who was a complete waste of space. Indeed, Nick reckoned he'd probably done the world a favour.

As he pulled into Crown Avenue, Nick turned towards his father. John Kelly looked tired and wan but there was a kind of resignation about him. He too must realise that at least it was over now, thought Nick. And he was clean and sober, and likely to remain so. A darn sight more likely than he would have been with Angel around, that was for certain.

Nick was happy. He'd fixed it. Angel was out of the picture. His father had his life back, which meant Nick had his father back.

Quite suddenly he felt Kelly's hand on his shoulder.

'I'll never let you down again, son,' his father said.

'I know, Dad,' replied Nick. 'I won't let you.'